D0724436

Martin Hocke studied at the
Royal Academy of Dramatic
Art and, after a spell in the
Norwegian Merchant Navy,
taught English, translated
and became senior language
consultant to several major
companies in Europe. Martin
has also worked for film and
radio, and has spent much
time in remote places,
writing stories.

The Ancient Solitary Reign

MARTIN   HOCKE

GRAFTON BOOKS
A Division of the Collins Publishing Group

LONDON GLASGOW
TORONTO SYDNEY AUCKLAND

Grafton Books
A Division of the Collins Publishing Group
8 Grafton Street, London W1X 3LA

Published by Grafton Books 1989

Copyright © Martin Hocke 1989

A CIP catalogue record for this book is available
from the British Library

ISBN 0-246-13469-0
ISBN 0-246-13498-4 (Pbk)

Photoset by Rowland Phototypesetting Ltd
Bury St Edmunds, Suffolk
Printed in Great Britain by
William Collins Sons & Co. Ltd, Glasgow

Illustrations by Shirley Barker
Map by Ursula Sieger

All rights reserved. No part of this publication may be
reproduced, stored in a retrieval system, or transmitted,
in any form or by any means, electronic, mechanical,
photocopying, recording or otherwise, without the prior
permission of the publisher.

Extract from the poem 'Owl' by George MacBeth
© George MacBeth 1965, reprinted with kind
permission of the Author and Anthony Sheil
Associates

For Pauline

and with many thanks
to Jenny Picton,
without whose help, etc.

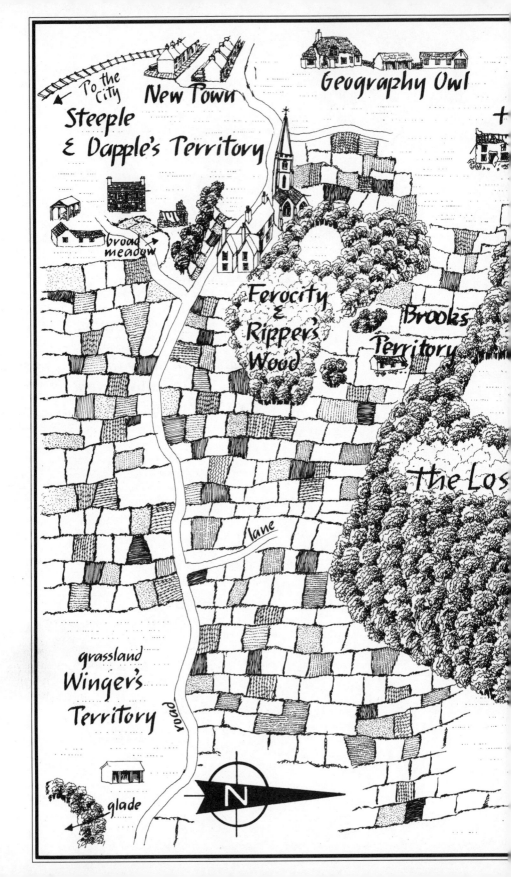

To the City

Steeple & Dapple's Territory

New Town

Geography Owl

broad meadow

Ferocity & Ripper's Wood

Brooks Territory

the Los

lane

grassland

Winger's Territory

road

glade

N

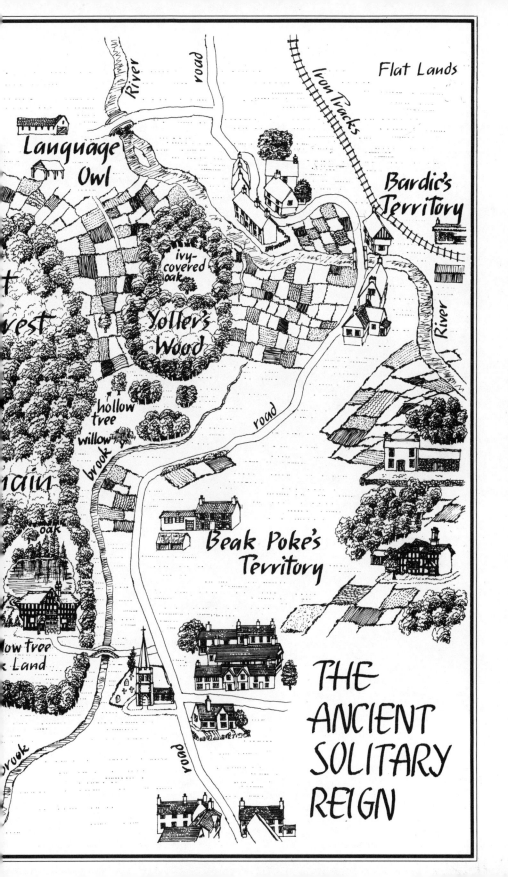

Part One

Save that from yonder ivy-mantled tow'r
The moping owl does to the moon complain
Of such, as wandering near her sacred bow'r,
Molest her ancient solitary reign.

Thomas Gray
Elegy Written in a Country Churchyard

...In the reign
of the chicken owl comes like
a god.
Flown wind in the skin. Fine
rain in the bones. Owl breaks
like the day. Am an owl, am an owl.

George MacBeth
Owl

CHAPTER 1

In the beginning there was a shaft of sunlight in which danced tiny particles of dust and hay as the beam filtered its way through the rafters of the barn where Hunter first saw the light of day. Drowsy and secure, he dozed the late daylight hours away, warmed by the presence of his mother and the two little ones who soon appeared beside him in the nest.

As the days waned and dusk thickened into night, a ray of silver moonlight would take the sunbeam's place, wake the three fledglings and set them clamouring for food. In the nights that followed, the shaft of moonlight would be blotted out three times or more before the dawn by the huge shadow of his father returning from the hunt.

Being the firstborn, Hunter was served first at mealtimes and, after his parents, he had the lion's share. This seemed quite natural to him, though sometimes he felt sorry for his little brother Quaver, who took a long time to learn to eat properly and still had to be beak fed long after Hunter and his sister had learned to swallow whole. Hunter was also the first to learn to walk and the first of the three to be allowed outside and encouraged to make a clumsy, uncoordinated attempt at flight around the safety of the barn. He took all of this for granted and was happy, for it seemed to him that the pattern of his early days and ways had been well and benevolently preordained.

The words were difficult, of course, but less difficult for him than for Dawn Raptor or his little brother. Hunter listened carefully when his mother recited them at dawn and twilight every day and could soon repeat the credo without thinking and without making a mistake. He did not understand the words but in the beginning that did not seem to matter. They were part of his life, like the warmth of his mother, the regular appearance of his father bringing food and the first shaft of sunlight that filtered through the rafters before he went to sleep. It was not until the day little Quaver finally succeeded in squeaking through the words without stuttering or making a mistake that Hunter realized for the first time that life might not always be so simple and straightforward as it seemed.

'Congratulations, Quaver,' his mother said, when he had finished his recital. 'That was very good indeed. Now, I want to ask you all a question before you go to sleep. But before I ask the question, listen carefully to the words again. Dawn Raptor will say them this time and I want you to concentrate carefully, not just on the sound of them, but on exactly what they mean.'

Puzzled, Hunter shifted on his perch and listened while his sister said the words again in that detached and rather supercilious tone she had been using almost from the first day that she learned to speak.

> 'Hoard and covet not
> But be brave and free.
> Quest always after knowledge
> And slowly learn to know
> What science cannot see.
> Seek and strive for learning,
> Be temperate and wise
> For skill and wisdom only
> Will help us to survive.'

'Thank you, Dawn Raptor,' Dapple said when she had finished. 'Now, Hunter, what do you think "knowledge" means?'

In the early dawn light this question came like a bolt from the blue and took Hunter by surprise. He steadied himself on his perch, thought for a moment or two and then looked at his mother with eyes wide open and replied. 'It means knowing things,' he said, taking care to speak slowly and precisely without squeaking like little Quaver or sounding flat and supercilious like his sister Dawn.

'What things?' asked Dapple, patiently.

'Oh, all sorts of things,' Hunter answered vaguely, gazing at the first ray of faint dawn light as if the answer lay among the dancing particles of hay and dust.

'Give me an example,' Dapple said, and though her tone was gentle, it was also very firm indeed and Hunter knew that he would have to think again.

'Oh, you know,' he said, affecting a somewhat careless manner to cover up his ignorance, 'it means knowing all about hunting and about what sort of food to eat. That's the most important kind of knowledge. And where to live and where to sleep and how to look after owlets and all that sort of thing.'

'What else?' his mother asked. 'What else does knowledge mean?'

Perplexed, Hunter looked at her and racked his young and as yet unpractised brain. He found this sudden change in Dapple most disturbing. In front of his very eyes, his warm and loving mother appeared to be turning into a strict and relentless inquisitor. Then he had a flash of inspiration and blurted out his answer very quickly, before his sudden glimpse of vision faded in the rising sun. 'It means knowing all about foxes, weasels, men with firesticks and most of all about the monster owl. It means knowing all about the creatures that can do us harm.'

'Good,' said Dapple, smiling at him gently. 'That's not bad, Hunter. Not bad for a beginning. But knowledge means a great deal more than that. Knowledge means understanding why we Barn owls behave in a different way from our neighbours the Tawnies and the Little owls, and why owls in general are superior to all other birds of prey. It means understanding ecology and learning about man and the environment. It means studying the history of all owl species and understanding why they are the oldest and the highest form of life on earth. And then, of course, there is religion, but your father will attend to that.'

Hunter listened to all this in wide-eyed fascination. On the one hand, the prospect of acquiring all this knowledge was a stimulating challenge, but on the other hand how would he ever learn, much less remember, all these thousand different things? He asked his mother this and she smiled at him as the sun rose higher in the sky outside and slanted in a second beam of light to dance and mingle with the first and dazzle their night eyes.

'You will learn all these things by a process we call education,' his mother answered, blinking a little in the sunlight as she spoke.

'And what is education?' piped up little Quaver. 'Does it hurt much? Where does it happen and how long does it take?'

'No, it doesn't hurt much,' said his mother, laughing. 'In fact, if you are enthusiastic and study very hard, it doesn't hurt at all. And you needn't worry, Quaver. You don't have to travel yet because the first part of your education happens here.'

'Who teaches us? How does it happen?' asked Hunter.

'I teach you,' Dapple said. 'I teach you the basic theory of everything except religion. Since your father is Religion Owl on the Barn owl council, he is much better qualified to teach you that.'

'How many subjects are there?' Quaver asked.

'Eight, altogether,' Dapple said. 'History, geography, ecology, religion, human studies and owlology. I've already told you . . .'

'What is owlology?' interrupted Hunter, who wished that Quaver and his mother would not tear away at things with such bewildering speed.

'Owlology is the study of owl behaviour patterns and philosophies,' said Dapple. 'Not only Barn owls, but all other species, too, especially our neighbours the Tawnies and the little immigrants, since with both of these we have to co-exist.'

'And human studies?' asked Dawn Raptor, who managed to sound cool and aloof even at that early age.

'I told you that before,' said Dapple. 'Human studies are about man's habits. Remember that we have to co-exist with him as well.'

'That's only six, so far,' said Quaver, who had been counting slowly on his little talons. 'What are the other two?'

'I'll tell you that at twilight,' Dapple said. 'The sun outside is high and this blazing light will make your head ache. Sleep now, and this evening, after twilight, we'll begin.'

'Just one more thing!' begged little Quaver, bouncing with excitement on his perch. 'You haven't answered all of my first question yet. You haven't told us how long it will take?'

'There are three stages,' Dapple said. 'Basic education will last till you are grown up and old enough to fly away from home. The second stage will take at least four seasons with an expert tutor at his seat of learning.'

'What shall we study there?' asked Hunter, blinking as the double beam of sunlight shifted and shone directly on his perch.

'The subject you prefer,' said Dapple. 'Always assuming you are fortunate enough to find a place.'

'And the third stage,' enquired Quaver, still hopping up and down as if he had a flea. 'How long will the third stage take?'

His mother looked at him and smiled, in spite of the sunlight in her eyes. 'The third stage will take a lot longer,' she said. 'If you wish to go on surviving, the third stage will last all through your life.'

'But what is education for?' Dawn Raptor asked, sounding sceptical and unimpressed. 'In the words you taught us it says that only knowledge will help us to survive. And yet so far you have spoken only of theory. Of history, owlology, religion and the like. What about hunting, having fledglings and finding them a place to live? Surely those are the most important things?'

'You have already started learning those,' said Dapple, remaining cool and calm in the face of Dawn Raptor's provocation. 'That is what we call the Practice, as opposed to Theory, and you will learn it from your father. He will take you on field studies related to every subject that I teach. You are right, Dawn Raptor. The words sum up our religion and mean exactly what they say. Education is about survival. Everything you do and everything you learn is directed to that end. Other creatures come and go, but owls have inhabited this earth for more than sixty million springs. Which brings me to the hardest lesson. Most parents and teachers leave it till the end, but since you are such a little iconoclast, I will teach it to you now.'

'What's an iconoclast?' squeaked Quaver, taking the question right out of Hunter's bill.

'Dissident, awkward, call it what you will,' said Dapple, who was obviously annoyed in spite of her outer calm. 'It means that your sister has a tendency to break images, contradict the wisdom and tread on the dreams of great owls who have been dead for centuries, all before she's had the chance to learn one single lesson.'

'Teach us then,' Dawn Raptor said, taunting Dapple with her aloofness and composure. 'Teach us the hardest lesson now. Make us afraid and unhappy before we have begun. Frighten us. Perhaps that way we'll be easier to teach.'

'Your father will hear of this,' hissed Dapple, looking suddenly much older as the kindness vanished from her eyes. 'Your father will hear of this, but in the meantime, I will satisfy your wish. The hardest lesson means that you can't come home again.' Dapple paused and as she looked at each of her fledglings in turn, the anger slowly faded from her eyes and a gentle sadness took its place.

'What, never?' Quaver asked, while Hunter sat silent on his perch, trying to absorb the dreadful shock.

'Not to live,' his mother said. 'You can come and stay for short visits, but once you've grown up and flown away from home, you can never come back here again to live.'

'What happens if we can't find territories of our own?' asked Quaver. 'Or even before that, what happens if we can't find a place to study for our further education?'

'It will be arranged for you,' said Dapple. 'Or at any rate, you will be helped. Your father is a member of the council, after all.'

'Why can't we stay?' Dawn Raptor asked. 'I don't want to, but just supposing that I did?'

'It's against Barn owl philosophy and lore,' her mother answered. 'In the interests of survival, you must become fully independent as soon as you are able.'

'In the interests of whose survival?' asked Dawn Raptor. 'Mine, or the whole species?'

'The whole species,' Dapple said, 'but yours as well. Even in times of plenty this territory cannot feed five adults and when there is a slump in the food supply, or heavy competition from daytime birds of prey, it barely provides sufficient for two adults and three chicks. So when you mate, you will need a territory that will provide enough food for your partner and for a family of your own.'

'What if we promise not to mate and have a family?' asked little Quaver. 'Would it be all right for us to live here then?'

'No, Quaver,' said his mother, smiling and blinking in the sun again. 'You will want to mate one day. It's only natural. And when that time comes, you will be the first to want a place that you can call your own. I know it's hard. It's the hardest lesson that a mother has to teach, but I teach it to you in the interests of survival. And for that same reason you must study very hard. For as the words say, without knowledge, skills and wisdom you will find it hard to stay alive. Sleep now and this evening, after twilight your new adventure will begin.'

CHAPTER

2

The fresh spring days of Hunter's early youth melted away into the haze of a long, hot summer. After twilight, when darkness came alive with the seething and throbbing of the thousand creatures of the night, the three fledglings flew with their father Steeple in ever-widening circles round the barn, learning to develop the secret owl skills for identification, for navigation and above all for the hunt. In that long, idyllic summer they learned the names of many animals and trees and with their heightened senses they smelled the bee-sucked linden, wild rose and honeysuckle even as these flowers slept.

At dawn, they studied under Dapple in the barn, while outside the sun rose and beat the golden corn to ripe burnished copper ready for the cutting. Being the oldest and the strongest, Hunter was the best of the three at field work and generally stayed ahead of the others in the academic subjects that his mother taught. The exceptions were ecology, at which Dawn Raptor made slightly better progress, and poetry and singing, for which little Quaver showed a very special flair.

Hunter's favourite subject was owlology. It fascinated him to hear about the ancient Tawnies who ruled their woodland kingdoms so close by and about the fierce little immigrant owls who were condemned to live in no man's land or else to squat on any vacant spot of land that they could find. He longed to meet one of these lords of the secret darkness like themselves, but though he heard them calling far across the cornfields in the summer nights, none came close enough for eye contact to be made. In fact, no hazards and no threat of the unknown came to endanger the three fledglings as summer wore on to its end and they waxed strong and vigorous, both in body and in mind.

Then, late one twilight, shortly after they had eaten breakfast, Steeple cleared his throat, called for attention and made an announcement that took them by surprise. 'You have all three led very sheltered lives,' he said, most unexpectedly. 'Not only you, Dawn Raptor, but both your brothers here as well. You come from a good home where you have enjoyed all of the essentials – food, love, shelter and a better than average general education. But before you move on to the last stage of your studies here with us, there is one very basic lesson you must learn.'

'Tell us now, father,' demanded little Quaver, sounding eager and impatient. Though the youngest of the three, he seemed even more anxious than Dawn Raptor to quit the family constraints and fly away to his new freedom and his higher education.

Steeple looked at each of the three young owls in turn. His expression was graver than ever and he waited until the attention of his offspring was fully centred on his words. 'You must learn about danger,' Steeple said. 'And, more important still, you must learn to come to terms with fear.'

'But we know all about danger,' protested Quaver, making an effort to keep his tone reasonably submissive and respectful. 'Dapple has taught us all about the various dangers we may meet, whether from hawk or falcon at dawn or in the early twilight, from the atavistic Tawnies that may attack us if we stray too far into their precious woods, from man and his firesticks, from four-legged killers such as weasel, stoat and fox . . .'

'Stop!' said Steeple in his sternest tones. 'You have proved my point. You are merely reciting facts that you have learned by rote. None of you has any direct experience of danger, or of the thrill of fear.'

'But Dapple really did teach us the theory exceptionally well,' said Hunter. 'She made it all seem very real. And on our reconnaissance flights with you, we've already learned to identify many of the dangers that Quaver has just mentioned.'

'That's true,' chipped in Quaver. 'At night I've seen a stoat and a fox, and twice at dusk I've seen a man. He was a long way off, but I saw him just the same.'

'Stoats and foxes cannot fly,' said Steeple, patiently. 'They cannot hurt you when you're high up in the air. And the man you saw is one of those with whom we co-exist on and around the territory that they farm.

They tolerate us because we kill mice, sparrows, moles and other creatures they do not eat – food which for their own reasons they eschew.'

'Dawn Raptor met a kestrel face to face,' said Quaver, his voice rising still higher in excitement. 'You can't say that wasn't dangerous!'

'All right, we'll ask your sister what she felt,' said Steeple, leaning back on his perch and raising his eyebrows at his daughter to indicate that the floor was hers.

Dawn's eyes moved quickly from Steeple to her two brothers and then back again as if she intended to sum up her audience before she gave an answer. Then she shrugged and glanced sideways through a chink in the rafters and stared out into the rising dawn. 'Dapple was with me,' she said, in a voice that sounded superior and almost bored. 'I did feel a thrill – some excitement, yes – but there were two of us and I knew my mother would scare the kestrel off if it attacked us.'

'Exactly!' said Steeple, leaning forward on his perch. 'You were not afraid, then?'

'No,' said Dawn Raptor, shaking her head twice as she looked at her father. 'For the moment, fear, for me, is just a word.'

'What about Hunter?' demanded Quaver, as his sister settled back into her rather supercilious listening posture. 'Hunter was on his own when those two crows attacked him for flying too near their nest. He was in danger. He must have felt afraid.'

Steeple turned to the oldest of his offspring and raised his eyebrows once again. 'Well, Hunter,' he said, in serious level tones, 'tell your brother what you felt.'

'I'm not sure,' said Hunter, 'only I don't think it was really fear. Perhaps I felt a pang when they first flew at me with all that mindless squawking. Certainly, I would have been afraid if I hadn't identified them as crows and therefore belonging to a lower form of bird life with no brain to speak of and with vastly inferior weapons to our own.'

'And after this initial shock?' asked Steeple, seeming pleased with what Hunter had said so far.

'I was indignant,' Hunter said. 'Maybe even angry. My impulse was to turn and rip them with my talons, but I merely hissed at them and flew on by.'

'It was fear you felt, initially,' said Steeple, nodding wisely. 'It was only a touch, admittedly, but for a moment or two it was unpleasant enough for you to realize what real fear can do.'

'You mean it can petrify you, like a rabbit and a stoat,' asked Hunter, remembering a lesson that his mother had taught them on the subject.

'Precisely,' answered Steeple. 'Fear can paralyse the body's functions. It can freeze your wings and talons. It can cause you to shed pellets accidentally and, in the case of a very old or a very weak owl, it can stop your heart and even kill you.'

'What a dreadful thing,' said Hunter, who was now almost afraid of fear itself. 'Is there no way it can be avoided?'

Steeple looked at Hunter and slowly shook his head. 'No,' he said. 'Fear cannot be avoided. And since it cannot be avoided, you must learn to live with it and to accept it as essential for survival. For fear, like pain, is just as much a part of life as comfort, warmth or love. Do not attempt to ignore it, because, like pain, it is a warning. Only the very stupid are never afraid and the very stupid don't survive.'

'How will you teach us to come to terms with fear?' asked Dawn Raptor, speaking for the first time of her own accord. 'Surely it is something we must feel for ourselves, or do you believe, as usual, that more briefing, teaching and theory will make the problem disappear?'

'We can prepare you for it,' answered Steeple, ignoring the sarcasm in Dawn Raptor's tone. 'But this time you are right. The real impact of fear comes always from the unexpected, and the worst fear of all is fear of the unknown.'

'The only thing that I'm afraid of is the monster owl,' chipped in Quaver. 'I have bad dreams about him sometimes. Suddenly he appears above me, blotting out the sky.'

'That proves my point,' said Steeple. 'The monster owl frightens you because you've never seen one. In these territories, at least, it is extinct and therefore unknown and because it is unknown your imaginings make it seem more terrible than it really is.'

'Have you ever seen one?' asked Quaver, who was slightly frightened by the legend of the monster, even when awake.

'No, of course not,' Steeple said. 'But I once met a Short-eared nomad owl who had travelled very far and he had seen one. He told me that our cousins across the salty waters had also seen giant owls and even fought against them, but that was long ago.'

'Do you think they might return one day?' asked Hunter, who was almost as fascinated as his younger brother by any mention of the monster owl.

'No, I don't think so,' said Steeple, smiling his usual grave and solemn smile. 'No giant owl has invaded these territories for many hundred springs. You are all fortunate to be growing up in a time of peace and plenty. Of course, there is danger all around us always, but for the moment our only real problems are internal, either within the Barn owl community itself or with our neighbours the Tawnies and the little immigrants that live in no man's land. For the moment, there is no danger from outside.'

'So how do you propose to teach us about fear?' asked Dawn Raptor, returning to the point from which they had strayed.

Her father looked at her for a moment or two before replying. 'Before you leave home,' he said, eventually. 'I'm going to take you into danger, one by one, and in the midst of danger you will for the first time begin to come to terms with fear.'

'But it will only be a training exercise, won't it?' asked Quaver, sounding rather worried. 'You will protect us if we get attacked by something we can't handle?'

'Of course,' said Steeple. 'But to be successful, the exercise must also contain an element of risk. Otherwise, as Dawn Raptor suspected, it would be theory only and as such would prove to be quite futile.'

'Doesn't it worry you?' Dawn Raptor asked. 'A father who must deliberately lead his offspring into danger?'

'Naturally it does,' said Steeple, rather brusquely. 'It is the hardest lesson that a father has to teach.'

'Like Dapple when she explained to us that when we were grown up we had to leave home and take care of ourselves,' said Quaver. 'When she told us that we could never, ever come and live at home again?'

'That is even worse,' said Steeple. 'To face danger is always better than to lose the ones we love. Both for a mother and her young ones, that is truly the hardest lesson of them all.'

'Why teach it then?' Dawn Raptor asked. 'Why must we all conform to this conditioning – to this eternal Barn owl dogma? Shall we never be permitted to think and make decisions for ourselves?'

'It is natural, not dogmatic,' answered Steeple, who seemed quite unruffled by his daughter's challenge. 'We teach it against our individual wills, in the interests of survival. And for the same reason I must teach you how to come to terms with fear.'

'When?' asked Hunter, already attempting to steel himself for the ordeal that lay ahead.

'You are the first, Hunter,' said his father very firmly. 'You fly with me tonight. We shall fly from twilight until dawn, or until danger finds us. And when danger finds us we will pause and you will come to terms with fear.'

CHAPTER

3

Soaring above the territory that he knew and loved so well, accompanied by the steady wing beats of his father, Hunter felt a deep sadness at the thought that he must soon leave this peaceful homeland of copse, field and meadow for the great unknown – vast tracts of land he must learn to chart and navigate alone in the interests of survival.

The flaming harvest moon shone full as they flew, shedding a ghostly light on the fields, some of stubble, some still thick, golden corn, and on the dark trees that drooped drowsily with the weight of leaves, fruit and flowers that were about to fall. Even at this time of ripeness, Hunter sensed the autumn ·lurking somewhere behind the flaming moon, waiting to bring change and to reclaim the spoils of summer to the pungent, acrid earth from whence they came.

Midnight came and went as they flew on in ever-widening circles until at last they came to the ruined church where Steeple told him their ancestors had once settled, bred and for many generations had their being. As they glided high above the church's broken tower, Hunter sensed a sudden change in his father's flight path. He had picked up something down there in the lower world. Though receiving nothing yet, Hunter swerved alongside his father as their flight path changed and they veered east before beginning to drop silently downwards towards the long, dark copse that straggled the borders of their territory. Then Hunter picked up the danger, too.

Somewhere on the edge of the copse prowled a large predatory mammal, still out of sight in the distant darkness, but pinpointed by the owls' superb sensory skill.

'Have you got it yet?' asked Steeple, in a whisper, as they glided downwards in the direction of the unseen killer.

'Yes, I've got it,' Hunter answered softly. 'It's a fox, or else a wild dog.'

'Fox,' his father said. 'Or a big vixen, to be more exact. In a moment you'll come in range and get the rankness of the smell.' No sooner had he spoken than the stench drifted up and threatened to engulf Hunter as the two owls drifted closer to their quarry. 'Silence now,' whispered Steeple softly. 'When we get near enough to see her, circle with me and watch closely. She's found something she intends to kill.' They dropped still closer to the ground until the vixen came in sight, moving her haunches slowly and purposefully along the edges of the copse, her yellow eyes fixed on some point in the open field beyond. Hunter decided that what frightened him most was her strange, primeval beauty and the rank smell that rose up from her, transmitting an untamed and wanton lust to kill.

Suddenly Steeple turned on a surge of power and rose almost vertically till he was high in the night sky, remote from the slinking predator below. Hovering, he waited there till Hunter joined him and then began to circle once again. 'I have decided,' he said. 'We need fly no further this night in search of danger. We have found it here. Listen carefully to my briefing,' he continued, 'and do not interrupt me till the end. Then ask me to clarify what you have not understood.' Hunter nodded as they circled high up in the sky, keeping the vixen's stealthy movements monitored with their inner vision.

'You should know already,' Steeple said, 'that there are certain types of owl that do not live in fixed abodes as we and the Tawnies do, but camp out on the ground wherever they can get a living. To combat the constant danger from four-legged raptors they have developed ground defence techniques that are occasionally useful even to those of us who live in proper, well-protected homes like churches, barns or hollow trees. What we are going to do now is to pretend to be two nomadic, Short-eared owls who have nested on the ground. I shall play the part of the mother and your role will be that of the young owlet who has not yet learned to fly. We shall drop now into the field of stubble, midway between the copse and the family of rabbits that the vixen is preparing to destroy. She will come upon us as she steals towards the rabbits from her down wind position in the copse. Seeing that you cannot move, she will attack. I shall employ the decoy ground defence technique to distract her just as she reaches the critical distance, ready to spring, and it is already too late for you to fly away. Remember that you must not move, however close she gets. Use the static defence display, but do not take off until I tell you. Any questions?'

'Yes,' said Hunter, as they continued to circle high in the late summer sky. 'I've never used the static defence display before. What if it doesn't work?'

'It will work,' said Steeple. 'Just before the vixen reaches the critical distance – the point of no return, when she is so close that you no longer have time or space for flight – the sudden increase in fear will send a message to your brain and the rest will happen automatically.'

'Supposing that it doesn't?' said Hunter, who had begun to wish that his father had been a much more common owl who took less interest in his education and let fear find him by itself.

'If it doesn't work, I shall attack the vixen from behind,' said Steeple, sounding quite calm and sanguine, as if he relished the prospect of battle with any vicious beast, in spite of his religion and his position on the Barn owl council.

'Very well,' said Hunter, closing his eyes and taking a deep breath. 'Ready for action stations when you are.'

'Right!' said Steeple. 'Action stations now.'

There was no more time to think, for Steeple veered west and dived down towards the field where they would meet the vixen face to face. Hunter followed close behind and as they plunged earthwards he came to understand what his father had meant earlier by the thrill of fear, for as danger seemed to spring up from the darkness down below he knew in those few moments that he had never before seen so clearly or felt so vividly alive.

Steeple and Hunter dropped so swiftly from the sky that the vixen did not see them land, though she had already begun her stealthy, slinking course across the field. But she sensed them soon afterwards, almost before they had taken up position, with Hunter sitting tall and huma-noid directly in her path, while his father lay down outside the vixen's line of vision, behind a mound of earth, with one wing half trailing on the ground as if it had been broken.

The she-fox paused in her slow approach, lifted one front foot from the ground and cocked her cruel head slightly to one side. As she spotted Hunter, straight ahead, her foot came down again, her body stiffened, she snarled softly and her yellow eyes burned brightly with the lust for blood.

Faithful to his brief, Hunter sat quite erect and still as the vixen crawled closer and closer to him until the rankness of her smell grew almost overpowering. Soon she was only ten lengths away, head lowered, teeth snarling and her tongue lolling only inches from the ground. The ten lengths dwindled to eight, seven, six and still Hunter did not attempt to take off and fly away. At five lengths distance the vixen paused and snarled, glaring at Hunter with eyes that glowed and swam with lust for blood. Though almost petrified, Hunter obeyed his orders and continued to stare back into those dreadful eyes.

'She's nearly there,' he thought. 'She's nearly reached the point of no return. Just one step more and she can spring. Oh, please, please let my instinct function now!'

As the vixen moved her haunches slowly, limbering to spring in for the kill, Hunter's body plumage suddenly began to ruffle and swell so quickly that in a split second he seemed almost twice his size. At the same time, his wings spread and rotated forwards like a giant fan.

The vixen wilted at this apparition and jumped half a pace backwards as Hunter clappered his bill, hissed, screamed and snorted at her with a terrifying battle cry. 'It works,' he thought, delighted with himself. 'I've done it, I've done it.' And he felt life flowing back through his body and firmness forming in those parts of him that had been liquefied by fear.

Frustrated, the vixen snarled, dropped her head and began to edge forward once again. No longer very young, she was experienced and exceptionally vicious, but realized now that dealing with this apparition was going to be a very different proposition from the killing of an ordinary farmyard cock. Yellow eyes glowing and her predator's heart now touched by fear, she nonetheless stole forward determined to tear Hunter limb from limb.

Hunter swelled and snorted ferociously as she reached the critical position once again, baring his talons ready for battle as she moved her slow haunches ready for the spring. Then a louder and more fearsome screech than Hunter's shattered the air as if it meant to carry to all the owls in creation and beyond them to the pale moon that bathed the night-time fighters in its light. From the corner of his eye, Hunter saw

Steeple emerge from behind his clump of cover, dragging himself on his belly with both wings limp and trailing as if they had been broken.

The vixen leaped like a hare on all fours and spun round to face the new intruder. Then her head turned and her eyes flashed back to Hunter, who was, after all, so much closer to those cruel and practised jaws. At that moment she was distracted once again by a piteous mewing from behind her. She turned again and stared at Steeple as he dragged his clumsy, broken-seeming body across the cornfield stubble. Even in the midst of fear, though still ready to do battle, Hunter was fascinated by his father's histrionics.

'What a performance,' he thought proudly, as the crumpled body flopped and dragged its way along the ground accompanied by heart-rending mews of pain and fear.

The killer cast one quick glance back at Hunter, who still stood war-plumed and erect, whereas the other creature was clearly maimed and half-dead already. Lured by the prospect of an easy kill, the she-fox leaped towards Steeple and bounded the few remaining paces that separated her from an orgy of bloodletting and revenge. Hunter held his breath. Would his father take off before the vixen reached him, or would he turn and fight?

In a split second that seemed like all eternity, Hunter saw the vixen cross the critical divide and spring while at the same instant Steeple bunched up all of the power and strength within him and thrust forwards up into the air. For one moment neither fox nor owl was in contact with the ground. Then the fox crashed nose first into the field while Steeple rose gracefully up into the air, circled and then gave word for Hunter to follow him.

The vixen gnashed her teeth and howled with rage, thus warning all prospective prey for many meadows round. She saw a great white shadow as Hunter soared above her on the ascending flight path towards his father and howled once more at the sky, part in rage and part in that strange fear of the unknown that Steeple had described at twilight. Then she stopped her futile baying at the moon and snapped in frustration at the stubble across which her maimed and easy prey had dragged itself before some magic had spirited it away into the air and into a realm that lay far beyond the vixen's ken.

Snapping at the stubble with her teeth, the vixen became aware of something long and greyish white that brushed and tickled her nose as it stuck up from the ground. At first, she drew her head back in surprise and then bent closer to examine this curious feather which was all that was left now to testify to the passing of those secret creatures from another world, suspended somewhere between heaven and earth, a world of which men and foxes know so very little.

CHAPTER 4

Not long afterwards, when the first leaves had begun to fall, Hunter sat in the barn with his mother, his brother and his sister anxiously awaiting Steeple, who was due to return sometime before dawn from the biannual session of the Barn owl council with news of the arrangements that had been made for their further education.

Day had just begun to break up the darkness with faint stripes of pink as their father flew in after his long journey from the west, settled on his favourite perch and greeted each of them in turn. Quaver was bouncing up and down on his perch, unable to mask his excitement. Hunter fidgeted, full of curiosity and only Dawn Raptor sat still and aloof, as if her father's homecoming with the news that was about to determine all their futures was of little or no concern to her, but merely some new ritual or protocol that must be borne with all the rest.

'Well, father?' asked Quaver, unable to stand the tension for a single moment longer. 'Am I to study poetry and singing? Has Hunter been accepted for owlology? Where is Dawn Raptor going? For the Great God Bird's sake, tell us soon or else we shall go mad. We've hardly eaten all night long. We just kept flying back here all the time to see if you'd arrived. I know you must be tired, but please, please don't keep us in suspense!'

'One at a time,' said Steeple, turning his grave smile from Dapple to his youngest fledgling. 'We'll start with Quaver, since as usual he seems to be the most impatient. You, Quaver, will indeed be studying poetry and singing and you will be taught by Bardic, our current expert on the Barn owl council.'

'Not the Bard Owl himself?' asked Quaver, his eyes almost rounded with a surfeit of surprise and pleasure.

'Yes, indeed,' said Steeple, smiling once again. 'You have been very lucky, though I must warn you that you may not find Bardic as tolerant and easy to get on with as you might expect. Like so many poets and composers, he has his own little habits and eccentricities that you will almost certainly find difficult to adjust to, especially after the more conventional environment you've been used to here.'

'I shan't mind at all,' chirped Quaver, cheerfully. 'It will make a change and you have always told us, father, that change is an essential component in any form of higher education.'

'That's quite true,' said Steeple, whose expression had become a trifle graver, 'but there is change and change, and not all change is always for the better. However, I will give you the best briefing that I can before you leave and I'm sure you will behave sensibly and make the best of this great opportunity. As for Hunter, he too has been very lucky. He will be taught by Beak Poke, who is the longest serving member of our council and has been incumbent Owl Owl now for more than twenty springs.'

'What kind of bird is Beak Poke?' asked Hunter, who felt elated and anxious both at the same time.

'He's very old of course,' his father said, 'but he's certainly one of the greatest living experts on his subject. He's a pragmatist and when he was younger not everyone approved entirely of his methods. He's said to have lived for a while with a colony of immigrants and to have spent so much time in a woodland domain with the Tawnies that he almost went native. Yet his store of knowledge is immense, not only in his own subject, but in other fields as well.'

'What about Dawn Raptor?' asked Hunter, glancing at his sister who sat listening quietly, only her eyes moving slightly back and forth between her father and her brother. Both her body posture and the expression in her eyes seemed to suggest that she expected a disappointment but was determined to show no reaction whatsoever when it came.

'It's different for your sister,' said Steeple, frowning seriously at his daughter. 'She has not yet shown any special aptitude or ambition to excel in any one specific field. She's a good all-rounder who might benefit from a more practical form of higher education. For the moment, she'll stay on with us, at home, until she develops a new interest or until something suitable turns up.'

Both Hunter and his younger brother gazed solemnly at their sister to see how she might react to this decision, but Dawn Raptor sat quite calm and still and gave no sign of disappointment or displeasure. It seemed as if either Steeple or her mother had already prepared her for this decision, or else she herself had already guessed.

'Of course,' said Steeple, raising his eyebrows and scrutinizing Dawn Raptor with the sort of gentle severity that they knew so well, 'it may be that your sister is a late developer. She may discover a special talent or a keen interest in one particular subject at some time in the near or distant future. That quite often happens, and in such cases it is always useful to have as much practical experience as possible to fall back on. In education, as in life itself, theory without practice is seldom of any great advantage. So in the meantime, Dawn Raptor will stay on here with us.'

Watching his sister, Hunter saw a wry, ironic smile flit across her features and he felt that he could tell what she was thinking from a series of disturbing little things that she had whispered to him from time to time either during or at the end of Dapple's lessons. 'Indoctrination she means, not teaching,' was one that had quite shocked him, or, 'Why should we be burdened with this traditional mumbo jumbo that goes back twelve million years when all the world around us is changing into a new, exciting place?'

'Couldn't Dawn Raptor go as apprentice to the Dissident Owl?' piped up Quaver, whose mind had obviously been running along the same lines as Hunter's.

'Impossible,' said Steeple, as a frown once more engulfed his features. 'You can only become an official iconoclast as an adult, after taking at least two types of further education. Dissidents simply happen, they are never made.'

'Then why do you always have a Dissident Owl on the council?' asked Quaver. 'If he doesn't agree with traditional Barn owl lore, philosophy and religion, surely the Dissident member can be nothing but a nuisance?'

'Certainly the Dissident Owl can be a nuisance,' said Steeple, with a tolerant little sigh, 'but, don't you see, it is his role. It is Barn owl policy to give every point of view a hearing on the council. It would be very dangerous to deny any minority the chance of a lawful hearing. Without an official opportunity to air their views, the dissidents might feel frustrated and form some kind of clandestine, subversive movement.'

'I see,' said Quaver, who seemed most impressed by his father's logic. But as Hunter watched his sister, he sensed a stubborn, deep-rooted rejection of this thinking. Perturbed, he pondered to himself that it was perhaps a good thing she was being forced to stay for what she obviously thought of as a further process of conditioning.

His worries about Dawn Raptor were cut off as Steeple coughed and raised his head to command their full attention. 'I am tired now and I want to sleep,' he said. 'But at twilight, Hunter, the briefing for your journey will begin. It will last from twilight until dawn and you will leave for your seat of learning tomorrow when night falls. Your briefing will be vitally important because the journey from here to Beak Poke's domain is to some extent a dangerous one.'

'Why is it dangerous, especially?' asked Hunter. 'You have taught us that the worst fear is fear of the unknown, so please tell me now, lest my imaginings turn into nightmares like the ones that Quaver has about the monster owl.'

'You will have to cross the lost domain,' said Dapple, unable to mask a motherly concern. 'That will be the worst part, I imagine.'

'What is the lost domain?' demanded Quaver, as eager and curious as if he were about to fly across the place himself.

'The lost domain is a forbidden territory where no owls ever fly,' said Steeple. 'It contains the secret forest and a vast, fertile stretch of parkland leading to a lake and to the largest man-made edifice that any owl in these territories has ever seen.'

'Why do no owls live or hunt there?' Hunter asked. 'Why are there no Tawnies in the forest or Barn owls in the parkland, if the territory is as rich as you suggest?'

'Tawnies inhabited the forest until several hundred springs ago, but that is another story. The peril, Hunter, comes from men with firesticks who patrol the place in daylight hours, but very rarely in the night. The other, much lesser danger you will face from the Tawnies in the woodland you must cross at the outset of your journey, soon after you have flown by the broken church, skirted the village and crossed the no man's land beyond.'

'Why the Tawnies?' Hunter asked. 'We have territorial conventions and agreements with them that go back for many hundred springs.'

'Tawnies vary, like Barn owls or any other creatures,' said Steeple, with a patient little smile. 'Only Tawnies vary more than we do because some are privileged and some are not. Those who live in our neighbouring woods have had few advantages and very little education. They are primitive, atavistic and unfriendly birds, though not dangerous if you follow the correct procedures. But again, more of that at twilight. I am weary after the council meeting and my long journey from the west. Rest now, Hunter, for you will need all your strength and energy for the new beginning and for the days and nights that lie ahead.'

CHAPTER

5

Hunter left home as dusk deepened on the following day. He flew over the fields of stubble, the broad meadow and the ruined church and then across the sloping copse that led down to the village in the valley. He skirted round the village, keeping well away from the few house lights that shone dimly in the ever-deepening autumn twilight and then struck out boldly across the open fields on the other side, heading for the opposite slope and the vast range of woodland where the fierce Tawnies lived.

As he sped silently through the darkness on his now practised wings, Hunter tried to steel himself for a sudden encounter with the atavistic lords whose ancestors had ruled that deep stretch of woodland for more than forty million springs. Oddly enough, his immediate fear was not so much of being savaged by their cruel talons as of having to communicate and explain his mission to these fierce primitive creatures of the forest.

'Those particular woods are controlled by a couple called Ferocity and Ripper,' his father had explained in the course of the briefing that had lasted all the previous night. 'Ferocity is even more belligerent than her mate, and her simple-minded brother, Stoop, is also quite a killer. Though their territory is large, one of them will almost certainly pick up your flight path and rise to challenge you. You can outfly a Tawny if you stay above the tree line, but you must on no account attempt it. Their communications are excellent and one of the others will be called to cut you off before you reach the boundary of the woods and no man's land beyond.'

'What if they attack me?' Hunter asked, having already formed a terrifying mental picture of the Tawnies and especially of the bellicose female called Ferocity.

'They won't attack you,' Steeple had replied. 'They will be hostile, frightening and unfriendly, but because of our territorial convention with the Tawnies, they will let you pass.'

'That's all very well,' thought Hunter as he entered the woods that seemed to loom ahead forever into the unfathomable distance, 'but what if I should have a language problem? What will happen if I can't make myself understood?' As he glided onwards, steering a straight course just above the upper branches of the trees, he silently rehearsed the words that he must say to guarantee him a safe passage, praying at the same time that he might cross the territory undetected.

But before he had finished practising his message for the second time, he heard the loud cry of a Tawny from across the woodland to his west. As he flew on with swifter yet still silent strokes of his powerful wings, an answering call came from slightly farther to his east. After Hunter's instincts had made a rapid calculation of the angles, distances and speeds, he realized that if the two Tawnies decided to intercept, they might just cut him off before he reached the safety of the no man's land beyond the Tawny woods.

Panic seized Hunter and in spite of his father's warning he decided to outfly them. Accordingly he switched his trajectory a little to the east, away from the nearer Tawny, hoping to steer a flight path between them and emerge from their domain without a confrontation. 'I'll soon be out of the wood,' he told himself as his wings whispered swiftly through the dark and silent trees. 'I'll soon be flying over copse and spinney and then out into Barn owl country and the open fields.'

When the Tawnies called again, Hunter realized they had picked up the variation in his flight path and were closing in rapidly in an attempt to cut him off before he reached the limit of the woods. 'Some day I'll come back here and face them,' thought Hunter, even as he strained every sinew to escape from their ancestral home. 'Some day, when Beak Poke has taught me all about them, I will come back and see for myself how these lords of the woodland thrive without the need of man and without the burden of a complicated education for survival.'

When the next calls came the Tawny to the west of him was so close that Hunter wavered in his flight, expecting at any moment to see enormous, rounded wings spread out against the night sky and talons stretched to bring him to a halt. Then almost to his surprise, Hunter found that the trees were thinning out and soon he could see the scrub and copse of no man's land that led down to Barn owl territory beyond. Even when Hunter had cleared the copse and left the danger well behind him, he did not slow down for several meadows' distance until he was almost halfway across the open farmland and heading for the forest of the lost domain. Only then did he ease his wing beats and begin to take stock of the fertile terrain below him. As Hunter relaxed, his appetite returned and was further whetted by the rustling and scampering of abundant food beneath his feet.

For a moment or two he was tempted to pause and catch himself a tasty snack. At least that way he would arrive at his new seat of learning with something in his belly. He knew very little about Beak Poke, except that he was a learned, desiccated bird who had grown very old and vague and was presumably no longer encumbered with anything so trivial as an appetite. Brilliant and eccentric as Beak Poke was famed to be, Hunter did not suppose that the venerable Owl Owl concerned himself with regular mealtimes or with the provision of food and comfort for his pupils. He might even decide to start his first lecture as soon as Hunter arrived and then forget all about eating until twilight the next day.

As he heard another short-tailed vole stir beneath his talons, the temptation to swoop down and eat it grew even more acute. There was no sign of Brook, the rustic Barn owl who occupied this isolated stretch of farmland wedged between the Tawny woods and the forest of the lost domain. 'He and his mate wouldn't miss a short-tailed vole or two,' thought Hunter, as his belly rumbled louder with the thinking about food. 'This is obviously fertile land and they have enough in their larder as it is, but to a hungry traveller like me a tasty little snack would make all the difference.'

Instinct and temptation make a potent combination, but Hunter's education and what Dawn Raptor called conditioning provided an even more powerful deterrent. Preparing to hover for the kill, Dapple's voice rang as loud and clear in Hunter's ears as it had done on the day when she had first taught him the six Barn owl commandments. 'No owl shall steal from another's territory, nor trespass there without good reason, nor fight or kill another owl of any kind unless in self-defence. This is the first rule for the survival of our species.' Driven by this inner voice, Hunter gained height so as to be in less direct contact with temptation, increased his speed again and flew purposefully onwards towards the looming forest of the lost domain.

'It is a place where men keep vigil in the moonlight whilst others of their species lie asleep,' Steeple had warned him during the course of the long night's briefing. 'Their task is to stay awake and prowl for fox and owl that feed on pheasant, partridge, woodcock or any other fodder that these men may wish to kill and eat themselves.'

'Strange that they should be so different from the men we know,' Hunter had replied. 'We have learned that humans welcome us for controlling the rodent population in the places where they live. Perhaps those who live in the lost domain are a different species from the ones with whom we co-exist. Perhaps they differ from others of their kind in the same way as we differ from the Tawnies, the nomad Short-eared owls or the little immigrants that live in no man's land?'

'The Man Owl doesn't think so,' his father had replied. 'He believes that they are just men, like any others, but with different behaviour patterns. Owls who have studied men say that such territories exist everywhere – places where no owl or other bird of prey is ever welcome.'

So Hunter flew on towards the forest that rose up before him in the darkness wondering whether the men in the lost domain or indeed elsewhere could distinguish between the different types of owl. 'Who knows?' he wondered, as the first line of trees loomed up ahead, 'They are earthbound, upstart creatures, yet they have their firesticks and the power to make the darkness light. Perhaps they have an Owl Man on their council whose job it is to study us as our Man Owl studies them?'

Once he had entered the forbidden territory, Hunter flew on swiftly just above the tree tops and did not look around him, as if ignoring danger would somehow make it go away. The forest below him seethed and teemed with life and though this was no man's land where he might kill and eat whatever he could find, Hunter was determined to take his father's advice this time and not linger till he had put the perils of the lost domain behind him.

The secret forest was both wider and deeper than the stretch of Tawny woods he had crossed before and it seemed an eternity before the trees began to thin out again and Hunter found himself flying over a broad expanse of parkland. Here, too, the ground was thick with food. Hunter sensed a dog fox on the prowl below him, and far across the parkland he picked up two immigrant owls, both of them males and both obviously out hunting. Although this surprised Hunter, in view of what he had heard about the lost domain, he did not pause to speculate but flew on high above the parkland till he saw the waters of the man-made lake glistening in the darkness and, beyond it, the stately gardens that swept up to the most enormous building he had ever seen. Hardly daring to look down as he flew above the house, Hunter nonetheless glimpsed two or three lights glowing from the mass of stone below him and climbed still higher in his onward flight until the crescent moon seemed to glimmer within easy reach in the expanse of eternity ahead.

Hunter did not drop his altitude again until he had cleared the smaller stretch of woodland on the far side of the lost domain and saw the tall steeple that marked the end of the forbidden territory and the beginning of the second village he must cross before he reached Barn owl country and his destination at Beak Poke's unusual seat of learning. Gliding downwards, Hunter flew due west above the sleeping hamlet, crossed a narrow strip of no man's land and then found himself flying over open farmland once again. In accordance with his father's briefing, he travelled onwards till he saw more woodland looming in the darkness far ahead and he knew then that somewhere just below him lay the abandoned farmhouse which was henceforth to be his seat of learning and his temporary home.

'Remember that Beak Poke lives in the house and not the barn,' his father had told him, to his great surprise.

'But that's incredible,' Hunter had replied. 'I've never heard of an owl living in a house before.'

'I warned you he was eccentric,' Steeple said, 'though in this case it was probably the most logical thing for him to do. You see, four or five springs ago his men abandoned the house and went to live elsewhere, but they still use the barn for storing straw and hay. So Beak Poke moved into the house and now he says he likes it there.'

Flying at tree-top height, Hunter soon located Beak Poke's isolated house and barn. He approached the ramshackle buildings with the greatest caution and flew around the abandoned farmhouse three times, calling out once to announce his arrival, but there was no sign of Beak Poke nor did any other creature stir to break the silence of the autumn night. On his fourth and closest circle round the house, Hunter called out louder, but there was no response from the silent house and barn or from the sleeping countryside around them.

'That's odd,' thought Hunter, with a sense of anti-climax now that he had finally arrived and found no one there to greet him. 'I suppose that he's gone out to get some food, and yet if he's anywhere in this territory, he must have heard my call.'

On his next circle round the old farmhouse Hunter spotted what he took to be the entrance to his temporary home. One of the upstairs windows had been torn off its hinges by the wind, leaving a gaping aperture in the wall. Hunter screwed up his courage, wheeled in mid-air and flew straight through the hole in the wall into what had once been the main bedroom of the house. Once inside, he settled on a ledge some three feet from the window and looked about him in a mixture of wonder, doubt and trepidation at the wondrous objects in the room.

The ledge on which he had found such a perfect perch was the wooden headboard of an old and damaged double bed, and from this vantage point he saw an armchair with bent springs pushing through the torn upholstery, a small table, a chair with a broken leg, a massive old oak wardrobe and a chest of drawers which stood against the wall in the opposite corner of the room. In between his wide-eyed inspection of these wondrous objects, whose purpose he did not begin to comprehend, Hunter cast frequent glances back at the aperture through which he had entered to make sure that it still afforded him unhampered access to the night outside.

As time passed Hunter grew more accustomed to his new surroundings and the novelty began to fade, whilst the hours of suppressed hunger made him feel more than a little peeved that there was no one there to make him welcome. There was nothing to eat and only the Great God Bird knew when Beak Poke might come back.

'I must get my own supper,' Hunter thought. 'I'm on my own now. It's no use waiting here for someone or something to turn up.' He gazed around the room once more, reluctant to leave the safety and comfort of his new quarters. Then, spurred on by appetite and curiosity, he left his perch and glided through the open window to explore the unknown territory outside.

After twenty circles round the abandoned house and barn, Hunter had found nothing edible in meadow, field or hedge. 'I bet a pair of kestrels came this way this morning and cleared up whatever food there was,' he thought, beginning to feel quite sorry for himself. 'It's all very well for the older, established owls to preach independence at us, but they already have mature and desirable territories of their own, together with years of experience to help them make the best of their rich pickings. We younger ones have nothing. We didn't ask to be born, so why should we be thrown out to fend for ourselves so soon and with so little help?'

Hunter's ever-widening circles took him to the borders of Beak Poke's barren territory and as he flew around its outer limits, he remembered the advice his sister had given him on the night before he left the safety of their family home. 'All this lore and religion that they teach us is really just conditioning,' she had said, speaking softly but with a sardonic contempt that Hunter had found quite disturbing. 'They don't want us to live naturally,' she'd continued. 'They don't want us to live and love how and where we please because it would threaten their own smug little lives and the precious standards of living that they've hogged and cornered for themselves. They don't educate us for survival, as they claim. They condition us to stop us causing trouble. If I were you, dear brother Hunter, I'd wake up and use your head. It's a hard world out there and you won't survive for long by just doing what you're told. That, dear brother, is called exploitation. Just remember that unofficial little rule and you'll stand more chance of survival than by obeying any of the rest.'

Hunter had been shocked at the time, but now, as he completed his final weary circuit of Beak Poke's domain, he was no longer quite so sure. Perhaps Barn owl lore, religion and philosophy were not quite perfect after all.

At the end of his final circuit he paused on the borders of Beak Poke's land and hovered above the banks of the muddy little brook beyond which a no man's land of copse and spinney led up a gradual slope and then thickened into a dense expanse of Tawny forest. 'I'll try the copse,' Hunter decided recklessly. 'It's no man's land, it borders on my territory and I'll explore it right up to the edge of those sacred Tawny woods.'

With this bold project in view, Hunter flew across the narrow brook and into the sparsely wooded slope that lay on the far side. Now desperate for food, he flew low down above the ground, listening for telltale rustling sounds below his eager talons. Intent and concentrating on his search for food, Hunter did not hear the almost silent whispering of huge wings in the sky above him and was quite unprepared for the giant shadow that suddenly obliterated the pale moonlight overhead.

Panic gripped Hunter for the second time that night and for one long moment stopped the beating of his heart. He dared not look up but flapped numbly onwards near the ground whilst the giant wings powered effortlessly along the same flight path some six or seven feet above his head. 'It is the monster owl, returned to claim its own and to kill all other raptors that dare to challenge him by flying the night sky.' This thought penetrated Hunter's panic-stricken mind, to be followed at once by a great surge of self-pity that flooded through him and filled his soul to overflowing. 'I don't want to die,' he gasped feebly to himself. 'It's not fair, on my first night away from home.' But even in the midst of all this terror and self-pity, the voice of Barn owl training and education spoke clearly to his inner ear. 'When you are trapped, fight back. At the critical distance, turn and sell your life as dearly as you can. Hiss and scream your battle cry so that others may hear you and be saved.'

With a choked-off little sob, Hunter wheeled in flight and turned upwards to face his mighty foe.

CHAPTER

6

To his amazement, Hunter was greeted by a low, melodious hoot and found himself face to face with an enormous Tawny. He flapped his wings, hovered and had no idea what he should do.

'Hello,' the Tawny said. 'Did I take you by surprise? I'd have hooted before, but I thought you'd heard me coming.' The rugged, handsome young bird spoke in a very aristocratic way, drawling the words out with that strange cadence and intonation that all highborn Tawnies seem to use instinctively from hatching unto death.

'To tell you the truth, you gave me quite a shock,' said Hunter. 'Your shadow felt so big that for a moment or two I thought you were the monster owl come back to claim his own.'

'Good heavens, no!' the Tawny said, dropping a little in the air so that he could converse on the same level. 'The monster owl is at least three times as big, and if I'd been him you'd have been dead and torn to pieces ten times over before you realized what was happening.'

'I suppose I would,' said Hunter, doubtfully. The handsome young Tawny seemed friendly enough, but then, with Tawny owls, you never really knew.

'In any case,' the Tawny said, 'it's at least nine hundred winters since a monster owl was seen in any of these territories. The general theory is that they are quite extinct.'

'Oh no,' said Hunter, anxious not to appear ignorant in front of this rugged yet highly sophisticated creature. 'Many of them are still living, but in other countries, far across the salty waters, though one was seen two thousand meadows north of here not more than fifty springs ago.'

'So you Barn owls say,' the Tawny drawled in his rather condescending tone. 'But then, we Tawnies only travel when we have to. We think abroad is awful, so we never ever go. But if you ask me, all that business about being seen fifty winters back is all an old crow's tale. Probably just a story that your parents tell to frighten you and get you to behave. You know the sort of thing: "Behave yourself, little chap, otherwise the monster owl will gouge your eyes out," and all that sort of rubbish. If you ask me anything, it's all a load of billclap.'

'Shall we perch somewhere for a moment?' asked Hunter politely. He was very tired and since they were nearer Barn owl territory than the Tawnies', he felt that it was up to him to extend the invitation. For all he knew, the young aristocrat might consider this stretch of no man's land to be part of his domain, but at any rate, inviting him to take a perch seemed like a tactful and diplomatic way of finding out.

'Right ho, then,' said the Tawny. 'I don't mind if I do, though I can't stay long because I haven't had my dinner yet. I just thought I'd hop over this way and see whether you'd arrived and how you're settling in.'

'You knew I was coming?' asked Hunter in surprise, as the two of them settled side by side on the sturdy branch of an ancient willow tree.

'Of course I knew,' replied the Tawny in his rather condescending drawl. 'By the way, my name's Yoller. What's yours?' Hunter told him and replied as best he could to the Tawny's formal little bow.

'But how did you know I was coming?' he asked, wondering whether Ripper, Ferocity or Stoop had been able to transmit the message all that distance from the deep wood he'd crossed at the outset of his journey.

'Old Beak Poke told me just the other night,' said Yoller. 'By the way, I hope you're finding enough food. I'm afraid the poor old boy got rather feeble towards the end. He let the place run down pretty badly, I'm afraid.'

'Towards the end?' asked Hunter, as yet unable to grasp the significance of what the Tawny owl was saying.

'Poor old fellow,' Yoller said, as he shook his head and sighed. 'He was almost geriatric towards the end.'

'Geriatric?' asked Hunter, whose head had now begun to swim. 'What does that mean, please? I'm afraid I've never heard the word before.'

'Oh, it means senile, wobbly on the old pins – perhaps a bit sloppy and incontinent as well. You know, all that sort of thing. If you ask me anything, it's a wonder that the poor old boy didn't conk out a great deal sooner than he did.'

'You knew him well, I take it?' asked Hunter, trying to copy the Tawny's casual, sophisticated tone in spite of the implications that were bursting in his brain.

'Yes, of course,' said Yoller, airily. 'I was the one who found him in the road. Poor old bird, I bet he never even knew what hit him.'

'What did hit him?' asked Hunter, still struggling to grasp the fact that Beak Poke, his future mentor, had been killed.

'Oh, you know, one of those things that men tear about in on the roads. The things that have lights on in the night. I suppose the poor old chap was dazzled and just flapped straight into it, instead of veering to one side. I must say, I'm surprised you hadn't heard.'

'I didn't even know that he was dead,' said Hunter, who was still numbed by this dreadful news. 'When did it happen?'

'Two nights ago,' said Yoller, 'on the road that separates his territory from no man's land, about two meadows' distance to the east of where we're sitting now.'

'Did you actually see him die?' asked Hunter, who in spite of himself was filled with morbid fascination. He had never seen a dead owl, let alone been present at the moment of decease. He supposed that he would see many and become accustomed to mortality in the course of time, but the young Tawny's calm, offhand manner in the face of death struck him now as most adult and impressive.

'I didn't see the actual impact,' Yoller said. 'The thing with lights on it had just begun to move again when I arrived and saw old Beak Poke lying in the road. I flew down to him at once, but there was nothing I could do. The poor old bird was still semi-conscious, but quite obviously a goner.'

'Did he say anything before he died?' asked Hunter, remembering the first words he had ever heard and the last that must be spoken by every Barn owl before his journey to the great beyond.

'Not much, actually,' answered Yoller. 'Or at any rate, it wasn't very clear. He was half-stunned, I suppose. Anyway, he was babbling away to himself about something that sounded like knowledge and survival. I couldn't make head or tail of it myself, but it sounded like a kind of jingle, or else part of some sort of hymn or prayer. It gave me quite a turn, I can tell you, to hear the poor old boy mouthing all that gibberish just before he died. I mean to say, physically he'd turned almost senile, as I said before, but mentally he was still a very dry old stick – very wise and very clever, in his way. I suppose the pain and shock had addled his poor old brain and he probably had no idea at all what he was saying.'

Hunter turned away as Yoller spoke, so that the rugged young Tawny should not see the tears that had welled up in his eyes. The idea that Beak Poke, the pragmatic, intellectual Owl Owl he had never met, should have remembered and cared sufficiently to repeat the vital part of their credo even when battered, crushed and on the point of death, moved Hunter so much that he heard the first words then as clearly as the first time his mother had taught them to him in the springtime of his days.

'Hoard and covet not
But be brave and free.
Quest always after knowledge
And slowly learn to know
What science cannot see.
Seek and strive for learning,
Be temperate and wise
For skill and wisdom only
Will help us to survive.'

For several moments after Yoller had finished his account of Beak Poke's death, Hunter was too full and fraught with emotion to turn back towards the Tawny and too uncertain of his voice to speak. He was, after all, a very young owl and for the first time in his life a long, long way from home.

'I say, are you all right?' asked Yoller, sounding most concerned. 'You haven't caught some kind of rheum, or fever, have you? Your chest is going up and down as though you couldn't breathe.'

'Oh, it's nothing to worry about,' said Hunter, pulling himself together with a massive effort. 'I'm really quite all right. I was just thinking how awful it must have been. For him, of course, but also pretty harrowing for you.'

'Oh, it wasn't very jolly,' said Yoller, dropping an octave or two lower into a more serious, reflective tone. 'But then, he really was a very desiccated, ancient owl indeed. He could no longer look after himself properly, and when you come to think of it, he didn't suffer very long. It was a fairly quick, clean death and I suppose that's as much as any of us can hope for when the final moment comes.'

'I suppose so,' said Hunter, who was feeling less numbed now and beginning to ponder the implications for his own immediate future. 'Well, there goes my further education, anyway,' he said, with a little sigh and a shrug. 'They won't be able to find me an alternative seat of learning until the next council meeting, and even then there may not be any other places going till next spring.'

'I'd look on the bright side, if I were you,' said Yoller, raising his eyebrows slightly as he looked back at Hunter. 'There is at least one consolation. With Beak Poke still alive, there'd hardly have been enough food to go around, especially not with that little immigrant on the scrounge.'

'Immigrant?' asked Hunter, more than a little bewildered and wondering how many more surprises this long, hungry night might hold in store.

'I'm afraid so,' said Yoller, drawling the words out in disgust. 'You've got a blasted immigrant squatting on your land. I saw her lurking around the edges of this copse about fifteen nights ago and then again the day before poor old Beak Poke died. At least, I think it was a female. From that distance I couldn't really tell.'

'You mean a Little owl?' asked Hunter, to make certain that he had understood.

'I mean a blasted immigrant, old boy,' said Yoller sharply. 'Another bloody scavenger from overseas. Think what you like, but if you don't scare that one off your land, or kill it, you'll get damn all to eat.'

'What is overseas?' asked Hunter, wondering how much worse the news would get before the night was through.

'Overseas means from across the salty waters,' Yoller said. 'That's where those blasted squatters came from, less than a century ago.'

'Why didn't Beak Poke scare her off?' asked Hunter, feeling more and more confused.

'Oh, you know Beak Poke,' answered Yoller, who obviously did, or had done, very well. 'He was old and feeble, and in any case he liked talking to the wretched little things. You know, finding out how they lived, where they came from and all that sort of thing. As if we didn't know already, without all that blasted empirical research, or whatever it was he used to call it.'

Hunter opened his bill to say something and then thought better of it. It had been a long, hard night and he had no desire to argue with the Tawny at this stage. 'Will you be around this way about the same time tomorrow night?' he asked instead, as Yoller yawned and spread his enormous, rounded wings.

'I might be,' his new friend replied. 'Though of course, only with your permission,' he added, bending his head in a patronizing and ironic little bow. 'After all, although this is officially no man's land, it's much more your territory than mine.'

'Oh, please, do come,' said Hunter, urgently. 'I've enjoyed meeting you and I should so much look forward to seeing you again this time tomorrow.'

'I'll drop by, if I'm in the district,' said Yoller casually and then flapped his big, strong wings and sped away.

CHAPTER 7

Hunter's feelings were very mixed as he watched the big owl wing his way up the slope towards the dense Tawny woods from whence he came. He liked him, there was no denying that. Though obviously very young, Yoller was confident, composed and debonair. He seemed to know an awful lot and his suave manner did not altogether fit with the image of a Tawny that Hunter carried with him from his education.

Now that he had gone, a host of questions flooded into Hunter's mind. For example, why did Tawnies count the ebb and flow of time in winters, not in springs? Was it true that Tawnies did not believe in higher education, and if that were the case, how come Yoller knew so much? Could his new friend really bring himself to kill an immigrant that he found trespassing on his land? He knew some Tawnies did, but would Yoller? 'I'll ask him tomorrow, or when I've got to know him better,' thought Hunter. 'I know I oughtn't really to approve of him, but on the whole I'd say he was just about the most impressive creature that I've ever met.'

Hunter sat on the willow branch for quite some time, ruminating on the events of the long night and trying to make up his mind between the rival claims that hunger and fatigue were making on his body and his mind. Fatigue wanted him to fly the shortest route back to the farmhouse, re-establish himself, rest and then sleep in the safety of what was now to be his home. Hunger and curiosity, on the other hand, urged him to make a brief detour to the place where Beak Poke had perished and to try for a morsel of food in the overgrown hedge beside the road.

Eventually, hunger and curiosity won the battle for the second time that night and not long before dawn Hunter took off from the branch that he had shared with Yoller, flew out of the copse on the eastern side and began to glide slowly over the dark tarmac and the unkempt verge, half-dreading and half-hoping to spot a feather or some other evidence of Beak Poke's passing.

Suddenly he heard a rustling in the verge below him, as if a small animal had heard him coming and was dashing to take cover in the hedge. Hunter wheeled, climbed a little higher above the sound and waited for his radar to locate the prey. As he fixed it in his sights and prepared to dive, a ragged, round-winged shape burst from nowhere and dived into the unkempt grass below. He heard a strangled squeak and then saw the scruffy yet somehow graceful shape rise upwards from the verge and bounce back quickly to its perch on a five-barred gate across the road.

Still soaring silently and hoping the intruder had not spotted him, Hunter looked long and closely at the nocturnal poacher on his land and saw that Yoller had been right. The intruder was an immigrant, a Little owl, and from her markings and the way she wore her feathers, Hunter decided she was a female and still quite young.

Confused and uncertain as to how he should react, Hunter circled again on the dark side of the moon and watched the poacher make a dainty meal of the morsel she had just pinched from under its rightful owner's very nose. One part of him wanted to stay out of the way and watch this ragged Little owl without attempting to challenge her or to communicate in any way. Hunter was still very shy and he felt that he had already had enough adventures on his first night away from home. On the other hand, this was his territory, not hers, and if he wanted to survive, he must start as he intended to go on,

'I must look very fierce,' thought Hunter, as the little female finished her snack and then sat preening herself quite prettily on top of the five-barred gate. 'I must be assertive, but not aggressive,' Hunter reminded himself. 'If I frighten her too much, she might attack me. Then I'd have to fight her, and we don't want anything like that. It's against our laws to kill another owl, except in self-defence, and in any case, I couldn't bring myself to do it. But I must go down there and tell her to keep off my land. Of course, I know that we Barn owls sympathize with the little immigrants' plight, but if they move in and settle on someone else's territory that would mean pure anarchy, or the beginning of the end.'

Thus armed with righteous indignation and puffed up by the centuries of lore, learning and tradition, Hunter caused his breast feathers to swell, bared his talons and swooped down resolutely from the sky to challenge his pretty, unwanted little squatter. As he homed in on the five-barred gate, his wings spread wide, the Little owl cocked her head calmly to one side and watched him alight on the top bar of the gate beside her. She did not move her body as he landed, but turned her head at right angles and gave him a bright but rather wistful little smile. 'Hi!' she said, 'I was wondering when you'd come down from the sky and say hello.'

This approach disarmed Hunter altogether. In spite of her accent and the strange, lilting cadence, the Little owl spoke very clearly and there was no doubt at all as to what she had said. 'Pleased to meet you,' Hunter stuttered, feeling rather foolish. 'My name's Hunter and I thought I'd introduce myself, since this is my territory that you're poaching on.'

'Poaching?' the little immigrant replied, turning her head sideways again and widening her big, attractive eyes in the prettiest and most innocent manner. 'Oh gee, I'm sorry. I didn't know you were the new landlord here.'

'Well, I am,' said Hunter, as flustered as before, 'so if you don't mind, I'll have to ask you not to hunt here any more. I've only got just enough land to live on as it is.'

'Oh well, lucky you,' the little female said. 'I don't have any land at all.'

'You must have some,' said Hunter, unsure of himself and not wanting to confuse the issue. 'All owls have some territory allotted to them even if it's only no man's land. Otherwise they couldn't live.'

'You're so right,' the little immigrant replied. 'Some owls can and some owls can't.'

'Can't what?' asked Hunter.

'Can't live, I guess,' the immigrant said, cocking her head sideways with an ironic little smile.

'Well, you seem to manage somehow,' said Hunter, who had an uneasy suspicion that things were not working out quite the way he wanted. 'At any rate, there seem to be enough of you Little owls around.'

'Oh, we manage,' she replied, 'but it's tougher than you think.'

'It's hard for all of us,' said Hunter, feelingly. 'Surely there must be some stretch of no man's land where you can find a living? Why do you have to come and poach on patches that belong to someone else?'

'No man's land is kind of lonesome,' replied the Little owl, opening her big eyes wide and looking very wistful. 'It's lonesome, it's dangerous and you never know what's going to happen next. I guess that's why other owls don't want it. I guess that's how it got to be no man's land from the beginning.'

'That's all very well,' said Hunter, determined to be firm and stick up for his rights. 'But what would happen if I let you and your family move in here on my land? I'd starve to death, wouldn't I? And in any case, you can't simply wander around squatting on other people's property. It simply isn't done.'

'Beak Poke didn't figure things that way,' the little female answered rather sadly. 'He was a sweet, kind, wise old bird and he encouraged me to stay. Sure, he was kind of decrepit and dilapidated, all old bones and bits of white, wispy feather, but he knew more about the different owl cultures than any other bird I ever met.'

'Funny he didn't mention anything about it to my father,' said Hunter, shaking his head and fidgeting nervously on the five-barred gate. 'My father gave me a very thorough briefing before I started out. I'm sure he'd have mentioned an immigration problem, if Beak Poke had explained the situation to him first.'

'Maybe he wanted you to have a nice surprise,' the Little owl said, turning sideways again and smiling at him in a rather mocking fashion. 'Beak Poke was devoted to his subject, as you surely know, and he may have thought it would be kind of useful for you to meet someone from another species on his land.'

'What's your name?' asked Hunter, having suddenly conceived what he took to be a very clever plan.

'Alba,' replied his unwanted guest, with a pleasant little grin.

'Alba?' repeated Hunter, hesitantly. 'That's unusual, isn't it? I don't think I've ever heard that name before.'

'You wouldn't have,' said Alba, still smiling at him, but seeming suddenly remote, her thoughts a long way from Hunter and the five-barred gate. 'It's a name from the old country, and in our language it means dawn.'

'Dawn is a common name among our female Barn owls,' Hunter said, only just resisting the temptation to mention his sister and thus strike up a familiarity that under the circumstances would obviously be out of place.

'I'm sure it is,' said little Alba, tossing her pretty head and glancing round the darkened countryside. 'In spite of all the different species, different languages and different customs, all owl culture is always basically the same.'

'That's not true,' cried Hunter, hotly. 'You immigrants don't have territories, Short-eared owls are nomads, Tawnies rule the woods and believe in the survival of the fittest and we Barn owls believe in equal opportunities for all.'

'Those are merely superficial differences,' said Alba. 'Deep down, all owl joys and sorrows are basically the same.'

Hunter pondered on this and could not find an answer. Superficial and profound, what was the difference? Was it merely a question of semantics, or did it depend on different traditions, climates, ecologies, religions, politics or what? 'That's all very well,' he said, using one of his mother's favourite phrases yet again, 'but what is superficial for some owls, for others is both fundamental and profound. You could say that owl values were relative, I suppose, but that is all.'

Little Alba smiled at Hunter sweetly, making him feel even more confused and bewildered than before. 'I guess you must be hungry?' she asked, moving her head slightly to one side in that wistful, winning way she had.

'Starving,' said Hunter, with great feeling. 'Since starting out at twilight, I haven't even had a snack.'

'Poor you,' said Alba, with another wry and sympathetic little smile. 'Just you sit tight right where you are, little Hunter, and I'll see what I can do.'

As soon as she had spoken, Alba took off with her funny, bouncing flight and disappeared into the copse on the other side of the narrow country road. Weak with hunger and fatigue, Hunter sat where he was and watched the spot where she had disappeared, while a series of random thoughts flooded through his tired mind. 'All this talk of relative values and different owl cultures is all very well,' he concluded, 'but it doesn't get us any nearer to the basic issue. It may be both educational and edifying, but it isn't going to solve a single thing. When she comes back, I'll simply knock it on the head and tell her that she's got to go. Yoller was right. If I let her sidetrack me like this, she'll not only stay around herself, but she'll have all her uncles, her aunts and her cousins here as well.'

Having made his decision, Hunter sat up tall on the five-barred gate, plumed his young breast feathers and stared resolutely at the spot where little Alba had disappeared into the copse. But in spite of himself, as he sat there waiting for the undesirable immigrant to reappear, little, nagging doubts and regrets began to tug and fret at the corners of his weary mind. 'She's quite nice, really,' was the first one that he sternly put away. 'It's a shame that they have to live in no man's land,' was the second notion that he crushed, and, 'Of course, she's quite pretty, in a funny foreign sort of way,' was dispelled by the sight of round, ragged little Alba bouncing back from the copse with a small snack held firmly in her bill. 'She's not pretty at all,' he thought. 'Not when you look at her objectively. She's just small, round and rather scruffy, and she hops about the place like some lower form of bird life. At the end of the day, she's got no more about her than a clumsy, soppy little sparrow.'

'Here you are, my hungry chick,' said Alba, landing quite gracefully beside him on the five-barred gate. 'Here's a little something for your supper.' Leaning forward, she placed what was obviously a common shrew between them on the top bar of the gate.

Hunter looked at the offering with great distaste. The rear portion of a shrew was very bitter, and in any case, all self-respecting owls kill what they eat and do not feed on carrion. Hunter was at one and the same time hungry, embarrassed and bamboozled, and on top of it all he had the recurring suspicion that he was being outmanoeuvred.

'Go on,' said little Alba. 'It's still good and warm, and you look like you're starving. Sure, it's no pheasant chick, but it will do you good. See? I'll bite off the bitter back part, and you can have the tasty bit up front.'

'Please don't,' said Hunter, shaking his head in acute embarrassment. 'I'm quite old enough to feed myself.'

Alba sat back on the five-barred gate and looked at him with a tolerant, amused expression on her face. 'OK, Hunter,' she said. 'If that's the way you want it. But you took food from your mother, otherwise you wouldn't be alive. And I guess she only stopped feeding you a short while ago.'

Hunter was nonplussed. The hungry part of him very much wanted to devour the shrew, bitter bit included, while the rest of him rebelled.

The food lay on the five-barred gate between them while he stared at the hedge across the road in an agony of indecision. Suddenly he heard little Alba move, turned to face her and saw that she had butchered the shrew and was offering the front part to him with her bill. She leaned closer to him as he stared, making it easy for him to take the food without even moving. Hunter let out a little sigh as his upbringing and his pride finally gave in to hunger, and he opened his bill, took in his little bite of supper and swallowed it whole.

'There's a good boy,' said Alba, sitting back again on the top bar of the gate. 'That's no banquet, but I guess it will help to keep you going.'

'Thank you,' said Hunter, eventually, as he felt the morsel of food warming him inside. 'That was very kind of you, but it doesn't really solve our little problem, does it?'

'What problem?' asked little Alba, cocking her head to one side and opening her eyes wide again.

'You say Beak Poke let you stay here on his land,' said Hunter, who was determined to get to the bottom of things and sort the matter out. 'But how do I know what he said, or didn't say? The poor old bird is dead.'

'I guess he might have told your father,' said Alba, hopefully. 'Maybe you should check with him?'

'I'm not going home,' said Hunter. 'At any rate, not yet. But I shall check with him, eventually. That's why I asked your name.'

'I knew it,' said little Alba, half-sad and half-reproachful. 'You've been listening to all these stories about Little owls not sticking to territorial agreements that are made with other species.'

'Please don't think I'm taking any notice of rumour or hearsay,' Hunter answered. 'I don't want you to think that I'm prejudiced in any way. But even if Beak Poke did make some arrangement with an immigrant owl, how do I know that immigrant was you? It might have been your cousin, or your sister or your aunt. Or supposing that you simply changed your name? I mean, there could be dozens of Little owls on this patch of territory, each claiming Beak Poke said that she could stay.'

Little Alba looked back at him with a hurt expression in her big, round eyes. 'My oh my, what a suspicious young owl you are,' she said, shaking her head a little as she spoke. 'You've been listening to too much propaganda, young Hunter. So now you're going to hear the truth. To start with, our civilization is older than yours. And how! We've been around since the beginning of recorded time. OK, so we've only been in this lousy district for about a hundred summers, but my parents and my grandparents were all born here, and being immigrants doesn't mean that we're savages without any kind of culture.'

'That may very well be so,' said Hunter, feeling that perhaps he had gone a little far on the subject of the cousins and the aunts. 'But what we're discussing here is not genealogy, religion, culture or tradition. What we are trying to establish is whether you have any right to stay here on my land or not.'

'Why don't we talk it through tomorrow night?' asked Alba, with a little smile. 'You must be exhausted and it's very nearly dawn. Why don't we meet some place, say tomorrow twilight, and continue our discussion then?'

Though it was true that day must shortly break, Hunter knew that in reality his little female immigrant was merely playing for time. But he was tired and he did feel that he might be able to order his thoughts and acquit himself better after a long rest and with a lot more nourishment inside him.

'Very well, then,' he said. 'Where shall we meet?'

'Right here?' said Alba, tilting her pretty head into a question. 'And don't be late,' she added, when Hunter nodded his assent. 'Because tomorrow, Hunter, I'm going to set your heart at ease. I'm going to show you how survival in this district can be simple. I'm going to prove that there's enough food for you, me and maybe a dozen young owls with healthy appetites as well.'

'Tomorrow, then, at dusk,' said Hunter, who did not really believe her, could not say no and was troubled deep inside by a feeling that he might be making a very great mistake. 'Where will you sleep?' he asked, turning for a last look at this funny little female before he took off on his direct flight path to the farmhouse.

'Where the dawn finds me, I guess,' Alba said. 'There's a vacant hollow tree behind us in the copse. I occasionally use it when I'm round this way.'

'Goodnight then,' said Hunter, spreading his long wings prior to take off. 'And thank you for the shrew.'

'Stay loose, Hunter,' the Little owl replied. 'Fly home safe and have a restful day.'

Not quite certain what she meant by 'stay loose', Hunter took off and flew straight back to his new home in the abandoned farmhouse, arriving there as dawn began to colour the night sky. He flew in through the window and flopped on to his safe headboard perch, nearer to complete exhaustion than he had ever been before in the course of his young and somewhat sheltered life. Though his mind was still teeming with vivid impressions of his first long night away from home, sweet fatigue completely overcame him and he fell asleep at once, with a dozen different questions still buzzing in his brain.

As Hunter slept, he dreamed of little Alba, tucked up snugly somewhere in the middle of her hollow tree, 'Stay loose, Hunter,' she said to him once more, in the middle of his dream, but before he could ask her what it meant, Yoller swooped down from the sky and forbade him to let the little poacher stay a single moment longer on his land.

'They're all the same, these blasted immigrants,' he said, in his drawling, aristocratic tone. 'Give them one hollow tree and they'll take over half the forest.' Then, suddenly, he was in the middle of the lost domain, flying for his life from Ferocity and Ripper who were closing in on him fast with their talons shining, sharp and at the ready. Just before they caught him, the sky blazed with man-made light and a thousand firesticks exploded, sending flames of death high up into the air around him.

He fainted with fear then in his dream and came to in the barn back home where his mother sang softly as the first rays of sunlight filtered through the rafters in the roof. 'Shall I make it?' thought Hunter, in his dream. 'Shall I survive to be a fully-fledged expert owl like Bardic, Beak Poke and my father, or shall I fall somewhere by the wayside and die half-formed and soon forogotten like so many of my kind?'

Hunter woke then to find himself bathed in real sunlight which was pouring through in a much wider shaft than he had ever known at home. The whole of his room was flooded with bright light from the gaping window, and from the sun's position Hunter knew that he had slept and dreamed until late into the mellow autumn afternoon.

He stirred himself on the bedstead perch, preened his ruffled feathers and stretched his sleepy, tingling legs and wings, listening to the song of day birds on the farmland round about him and to the loud hum of country life that human ears are too insensitive to hear. He no longer felt sorry for himself, or lonely, but relaxed, warm and tingling at the thought of the fresh adventures that lay in store for him at twilight. He knew that sooner or later he would have to fly home to consult with his father on the matter of Beak Poke's death and the new arrangements that would have to be made for his further education.

'But not yet,' he thought. 'Not so soon after my first taste of freedom. I'll stay here a little longer, resting until daylight fades. Then I'll go out to meet whatever nightfall and my good fortune may bring forth.'

CHAPTER 8

Little Alba was not there when Hunter arrived at their trysting place, so he perched on the five-barred gate, feeling rather conspicuous and vulnerable as the last glimmers of light faded slowly in the darkening sky.

As he waited for the little immigrant to appear, Hunter rehearsed what he intended to say to her. Now that he had slept and eaten, he felt much firmer in his original resolve to remove her from his land. It was his duty as a Barn owl to preserve Beak Poke's territory intact, for himself and for other members of his species. Besides, what would Yoller think of him if he allowed the immigrant to stay? Nevertheless, and in spite of himself, he was interested in the secret concerning his new territory. If there really was a secret, how would he ever know it if he turned her off his land?

As Hunter was speculating on this problem, little Alba suddenly appeared from nowhere and perched beside him on the five-barred gate. 'Hi, Hunter!' she said, smiling her wry and cheerful little smile. 'How did it go, then, the first day on your own?'

'Very well, thank you,' replied Hunter, quite politely.

'Sleep OK?' enquired Alba.

'Like a dormouse in the hay,' replied Hunter, protecting himself with a Barn owl cliché that he normally refrained from using. 'How about you?' he asked, feeling that these nugatory preliminaries were perhaps useful after all before getting down to the nitty-gritty business of evicting the squatter from his land.

'Just fine,' said little Alba. 'The hollow tree back there in the spinney is no place to bring up a family, but it makes a neat little pad for the single female.'

'Why not a family?' asked Hunter, still thinking it politic to be polite and play for time. 'Is it too small, or is the district not suitable for chicks?'

'Both, I guess,' said Alba. 'The tree is kind of small and the hollow in it is too low down and near the ground. Then the Tawnies are too close for comfort and there's a family of weasels living about a quarter of a meadow's distance from the tree. They'd soon polish off any chicks that were left unattended.'

'What about this secret you were going to tell me?' asked Hunter, almost surprised that he had been able to get the question out so soon. 'We have to discuss the question of your staying here, you know, and before I can make a decision I must be in possession of all the relevant information. We learn that,' he added, a trifle pompously, 'as part of our basic Barn owl education.'

'Ready when you are,' said little Alba. 'Only it's quite some flight away and I guess you haven't eaten yet?'

'As a matter of fact, I have,' said Hunter. 'I've already had two field voles and one common shrew. And the secret can't be that far away, not if it's connected with my territory.'

'Where we're going isn't part of Beak Poke's old domain,' said Alba, looking at him with a grave expression in her big, wide eyes. 'But you could annex part of it to your territory, if you wanted. And you've got to believe it, Hunter, it may be risky but there's more food where we're going now than in any other place I've ever seen.'

'Let's go then,' said Hunter, who was excited, but also rather sceptical. If such a territory existed, so close to Beak Poke's land, then surely his father would have told him?

'OK, Hunter, follow me,' said Alba, and took off at once with quick movements of her blunt, rounded little wings. Hunter followed, keeping pace easily with slow beats of his long, powerful wings, wondering at the funny, bouncing flight of the little female as she hopped along ahead.

They flew over the fields to the south of Hunter's abandoned farm-house and then still further south until the terrain below them changed from field and meadow into wooded parkland and Hunter realized with a sudden shock of fear that little Alba was leading him back into the lost domain.

One part of him wanted to turn at once and speed back to the safety of Beak Poke's abandoned farmhouse but, for some reason that he could not explain, Hunter flew on behind little Alba as she penetrated deeper and deeper into the lost domain. Was it curiosity, was it a sense of adventure, or was it because he did not want to show the female immigrant that he was afraid? Hunter asked himself these questions briefly, in his panic, but forgot to answer them as the forbidden territory engulfed them both and yielded up its secrets.

Flying lower now, below the top branches of the trees, Hunter saw things that he had only been able to imagine on his previous high, fast crossing, closer to the pale moon, it seemed, than to the earth beneath. Soon they emerged from the trees and came in sight of the biggest house that anyone could possibly imagine. From high in the sky it had looked huge, but there, at tree-top height, the sheer size and grandeur of the place took Hunter's breath away. As the great house loomed up ahead of them, Alba turned for the first time and closed one eye in a solemn little wink. Then she bounced back into flight and veered west, away from the huge building, with Hunter gliding silently behind her. Though the rest of the house was in total darkness, two dim lights shone from ground floor windows in the east wing of the building and Hunter held his breath until these were well behind them and they were flying towards the parkland that stretched away beyond the vast expanse of lawn and the big lake whose waters glistened softly in the moonlight.

Halfway up the sloping parkland, Alba ceased to move her rounded, stubby wings and disappeared with surprising skill and grace into the middle branches of a tall and stately oak. To follow her, Hunter was obliged to brake, wheel sharply and then manoeuvre through the outer foliage to perch beside her near the centre of the tree.

'Are you OK?' asked Alba, as he settled beside her on the sturdy branch. 'I hope you didn't scratch your wings. I guess I forgot how long they were compared to mine.'

'It doesn't matter,' said Hunter, preening his feathers and plucking bits of leaf and twig off with his bill. 'It's a safe place, here in the centre of this oak. I shouldn't think that even man-made light could find us here.'

'It's a good place when you're hungry,' little Alba said. 'Look down there, at the parkland. On wettish nights the whole place comes alive with short-tailed voles.'

'That's all very well,' said Hunter, his mouth beginning to water in spite of the fear that he had so far kept at bay, 'but what about the firesticks?'

'Oh, so you've heard about this place?' said Alba, cocking her head and looking up at him in mock surprise.

'Of course I have,' said Hunter. 'It's known as the lost domain and it's strictly off limits to our species. It's said to be the most dangerous place for many thousand meadows round.'

'There's lots of goodies, though,' said little Alba, half-teasing him and half-apologetic.

'That's as may be,' said Hunter, striving to suppress his appetite as he sensed the voles seething in the grass below them. 'But goodies or not, I'd rather go hungry than be blasted by a firestick. You can stay here if you want, but I'm off back to Beak Poke's as fast as I can go.'

'Just have a little snack before you leave,' said Alba, in a teasing and ironic tone. 'You sit here out of sight and I'll bring you something for a starter and then something for you to take back home.'

Hunter opened his bill to protest, but before he could utter a single word Alba had bounced off her perch and was drifting five or six feet above the long grass in the parkland. Hunter noticed that her wings looked far less ragged when she was in flight and in spite of himself and his fear he was impressed by the way she quartered the ground below her, all reflexes ready to strike at the first sign of prey beneath her talons.

He looked away from her and scanned the darkness of the parkland, waiting for the bang and the blinding flash of light which his father and mother had warned him about and described so well. But instead of an explosion he heard a little screech of glee and looked back to see Alba lifting from the ground with a large vole held firmly in her bill. In no time at all she landed on the branch beside him, deposited the vole, said 'Eat, Hunter!' and then flew off again. Hunter watched her go, then examined the succulent vole beside him, sighed and looked back to the parkland, where Alba was now quartering the ground a little further from the tree. Almost at once she swooped, gave another gleeful little cry and bounced swiftly back up to the branch bearing a second vole, even larger and more tasty-looking than the one she had caught before.

'Eat, Hunter,' she said again, placing the second morsel daintily beside the first. 'Eat, before the food goes cold.'

'What about you?' asked Hunter, whose appetite had temporarily overcome his fear.

'Oh, don't worry about me,' said Alba, smiling. 'I'll be right back with my first course before you're halfway through. We're going to have ourselves a real vole banquet before you start your journey home.' She paused then before take off, glanced back at him, winked mockingly and said: 'Just remember, Hunter, if the firestick's going to get you, then make sure it gets you when your belly's full. That way you die quicker and happier and it doesn't hurt so much, they say.' Then she bounced off again and as soon as she had gone Hunter devoured the first vole, which was delicious.

'I'd better wait and see if she catches another for herself before I eat the second,' he thought shamefacedly, and then swallowed the remaining morsel anyway.

This time it was much longer before Alba landed beside him, deposited a third vole on the branch between them and then patted him gently with the edge of her rounded little wing. 'There's a brave young Barn owl,' she said, smiling brightly. 'Now you eat this one, too. There's plenty more out there, not to mention all the other food that's running around in the garden or up there in the forest.'

Hunter shook his head, overcome with guilt, and braced himself for action. 'No,' he said. 'You sit here and eat. It's my turn now.' And before Alba could reply he pushed off from the safety of his branch to fly out of the tree and across the open parkland. Exposed in free flight he felt terrified, expecting that bang and blinding flash of light which Steeple had described so well. But then he remembered his father's hardest lesson and how he had been taught to come to terms with fear. 'I'm afraid now of fear itself, and not of firesticks,' he realized, and this helped him to concentrate on hunting and to forget the hidden dangers of the lost domain.

Being a Barn owl, Hunter flew higher and circled wider above the ground than little Alba and this took him quickly to a greater distance from the safety of the tree, yet the grass beneath him now seemed bare of voles, as if they had all vanished into hiding. 'I can't go back with empty talons,' thought Hunter, skirting still wider and farther from the tree. 'There must be something down there for me to catch.'

And then Hunter picked up the mole emerging from his little hill only thirty feet below. Hunter set his systems, dived, killed his prey instantly and bore the prize joint skywards while his brain raced with the food conversion factors that he had learned from Dapple. 'One vole and one house or wood mouse have a unit weight of one, but a mole weighs five times that amount, so I've caught five units in one go compared to Alba's three.'

Glowing with pride, Hunter flew back to the oak with his heavy piece of meat and set it down on the thick branch between himself and little Alba.

'My, what a big strong owl you are!' said she. 'A mole is something really rare and the taste is quite delicious.'

'A bit of luck, really,' said Hunter proudly. 'Anyway, it should keep you going quite some time. I do hope you enjoy it.'

'Oh, it's much too much for me!' exclaimed little Alba. 'You'll just have to stay and share it with me before you set off back to Beak Poke's place.'

Hunter was still hungry and in any case it seemed churlish to refuse. He still had plenty of time to make his predawn appointment with Yoller, and if he was to be blasted by a firestick on his way back home, then Alba was quite right. It would be much better to meet the Great God Bird in the sky after a banquet than on a semi-empty stomach.

'I'll carve,' said Alba, with a pretty little smile. 'Which part do you like best? Rump, fillet, leg or sirloin?'

'Oh, it's all the same to me,' said Hunter, who had only ever eaten mole twice in his life before and had been given fillet on both occasions, as befits the firstborn. 'Just have whatever you prefer and I'll eat up the rest.'

'Well now, let's see,' said Alba, carving the meat quite daintily. 'Let's have a sort of mixture, shall we? I'll just cut everything in half so that we can share the rough bits with the smooth.'

'You're right,' said Hunter, watching as Alba divided the different cuts of meat into almost equal portions. 'At five times the weight of a wood mouse, it's a bit too big to swallow whole.'

'There you are,' said little Alba, placing the slightly larger portions on the branch in front of him. 'Enjoy your banquet, Hunter, and afterwards I'll tell you why there's no need to be afraid here in the lost domain.' Hunter glanced up at her quickly, but she smiled and shook her head.

'Eat first,' she said, 'and then I'll tell you something that the other owls don't know.'

The food was so delicious that for some time Hunter forgot all about his fear. Closeted there with little Alba on the hidden branch in the centre of the mighty oak, he felt very safe and cosy – in fact, altogether better than at any time since he had left his family home. They finished the food quite quickly, pausing only to exchange pleasantries and to comment on the different cuts of meat, while Hunter wondered at the little immigrant's table manners, which were almost as good as his own mother's. When they had finished, each sighed, almost simultaneously and smiled with deep satisfaction into the other's eyes.

'Still feeling scared, Hunter?' asked Alba, her eyebrows raised in that quizzical, half-mocking way she had.

'Yes,' said Hunter. 'I feel better for the banquet and safe enough here in the centre of this tree, but deep down inside I'm terrified and shall be until this place is far behind me. Playing around with firesticks may be your idea of fun, but I can tell you that it doesn't in the least appeal to me.'

'There are no firesticks anymore,' said little Alba. 'The men have gone away.'

'I saw two lights in the great house beyond the lake,' said Hunter, angrily. 'Man-made lights, they were, or have badgers learned to light up the night sky in this mysterious domain?'

'They no longer come to kill the pheasant and the partridge in the parkland and the wood,' said Alba. 'So the whole place is alive with game. On the lake there are mallard, moorhen and other water birds as well. Most of them are too big for me to kill, but think of the chicks there'll be in spring!'

'If you stay here you won't be alive to see the spring, let alone taste your mallard or delicious duckling,' said Hunter, with passionate conviction. 'If you want to survive, for the Great God Bird's sake get back to your weasel-ridden hollow tree. You'll be a great deal safer there.'

'You don't believe me, do you?' asked little Alba, sadly.

'Of course I don't,' said Hunter. 'How can you know more about this territory than the Tawnies, who lived in the secret forest for many million springs before man usurped it from them? Or than we Barn owls, who have studied man's habits since he hunted the forest on all fours, all covered with hair like a clumsy daytime badger? On our council we have a Man Owl whose job it is to study human ways, just as our Owl Owl studies you, the Tawnies and all other types of owl. You immigrants arrived here fewer than a hundred springs ago and yet you pretend to know more about the habitat than our learned specialists who have studied these phenomena and handed down each piece of wisdom from one generation to the next since man first appeared on earth among us.'

'I guess necessity is the mother of invention,' said little Alba, patiently, when Hunter's long diatribe had ended. 'We didn't pick the danger zones, you know. We only used them because there wasn't any other place to go. Me, for instance, I was born right here in the middle of your so-called lost and dangerous domain.'

'Born here?' exclaimed Hunter, who could hardly believe his ears. 'But that's impossible. It's one thing to come hunting in the lost domain at dead of night. It's a challenge that sets a thrilling tingle in your every fibre. But to be born and bred in the midst of such appalling danger – why, that's quite beyond belief!'

'My first home was in a hollow tree, across the parkland over there,' said little Alba, pointing with one ragged, rounded wing. 'Right on the edge of the slope, just before the beginning of the secret forest.'

'What about your parents?' Hunter asked, still trying to grasp the full implications of what little Alba had just told him. 'Do they still live here, in the lost domain?'

'No,' said little Alba, sadly. 'They don't live here any more. They don't live anywhere at all. They were killed three falls ago, on the edge of the woodland, right next to where we'd made our home.'

Hunter looked at the little immigrant in dismay, fearing the pain and sorrow in her eyes. He was very young and still embarrassed by the stark, uncomfortable realities of birth, accident and death. 'How did it happen?' he muttered, seeking refuge from discomfort by gazing far out into the darkness towards Alba's birthplace on the borders of the secret forest.

'The men with firesticks came,' said little Alba. 'It was the first and last time that I ever saw them. No firesticks have been here since my mother and my father fell to them.'

'How old were you when it happened?' asked Hunter, who really wanted to console her but was too unsure of himself to find either words or body language with which to communicate the confused emotions in his breast.

'Oh, I was very small,' said Alba. 'I'd only just learned how to hunt and my little brother was so uncoordinated that he couldn't even catch a butterfly.'

'How did you manage?' asked Hunter, wondering why he went on asking questions instead of putting one wing around her and expressing his heartfelt sympathy with a gentle hug.

'Oh, somehow we got by,' replied Alba, with a brave little smile. 'My big brother and my elder sister could both hunt a bit and there was plenty of food to catch, as you can see. It was hard, I guess, but we made out OK.'

'You can come and stay at my place, if you like,' Hunter blurted on a sudden impulse. 'There's enough food for two. There must be, if you and Beak Poke shared the place before.'

Little Alba smiled at him and shook her head. 'Beak Poke was a very old, emaciated owl,' she said. 'He ate hardly anything and wasn't really interested in food. Sometimes he was so busy thinking that he forgot to eat for days on end, until I took him something, or at least reminded him to try and catch a bit of something for himself. But you're young, Hunter. You haven't really finished growing and you need all the food that you can get.'

'But it's not safe here,' Hunter insisted. 'The men with firesticks may come back at any moment.'

'I guess that's possible,' said Alba, with another of her ironic, teasing little smiles. 'But no owl can live forever, and while the going's good I guess I'll stay on here and enjoy the riches of the lost domain. The winter's coming, Hunter, and food will be in short supply. Feel free to come over here and hunt with me if you run short at Beak Poke's place.'

'Thank you,' said Hunter, who was quite moved but did not want to show it. 'Does that mean that you won't be coming back to my territory, or sleeping in your hollow tree?'

'Oh, I'll come back and look you up from time to time,' said Alba. 'Two or three times, at least, before the fall is through. But when winter comes, you'll need the whole territory for yourself. You said so yesterday, remember?'

'I'm going now,' said Hunter. 'Do come and see me soon. And, Alba, I'm very sorry about what happened to your parents.'

'Stay loose, Hunter. Fly home good and straight, and have a restful day.'

'Same to you,' said Hunter, giving her one last, shy smile before he took off from the safety of the stately oak and flew back across the parkland towards the gardens and the lake, skirted the enormous house, now plunged entirely into darkness, and then headed back above the tree tops towards the open farmland where he would once again feel safe.

He thought about little Alba as he flew and concentrated on her language as a kind of antidote for fear. 'Fall is a better word than autumn,' he surprised himself by thinking. 'Leaves fall in autumn, the light dies earlier in the day. Fall means something whilst autumn's just a word. But why does she say "Stay loose" and "Have a restful day"? And why does she always say "I guess", when what she really means is "I suppose"?'

'I guess I'll have to ask my father,' Hunter thought, feeling a funny little thrill as he used a non-Barn owl expression for the first time in his life. 'Even if he doesn't know, he can ask the Language Owl at the next session of the council and then tell me later on.'

Of course, the main thing in Hunter's mind was not so much Alba's language but the little immigrant herself, the night's adventure they had shared, her change of mind about living on his territory and the things she had told him about her family, the firesticks and the lost domain. 'I wonder why I offered to let her come and live at Beak Poke's place?' Hunter asked himself, worried now by his own impetuosity. 'I'm too impulsive, that's my trouble. What on earth would Yoller say, if he knew about my invitation? Let alone my parents!'

Hunter flew out of the wood, left the dangers of the lost domain behind him and tried to put aside his confused impression of the night's events. Later, alone on his perch at home, he would relive and savour them again, able, perhaps, in peace and quiet, to learn, digest and draw conclusions from the experiences that had befallen him. For the moment, as he flew over Beak Poke's abandoned farmhouse and headed for his trysting place with Yoller, he needed a clear head and at least an appearance of composure for his meeting with the young, strong and most impressive Tawny.

CHAPTER

9

Hunter had no difficulty in finding the willow tree where he and Yoller had got to know each other on the previous evening, but when he settled on the same, comfortable branch there was no sign of the Tawny's presence.

In a way, Hunter was relieved. It gave him more time to compose himself and more time to work out how much to tell his new friend about little Alba and the lost domain. He wanted to question Yoller on these matters, but he was anxious not to give away too much information in return. Hunter was also worried about going home. He knew that sooner or later he would have to report back to his father about alternative arrangements for his further education, yet instinctively he wanted to stay in his new territory for a few more nights at least. The perils of the journey were now more real to him than they had been when he had first left home, and the prospect of crossing the deep woodland where Stoop, Ferocity and Ripper reigned filled him with a very special dread.

Lost in his private worries, Hunter was not aware of Yoller's arrival until he heard a faint rustle of those big broad wings a moment or two before the Tawny made a perfect landing on the branch beside him.

'Hello there,' said Yoller, with a friendly smile. 'How are you settling in?'

'Not too badly, thank you,' said Hunter, nodding rather shyly in reply to Yoller's greeting.

'Are you finding enough to eat?' the Tawny asked, yawning in a relaxed sort of way as he stretched himself and preened his splendid feathers. 'Your predecessor, Beak Poke, let things run down pretty badly, I'm afraid. As I told you yesterday, he got pretty feeble towards the end.'

'Oh, things could be worse,' said Hunter, doing his best to imitate Yoller's offhand, sophisticated tone.

'What about your little squatter?' the handsome Tawny asked. 'Have you seen her yet?'

'Oh yes,' said Hunter, still trying to sound casual. 'I saw her last night. She was hunting near the place where Beak Poke died.'

'You confronted her, I hope?' asked Yoller, raising his eyebrows in a friendly sort of challenge.

'Of course,' said Hunter, sounding much calmer than he felt.

'And what happened?' asked Yoller, immediately, thus confirming Hunter's worst fears about the ratio of information to be given and received.

'I told her she couldn't stay,' said Hunter, looking the Tawny straight in the eyes to show that he had taken up the challenge.

'I suppose she told you Beak Poke had granted squatter's rights?' asked Yoller, with another discreet little yawn.

'She did,' Hunter answered carefully.

'And?' asked Yoller, his eyebrows going up again.

'I told her that since Beak Poke was dead there was no way I could get confirmation of her claim. She argued a lot, of course, and I must say that in some ways she sounded quite convincing, but I met her again tonight and told her that as the new landlord my decision must be final.'

'Good chap,' said Yoller. 'I wonder where she's gone?'

'Maybe to the lost domain?' said Hunter, tentatively getting in his first question of the night's encounter. 'You know the place, of course?'

'I think so,' Yoller said. 'You mean the great manor house, the parkland and the forest that lie beyond Beak Poke's territory, between the village and Ferocity and Ripper's wood?'

'That's the place I mean,' said Hunter. 'I understand that the forest was Tawny territory once?'

'Of course it was,' said Yoller. 'It belonged to my ancestors until the men built that house there about four hundred winters past. As a matter of fact, we are thinking of taking the place back again.'

'What about the firesticks?' asked Hunter, stalling for time while he thought hard and very quickly. 'Surely it would be too dangerous for you Tawnies to move back and reclaim it?'

'We're not sure,' said Yoller, 'but we know that for three or four winters past the men with firesticks have stayed away. In fact, our intelligence service tells us that in the recent past men's behaviour patterns have been the subject of very drastic change. In my view it's still too risky, but if our survey should show that the men have gone away for good, then some of my cousins will probably recolonize the place. As you are probably aware, we have been losing woodland territories steadily for many thousand winters now, and we're keen to reclaim and resettle any traditional forest we can find.'

'I see,' said Hunter, rather sadly.

'Oh, don't worry about your patch,' said Yoller, picking up but totally misunderstanding the disappointment in Hunter's tone. 'We shan't interfere with Barn owl land. And even when we have resettled what you call the lost domain, you would still be able to hunt on this side, if you wanted, around the house, the gardens and the lake. That will still be classified as no man's land. We shall resettle only in the ancient forest, which is ours by right.'

'Have you any idea when this resettlement might happen?' asked Hunter, still looking very worried. 'I've just got rid of my little squatter, and if she's gone there, which is possible, I'd much rather that she stayed.'

'I take your point,' said Yoller, gravely. 'However, I can't be too encouraging. I'm afraid it might happen very soon. Ripper and Ferocity have already been given the job of reconnoitring the place. They'll be leaving Stoop at home to guard their own territory. All the arrangements have been made and their survey starts tomorrow night. However, they'll kill anything they find there, that's for sure. I mean, although they're my own kind and I suppose I shouldn't say so, they really are the most frightful atavistic thugs, those three. Positively barbaric, you might say. For them, killing things is more than necessity or sport. For them, mindless, indiscriminate slaughter has become more like a religion or a way of life. And the funny thing is that Ferocity, the female, is the worst. A huge, bad-tempered, bony bird she is, and what a warrior! She's killed three kestrels that I know of and they say she once took on a peregrine, though she couldn't kill the thing, of course. Ripper, her mate, is just about as vicious, only lazier, you might say. A trifle less dedicated to carnage than Ferocity. After all, slaughtering birds of prey is a risky and exhausting sort of business.'

'What about the third one?' asked Hunter, trying not to let the horror that he felt express itself in his body language or his tone of voice. Most of his fears were for little Alba, but some were for himself and for the two journeys he must make across the woodland ruled over by these frenzied killers.

'Oh, poor old Stoop is rather simple-minded,' Yoller said. 'He's Ferocity's younger brother, you know, and they say she used him as a sort of sparring partner when both of them were fledglings. She taught him how to fight extremely well. He's as tough and able as the other two, but he isn't awfully bright. They say it comes from Ferocity using his head for target practice when he was a chick.'

'Would they kill another owl?' asked Hunter, who knew the answer but wanted to be sure.

'That depends,' said Yoller. 'On their own territory, they'll kill anything that moves, except a Short-eared owl or a Barn owl with a transit permit, like yourself. But they'd never trespass on a Barn owl's territory, let alone another Tawny's. They believe in an eye for an eye, a talon for a talon, and all that sort of thing.'

'But would they kill a kestrel or a Little owl in no man's land?' asked Hunter, coming finally to the specific question that he dreaded.

'They might just leave a kestrel,' Yoller answered. 'That would depend on the level of their blood lust at the time. But they'd tear a Little owl to pieces, you can bet your life on that!'

'But why?' asked Hunter. 'After all, the immigrants are owls, like us, but hawks and falcons are a lower form of bird life. Only one rung below us, I admit, but they still can't be classed as the equals of any kind of owl. They also compete with us for the same prey, even though they never hunt at night.'

'Theoretically, you're right,' said Yoller. 'But there are Tawnies I know who would argue that almost any other form of life is preferable to those blasted little immigrants. They've only just arrived, they're tough, they're clever, they breed like wretched rabbits and they don't have any land. So what you get is squatters, overcrowding and a shortage in the food supply. That's why we chase them off our land.'

'Chasing them off your land is one thing,' said Hunter. 'In the interests of survival, I quite agree with that. But killing another owl is quite a different thing. It's totally against our credo and I strongly disapprove.'

'My dear chap,' said Yoller, cocking his powerful head to one side and looking at Hunter with a hurt and reproachful expression on his handsome face. 'You don't think I do, do you? Approve of killing them, I mean. But fear, instinct and prejudice are very hard to overcome. And in spite of your so-called credo, you Barn owls are a tiny bit hypocritical about the immigrant question, don't you think?'

'What do you mean?' asked Hunter, resenting the aspersions that Yoller was casting on his culture and his way of life.

'I mean that you don't agree with killing them,' said Yoller. 'The final solution doesn't appeal to your sensitive, educated conscience any more than it does to mine. But, on the other hand, you won't let them settle on your territory and thereby condemn them to no man's land, which more often than not means an inadequate diet, or death by starvation, firestick or pollution.'

Though Yoller's logic was irrefutable in general terms, Hunter felt the personal injustice of it very deeply and was seized with a sudden impulse to tell his Tawny friend all about little Alba and the lost domain. However, he guessed wisely that it was too soon and that Yoller would almost certainly disapprove, so he refrained from saying what was in his heart and mind and turned the subject back to Ripper, Ferocity and Stoop.

'You may be right,' he said, against his every instinct, 'but what I'm more concerned about at this very moment is how I'm going to get home to see my father and ask him what's to happen now that Beak Poke's dead. From what you tell me, I'm liable to be torn to pieces if I attempt to cross Ripper's wood without a transit permit.'

'Oh, I'll fix that for you,' said Yoller, in a friendly though rather condescending tone of voice. 'If you like, I could fly with you to the lost domain, when they begin their survey. That way you could get to know them and fix yourself a permanent transit permit, so to speak.'

'That's kind of you,' said Hunter still trying to sound unconcerned and casual, though he was desperate to fly back to the lost domain and warn little Alba before dawn came and it was too late to make the dangerous journey. 'I'll meet you here at nightfall, then? But now I really must be going.'

'Hold on a moment,' Yoller said, half-joking and half-offended. 'Don't be in such a rush. There's something I want to ask before you go.'

'What is it?' asked Hunter, barely able to disguise his anxiety and impatience.

'What do you think your father will say about your further education?' Yoller asked. 'Do you think he'll let you stay on here, at Beak Poke's place?'

'I don't know,' said Hunter, honestly. 'But there's a good chance that he might ask me to come back. You see, there won't be another meeting of the Barn owl council until the new moon after next, and all decisions on changes in further education will be taken then.'

'Oh, I know all about that,' Yoller said, impatiently. 'The question is, do you want to come back, or are you hoping that they'll find you another tutor somewhere else?'

'How do you know about it?' asked Hunter, who was quite surprised.

'Beak Poke told me.' Yoller said. 'He used to go on a lot about your Barn owl education system – all the different subjects that you study, the specialists that you have and all that sort of thing. Though I can't say I see the good of it myself.'

'You Tawnies don't believe much in higher education, do you?' asked Hunter, remembering one of his owlology lessons about habits and behaviour patterns. 'I was taught that you leave home and learn to fend for yourselves as soon as you are able. It's called the pragmatic approach to life,' he added, rather proudly. 'Your species is quite famous for it, really.'

'That's all a load of crow dung, frankly,' said the Tawny, turning his head and looking at Hunter with a supercilious air. 'The whole point is, we don't approve of higher education for the masses. We don't see the point of having all the woods around here filled with poets, philosophers, experts on ecology, learned historians and all sorts of other egg-headed, absent-minded creatures who are so impractical that they can hardly cut their food up, let alone go out and catch it for themselves.'

'I see,' said Hunter, rather doubtfully. 'You mean that you believe in an élite?'

'You could put it that way, if you wanted,' Yoller said. 'Though I admit, it does sound rather snobbish. We don't believe in a general smattering of higher education. It's less useful for Tawny owl survival than a few real experts and decision-makers, on the one hand,

and a healthy respect for knowledge and leadership on the part of the untutored masses.'

Though he was itching to get away, Hunter listened carefully to what Yoller had to say, analysing the content and searching for a fatal flaw. To his great relief, he found it as soon as the Tawny finished speaking. 'That's all very well,' he said, 'but too little education produces obedient barbarians like Stoop, Ferocity and Ripper. Only just now you referred to them as atavistic thugs and said that they were too ignorant and too bloodthirsty for your taste.'

To Yoller's credit he did not twitch, flinch or turn away as Hunter cut down his argument with this foolproof logic. Instead he gazed back at Hunter, raised his eyebrows and said, very quietly: 'Obedient barbarians they may be, Hunter, but they have their uses. They'll rid you of your unwanted little squatter and that way your precious Barn owl conscience will stay clear.'

Unlike the Tawny, Hunter turned away at once to hide the pain and disappointment that he knew would be sculpted on his face. 'I must be going,' he said, trying to keep his tone as casual as he could. 'It's already very late and I haven't had my supper yet.'

'See you when twilight dies tomorrow night,' said Yoller, sounding kinder and more gentle now that he had scored a point. 'And by the way, old boy,' he added, as Hunter geared himself for take off, 'I do hope you are allowed to settle in at Beak Poke's place. You're a good chap and I should be sorry to lose you quite so soon. After all, good neighbours are important and you never know who might take your place. Like Tawnies, you know, not all Barn owls are the same, and not all Tawnies think like Ferocity and Ripper. In fact, we have a saying about it. "If a Tawny does not think like a Barn owl when he's young, then he has no soul, but if he still thinks like one when he's fully fledged, he's unlikely to survive for very long."'

Hunter glanced back to Yoller and nodded in acknowledgement, though he did not trust himself to speak. He took off swiftly, climbing high and set his course directly for the lost domain. 'This is paradoxical,' he thought, as he winged his way out of the copse, across the fields, above the deserted farmhouse and through the darkness towards the secret and forbidden territory. 'Here I am, risking my life to save someone that I wanted to get rid of.' It was really quite absurd, and in his head he knew it. 'This is quite contrary to all I have been taught about survival,' he reminded himself, severely, 'and I must remember that survival of the Barn owl species, including me, should be my first and most sacred duty.'

But in spite of this solemn warning from his brain, Hunter flew on towards the lost domain, his reason and his conditioning for once overruled by a stronger impulse from the heart.

CHAPTER

 10

There was no sign of Alba when Hunter flew into the stately oak in the middle of the parkland and sat on the same branch where he and the little immigrant had banqueted on vole and mole at the beginning of that long, eventful night.

He waited patiently at first, and then with rising anxiety as the dark sky began to lift a little to herald the approaching dawn. 'I'm not staying here a moment longer,' vowed Hunter, eventually, for no good reason feeling both hurt and let down by little Alba's absence. 'I'm not flying back across the house and garden in the daytime, nor even in the first light of dawn. If she gets torn to pieces, then that's her fault. I've done the best I can. To stay any longer would be worse than madness.'

Yet still he lingered, shivering with disappointment and frustration while the first faint streak of pink smudged the dark sky above him. All systems straining and alert for little Alba, Hunter picked up nothing but the rustling of short-tailed voles in the parkland grass below him. 'I might as well grab myself a snack before I go,' thought Hunter, subconsciously seizing on any excuse to put off his departure till the first flood of daylight meant that all hope must truly be abandoned.

He swooped down from the oak, caught a vole, devoured it on the spot, then rose again and dived down for a second. When he had swallowed that he flew back to his perch in the great oak and glanced fearfully upwards and behind him at the eastern sky. To his great relief, day seemed to be breaking very slowly and no more stripes of red or pink had yet appeared. Then suddenly, he heard her coming from the woods beyond the parkland and a few moments later she alighted neatly on the branch beside him.

'Hi Hunter,' she said, as yet unaware of his frustration and anxiety. 'It's great to see you back again so soon.'

'I've been waiting ages,' Hunter snapped ungraciously. 'Where on earth do you think you've been?'

Alba cocked her head to one side and looked at him steadily while the warm smile of welcome faded from her face. Then, instead of being angry or offended, she said very gently: 'What is it, Hunter? Somebody has hurt you, or something bad has happened. Please tell me what it is.'

'Nothing has happened and nobody has hurt me,' answered Hunter, rather gruffly. 'But if they catch you here, it's you they're going to hurt.'

'Who?' asked little Alba, her eyes widening in apprehension and surprise.

'The Tawnies,' Hunter said. 'They want to reclaim the lost domain. They claim it was their territory until men built the house here four hundred springs ago, and they're sending two of their most ruthless owls to carry out a survey.'

'When?' asked Alba, calmly.

'Tonight,' answered Hunter. 'They start their survey shortly after dark.'

'How do you know?' asked Alba, who was concentrating very carefully on every word he said.

'Yoller told me,' Hunter answered. 'Have you ever heard of him?'

'Sure,' said little Alba, nodding her head slowly and rather sadly. 'He's the firstborn in that aristocratic family of Tawnies that live in the woods beyond your land.'

'Right!' said Hunter, sharply. 'Well, he's the one that told me and he also said that if Ferocity or Ripper find you here, they'll tear you into pieces. So I thought perhaps you ought to know.' Alba again nodded slowly and then looked up at Hunter, her eyes widening into a gentle little smile.

'I'm very grateful to you, Hunter,' she said softly. 'It was big of you to take the risk.'

'What are you going to do?' asked Hunter, after they had looked at each other in silence for a while. Alba sighed and shrugged her rounded little shoulders.

'I guess the first thing I have to do is warn my kinsfolk,' she said. 'If they want to stay and fight, then I guess that's their affair, but I have to let them know.'

'What kinsfolk?' asked Hunter, remembering the two Little owls he had become aware of on the first night he had left his father's home. 'You mean there are more immigrants living here, in the lost domain?'

'Sure,' said little Alba. 'A cousin of mine and a guy who dropped by here sometime last fall. They hang around the woods up there, and sometimes by the garden and the lake.'

'You didn't tell me,' said Hunter, surprised and once more rather hurt.

'You didn't ask me,' said Alba, with a bright, frank and friendly smile, while Hunter again began to suspect that all the bad things he had heard about the squatters might be true.

'You don't think they'll stay, do you?' he asked. 'They wouldn't stand a chance against any two Tawnies, let alone Ferocity and Ripper.'

'I guess not,' Alba said. 'I guess they'll move on some place else.'

'And you?' Hunter asked, sneaking a glance above him at the slowly breaking dawn. 'What are you going to do?'

'I'll move out, too,' said little Alba. 'With your permission, I guess I'll go back to my hollow tree. It's a useful funk hole at a time like this.'

'Why don't you move on with your cousin and his friend?' asked Hunter, beginning to fear that Alba might intend to introduce her two kinsfolk as extra squatters on Beak Poke's barren and unfertile patch of land.

'No way,' said little Alba, as though she had read his thoughts. 'There's no way I'm going anywhere with them.'

'Why not?' Hunter asked. 'You live here with them, don't you? Though you never mentioned it before. And you Little owls do have a reputation for crowding everywhere together, don't you?'

'Dawn is breaking, Hunter,' said little Alba, gently patient in the face of Hunter's provocation. 'You'd best be on your way. When you're older, more experienced and less hung up on your Barn owl education, I'll tell you why I won't go anywhere with them.'

'Come to the farmhouse,' Hunter blurted suddenly, unable to resist his impulse. 'You can stay at Beak Poke's while I go home to see my parents. At least you'll be safer there than in your weasel-ridden hollow tree.'

'When are you leaving?' asked little Alba, looking at him coolly, with her pretty eyebrows raised.

'That depends,' said Hunter. 'I have to cross Ferocity and Ripper's wood, so Yoller is bringing me here to get a transit permit as soon as they start their survey.'

'OK,' Alba said. 'I'll take you up on that.'

'You know where it is?' asked Hunter, his heart beating faster at the speed with which events were suddenly precipitating.

'Sure,' said little Alba. 'I visited there with Beak Poke on several occasions.'

'Right,' said Hunter. 'Come as soon as you are ready, and if I'm sleeping, please try not to wake me up.'

'I'll try not to,' Alba said. 'Have a safe trip home, Hunter. And thanks again for coming.' The little immigrant smiled at him and then suddenly took off, setting her funny, bouncing flight path for the secret forest of the lost domain. Hunter watched her vanish into the darkness, then took off himself and flew swiftly, safely home, arriving just as the last of the darkness disappeared and dawn flooded Beak Poke's abandoned farmhouse in misty, autumn sunlight.

The same sun was still shining when Hunter woke in the late afternoon. He yawned, blinked, stretched and tingled with contentment. 'How nice it is to have a safe home of one's own,' he thought. 'How comforting to be hidden from danger, all tucked away in one's private den, yet with the whole of the teeming, seething world beyond this house and farmland just waiting to be left or taken, according to one's whim.' He blinked again, stretched for a second time, remembered little Alba with a shock and then saw her asleep on the chest of drawers across the room from his bedstead perch. She was untouched by the shaft of sunlight from the window, her head was tucked prettily to one side and he could see the gentle rise and fall of her breast in the breathing of her sleep. He screwed his eyes tight shut and kept them closed for quite some time, but when he opened them again little Alba was still there and still breathing gently in her sleep.

'I can't just sit here watching her like this,' he grumbled to himself. 'And yet it might be ages before she wakes.' Hunter fidgeted on his perch and found himself resenting little Alba's presence, which was really quite illogical, since he had invited her himself. 'If she's got to be here, then she might at least wake up and talk to me or take some part in the proceedings,' Hunter brooded. 'As it is, I'm trapped on my own perch and dare not even fly across the room for fear of waking her.'

Still little Alba did not stir and Hunter's irrational resentment grew and grew. 'What if my father should drop by to see me?' he thought, with sudden horror. 'How on earth would I explain it? Or Yoller? Supposing he came by to give me some kind of message? It would be horribly embarrassing, to say the very least.'

Hunter shifted on his perch and stared across the room at the intruder, regretting the kind impulse that had prompted him to offer little Alba shelter. 'If the Tawnies do reclaim the lost domain, how will I ever get rid of her?' he asked himself, as his heart sank and sank still further. 'Face up to it, Hunter,' he sighed in the depths of his discomfort. 'She's a ragged, scruffy alien who uses funny language and frankly I'd be ashamed if Yoller or my parents knew that we were friends.'

This confession depressed Hunter even more. She had been kind to him, after all, and it was not her fault if her species was smaller and less graceful than his own. And in her own odd way, she was quite pretty, really.

'I can't bear it any longer,' Hunter decided, as the daylight began to wane and the shadows lengthened in the coming twilight. 'I'm going out now, even if she does wake up.' But Alba stirred then, as he stretched his wings for flight, so Hunter checked himself and sat back on his perch to see what would happen next. Alba yawned, sighed and then smiled at Hunter from across the room.

'Hi,' she said. 'Did you sleep well?'

'Yes, thanks,' answered Hunter, trying to sound as composed as she did. 'And you?'

'Fine, thanks,' said Alba, shaking her feathers and beginning to smooth them slowly into place. 'Only I guess I got here pretty late. It took me a long time to find the other two.'

'Where are they now?' asked Hunter, still secretly dreading that one or both might have taken up residence on the edge of his territory in little Alba's hollow tree.

'They're heading east,' she answered. 'They say there's a stretch of no man's land beyond the lost domain, before you get to the next village. I guess they'll be OK if they can cross the Barn owl country in between.'

'That should be possible,' said Hunter, rather stiffly, 'We Barn owls don't maltreat immigrants, as you can see.'

'Come on, Hunter, own up to it,' said Alba, still preening her pretty, ragged feathers, 'you were worried and uptight because you thought that I was going to bring them here.'

'I must confess it crossed my mind,' said Hunter. 'Not here, exactly, but to the hollow tree.'

'Oh, my poor, doubting Hunter,' Alba said. 'Now would I do a thing like that, especially after what I told you yesterday?'

'You didn't tell me anything yesterday,' Hunter replied. 'You just said you weren't going anywhere with them and when I was older you would tell me why.'

'Well, little Hunter, try using your imagination,' said Alba cheekily. 'You're already one night older and if you think hard enough I guess you'll come up with the answer by yourself.'

'Is there an old family feud, or something?' asked Hunter, who was really very puzzled. 'I'm supposed to be studying owlology, you know, only with my tutor dead it isn't going to be that easy. But from my basic education I seem to remember that you Little owls are susceptible to violent family blood feuds that go on from one generation to the next. Is that true? Is that why you didn't go with them?'

'Education, education, education,' said Alba, sighing once more as she finished preening her feathers and looked up at him across the room. 'In education you learn how things ought to be, not how they really are, so education is only any good if you adapt it to reality.'

'But I want to learn,' insisted Hunter. 'Knowledge is survival, even you immigrant owls must be aware of that.'

'Oh, don't be so pompous, Hunter,' said Alba, in tones that were teasing rather than unkind. 'That's the trouble with you Barn owls. You're tortured by self-doubt. None of you can ever forget about education, religion and politics, not even for a single moment. Why can't you just relax and be natural? Life's much more fun that way.'

'You haven't answered my question,' said Hunter. 'You see, I want to understand, I really do.'

'OK, Hunter, there's no family blood feud. We used to have them back in the old country. From time to time they break out even here. But they're relics from the past. Most of the time we're much too busy trying to survive.'

'I wouldn't have gone with them, of course,' said Hunter. 'Not if I'd been in your place. But we learn that you Little owls live in very large families. One might almost say in tribes.'

'In the old country we did,' said little Alba. 'There was more space there and fairly large families could still afford to live together. But here space is hard to find, so we have to leave home early and manage on our own, like you.'

'But surely that's much more civilized?' said Hunter. 'I mean, all crowding together on one tiny patch of land – to our way of thinking that's positively manlike.'

'What do you mean by manlike?' Alba asked. 'We have that word as well, but I guess we use it in a different way.'

'Manlike means all swarming together like a mob of mindless peewits,' said Hunter, feeling very knowledgeable and clever. 'It means all living on top of one another and getting in each other's way.'

'We have another word for that,' said Alba. '"Gregarious". It comes from the old language. "Gregge" means flock and gregarious means wanting to be with others, but it also means getting on with others, too. So it's not an insult in the way your manlike is.'

'But don't you feel diminished?' Hunter asked. 'I mean, we have the word sheeplike, too, but in our language it means the same as manlike, and both of them are used in the derogatory sense.'

'Oh no,' said Alba, shrugging a little and putting on her wistful look. 'I wouldn't feel at all ashamed to be gregarious. I think it's very sad to be all alone with no one to love and no one to care for you. I think all owls need love and affection at least as much as they need independence. What they need is belonging, commitment and for other owls to care. That might not sound very intellectual or brave, according to your Barn owl way of thinking, but I believe it's true and that it's hypocritical to pretend that things are otherwise.'

'Then why didn't you go off with your cousin and his friend?' asked Hunter, yet again. 'If you like collective living, why didn't you head east with them? I don't understand it at all. It's what we'd call an anomaly in your behaviour pattern.'

'For the Great God Bird's sake!' exclaimed Alba, impatiently. 'If you used your famous Barn owl brain you'd realize that by not going with them I'm trying to avoid the most basic behaviour pattern of them all.'

'I don't understand,' said Hunter. 'I don't know what you mean.'

'You'll find out soon enough, I guess,' said little Alba. 'But right now, why don't we stop philosophizing and get ourselves some breakfast? Philosophy, education, politics and religion all take second place to breakfast, lunch and dinner. If you want to survive, Hunter, that's one priority that you've just got to learn.'

'You go,' said Hunter, somewhat offended that she thought him so naive. 'I'll get mine later on, with Yoller in the lost domain. That way there will be more food left round here for you.'

'That's very sweet of you,' said little Alba, with a smile. 'But I'm sure there's more than enough out there for two.'

'I've no time, anyway,' said Hunter, glancing through the window at the lengthening shadows and the quickly fading light. 'I must leave for my meeting very soon.'

'Are you going straight back to your father's from the lost domain?'

'I don't know,' said Hunter. 'That will largely depend on Ferocity and Ripper.'

'And if you do go straight home, do you reckon your father will want you to come back?'

'I think so,' Hunter said. 'At least until the new moon after next.'

'I sure hope so,' little Alba said. 'You're a nice guy and nice guys are pretty thin in the sky, whatever species they belong to. I guess I'd kind of miss your silly questions if you stayed away.'

'Will you explain the anomaly in your behaviour pattern when I come back?' asked Hunter, blurting out another silly question instead of responding to Alba's pretty little speech.

'Figure it out for yourself,' said Alba, with a cheeky little grin. 'It will give you something to think about on the long journey home. And remember, you don't need your precious logic to help you work this one out. You just need an elementary notion of biology.'

'I see,' said Hunter, who did not see at all, but suddenly felt very sorry to be leaving his new home and his funny little friend. It was surprising, he thought, how quickly one got used to things. 'I must be going now,' he said. 'Yoller is doing me a favour and I don't want to keep him waiting.'

'Good luck then, Hunter, and take care,' said Alba, with a wistful little smile. 'I'll look after your homestead for you while you are away.'

'Goodbye, Alba,' Hunter said, and very nearly added that he was already looking forward to seeing her again. But he could not get the words out, so he merely gave her a shy smile, nodded and then took off and flew out into the deepening autumn twilight.

As he flew towards the copse at the edge of Beak Poke's territory, Hunter had much to speculate upon, apart from the anomaly in Alba's behaviour pattern. In particular, her use of language fascinated him. The things she said were different, yet basically the same. He decided that he would willingly switch from owlology to study languages and the science of linguistics if a place could be found for him under the incumbent Language Owl. 'One would learn much about other owls by studying the way they speak,' he pondered. 'And most of all, one would learn more about Barn owl language.'

Hunter was also curious about little Alba's reference to a Great God Bird in the sky. From this it was clear that the immigrants also worshipped a deity of some kind. Could it be the same as the Barn owl God Bird, the one his father represented? Why had he not been taught these things as part of his basic education? Comparative religion, after all, was one of the subjects on the syllabus that all young Barn owls had to follow. 'Perhaps Steeple did teach us that,' thought Hunter, 'but maybe I was dozing at the time. Or perhaps I learned it all by heart, as we often used to do, and then quite simply forgot.'

As he flew towards the beginning of a long period that was to prove more eventful and dramatic than he could ever have imagined, Hunter thought one more time of little Alba and about the need for commitment and for other owls to care. He remembered the hardest lesson and how lonely and let down he had felt on his first night away from home, with no one to talk to and no one with whom to share his new experiences. Though he suspected that Yoller, for one, would class this as weakness and self-indulgence, at the bottom of his heart he could not help beginning to wonder whether his little immigrant friend might not after all be right.

Hunter slowed down as they approached the lost domain, while Yoller glided silently and effortlessly along beside him. 'This is where it starts,' whispered Hunter. 'Beyond those woods lie the enormous house, the gardens and the lake. Beyond the lake there is the parkland and the secret forest.' Yoller looked ahead of him into the darkness and then nodded twice.

'Let's go then,' he said, in steady, level tones. 'Ferocity and Ripper will be up there somewhere in the forest. They won't hang around the parkland or the lake.'

Hunter glanced at him and whispered back: 'Right, Yoller, I'll take you to the beginning of the secret forest. From that point on, it's up to you.'

'Lead on, old boy,' said Yoller, softly. 'I'll be right behind you all the way.'

As they flew into the forbidden territory and then on around the great house and across the gardens and the lake, Hunter felt exhilarated and almost unafraid. Yoller's powerful presence close behind him gave him a sense of security and he felt that together the two of them could tackle almost anything, come what may, except, of course, the firesticks, though even they now seemed more legendary than real.

They flew swiftly across the vast stretch of parkland and soon the outline of the great woods loomed nearer and nearer until eventually they penetrated the first line of trees and soon found themselves well inside the dense, rich forest of the lost domain. Hunter slowed down,

Yoller immediately drew level and by tacit consent they alighted on the branch of a tall and ancient beech tree. For a moment or two Yoller said nothing, but looked at the forest all around them and then back towards the now invisible and dangerous route that they had taken. It was his first direct experience of the lost domain and it was evident that he needed a little time to take it in.

'Quite a place, this,' he said, eventually. 'Though I must say I admire you, young Hunter. I bet it takes a lot of guts to come here on your own.'

'Oh, one gets used to it,' said Hunter, in the same casual, offhand tone that Yoller might have used, though in reality he was thrilled to bits and it was as much as he could do to stop the feathers of his chest from swelling up in pride.

'I'll call them now,' said Yoller. 'Softly, to begin with, so they'll only hear me if they're somewhere fairly near. If that doesn't work, I'll send out a middle distance call.' Yoller paused for a moment, breathed in deeply and then emitted a low, vibrant hoot that quivered and seemed to hang mysteriously in the still and pungent darkness of the autumn night. After the last tone had faded away there was silence for a moment or two, save for the barely audible rustling and scuffling of the thousand secret night lives that surrounded them. Then came two answering hoots, both of which sounded raucous, harsher and less modulated than Yoller's opening call. 'They're here,' he said. 'Quite close, really. Brace yourself, old boy. They'll be with us in no time at all.'

Hunter also took a deep breath in order to compose himself and then waited with some trepidation for the coming of Yoller's fierce and atavistic kinsfolk. Soon two huge shadows loomed in the sky above the beech tree and a moment later the two great birds landed side by side on a branch opposite the one where Yoller and Hunter sat. 'Greetings, young master Yoller,' Ripper said, glaring at Hunter with animosity and deep mistrust. 'What be that strange critter you've got with you there?'

'His name is Hunter,' Yoller answered, sounding his usual, sophisticated self. 'He's my new neighbour now that Beak Poke's dead.'

'Fine-looking young specimen, ain't he?' Ripper said in a sarcastic though slightly less hostile tone of voice. 'A well bred young bird, I reckon. Comes from good, 'ealthy stock, you can tell that straight away.' As Ripper spoke, Hunter was conscious of Ferocity's fierce, unsmiling eyes scrutinizing him with frank suspicion and dislike.

'He has to cross your territory to fly back to his father's home,' said Yoller, in the rather bored, affected drawl he used when giving orders. 'So I'm afraid you'll have to let him through. And back again, of course.'

'Tell the young cocksparrow to let us know next time,' Ferocity snapped back, scraping her cruel talons on the harmless branch beneath her.

'That's right,' Ripper said, reproachfully. 'If 'e be the same young 'un as flew over us a short while back, then 'e can thank 'is lucky stars we never caught 'im. Just flew straight through, 'e did, and never said a word.'

'Never announced 'imself, nor nothing,' snapped Ferocity. 'Just flew across as if 'e owned the land we live on!'

Yoller cast Hunter a quick, surprised glance as if expecting his friend to deny the charge. Hunter opened his bill and then closed it again in sheer mortification, feeling all his newly acquired self-confidence and pride ebbing rapidly away at this revelation of his former cowardice. 'Yes, well, that won't happen again,' said Yoller casually, as if the matter were of no consequence at all. 'As you well know, Barn owls have rights of passage anyway.'

'Not unannounced, they don't,' Ferocity riposted.

'Not if they want to be alive when they come out on the other side,' said Ripper, though he took the opportunity to wink secretly at Hunter as he spoke, as if to say 'Don't take too much notice of her. She'll get over it in time.'

'Right,' said Yoller, looking at Ripper and Ferocity in turn, 'I'll fly Hunter over to your territory and introduce him to Stoop while you two get on with your survey. How have you found things up to now?'

'Ain't 'ardly started yet,' said Ripper, scratching his formidable stomach muscles with one lethal-looking talon. 'Can't say I like it, though. Not from what I've seen so far.'

'Why not?' asked Yoller. 'Have you heard or seen a firestick?'

'Not yet I ain't,' replied Ripper. 'But these 'ere woods be full of game. Pheasant, partridge, woodcock, rabbit – you name it and you'll find it 'ere.'

'What's wrong with that?' asked Yoller, with a faint smile. 'Or don't you care for delicacies of that kind? You prefer a plain diet of dormouse, shrew and rat?'

'It ain't natural, that's what's wrong with it,' said Ripper. 'I ain't never seen so much fancy food in all my life as I seen since I flew in 'ere at twilight.'

'There be a deal of game 'ere, that I don't deny,' snapped Ferocity, who made Hunter tremble almost every time she stirred or spoke. 'But that's because there ain't no other raptors 'ere. There ain't nothing 'ere to kill it.'

'There is, and all,' said Ripper, for once making no attempt to placate his formidable mate. 'What about them Little owl pellets as we found? And feathers, too? I reckon these 'ere woods be riddled with them bleedin' little squatters, only they ain't big enough to kill pheasant, rabbit and the like, leastways, not once they're fully grown.'

'Have you been down to the gardens and the lake?' asked Hunter, at last summoning up enough courage to contribute to the conversation.

'You bet I ain't,' said Ripper, with great feeling. 'If there still be firesticks in this creepy place, then that's where you'll surely find them. No, my young cocksparrow, wild eagles wouldn't drag me more than half a meadow's distance past the edges of this wood.'

'That's a pity,' said Hunter, trying to copy Yoller's casual tone, yet inwardly quaking as he spoke. 'They say that in spring there is an abundance of moorhen chicks and ducklings on and around the lake. They're supposed to be the greatest delicacy of them all. And I believe that a healthy duckling has a food conversion factor of four or five, so they're exceptionally nourishing as well.'

'So our young friend 'ere 'as found a tongue,' said Ferocity, almost spitting with contempt and loathing as she spoke. ''E ain't a dumb mute, after all. 'E's just stuck up and rude.'

'Actually, he's right,' said Yoller. 'I spotted several tasty-looking water birds as we flew over.'

'Begging your pardon, young master Yoller,' said Ferocity, 'there b'ain't no Barn owl as could hunt that lake and live to tell the tale.'

'Oh, Hunter goes there often,' said Yoller, affecting a tolerant little yawn. 'Don't you, old chap? Of course, to me it seems quite suicidal, but then I thought that was the purpose of this survey. To find out if this territory is safe enough for us Tawnies to resettle.'

'Us'll do the best we can, young master,' Ripper said. 'But don't you ask us to inspect them there gardens and that lake. Leave that to them cousins of yours as wants to settle 'ere. We'll check the forest for you, that's our duty, and we'll kill any illegal squatters as we find. But we ain't going near the gardens and the lake. It ain't natural.'

'Very well,' said Yoller. 'I'll tell my father you're doing all you can. We'll be on our way now and I'll be back from your territory later on tonight. I'll bring you word of Stoop and I'll have a snack with you as well. I'm very keen to try some of the delicacies you've found here. See you both later then?' With that Yoller nodded to Ferocity and Ripper and then took off, with Hunter following very close behind him. They travelled very fast, at tree-top height, flying much lower than Hunter had done on his first journey across the lost domain. The whole of the woodland seemed to be alive with game and the secret forest seemed even larger and more forbidding than Hunter had previously imagined.

In the heart of the forest, Yoller slowed down, hovered for a moment and then swooped down and perched in the centre of another ancient beech tree. Hunter followed and landed beside him on a branch that gave them a good view of a little clearing that lay just ahead. 'I'd like to perch here for a little while, just to get the feeling of the place,' said Yoller, by way of explanation for the landing. 'Look at that clearing. You can see a path there that man once used. Until quite recently, I'd say. It's overgrown now, but up until three or four winters ago they must have used it to travel to the centre of what they now think of as their forest.'

'I've seen others,' Hunter said. 'All overgrown to more or less the same degree.'

'Soon the paths will vanish,' Yoller said. 'Then we can safely return and reclaim what has always belonged to us by right.'

Hunter shivered and took a deep breath to calm himself. Whilst he was overcome with the ancient beauty of the place, it was not his natural environment. Surrounded by the deep, dense woodland, he began to long for the open country and for the field, meadow, copse and spinney that he knew so well. 'Thank you for helping me with your friends Ferocity and Ripper,' he said. 'And thank you for taking me to Stoop. I honestly don't think I could have managed on my own.'

'Don't mention it, old boy,' said Yoller, airily. 'I told you, it's time I had a good look at this famous lost domain. And you can't trust Ferocity and Ripper. On their own territory, they're magnificent. Almost invincible, you might say. They know every inch of their own woods and would defend them to the death. But they don't travel well, as you probably discovered for yourself.'

'They are very fierce,' admitted Hunter. 'But I don't like their manners and I find their threats preposterous. Just because we Barn owls don't make a habit of killing everything that moves, it doesn't mean we couldn't if we tried. I mean, there's no record of any Tawny ever having killed a Barn owl. Not that I've heard of, anyway. Presumably that means that we're as strong as you are, otherwise I'm sure that Ferocity and Ripper would have tried. And then, of course, there's the treaty that you mentioned. It's against our laws and yours for us to fight, so why do they bother with their silly threats?'

'I wouldn't be too sure, old boy,' said Yoller, carefully. 'The treaty is one thing, but that depends on each of us keeping to our separate territories. I'd say the balance of power you mentioned is the thing that really keeps the peace. You're as strong as we are, as you say, though Ferocity, Ripper and the like would never once admit it, not even to themselves. But if your numbers dwindled, or ours did, and if we were both desperately in need of the same territory, then I dare say there'd be a war.'

'I don't believe it,' said Hunter emphatically. 'Can you imagine the two of us fighting, for example? Why, it's quite unthinkable, and in any case, this treaty between us has lasted now for centuries. Why should it ever break?'

'Things change,' said Yoller, staring out into the forest that surrounded them, 'and centuries go by very quickly, even with a short history of twelve million winters, like yourselves.'

'I don't believe it,' Hunter repeated with conviction. 'You might get local squabbles, even deaths. We have types like Ferocity and Ripper, too. Though I must admit I've never heard of a Barn owl being quite so atavistic as those two. But a war is quite unthinkable. It would be the end of civilization as we know it.'

'Oh, I agree,' said Yoller. 'But all good things must finish sometime, I suppose. Look, why don't we get back to the nitty gritty and let me give you a briefing for your encounter with old Stoop? You won't have any problems when we get there, but by the time you're ready to come back, he'll have forgotten who you are.'

'But if I do come back, it will either be tomorrow or the night after,' Hunter said. 'How can anyone forget as soon as that?'

'If Ferocity had done target practice on your precious head,' said Yoller, darkly, 'I don't suppose you'd remember your father, your mother or even who you were yourself.'

'I suppose not,' said Hunter, with a shudder at the very thought. 'How do I remind him, then? Or how do I get him to remember?'

'You don't,' said Yoller. 'You just tell him a story, or else you sing a song instead.'

'You must be joking,' Hunter said, annoyed with Yoller for making fun of his predicament.

'Believe you me, old boy, I'm being deadly earnest,' Yoller answered gravely. 'He's fierce all right, but feeble-minded, like a fledgling, and he loves anything like a story or a song.'

'I'm not very good at singing,' said Hunter, rather peevishly. 'And I'm afraid I'm not much good at telling stories. Not like my mother or my little brother Quaver.'

'That's a fault,' said Yoller. 'If you don't work on it, it could even turn out to be a fatal flaw. Everybody loves a raconteur. That's why the Short-eared owls are tolerated whenever they appear. They eat everybody out of house and home but nobody minds because they bring news of the outside world and provide such first-rate entertainment. It's important to be able to divert your friends and neighbours, and you're much more likely to survive if you can entertain your enemies as well.'

'I've never thought of it like that,' said Hunter, who was surprised that a highborn and aristocratic bird like Yoller should be counselling what appeared on the surface of it to be such base and dishonourable tactics. 'It seems a bit degrading,' he said, doubtfully. 'I mean, it does sound rather like singing for one's supper.'

'Never mind your dignity, old boy,' said Yoller. 'Just think about survival. You're not back in your father's Barn owl country now. In the real survival game, the rules are very different. And do try to be consistent. You can take on a feeble-minded killer, if that fits in with your credo, but in your place, I'd much rather sing than fight.'

Hunter thought about this as they flew on over the rest of the secret forest, across a stretch of Barn owl country and then over the no man's land of copse and spinney that led up to Ripper's wood. 'Alba was right,' he decided, as they entered the territory where he must choose whether to sing or fight for his transit permit. 'I must learn to be less pompous, and above all I must endeavour to adapt my little learning to reality.'

They flew a little way into the wood and then landed on the branch of a smooth-leaved elm, from which Yoller emitted a melodious hoot announcing their arrival. A loud answering call came at once from very little farther inside the wood and presently Stoop loomed out of the darkness, seeming at first sight even bigger and more powerful than Ferocity or Ripper.

He landed on a branch at a slightly higher level and stared down at them with a wide open bill, looking from one to the other, obviously unable to fathom what on earth a fellow Tawny was doing seated on a branch next to a strange young creature from another species.

'Hello, Stoop,' said Yoller, calmly. 'I've just come from the lost domain and am returning there at once to help Ferocity and Ripper with the survey. This is Hunter who has to cross your wood to return to his father's territory. He may be coming back tomorrow night. If so, you must grant him a safe passage, is that clear?'

Stoop continued to stare down at them with an open bill. He seemed so utterly perplexed that Hunter began to feel quite sorry for him and decided to say something that might help to break the ice. 'Greetings, Stoop,' he said, after a quick glance at Yoller to make sure that it would be in order for him to speak. 'It's very good of you to let me fly across your territory and I should like you to know that I really am most grateful.'

''E ain't no Tawny,' Stoop said, turning suddenly to Yoller. ''E be a Barn owl and we don't like them Barn owls on our land.'

'You may not like them,' answered Yoller, patiently, 'but the treaty says you have to let them pass. And anyway, this one is rather special. He's a friend of mine and he tells the most exciting stories.'

Stoop stared back at his young master for a moment longer and then looked back at Hunter. His bill was still wide open and his fierce features were somewhat softened by perplexity. 'I never 'eard of no Barn owls telling stories,' he said suspiciously. 'Nomad owls be the ones as tells the stories. Them as 'as no fixed abode and only little tiny ears.'

'Well, I've told you, this one's an exception,' Yoller said. 'His stories are the very best.'

'Then let 'im tell one now,' said Stoop. 'If it be a good 'un, then I'll let 'im through.'

'You have to let him through in any case,' said Yoller, with continuing patience, 'and he can't tell you a story now because he has to reach his father's territory before sunrise. He can tell you one on the way back.'

'And if 'e don't come back?' asked Stoop, assertively. 'You said as 'ow 'e wasn't certain.'

'Don't be awkward, Stoop,' said Yoller, speaking more severely. 'You know that nothing in this life is certain. Be a good chap and let him through at once. I'll stay here with you for a little while and you can give me any messages you want me to pass on to Ferocity and Ripper.' Stoop glanced dubiously at Hunter and then looked back to Yoller and sulkily nodded his assent. 'Off you go, Hunter,' said Yoller, giving him a sharp glance which suggested that he should fly on at once, before Stoop had a chance to forget or change his mind.

Travelling fast at tree-top level across the Tawny woods, Hunter wondered what kind of story he would be able to remember or invent to satisfy the simple-minded Stoop, who was obviously both demanding and discerning when it came to entertainment, in spite of Ferocity's target practice on his head. He little dreamed then that the story he would tell, though very short, would be both strange and true and would serve as the preface to an epic saga that would change his life, Stoop's life and the lives of all the owls they knew.

CHAPTER

12

When Hunter reached his family home he was surprised to find that everything seemed much smaller than he had remembered. The spinney and the fields he flew across seemed smaller, while both the farmhouse and the barn appeared to have shrunk in the short time he had been away. Inside the barn, where he found his parents and Dawn Raptor already back from the business of the night and safely hidden from the rising dawn, there was much less space than he had remembered and even Steeple and Dapple themselves seemed slightly less solid and impressive than before.

However, the sense of security was just the same and Hunter basked in this after his long, eventful journey, while his mother and his father welcomed him even more warmly than he had expected.

'Beak Poke is dead,' Hunter announced, as soon as the mutual greetings and enquiries about health were over. 'I've come home to tell you and to ask what I should do.'

'We know,' said Steeple, gravely. 'We heard about it the night after you'd left home.'

'It was tragic,' said his mother, softly. 'He was a great old owl and will be sadly missed.'

'Do I stay there, on his territory?' asked Hunter, looking at each of his parents in turn, while his sister listened quietly, moving her eyes from one speaker to another in her usual silent, enigmatic manner. 'Or shall I stay here while alternative arrangements are being made for my further education?'

His father hesitated and glanced at Dapple before attempting to answer his son's question. 'You go back,' said Steeple, after a longer pause than Hunter would have expected. 'The territory is yours for the moment, and no further arrangements can be made about your education until the Barn owl council meets again.'

'Tell us about it,' said his mother, a shade too quickly, Hunter thought. 'Is there enough to eat? Have you met any of your neighbours yet?'

'Oh, it's not too bad,' said Hunter. 'Beak Poke's abandoned farmhouse is both comfortable and safe and the territory should provide me with a living, especially if I don't have to share. So far I've met four Tawnies and a Little owl, and I think I can learn a great deal from studying their languages and above all their behaviour.'

Steeple nodded slowly and then looked at Dapple and Dawn Raptor, and suddenly Hunter was certain that something had happened, something that they did not want to tell him. Perhaps they had heard that little Alba was staying at the farmhouse, though for the life of him he could not imagine how. 'I'm still keen on owlology,' Hunter said. 'Perhaps even keener than before. And since meeting owls from other species, I've become quite interested in linguistics. Perhaps I could study under the Language Owl, if a place becomes available, or continue with owlology when the Owl Owl is appointed?'

'He's already been appointed,' said Steeple, quickly, while Dapple and Dawn Raptor exchanged a series of brief, significant little glances. 'You see, to some extent Beak Poke's death had been expected. His successor was chosen at the penultimate meeting of the council.'

'But if he takes over Beak Poke's territory,' said Hunter, 'perhaps I can study under him? There's not really enough food for two to live on, but if he's old, like Beak Poke, I dare say we could manage.'

'On the contrary, he's very young,' said Steeple, with a worried little frown. 'As a matter of fact, he's one of the youngest Barn owls ever to be appointed to the council.'

'I see,' said Hunter. 'Well, I suppose I'll just have to be patient, like Dawn Raptor, and wait for a free place, either there or somewhere else. By the way, who told you about Beak Poke's death?'

This time more rapid, almost furtive glances flew from Steeple to Dapple, from Dapple to Dawn Raptor and then back again. 'Your sister has been very fortunate,' said Steeple, with another grave and worried frown. 'In fact, we have two pieces of news for you, Hunter, one of which is good and the other very bad, or may be very bad, though no one can be quite certain yet.'

'I thought there was something wrong,' said Hunter. 'What is it? What's happened? Is it little Quaver? Don't tell me he's been hurt or killed?'

'Your brother is all right,' said Steeple. 'Or more or less all right. The bad news is about a possible invasion.'

Hunter stared at his mother and his father and the worry in their eyes convinced him that he had heard correctly. 'An invasion?' he asked. 'What on earth do you mean?'

'A monster owl,' said Steeple. 'The news is that several territories have already fallen to the south and east of here and that the enemy appears to be moving rapidly in this direction.'

Hunter was speechless. He stared at his father, then at Dawn Raptor and finally at Dapple. 'But the monster owl never comes here,' he heard himself saying weakly. 'You taught us so yourself.'

'We were brought up to believe it,' said Steeple. 'Now it seems that we were wrong.'

'It's not certain yet,' said Dapple, quickly. 'And even if it's true, he may be satisfied with the territories he's already conquered. He may stop before he gets as far as this.'

'Wishful thinking, mother,' Dawn Raptor said, speaking for the first time since she'd greeted Hunter on arrival. 'You know what Winger said.'

'Winger? Who is he?' asked Hunter, who had never heard the name before.

'The new Owl Owl,' said Steeple, gravely. 'He came here to give us the news and to tell us of poor Beak Poke's death.'

'Winger tells us there are two types of giant owl,' Dawn Raptor said, sounding supercilious and very sure of herself indeed. 'One type, our present enemy, is like a monster Tawny owl, and the other is a gentle giant from far to the north-east of here. He says that nothing will stop the monster owl until he reaches the Snowy territory, where the climate and giant Snowy owl will finally destroy him.'

'The information needs to be verified at source,' said Dapple, glancing sharply at her daughter. 'We have no proof yet that this news is true. For all we know it might be just one of Winger's many interesting theories.'

'Winger is the new Owl Owl,' Dawn Raptor said, brushing off her mother's argument with a supercilious little shrug. 'If he says it, then it must be true.'

'Even experts sometimes make mistakes,' said Dapple tartly. 'Ask your father. He's an expert and he knows.'

'Did Beak Poke ever talk about the monster owl?' Hunter asked his father. 'Everyone seems to agree that he was one of the greatest Owl Owls that ever lived. If all this were true, surely he would have been the first to know?'

'Beak Poke was very old,' said Dawn Raptor, smugly, 'and everybody knows that he was almost senile towards the end.'

'That's enough, Dawn Raptor,' Dapple snapped. 'It's time you learned respect for your elders and your betters, and especially for the dead.'

'Beak Poke was truly a great expert on his subject, and on many other things as well,' said Steeple, speaking very slowly, almost as if he was thinking to himself out loud. 'But he was also very wise. He never said anything to suggest that the monster owl might not be extinct. But even if he had suspected that they were still living somewhere far away across the salty waters and might one day return, he would not necessarily have told us so.'

'Why not?' asked Hunter, in surprise. 'Surely that's what the Owl Owl's for? To provide information on all the other species, and especially the very dangerous ones.'

Steeple looked at the three of them in turn and slowly shook his head. 'I must remind you, Hunter,' he said solemnly, 'and also you, Dawn Raptor, that as fledglings you both led very sheltered lives. In reality, the world around us is full of unpleasantness and danger. And as you already know, the worst thing of all is fear of the unknown. It fosters suspicion, prejudice and myth. If the monster owl had been a threat while Beak Poke lived, then he surely would have told us. But if it had been merely rumour, he would have kept silent, avoided senseless panic and let us all live on in peace.'

'It may still be nothing more than rumour,' said Dapple, looking at her daughter. 'The new Owl Owl is young. He has to make his reputation. He's bound to come up with some new theory or some revolutionary discovery to give him greater status. All experts and council members are the same.'

'You are exaggerating again, my dear,' said Steeple. 'Regrettably, owl nature being what it is, some do conform to the pattern that you mention. Perhaps even the majority, but by no means all.'

'Oh well, you are an exception,' said Dapple crossly. 'And that's mainly because you're not ambitious.'

'It would hardly become the Religion Owl to be ambitious,' said Steeple, his eyes showing the suspicion of a twinkle as he spoke.

'The new Owl Owl is from the south,' Dawn Raptor said. 'You know he studied under a younger, much more dynamic expert than poor old Beak Poke. In this territory here we are too insular and too bogged down by tradition. That's why Winger was selected by the council, because he is progressive. If we are to survive at all, what this sleepy territory most needs is change.'

'Be fair, my dear,' said Steeple to his daughter. 'We only know what he has told us. And your mother is quite right about hypotheses and newfangled theories. They may all sound impressive, but not all of them are always true.'

'As for me, I've already had enough change to last me half a lifetime,' said Hunter, who was astonished by the transformation in the family scene. Here was his father treating Dawn Raptor like an adult and his mother openly casting aspersions on the Barn owl council, all amidst talk of such undomestic subjects as ambition, war and change. 'It's all too much for me,' he said with considerable feeling. 'I just can't take it in!'

'Never mind, Hunter,' said Dapple, using a soothing motherly tone for the first time since he had come home. 'None of it may ever happen. It's just that we must all be prepared in case it does.'

'An emergency meeting of the council has been called,' said Steeple, calmly. 'It takes place here two nights after next. If there is any real threat of invasion, decisions will be taken and a plan of action made. But in the meantime, we may have a refugee problem to contend with. If what Winger says is true, many owls will be flying north from the occupied territories and they will need both food and shelter. We must all be prepared. Your first task, Hunter, is to fly and warn the Bard Owl and your brother, Quaver. I'll tell you how to reach his territory before you leave. And on your way, you must take the news to Brook and his mate, whose territory you have crossed twice already. It lies between Ripper's wood and the beginning of the lost domain. They must be warned about refugees and about a possible invasion. Warned, but not frightened, do you understand?'

'Of course I do,' said Hunter. 'When do you want me to leave?'

'As soon as possible,' replied his father. 'Tonight, in fact, after you have slept and rested here with us.' Hunter nodded and saw from the broad shafts of light streaming through the rafters of the barn that the sun was already high and dawn had come and gone unnoticed since he had arrived home to such an unexpected and unpredictable reception.

'You mentioned good news, too,' Hunter said. 'Please tell me that as well, and perhaps I shall sleep sounder than with all this talk of invasion, war and change.' He smiled somewhat wearily at Dapple, Steeple and his sister, but none of them seemed anxious to reply.

His father looked at Dapple, who nodded, and then Steeple looked back at his eldest son and spoke. 'We've already told you that the good news concerns your sister,' he said. 'The fact is that she's been presented with a splendid opportunity for her further education. It came as a great surprise to all of us and I'm sure it will to you as well.'

'What is it?' asked Hunter, who sensed once again that although this was supposed to be the good news, his father did not really want to tell him.

'She's to study under the new Owl Owl,' Dapple said, not really succeeding in her attempt to sound enthusiastic. 'She's leaving for his seat of learning two nights after the emergency meeting of the council.'

'Dawn Raptor?' said Hunter, in amazement. 'But she's never been particularly interested in owlology. I didn't think she cared.'

'Well, she does now,' said Dapple, sounding rather cross. 'When the new Owl Owl was here, she hung on to his every word.'

'He has a stimulating mind,' Dawn Raptor said. 'His ideas are new and exciting. I have a feeling I shall learn a lot.'

'Some of his ideas are very new indeed,' Steeple said. 'For instance, he believes that we should have more female experts on the council. Not only the Feminist Owl, the one we have already to put the female point of view on issues that concern the second sex. Winger says that all the places on the council should be open to females, provided they can prove themselves as competent as males.'

'He's ahead of his time,' said Dapple. 'Full sexual equality may come someday, but not yet, and not even very soon.'

'Why not?' asked Dawn Raptor, raising her eyebrows and looking at Hunter and her father in a challenging, sarcastic sort of way.

'Because we're not ready for complete emancipation yet,' Dapple replied emphatically. 'And neither are the males.'

Steeple coughed and cleared his throat again. 'To be fair, my dear,' he said, 'the new Owl Owl believes in equality of opportunity, and with that we surely must agree.'

'Stuff and nonsense!' Dapple said. 'We Barn owls have had equality of opportunity for ages. It's just that the females have been too busy raising chicks to set up in competition to the males. Winger should go and preach his female emancipation to the Tawnies and especially to the Little owls. From what I gather, the immigrant females have hardly any rights at all.'

'Well, we won't go into it now,' said Steeple, trying to keep the peace. 'The thing is, Hunter, we hope that you won't be too disappointed. It's a very good opportunity for your sister, and with refugees almost certainly on their way, the opportunities for further education may be severely restricted, at least for the time being. And you have your own territory to protect from immigrants and maybe from Tawny refugees. Who knows, you may have to find room for a Barn owl fugitive before these troubles are over and you move on to study somewhere else.' Steeple paused at this point and looked closely at Hunter in an attempt to gauge his reaction to all this extraordinary news. 'We put your name forward, of course,' he continued, rather lamely, 'but the new Owl Owl had already decided on a female apprentice – to set an example to the council, as it were. He was very taken with your sister's intelligence and aptitude, and so, for her sake, we agreed.'

'It may be all right for Dawn Raptor,' Dapple said, 'but I must say that I think it is a shame for you. However, .disappointments are a part of life and one must learn to put up with them, the same as with injustice.'

'Oh, that's all right,' said Hunter, at last overcoming his bewilderment sufficiently to speak. 'I don't really mind at all. As you say, it's an excellent opportunity for Dawn Raptor. In the meantime, I can go back to my territory and learn about survival for myself and about other owls and owlology from the neighbours I've already mentioned. They've taught me quite a lot already. In fact, from the experience I've had so far, I'd say I was probably a pragmatist, like Beak Poke, and likely to learn much more from field work and direct contact than from pure academic theory.'

'That's as may be,' Dapple said. 'But to get anywhere in the Barn owl world you must have studied something somewhere under one kind of expert or another. As your father has just promised, you'll be found another place just as soon as this invasion threat is over. For the moment, though, it's time to get some sleep. The sun is already high and we shall need all our wits about us in the time that lies ahead.'

They settled on their perches then and Hunter tried to get some sleep, but tired as he was he could not stop his mind from racing round and round in a hopeless attempt to come to terms with all the surprising and frightening things that he had just heard. He could tell that Dawn Raptor, too, was still awake and he would have dearly liked to ask her more about the new Owl Owl called Winger, and what it was about his mind that had so much inspired her. But he did not want to disturb Steeple or his mother and knew that he must gather all his strength to face yet another journey fraught with the danger and excitement that had so quickly become the essence of his hitherto sheltered and innocent young life.

CHAPTER

 13

Hunter reached the farmhouse at dawn, worn out by his long and as yet unfinished mission. He flapped through the gap that had once been a window and was immensely relieved to see little Alba preening her feathers on the wardrobe perch opposite the wooden headboard where he made a weary landing. Too tired to sleep, he desperately needed someone to talk to – someone who knew him well, who cared and would share his troubled thoughts and soothe the various conflicting emotions that beset him.

He told her everything, right from the time he had left to fly with Yoller to the lost domain, and she listened carefully without once interrupting him until he came to the return journey and the point where Stoop challenged him and demanded a story or a song as the promised toll fee for his crossing. 'The trouble was,' said Hunter, 'everything had happened so quickly that I hadn't had time to prepare myself and to save my life I couldn't remember a single story or a song, except one of the owlet rhymes my mother taught me as a fledgling. So I just blurted out the first thing that came into my head.'

'What was that?' asked Alba, her eyes still wider now as she identified with Hunter's dangerous predicament.

'"They say there will be great changes in the future. Females will become our equals in all things and may yet become our masters."'

'"There ain't nothing new in that," Stoop answered, in that funny rustic accent that he has. "Our Ferocity rules the roost round these 'ere woods. She allus 'as and as far as I can tell, she allus will."'

'"All right," I said, in desperation, not knowing if I was doing the right thing. "I'll tell you something very new, but this is no story, this is true. They say a monster owl has occupied several territories to the south and east of here. They say he's heading in this direction and may attack us from one day to the next."

'"There ain't no such things as monster owls," Stoop answered. "They was all killed or scared away from 'ere more than nine 'undred winters since. And even if there be one left, 'e won't dare come near these 'ere woods. And even if 'e do, us'll see 'im off. Me, Ferocity and Ripper will. Us'll kill 'im all right. We'll tear his eyes out and rip 'im all to pieces. Now, you get on with it. If you can't tell a story, sing a song. And you be quick about it, or you ain't going through."'

'What did you do?' asked Alba. 'Did you recite your owlet rhyme?'

'Thanks to the Great God Bird in the sky, I didn't have to,' answered Hunter. 'At that very moment we both picked up a big, winged intruder on the south side of the woods, where I'd flown in.

'"There be that blasted kestrel back again," said Stoop. "Our Ferocity killed her mate two winters back, when he was 'unting after dark. She still comes back to look for 'im, from time to time. Nasty little brute she is, and all. I'll 'ave to go and scare 'er off. You sit 'ere and wait till I come back."'

'And did you wait there, like he said?' asked little Alba.

'You bet I didn't,' answered Hunter. 'I flew right through the Tawny woods, across the no man's land beyond and then down to the Barn owl territory in the valley before the beginning of the lost domain.'

'To give your message to the Barn owl known as Brook? Did you find him? How did he react?'

'Oh, I found him all right,' Hunter said. 'And I must say he made me very welcome. He asked me to his home, which is in the roof of an old, abandoned cowshed, and introduced me to his mate, called Melody. They were both very kind and courteous, but the way they reacted to the news surprised me. In a way it shocked me, I suppose.'

'Why?' asked little Alba, shifting to make herself more comfortable on the perch where she had sat and listened to his story for so long.

'Well, they seemed more worried about the refugees than the invasion. They said they already had enough problems trying to feed themselves, without the added worry of finding shelter for a refugee.'

'I guess that's only natural,' little Alba said. 'Most owls worry more about personal survival than ideals.'

'Of course they do,' said Hunter. 'But survival doesn't mean merely the individual or the family. It means the whole group – no, more than that, it means the entire species. So, at a time like this, how can you turn your back on refugees?'

'Or immigrants?' asked Alba, with one of her wry, ironic smiles. 'I guess that could turn out to be your biggest problem, Hunter. Knowing where to draw the line.'

'They didn't seem to have much confidence in our Barn owl council,' Hunter said, 'and I must say that rather shocked me, too. They seem to think that the experts on the council will simply talk about the crisis, but nothing will get done. They might eventually issue general directives about refugees and guidelines on what to do in case of an invasion, but according to Brook, no positive action would be taken till it was too late. In other words, they didn't seem to have much confidence in our leaders, which I found quite disturbing.'

'How can you blame them?' little Alba asked. 'I guess your mother was quite right. Most experts or leaders enjoy being chosen or elected, and they love sitting round at council meetings and just talking. But when it comes to doing things, then they're not quite so hot.'

'I don't know,' said Hunter, cautiously. 'Anyhow, let's hope Winger, the new Owl Owl, is wrong. Let's hope there won't be any refugees and this invasion never happens.'

'That reminds me,' Alba said. 'Gee, Hunter, I bet you're sick your sister got your place. Come on, confess it, now. Don't keep it all inside and let it chew your liver out.'

'I'm very glad for Dawn Raptor's sake,' said Hunter, feeling rather insincere. 'And I suppose it's only right that females should have the same opportunities as we do. Though I must say that since I was always better at owlology, I can't help being rather disappointed.'

'I bet you can't,' said little Alba. 'If I were you, I'd be madder than a cuckoo with no nest. Still, I've got to hand it to you Barn owls. You sure are progressive. Just like your mummy says, you're way ahead of time.'

'Not all of us,' said Hunter. 'And the most progressive that I've ever heard of is this new Owl Owl known as Winger.'

'Well,' said little Alba, 'the males of our species could sure use a little of his teaching. We female Little owls have hardly any rights at all. And in the old country, it was even worse. We had to stay at home until we mated. Even here it's still difficult for a female on her own.'

'Why is that?' asked Hunter. Having observed little Alba's independent lifestyle, it had never occurred to him that she might have problems of that nature.

'They can't stand the sight of an emancipated female owl, that's why,' said Alba, impatiently. 'They can't bear to see us make out on our own. I guess it hurts their egos. They just can't wait to see us mated and subservient to some chauvinistic male.'

Hunter listened carefully and reflected for a moment or two on a problem he had shelved since starting on his journey home. 'Is that why you didn't want to head east with your cousin and his friend?' he asked, eventually. 'Did one of them propose to you?'

'Bravo, Hunter!' little Alba said, with another of her wry ironic smiles. 'I guess I knew you'd get there in the end.'

'It explains the anomaly in your behaviour pattern,' Hunter said, nodding wisely to hide the embarrassment he felt. 'I also understand now why you needed your funk hole in that hollow tree.'

'Right again,' said Alba, with a rueful little grin. 'The males of our species pride themselves on being passionate and irresistible. They can't bear a female to refuse, so there are times when distance is the only thing.'

Hunter felt himself go hot all over as his embarrassment became acute, and he turned his head away in the hope that little Alba would not notice. 'Don't worry,' he said, watching a shaft of dawn sunlight play on the objects that the men had left in the deserted bedroom. 'You can stay here as long as you like. You'll be quite safe with me.'

'That's very sweet of you, Hunter,' said little Alba, softly. 'But what about the refugees? You'll have to take at least one here on your land and even as it is there's hardly enough food for two.'

'We'll manage somehow,' Hunter said. 'In any case, for all we know it may never happen.'

'Is your mother very religious?' asked Alba unexpectedly.

'I don't know,' Hunter replied, more than a little surprised by Alba's question. 'I think so. Sometimes I think she's more religious than my father. At any rate, she believes that good will overcome and that somehow things will come out all right in the end.'

'Wouldn't that be nice,' said Alba, with a musing, pensive little smile.

'Wouldn't it be nice to believe that the Great God Bird in the sky would protect us, come what may? It would make life so much easier. Easier to live and easier to die.'

'I'd like to believe it,' Hunter said, 'but there are many things I just don't understand. For example, if we Barn owls, the Tawnies and you immigrants all worship the same God Bird, whose side is he on when we all pray for the same thing and only one of us can have it? If we're all his fledglings here on earth and all equal in his sight, how in heaven's name does he decide?'

'According to Beak Poke, all three species worship the same God Bird, but in a different way,' said little Alba. 'And according to him, there are many other differences as well.'

'What are the other differences?' Hunter asked. 'I suppose I must have learned about them, but I can't remember now.'

'It's time to go to sleep,' said little Alba. 'We can talk about it when you come back from the next part of your mission. Right now, the sun is rising and you need all the rest that you can get. Sleep now, and I'll wake you at twilight when I've found something for your breakfast.'

Feeling much more relaxed, Hunter yawned and nodded gratefully. As he drifted swiftly towards a deep and dreamless sleep, he mused contentedly on the comforts of having someone to come home to – someone who shared one's troubles and who cared, even if that someone was only a ragged little immigrant who worshipped the same God Bird, but in a different way. How was it he had more in common with little Alba than with Melody and Brook, the two Barn owls he had just visited to warn about the possible invasion? Was it because he and Alba were both young and both very much alone, or was his affinity for the little immigrant based on some secret wavelength they both shared? A wavelength that transcended race, religion, politics and even history itself?

'I will protect her,' Hunter murmured proudly to himself as the deep fatigue of the young and innocent drew him gently to the brink of sweet oblivion. 'I will look after her somehow, in spite of what the others think. If we stick together, if we have faith in friendship and if there is a God Bird somewhere in the sky, then sometime, somehow, I know we'll both get by.'

CHAPTER 14

Soon after twilight Hunter flew to the borders of his territory and then on into no man's land and the spinney where he and Yoller had first met. He landed on a branch of the same willow tree that had been the scene of their previous meetings, rested for a short while and then called out loud and clear to announce his intended penetration of the Tawny wood.

There was no answer, so Hunter called out again and then sat and waited for what seemed a very long time, hoping that Yoller was somewhere within hearing and no longer engaged in reconnaissance of the lost domain. Still no reply came and eventually Hunter flew on through the spinney and entered the ever-thickening wood. When he had flown six or seven meadows' distance through the tall, dense trees he landed on the branch of a yew and called again, as loudly as he could. This time the answer came at once and the message was quite clear. 'Stay where you are and wait to be identified.'

The voice came from too far away for Hunter to be certain that it belonged to Yoller and not another Tawny, but he called back to say that he had received the message and would wait, praying that Yoller would appear in person and not send an atavistic kinsman like Ripper, Ferocity or Stoop. Soon he picked up a large predator, and shortly after, to his great relief, Yoller appeared, hovered for a moment and then landed on the branch beside him.

'Welcome to our woods, young Hunter,' he said, seeming genuinely pleased to see him. 'What crisis brings you so deep into our territory?'

'I have to cross,' said Hunter, and then told the young Tawny about the monster owl, the threat of invasion and the mission he must fly to warn his brother and to summon Bardic to the emergency meeting of the Barn owl council.

'We know,' said Yoller, nodding gravely when Hunter had finished speaking. 'In fact, we had word of this some nights ago, but up till yesterday it was merely rumour. Last night our first refugee arrived and now we know it's true.' The two young owls stared at each other for a moment and Hunter felt an icy chill of fear run down his back and stretch cold fingers round his stomach. 'He's still some way off,' said Yoller, sounding very like his normal, casual self. 'He still has one more territory to the south to conquer before he reaches us.'

'What else did your refugee tell you?' Hunter managed to ask, though his voice sounded thin and very shaky as he spoke.

'The monster is an Eagle owl,' said Yoller, still maintaining his admirable outer calm. 'As you well know, this is a species we all believed to be long since extinct, at least on this side of what you call the salty waters. Its estimated wingspan is approximately three times the size of ours, and it can kill almost everything that flies with only one stroke of its enormous talons. It takes no prisoners and seems to believe in the final solution as far as all other owl species are concerned.'

'The final solution?' asked Hunter, whose outer feathers were trembling visibly as the ice cold fear gripped deeper in his gut.

'Total extermination,' Yoller answered. 'Complete annihilation of every rival species. No compromises, treaties, pacts of reciprocal agreements. Absolute power over the night sky, in fact, and nothing less than that.'

'The final solution,' Hunter whispered. 'How awful! How appalling!'

'We thought that it could never happen here,' said Yoller, with a brave and rather bitter smile. 'Of course, we've heard rumours of this sort of thing often enough from across the waters, but nothing of this sort has happened here for nearly a thousand winters. We thought it never would again. Not here!'

They stared at each other for a moment longer and then Hunter came up with the inevitable question, 'How long?' he asked. 'How long will it be before he gets here?'

'He's moving very fast,' said Yoller. 'So fast that none of the fallen territories had time to organize effective defences. But the last free territory to the south of here has some very proud Tawny inhabitants. If they decide to fight, it may slow him for a while. According to our intelligence, for two or three nights at the very most. Also, their territory is very fertile and very pretty, too. There is much to look at and an abundance of fine food to eat. Our only hope is that the monster rests a while to enjoy the spoils of victory. But I don't think he'll stay for long. A barbarian like that is interested in one thing, and one thing only.'

'The final solution,' whispered Hunter, who found the concept almost too horrifying to comprehend.

'Exactly,' Yoller said. 'So we can expect him here in two to three nights' time.'

'Where will it end?' asked Hunter, who had now transcended his own personal fear and had a sudden vision of all the owls and all the fields, meadows, woods and streams in the whole world suddenly pillaged of all their freedom and their beauty and subjected to the tyranny of this one dreadful beast.

'It will end here,' said Yoller very softly. 'We have time to prepare. Not much time, I admit. But we shall stop him here!'

'But surely that's impossible,' said Hunter. 'Our new Owl Owl says that nothing can stop the monster till he meets another giant, a great white owl that lives to the far north-east of here. He says that the beast you call the Eagle owl can only be beaten when he reaches the ice and snow where the kindly white giant will destroy him.'

'What good would that do us?' asked Yoller, with a careless little shrug. 'In the meantime we should all be starving refugees, or much more likely, dead. And our intelligence service tells us that this giant Snowy owl is just as bad. He's not quite so powerful or so vicious as the Eagle owl, but in his own way they say he's potentially just as big a tyrant and just as interested in total world control. And he won't come here to help us, that's for certain.'

'Your intelligence service seems to know much more than ours,' Hunter said, astonished to hear himself conceding any kind of superiority to the Tawnies, even though the rivalry between their species seemed a trivial and ridiculous issue now. However, gathering himself to the defence of Barn owl pride, he added: 'At least, it seems to be more efficient at the present moment.'

'It always has been,' said Yoller brusquely, 'However, your Owl Owl might know something that would help us draw up a battle plan. Any information about the Eagle owl could be useful now.'

'I'll do my best,' said Hunter. 'He'll be at the emergency council meeting the night after next. I could get Bardic or my father to ask him for you when they meet.'

'That will be too late,' said Yoller. 'The monster may be here by then.'

'Then Bardic himself is the only hope,' said Hunter. 'If he knows anything, I'll report it to you when I fly back through tomorrow night.'

'I don't hold out much hope,' said Yoller, with a cynical shake of his head. 'If he's your head poet, minstrel or whatever, you can't expect him to be very practical. Artists hardly ever are, whatever species they belong to.'

'You never know,' said Hunter. 'An ancient poem or a ballad from the old days might give some sort of clue to the monster's behaviour patterns.'

'Come,' said Yoller. 'I'll fly with you to the borders of our territory and then I must go back to my father, my brother and the refugee.'

'What's he like, your refugee?' asked Hunter as they prepared for take off.

'A poor thing, really,' Yoller answered, more with compassion than contempt. 'He saw far too much carnage in his territory before he managed to escape. His mind is blown and his brain is addled with the shock. We'll keep working on him, though, until we're sure there's no more information he can give us.'

Yoller took off then and led Hunter swiftly and silently across his homeland woods until the trees began to thin out and Hunter glimpsed the open countryside beyond. Yoller slowed down as they crossed a clearing just inside the final line of trees and landed in an ivy-covered oak.

'You know the way from here?' he asked, as Hunter dropped down on the branch beside him.

'Yes,' said Hunter. 'My father gave me very clear instructions.'

'Good,' said Yoller, nodding quickly. 'It's a long way, though, and a dangerous journey at the best of times. But at least you're flying north, not south, so you won't meet the monster face to face.'

'Let's hope this invasion never happens,' Hunter said. 'But if the monster does attack, remember that you can count on any help that I can give.'

'There's an alternative,' said Yoller. 'You could stay with your brother and this famous poet owl of yours. Or better still, you could keep flying north. That way you'd stay two or three nights ahead of the monster, or even more, because I promise you that even if we don't stop the monster here, at least we'll put up a better fight than the owls he's conquered on his way.'

'No,' said Hunter, bravely. 'I'll be back. I am responsible for Beak Poke's territory. It is my duty to protect it and to stand by the Barn owl community, my family and my friends. In any case, no one can run forever. Sooner or later you have to turn and fight.'

'May the Great God Bird fly with you, then,' said Yoller, touching him briefly with one broad, powerful wing. 'We'll meet again tomorrow night.' With that Yoller turned and flew back to the heart of the deep woods where his ancestors had lived and hunted for more than forty million springs.

Hunter watched him disappear into the darkness and then took off and flew out of the trees and over the meadows that rolled downwards to the north, searching for the narrow strip of water that he must follow west until it flowed into a river. At this point he had to turn and travel upstream for fifty meadows' distance to the north. Flying fast and high by the dim crescent moonlight, Hunter paused only once to plunge gratefully down to the river bank and grab a vole, which helped to restore his flagging strength. Once the river wound round a tiny hamlet and once it flowed straight through the centre of a larger village which lay still and sleeping in the autumn night. Hunter did not flinch in either case but flew straight and true above the water, making no attempt to skirt the dark and silent rooftops that rose up on either side of him. Fifteen meadows past the second village Hunter came upon the narrow, iron tracks which for some distance ran northwards close beside the river's edge.

According to Steeple's instructions, he followed the rails until the river veered eastwards and the tracks led him due north towards two strange buildings that loomed ahead of him in the flatland darkness. These two buildings stood on either side of the iron tracks but there was no man-made light to be seen and no sign of any human presence.

'Announce yourself at least one meadow's distance from the buildings,' his father had warned him. 'Like most poets and musicians, the Bard Owl is very highly strung and every effort must be made to spare his nerves from undue strain or shock.'

In accordance with his instructions, Hunter landed on a tall, man-made tree beside the iron tracks, called politely and then waited. As he stared at the two strange buildings farther down the tracks, he saw a white shadow fly out of one of them and begin to head in his direction. As the owl drew closer and approached him, Hunter was relieved to recognize his younger brother, Quaver. 'Welcome, Hunter, follow me.' he said, veering as soon as he reached his brother's temporary perch and then turned and flew back in the opposite direction. Hunter followed him, flying above the tracks until they reached their destination and glided in through the wide downstairs entrance of the smallest building on their right. 'Welcome again,' said Quaver, perching on the back of a long, wooden bench in the deserted waiting room. 'Sit where you like. There's no one here but us.'

'And the Bard Owl?' Hunter asked, as he alighted on the back of another long bench opposite his brother. 'I have an urgent message for him – for both of you, in fact.'

'He lives on the other side,' said Quaver, nodding at the building opposite, across the iron tracks. 'I sleep here and he sleeps over there. I only go across for my tutorials.'

'Why's that?' asked Hunter.

'Wait until you meet him,' replied Quaver darkly. 'It shouldn't take you long to guess.'

'How are you getting on here?' Hunter asked, attempting to observe the niceties in spite of his urgent desire to unburden his bad news, eat, sleep and then start the long flight back to his endangered home.

'Oh, it's not too bad, all things considered,' Quaver said. 'Though the lessons haven't been quite what I expected. So far it's been mainly theory. You know, the history of music, the history of poetry and ballads, the technicalities of this and that and the music made by other forms of bird life and by man. By the way, did you know that men made music out of little boxes?'

'How?' asked Hunter, sceptically. 'Do the boxes have little tiny men inside, or what?'

'I don't know. I've never seen one, but Bardic says he has. On the whole, though, it's all been much more scholastic and less creative than I'd hoped.'

'At least you've got a tutor,' replied Hunter, anxious to get on with his business. 'Mine died before I ever met him.'

'I know,' said Quaver. 'Bardic was upset, or at least he said he was upset. At the moment he says he is composing a sort of dirge or lament to commemorate old Beak Poke's name, though if he takes as long over it as he does with most things, we'll all be dead and forgotten long before it's finished.'

'What else have you heard?' asked Hunter, sharply.

'Nothing,' Quaver answered, surprised at the urgency in his elder brother's tone. 'Why, is there something wrong?'

'Call the Bard Owl,' Hunter said. 'There's a lot wrong, and both of you must know at once.'

'All right,' answered Quaver, sounding a tiny bit offended. 'If it's really that urgent, then I will. But watch your manners. Remember the old boy thinks he's a celebrity. A star, in fact, as well as an elder statesman. And remember that he's used to holding forth for ages while others simply sit and listen.'

'Very well,' said Hunter, remembering his father's instructions and attempting to be patient. 'But I warn you, this is much more serious than you think.'

Quaver looked at his brother with a curious, worried little frown and then flew through the entrance and across the tracks to disappear inside the other building. While he was waiting, Hunter glanced impatiently around the room, which seemed large, bare and forbidding after the cosy den he shared with little Alba in Beak Poke's abandoned farmhouse. Anxious to return there, Hunter began to wonder whether he could get his mission over quickly and reach the edge of Yoller's woods before the break of day. He wanted to hear the latest news and most of all he was desperate to see little Alba and to warn her that the monster might invade at any moment.

Just then there was a rustling of giant, silky wings and a big, middle-aged and very portly Barn owl landed on the bench beside him, whilst Quaver alighted on the perch he had used before, thus keeping a respectful distance between himself and his tutor. 'Greetings and welcome to our humble seat of learning,' said Bardic, in more mellow and mellifluous tones than Hunter had ever heard in his whole life before. 'I take it you are Hunter, son of Steeple and brother to Quaver, my present Bard apprentice?'

'I am, sir,' Hunter said. 'I apologize for this disturbance, but it is my task to deliver a very urgent message.'

'And deliver it you shall, dear boy,' said Bardic, smiling gravely and bowing his large, extremely well-groomed head. Hunter noticed that every feather in his body appeared to be preened and arranged to perfection, as if his host had just completed a lengthy and most careful toilet. 'Well, Quaver,' the Bard Owl boomed again in his most melodious of voices, 'I trust you've made your brother welcome here, in our humble scholars' home. You've offered him some refreshments, I suppose?'

'Not yet,' Quaver answered, a trifle spikily. 'And in any case, there aren't any more refreshments to be had. You ate everything there was for your breakfast and your lunch.'

'Nonsense, my dear fellow,' replied Bardic in lilting though nonetheless reproachful tones. 'Go and fetch something for your brother at once, before he delivers his important message. You must learn, dear boy, that the laws of hospitality are sacred, especially to poets and musicians like ourselves.'

'Please don't concern yourself on my account,' said Hunter, quickly. 'I can eat on the way back and I'm afraid that my message cannot wait.'

'In that case I must hear it in my private quarters,' said Bardic, raising his fine head and taking the deepest of deep breaths. 'From your tone and your expression, I can tell that you bear ill tidings. My nerves are vulnerable to bad news, so I must hear your message in the comfort of my inner sanctum.'

Before Hunter could protest about this further waste of time, the Bard Owl drew himself together, readjusted his plumage with the prim dignity of a florid female owl in the middle of her age and then flew out through the entrance and across the iron tracks, followed closely by Hunter and his brother.

The Bard Owl flew into the opposite building through a similar entrance and then on through an open door into a much smaller room which contained a desk, three chairs and various other man-made objects whose sometime purposes lay well beyond the bounds of Hunter's wildest imaginings. Bardic seated himself on the centre of the desk and raised his fine head towards the ceiling in an attitude of prayer or meditation, while Hunter and Quaver perched on the backs of two separate chairs and waited. 'Do you like it?' Bardic asked eventually, lowering his head and waving a majestic wing to take in all of what he called the inner sanctum. 'This is where I have done some of my best work, since my talent was at last recognized and I was elected Bard Owl seven springs ago.'

'It's very nice,' said Hunter, and then added: 'It's really most unusual,' when he realized that Bardic had expected something more than his first lukewarm, conventional response.

'It is indeed original,' said Bardic, proudly. 'No one has ever heard of an owl converting a place like this into a residence and a famous seat of learning. You see, it suits my creativity, and as the official Bard Owl I felt that I must have a trend-setting lifestyle that would reflect my teaching and my compositions. Now, tell me your ill tidings. Surrounded by my memories and my life supports, I am ready for the shock.'

So Hunter gave them the message from his father and added the fresh intelligence he had gathered from the Tawnies on his way. In spite of his anxiety and his impatience to start back, he made every effort to give an accurate, objective report, as he had been trained to do, without allowing his own thoughts or emotions to influence the facts as they had been told to him by others. 'So if you have any information at all about the Eagle owl's behaviour patterns,' he concluded, 'it might help the Tawnies in drawing up their battle plan.'

Bardic, who had listened attentively from the beginning to the end, turned his handsome, well-groomed head towards young Quaver. His eyes were gleaming strangely with what looked more like exultation than the fear that Hunter had expected. 'Prepare yourself, dear boy,' Bardic said to his apprentice. 'Prepare yourself at once, for this will be an epic.'

'An epic?' asked Quaver, turning to his brother in bewilderment. 'It sounds more like the end of everything to me.'

'Nonsense, dear boy,' said Bardic. 'There will be a glorious battle and we shall record it for posterity.'

'What use will that be, if there's no one left to hear it?' asked Quaver, disrespectfully.

'Of course there will be Barn owls left to hear it,' said Bardic, sounding rather cross. 'The monster can't kill all of us, not in this day and age. The only ones to perish will be those who oppose him directly, or those who accidentally get in his way.'

'That's not what the Tawnies say,' objected Quaver, reminding his tutor of what Hunter had just told them. 'They say this monster believes in the final solution, for everyone.'

'Oh, you know the Tawnies,' said Bardic, airily. 'They're warmongers and they always have been. The fact of the matter is this: there will be an invasion and a battle. The Tawnies will either win the battle and destroy the monster owl, or more probably they'll lose it and be wiped out themselves. In either case, it will be an epic and we shall record it for posterity.'

'How?' asked Quaver, sceptically. 'What if we accidentally get in the monster's way?'

'That is always possible,' admitted Bardic. 'But as poets and official chroniclers, we must take precautions and avoid the battle zone. As the incumbent Bard, and therefore the only owl officially qualified to immortalize this great event, I shall conceal myself at a safe distance from the battlefield. You will fly backwards and forwards from the front, providing me with a blow-by-blow description of the conflict.'

'Is that really necessary?' Quaver asked. 'Why can't we wait until it's over and then get an account from someone who was there?'

'There may be no survivors,' said Bardic, crisply. 'Except for the monster owl, of course, and it would be a trifle risky asking him. In any case, survivors can never be relied upon to provide a full or objective account of the proceedings. To do full justice to this piece of history – to provide posterity with the epic ballad it requires – we must have the whole picture live, from the beginning to the end.'

'What about the Short-eared owls?' asked Hunter. 'I thought they were the media birds. I thought it was their job to report on any major news event?'

'Report is the word,' said Bardic sarcastically. 'That's all they are, reporters. And they only got that reputation because they have no fixed territory of their own, but wander everywhere like nomads in search of an easy living. And when they do report something, it has only transient value. It's news only for one night. No, it's the Bard Owl's job to marry art and history in the making, to record not only the events, but also the drama, the conflict, the hatred and the love – the tears, the cowardice, the bravery and the passion. In short, to create a work of eternal value – a saga – from what would otherwise be remembered as one dry, isolated fact or statistic among many others in the twelve million springs of glorious Barn owl history.'

'Oh well, if you put it that way,' said Quaver, with a little shrug of resignation. 'But what happens if we Barn owls decide to fight as well?

After all, these territories belong to us as much as they do to the Tawnies.'

'That's what I was thinking,' added Hunter. 'What would be expected of my brother then? Would he be asked to fight, or to stay and help you with the composition of your epic?'

'His place is at my side,' answered Bardic, without the slightest hesitation. 'A great work of this kind cannot be undertaken single-handed. Composing an epic poem and then setting it to music will take us many springs. And I am no longer young. Who else but Quaver could complete the task if it were still unfinished at my death?'

'What do you think the council will decide?' asked Hunter. 'To fight, or to flee and go into hiding in the hope that the Eagle owl will eventually be destroyed by the snowy giant in the north?'

'It's hard to say,' replied Bardic, with an effeminate little waggle of his portly, well-plumed body. 'The Owl Owl is the main expert in this case, so his views will be most carefully considered. The Owl for Ecology and Food will tell us what damage might be inflicted if we evacuate the land and the Man Owl will advise us as to what inadvertent help, if any, we may expect from these extraordinary two-legged creatures. The Geography Owl should be able to say how long it will take the monster owl to reach the Snowy's territory and the History Owl will be able to inform us of any precedent that might be of help. Then your father, the Religion Owl, will discuss the dictates of ethics and dogma when faced with a conflict of this kind, though I don't suppose anyone will take much notice, and finally the War Owl will estimate the forces at our disposal and advise us as to the chances of victory should the council decide to defend the territories by force. To sum up, the meeting will last all night – possibly two whole nights – until each expert has had his say and every facet of the crisis has been carefully discussed. After that a vote will be taken. There will be a show of wings and the final decision will be made.'

'Won't it be too late by then?' asked Quaver.

'Almost certainly,' replied Bardic promptly. 'But that is one of the problems inherent in our democratic constitution.'

'Please will you help,' pleaded Hunter, who now realized that it was too late for him to leave that night. 'Is there any information you can give me about Eagle owls? Information from old poems, songs and ballads? Anything at all that might help the Tawnies to draw up their battle plan?'

'Good heavens, dear boy, there are simply hundreds,' Bardic said. 'The first references to them go back to the beginning of recorded history and the last are as recent as thirty springs ago when there was a great war against them across the salty waters. Very many of our cousins were killed in that bloody conflict which was called the war to end all wars. In the end the monster was defeated when he met the snowy giant from the north. We have many poems, songs and stories from that period, which may well be the source from which the new Owl Owl got his theories.'

'Then there must be something you can tell me,' Hunter said. 'Something that could prove useful for the strategy and tactics of defence?'

'Sorry, dear boy, not my department,' Bardic said. 'I'm a poet and a minstrel, don't forget, and not a military owl at all. These things are much better left to the experts, don't you think? Now, if you'll excuse me, I haven't had my dinner yet. It's late and day will be breaking very soon. I must eat, rest and prepare myself spiritually for the great task that lies ahead. Go with your brother to the other side of the line, find something for your supper and then make sure you both get some sleep. Eat, sleep and be merry while you may, my two young heroes, for tomorrow we fly into danger and may die.'

CHAPTER

15

Hunter woke in the middle of the afternoon, prepared himself quickly and left Bardic's trendy, unusual domain before his brother Quaver or the Bard himself had stirred from what might well prove to be their last day's sleep on earth. As he set off to follow the iron tracks across the flat country towards the river, dusk had not yet begun to dim the autumn light and the last rays of sunshine hurt Hunter's eyes as he travelled onwards, determined to reach Yoller's woods soon after night had fallen. He flew a fast and true course, uncaring of the dangers still present in the fading daylight and taking the one single precaution of skirting round the larger village under cover of the lengthening shadows.

Such was his urgency and so swiftly did he travel that night had not yet fully fallen when he began his ascent from the river valley towards the dim and distant outline of Yoller's Tawny woods. 'Please let little Alba be all right,' he found himself praying as he flew. 'Please let Yoller and my family all still be alive. Please make the monster change his mind and stop this senseless killing. Or if it must happen, please let me see them all once more before I die.'

It was the first time Hunter had said his prayers since he was a fledgling and he could not help wondering why the Great God Bird should listen now, as he cried out in his hour of need, when he had been neglected and unworshipped for so long. 'Who knows if there is a God Bird, anyway?' Hunter asked himself as the Tawny woods loomed up ahead of him. 'And if there is one, does the monster worship him as well?

But if I'm killed,' thought Hunter as he approached the first thin line of trees, 'I promise that I'll say the words before I die. The words are true and beautiful and I believe them still.'

Hunter quickly found the same clearing, perched in the same ivy-covered oak and then called out to announce his presence. For a moment or two there was no answer and Hunter suddenly froze with terror as it occurred to him that the monster might already have invaded the territory and destroyed the Tawnies who opposed him. The Eagle owl might even now be lurking in the middle of Yoller's wood, bent on destroying all survivors before pursuing his path of devastation farther to the north.

Then came the answering call telling him to come forward and Hunter complied with it at once, filled with relief at the sound of Yoller's voice. He found his Tawny friend seated in another oak some three meadows' distance deeper in the wood and landed opposite him feeling a dreadful thrill of apprehension now that he was about to hear the latest news.

'So there you are,' said Yoller, sounding his usual suave, sophisticated self. 'You've been very quick. I hardly expected you so soon.'

'What's the news?' asked Hunter, who knew somehow it would be bad but was burning to hear it just the same.

'He's on his way,' said Yoller, in a matter-of-fact tone of voice that did not betray the fear he must be feeling. 'He'll be here before dawn, or tomorrow midnight at the latest.'

'How do you know?' asked Hunter.

'We've had another refugee. He claims to be the last one out. All the others have been killed.'

'What about the Barn owls?' Hunter asked. 'I believe there were many in that district.'

'The same story,' Yoller said. 'Some went into hiding and a few escaped, but most of them were hunted down, rooted out and put to death.'

'Our council meets at midnight,' Hunter said, 'I shall fly to my father's place just before dawn to find out what has been decided.'

'Do you think they'll put up an organized resistance?' asked Yoller, with a rather cynical little smile, as if he expected an answer in the negative.

'I don't know,' said Hunter. 'That will depend on the debate and on the final show of wings, but some individuals will fight. Of that you can be certain.'

'And you?' asked Yoller, raising his eyebrows quizzically. 'What have you decided?'

'I've come back, haven't I?' asked Hunter. 'I've told you, I shall fight with the Barn owls if the council is in time to organize an army. If not, I'll volunteer with you. And I'll bring any other Barn owls that will follow.'

'Good,' said Yoller, nodding as if that were the answer he had expected. 'Now listen carefully. This is our battle plan. If the invasion comes from due south, as we expect, the first place the Eagle owl will hit will be the lost domain. If it's slightly farther to the west, then the first place to fall will be Barn owl country, or more precisely the territory occupied by the owl that you call Brook.'

'Let's hope he hits the lost domain,' said Hunter. 'At least there's no one there for him to kill.'

'We think that's the way that he'll come in,' said Yoller. 'But you'd better warn Brook all the same.'

'There's another advantage of the lost domain,' said Hunter. 'There's so much food there that he may be tempted to hole up for a couple of nights and stuff himself with pheasant, hare and duck.'

'That's exactly what we're hoping,' Yoller said. 'But in any case, our battle plan remains the same. We intend to lure the monster from the lost domain to Ferocity and Ripper's wood. Those two and Stoop are the fiercest troops we have, but they fight much better on their own home front than in any other place. So we intend to send a decoy to the lost domain. This decoy, probably my brother, will allow himself to be spotted by the monster and will then lead him back to Ripper's wood where our troops will be assembled and the battle will take place.'

'What happens if he catches the decoy on the way?' asked Hunter.

'In that case, we send another,' Yoller said. 'And if the worst comes to the worst and he gets killed as well, we'll have a third decoy waiting to take over. If necessary a fourth and fifth as well.'

Hunter looked at the young Tawny, part in wonder at his capacity for sacrifice and part in grudging admiration of his iron will and of the ruthless single-mindedness behind the planning. 'What happens when the monster gets to the battle zone?' he asked, realizing with pride and fear that he would almost certainly be present at this bloody drama and that in all probability it would be the last part that he was ever asked to play.

'Our intelligence service tells us that the monster will fly into the wood at well above tree-top height,' said Yoller. 'His gigantic wings are far too long and wide for him to manoeuvre through the lower or even the middle branches of the trees. As he flies into their territory, Ripper, Ferocity and Stoop will rise up and attack him. Their task will be to bring him down among the branches, where the odds against us will be less impossible.'

'But surely if they confront him in the open sky, they stand no chance at all,' protested Hunter. 'The monster will strike them down as easily as one of us would kill three puny sparrows.'

'That may well be,' said Yoller, smiling grimly. 'But in every battle, someone has to lead the front line of attack, and as I've told you twice before, they are the fiercest troops we've got.'

'What happens if they don't succeed?' asked Hunter, dreading to hear his own name mentioned in the battle plan, but knowing that sooner or later the time would surely come.

'If they fail, another three go up,' said Yoller. 'The second line of attack will be composed of my uncle from the woods that lie some fifty meadows to the west of here, my younger brother and myself. That's always providing that my brother gets back alive and in one piece from his decoy mission. If he doesn't, his place will be taken by our second refugee.'

'And if the second assault wave fails?' asked Hunter, guessing that this time his turn had come.

'Then the third goes up,' said Yoller, as calmly as if he were listing what he would like for dinner. 'The third wave would consist of two peasant Tawnies from my uncle's area and you.'

'And if we bring the monster down?' asked Hunter. 'Who would be left to fight the second stage of the battle among the branches of the wood?'

'My father, my uncle, our first refugee and any other Barn owls you can muster,' said Yoller, looking at Hunter steadily, as if he knew what the young Barn owl was about to say. Hunter stared back at him and sadly shook his head.

'There aren't enough of us,' he said, surprisingly less afraid now that he knew the situation and realized that he was almost certain to be killed. 'Your plan is very well thought out and very brave, but the odds against us are too great.'

'Oh, I don't know,' said Yoller, still sounding as calm and casual as ever. 'In war, it's often quality that counts. It's no use having a big army or air force, if the birds in it have no stomach for a fight. I'd rather have a few trained fighters that I can rely on absolutely than hundreds of amateurs who either change sides or run away when things are beginning to go wrong. In any case, you don't have to fight. You can pull out, if you like. Nobody asked you to join us in the first place. You volunteered.'

'I'm not pulling out,' said Hunter, angrily. 'I'm merely expressing an opinion. In my view, we don't stand much of a chance.'

'Negative thinking,' said Yoller, with a reproving shake of his round, handsome head. 'Don't forget that Ripper, Ferocity and Stoop are all trained killers. My brother and I are not quite in their class, but I dare say that we'll acquit ourselves with honour. We have it in our blood. We have a great tradition to fall back on and behind us we have the courage and experience of many million springs. Personally, I think that we shall win. And if we don't destroy the monster in Ferocity and Ripper's wood, those of us who survive will go on fighting. We'll fight him in no man's land, in copse and spinney, and even in your Barn owl fields and meadows. We'll fight him everywhere, and in the end we'll win.'

'I'm sure we Barn owls will fight with you,' said Hunter, who could not help being inspired by Yoller's stirring rhetoric. 'This territory belongs to all of us and any differences between us seem ridiculous at a time like this.'

'Oh, by the way, that reminds me,' said Yoller, preparing to take off. 'Your little squatter has come back. She was seen last night, hunting on your land.'

'I gave her permission to come back,' said Hunter, looking his friend straight in the face and summoning up a second kind of courage. 'I didn't think it mattered any more. Not at a time like this.' Yoller raised his eyebrows and then, instead of answering, turned his head away.

'The only thing that matters now is victory,' he said eventually. 'After the war, there will be time to sort things out. Come, Hunter. I'll fly with you to the centre of our woods and then say goodbye until we meet again at dawn, in Ripper's wood.'

At dawn in Ripper's wood. The phrase recurred again and again in

Hunter's brain long after he had left Yoller and flown out of his territory and on across the spinney and then over the fields and meadows that he could now call his own. At dawn in Ripper's wood. The words had a ring of challenge and finality about them, pointing as they did to a time and place where everything he knew would end, or where the survivors would rise like a phoenix from its ashes and fly together towards a new beginning.

Tired and angry, yet still burning with that high-powered energy which is generated by excitement, fear and the sense of a great event, he flew into the abandoned farmhouse and found little Alba waiting for him on her usual perch. Without thinking and without knowing why, he flew directly to her perch, embraced her rounded little shoulders with one powerful wing and gave her a warm and heartfelt hug.

'Hunter,' she said, turning her sad, wide eyes to his. 'Oh, Hunter, I'm so glad to see you back.'

'There, there now,' he said, patting her gently with his wing, while to his great surprise and unexpected pleasure she snuggled up very close to him and brushed her head against his chest. 'It's all right,' he said, hugging her still closer with his wing. 'Everything is still all right. The monster hasn't got here yet and when he comes, we're going to fight him. And who knows, we might even win.'

'Oh Hunter,' little Alba said again, looking up at him with her wide eyes full of sorrow. 'Everything is not all right, it really isn't. Oh, do come quickly, please!'

'Come?' asked Hunter, who had no idea what she might mean. 'Come where? What is it? What's the matter?'

'It's a female Barn owl,' Alba answered, her eyes brimming full of tears. 'A fugitive, a refugee. She's dying, Hunter. She was too weak to fly in here. Oh, Hunter, do come quickly, please. She says she's too weak to say the final words, whatever that may mean, and she wants another Barn owl to say them for her.'

Hunter stared at little Alba for a moment while the news sank in. Then he pulled himself together, snapped into action and prepared for flight. 'Where is she?' he asked. 'And what's she dying of?'

'The monster owl,' replied Alba, almost in a whisper. 'It's horrible, Hunter! While she was still strong enough to speak, she told me that he'd only caught her a glancing blow with one single talon, yet it's ripped her back open from the neck right down to her hip. With that dreadful wound, I don't know how she managed to fly this far, or even go on living.'

'Take me to her,' Hunter said. 'The words may comfort her a little. Let's hope it's not too late.' Alba touched him briefly with her wing and flew out of the farmhouse, with Hunter close behind her. She headed for the nearby barn and landed in the yard, where Hunter saw the refugee at once. She was lying on her side in the dust and among wisps of straw that had fallen as the bales had been stacked into the barn above. Though she was facing them her eyes were closed and she was breathing quickly, with unnatural, heavy movements of her chest. At first he thought she was unconscious, but as he lowered his head to examine her more closely, she opened her eyes and smiled at him faintly from somewhere deep inside herself and very far away. Since she was facing him, the long gash all down her back was not immediately visible and Hunter thought that she was one of the most beautiful birds that he had ever seen.

'The words,' she said, softly, between one convulsive heave of her chest and the next. 'Please,' she whispered, trying to speak again, though it was obvious that each word she uttered caused her dreadful pain. 'Please, say the words!'

Hunter glanced at little Alba who perched beside him on the barnyard floor, looking down at the beautiful Barn owl with her big eyes filled with tears of pity. Then Hunter leaned forward over the female refugee, looked at her wounded back and then turned and stared at little Alba in sorrow and dismay. There was no doubt at all that the refugee must die and it was only a miracle of courage and endurance that had enabled her to fly so far and live so long after the dreadful wound had been inflicted.

> 'Hoard and covet not,
> But be brave and free,'

said Hunter, his voice sounding thin and rather shaky.

> 'Quest always after knowledge,
> And slowly learn to know
> What science cannot see.
> Seek and strive for learning,
> Be temperate and wise
> For skill and wisdom only
> Will help us to survive.'

Towards the end of the first words, Hunter's voice grew firmer, the refugee's breathing seemed to ease a little and the trace of a second faint smile flickered on her face. Hunter glanced at Alba again and then turned back and began the special words which are spoken only on the point of death, reciting them as clearly and calmly as he could.

'As you depart this earth and sky and go at last to rest, know that you are not alone. Know that our species will survive for all eternity, beyond the barnyards, fields and meadows where we live, beyond the twilight and the dawn, beyond the pale moon that glimmers and the stars that shine forever in the black and vibrant night.

'Through knowledge and self-sacrifice we shall survive until the sun no longer sets and until the moon fails to rise and give us light. Know, before you die, that with us and among us still you will survive for all eternity and beyond the boundless limits of all wisdom and all time.'

Watching her as he spoke, Hunter knew that the refugee had died soon after he began, but he went on to the end because that was what the protocol required and that was the way things had been done for many million springs. 'That's it,' he said, turning away from the refugee's body and back to little Alba. 'It's over now. She's gone.'

Alba sighed once and then nodded. 'What happens next?' she asked, sounding more like her usual self. 'Is the ceremony over now?'

'It's all over,' said Hunter. 'We go back to the farmhouse and get ourselves some rest.'

They flew the short distance back in silence and on arrival returned to their respective perches where they sat for quite some time without attempting to communicate, both drained of emotional energy and lost in their own private thoughts. 'You can't fight a beast like that,' little Alba said, eventually. 'If he did that to her with a glancing blow from one single talon, imagine what he'd do if he was trying.'

'Someone's got to have a go,' said Hunter, with a fatalistic shrug of his strong, young shoulders.

'If you try it, you'll be killed,' Alba said, her voice once more dropping to a whisper.

'Probably,' agreed Hunter, with a slow nod of his head. 'I only hope it's quick and clean, and that I get my share early, at the beginning of the battle.'

There was another long silence before little Alba stirred her feathers, raised her head and looked at Hunter across their cosy den in the abandoned farmhouse bedroom. 'I'll fight with you,' she said, suddenly, her voice sounding hard, dry and flat in the manner of one who has made an irreversible decision. 'I guess I don't want to be part of a world where things like that can happen. I don't want to live my life in fear of tyranny, knowing that I could be struck down like that poor female, from one moment to the next.'

Hunter looked at her in great surprise and then slowly shook his head. 'Best leave the fighting to us and to the Tawnies,' he said. 'If we lose, fly east and try to find your cousin and his friend.'

'What for?' asked little Alba. 'What would be the point of that? I'd just be putting off the evil day.'

'You're wrong,' said Hunter. 'In some ways you Little owls are lucky. At least, you're lucky at a time like this. You're used to travelling and you live in no man's land already. There's no reason for you to stay and face the danger. You don't have a territory to protect.'

'No,' little Alba said. 'I won't go on running. I'll stay and fight with you and with the Tawnies. If we win, then maybe after the war I'll be accepted. Maybe I'll be allowed to turn a piece of no man's land into a territory of my own. Or if they decide they don't want it, maybe the Tawnies will let me go on living in the lost domain. That's if we win. And if we don't win, I guess it won't matter anymore. I guess we'll all be dead.'

'You can stay here,' Hunter said. 'You can stay here and hide in the farmhouse till the battle's over. If we lose, you can take over the territory when the Eagle owl moves on.'

'Sure,' said Alba. 'Sure I can take the territory over, and then in the anarchy that follows I can fight to protect it from other Little owls, from Barn owl refugees and from the monster when he returns to claim his own. No, Hunter, I have to stay and fight. There just ain't no alternative.'

Secretly Hunter knew that she was right and for once he could think of nothing more to say. The unthinkable had happened, it had happened this time not to others but to them, and the only slender hope of survival lay in meeting the invader at dawn in Ripper's wood. 'Are you hungry?' he heard himself ask, after quite some time. 'Yesterday Bardic told us that at times like this we should eat, rest and be joyful while we may. I found it an odd notion at the time, but now I'm beginning to agree.'

'Sure!' said little Alba, enthusiastically. 'Let's go out and eat. And if this proves to be my last night on earth, then I'm happy to be spending it in the present company. Since my mother died, no other owl has ever been so sweet to me as you.'

Hunter was so surprised and moved by this unexpected compliment that he hardly knew what to say or do. He looked up at Alba shyly and saw that the little immigrant's eyes were brimming with friendship and affection. Instead of saying anything, Hunter found himself flying from his perch to hers, placing one wing around her little body and hugging her firmly but gently close to him. She snuggled up as she had done earlier that evening and rubbed her head against his chest.

'You're so sweet, Hunter, and so innocent,' she whispered. 'For both our sakes, I do hope you're not going to die.'

Hunter lowered his head and gently rubbed one side of his face against her upturned cheek. 'No more talk of dying,' he said, growing stronger and stronger the more he was needed. 'First we'll go and eat, then we'll come back here and sit on this perch until it's time for me to leave. I'll cuddle you like this, so you won't feel afraid. Daybreak is still some way ahead and daybreak can take care of the things unto itself.'

So they left then and went hunting, and they were lucky, finding an abundance of food almost at once, almost without searching and almost without effort. When they had eaten, they returned to Hunter's farmhouse den and rested there warmly, tenderly and very close together until the time came to say goodbye, perhaps forever, and Hunter set off for his father's home on the first stage of what he thought must be his final journey.

CHAPTER

16

Hunter sensed something different as soon as he entered the forbidden territory of the lost domain. As he flew fast across the lake and parkland halfway between midnight and dawn, there was an eerie, uncanny silence, as if all the creatures of the night had burrowed deep into whatever hiding they could find and were waiting with silent, bated breath for the apocalypse to come. Even the dark night air was tense with expectation and only the tall, ancient trees of the secret forest towards which Hunter sped seemed unaffected by the premonition of disaster. But when he left the parkland behind him, entered the forest and flew on at tree-top level among ancient sycamore, elm and oak towards Brook's Barn owl territory beyond, he found the same eerie stillness and sense of foreboding among the creatures of the forest floor. It was as if a giant, evil presence overshadowed the whole of the lost domain and as if all the living creatures there were struck dumb and petrified by the catastrophe to come.

As he flew deeper into the forest, Hunter felt more and more afraid until eventually his wings began to numb with fear and the very act of flying became an effort. As he struggled on, he was seized with a growing temptation to hide somewhere in the woods, freeze into oblivion and let history take its course without him. But then he thought of Yoller, of little Alba, of his family and of the twelve million years of Barn owl tradition that lay behind him. 'Know before you die that with us and among us still you will survive for all eternity and beyond the boundless limits of all wisdom and all time.' The words he whispered to himself warmed Hunter a little and he felt his strength and courage returning as he said them. Soon he was nearing the edge of the forest and not long afterwards the trees began to thin out and then gave way to the rolling fields and meadows of Barn owl country where he would normally have felt at home and safe from fear of the unknown.

But this time it was different. As he flew on over Brook's territory towards the abandoned cowshed inhabited by the Barn owl and his mate, he experienced the same sense of desolation and impending doom that had held the whole of the lost domain in thrall. With the chill of fear still clutching at his heart, Hunter sped towards the Barn owl's home, when suddenly he missed a wing beat and fluttered in full flight as he glimpsed, or thought he glimpsed, something quite dreadful in the meadow just below him.

Hunter slowed down, turned around and flew back slowly at a slightly greater height, not wanting or daring to look down again lest the sight he had seen was real and not merely a nightmare vision induced by a blend of fear and troubled fantasy. When he did finally look down, the shock of what he saw sent him shooting higher still, as if to escape from the unspeakable reality beneath him. He circled for a while, high in the night sky, unable to think or act as the panic in his brain threw all his sophisticated systems into a state of chaos.

Slowly, as he circled, the use of his shock-shattered faculties returned and he forced himself to drift slowly downwards and land beside the first of the two bodies he had seen. He recognized the corpse at once. The female owl lying in the grass beside him had once been Melody, Brook's mate, and her body was unmarked save for the single rent of one enormous talon, which had split her open from the chest down to the parting of her legs. The blow had killed her instantly and not very long ago, for the body was not yet entirely cold.

Hunter looked down at the corpse and the one dreadful wound for quite some time. Then he gathered himself together and said the last words quietly, in clear but trembling tones, before turning his attention to the second butchered body. In the course of his short life, this was by far the worst sight he had ever seen, a sight so gruesome and horrific that he had to fight back a panic impulse to fly away and go on flying till he could believe he had merely dreamed the dismembered, mutilated body in some one-off nightmare that belonged to youth and would never come again.

It seemed at first as if bits of what had once been Brook were scattered everywhere. The head was severed from the body and lay three lengths' distance from the mutilated trunk, to which one wing was still attached, while the other, ripped whole from the shoulder, lay with its feathers still intact on a little hillock nearer to Melody's body than to the one from which it had been rent by one tremendous blow.

'I must say the words,' Hunter muttered to himself, almost deranged by the appalling carnage that lay spread before his young, unwilling eyes. 'But to which part of the body do I say them?' he whispered weakly to himself, while his bill chattered uncontrollably and his faculties were once more chilled and numbed by fear. 'Which bit is the Brook that I once knew?' he asked himself, in near-hysterics. 'Is it the trunk and chest where his living heart once beat, or must I say the words to his severed head that once contained a brain?'

With a great effort of will, Hunter pulled himself together and muttered the last words incoherently over the remains of Brook's torn and battered torso. He then breathed in as deeply as he could, took off and headed blindly for Ferocity and Ripper's wood, not looking back and trying not to think at all until he had put at least five meadows' distance between himself and that piteous, dismembered corpse. As the valley began to slope upwards and the first line of trees loomed into sight, Hunter slowed down a little and began to reason with himself again.

'The monster must have come in this way, just as Yoller said he might,' Hunter muttered to himself, beginning to search once more for some hope of survival, however temporary and however slight. 'He must have come in through Brook's territory and taken poor Melody by surprise. Probably Brook tried to defend her and was torn to pieces for his brave attempt. But where is the monster now? Was he in the lost domain as I came through, or has he already invaded Ripper's wood, without a decoy and ahead of time? If I call to announce my presence, will a Tawny answer? Or will the Eagle owl emerge and will my life end now?'

Being a creature of habit, Hunter clung to what small comfort he could find by returning to the same branch of the same smooth-leaved elm where he had sat with Yoller after the two of them had flown across the lost domain. He listened for a little while, then summoned all his courage up, called and was overwhelmed with joy when Yoller answered from a short distance deeper in the wood. They met moments later in a small, natural clearing but by common, unspoken accord moved deeper among the dense trees before selecting a branch of a hidden sycamore on which to sit and talk.

'You've seen what happened?' Yoller asked, without preamble. 'You realize that the monster is already here?'

'I've seen what he did to Brook and Melody,' Hunter said, shuddering as he remembered, 'but I don't know where he's gone to since.'

'To the lost domain,' said Yoller, grimly. 'If you've just flown across there now, then you're a very lucky owl to be alive.'

'And you?' asked Hunter. 'I didn't expect to see you here till daybreak.'

'Our contingent decided to stagger its departure,' Yoller said. 'We forecast that he might arrive tonight and elected to fly here one by one. If we'd flown together in formation, he'd certainly have spotted us and wiped the whole contingent out, especially if he'd hit us over the parkland or the lake where there's no cover and no chance to bring him down among the trees.'

'How many of you made it?' asked Hunter, who could tell that some must be lost from the drawn and tense expression on the Tawny's face.

'Only my father and myself, so far,' answered Yoller. 'That leaves my brother and the two refugees to come.'

'There's still some hope then?' Hunter asked. 'If you left longish intervals between you, they may get here yet.'

'I doubt it,' answered Yoller. 'I left first, you see, but the second refugee was next in line, followed by the first. Both those two left well before my father. As I told you, he's already here but there's still no sign of them.'

'Perhaps they lost their way,' asked Hunter. 'They don't know the territory, after all.'

'We briefed them very well,' replied Yoller, with a slow shake of his head. 'There's still some hope for my brother. He was last to leave and by now should be somewhere in the middle of the lost domain. But I'm afraid both refugees are dead.'

'I hope not,' said Hunter, with another little shudder. 'With Brook gone, that would mean we'd lost three troops already, a long time before the battle has begun.'

'Some early losses were inevitable,' said Yoller, with a fatalistic shrug, 'though I admit it's a pity about our second refugee. He was a brave, strong bird and would have been most useful. But the first was still suffering from shock. It wouldn't have made much difference whether he'd got here or not.'

'It's also a pity about Brook,' said Hunter. 'He obviously put up quite a fight before he died.'

'That is a shame, I quite agree,' said Yoller, 'but my uncle and his two peasant neighbours should arrive all right. They're coming from the west and don't have to cross the lost domain.'

'I must be going now,' said Hunter, wondering at Yoller's apparent detachment and continuing outer calm. 'I'll have to hurry if I'm to reach the council meeting and get back here again before the dawn.'

'Yes, go now,' Yoller said. 'And if you bring back much-needed reinforcements, make sure they are as brave and disciplined as you are yourself. Remember, we need quality, skill and the capacity for self-sacrifice. Not hangers-on.'

'I'll do my best,' said Hunter, preparing to take off. 'And whatever happens, Yoller, you know that you can count on me.'

'I know,' replied the Tawny, gruffly. 'Go now, my friend. At dawn, we meet again.'

Hunter nodded quickly and then left. Without pausing for rest or refreshment he flew across the entire expanse of Ripper's wood, across the no man's land and around the sleeping village with its familiar steeple until he came to his father's territory and flew gratefully across field and meadow towards the barn where he had grown up in peace, surrounded by abundant love and shelter. In the face of all that had happened since, so suddenly and so soon, those fledgling seasons now seemed to have vanished like a dream that had died forever in the build-up to the coming war that would either see the end of all they knew or give the few survivors a chance to start a new life very different from the one they had known before.

As Hunter approached the barn, which stood firm and welcoming in the autumn moonlight, he was greeted by the unusual sight of his mother, Quaver and Dawn Raptor perched in a line of three along the roof. As he landed beside Dapple, he realized that the council meeting must still be under way inside the barn and that in all probability the assembly was still unaware that the invasion had begun.

'They've been debating solidly since well before midnight,' Quaver said, as soon as the greetings and the welcomes were completed. 'Bardic was right. It looks as though the meeting will go on all through the night and maybe tomorrow, too.'

'I bring important news,' said Hunter. 'Something they must know at once.'

'You can't interrupt a council meeting,' Dapple said. 'It's against the constitution. You'll have to wait until they take a break.'

'I can't wait,' said Hunter, angrily. 'The news I bear is a matter of life or death.'

'Oh well, rules were made to be broken, I suppose,' his mother said, after looking at him long and hard. 'But remember, if it's news they've heard already, they're likely to get very cross.'

'Well, since we'll all be dead quite soon, it doesn't really matter,' retorted Hunter, who was very close to breaking under all the strain and stress.

'Have you come to tell them the invasion has begun?' asked Dawn Raptor, who sounded infuriatingly calm, detached and uncaring. 'Because they know already, or at the very least, they've guessed.'

'Then why in the Great God Bird's name are they still talking and not acting?' demanded Hunter, beginning to quiver all over with frustration. 'Why do they go droning on while others are preparing for victory or death?'

'There, there now, Hunter,' said Dapple, in sad but soothing tones. 'Just be patient. They must break soon, if only for refreshments. A few moments more won't make any difference between life and death.'

'I think I hear them coming,' said Quaver, who was bending right over with his ear pressed against a big chink in the roof. 'In any case, there's a lot of movement going on down there.'

Sure enough, a few moments later the experts on the council began to emerge one by one from the barn below them, each flapping his long wings once or twice and then flying off in different directions in search of much-needed refreshments. Hunter had never seen so many owls together at one time and in spite of his frustration he was quite impressed. Steeple was the last to appear through the barn entrance below them and instead of following the others to stretch his wings in search of food, he flew upwards and sat beside them on the roof.

'What's happened, father?' asked Quaver, eagerly. 'Tell us! What has been decided?'

'Wait, Quaver,' said Steeple, glancing only briefly at his younger son

126

before turning at once to Hunter. 'Welcome back,' he said. 'You are a very brave young owl and you have accomplished your mission in the time allotted. Now, what news do you bring us?'

'Dire news, father,' said Hunter, with immense relief at the opportunity to unburden the dreadful tidings that he bore. 'The invasion has begun, Brook and Melody are already dead and the Tawnies intend to do battle at dawn in Ripper's wood, though they have already lost two or three of their warriors in the lost domain, where the monster now rules and prepares himself for further slaughter by gorging on rabbit, hare and full-grown pheasant.'

'We guessed as much,' said Steeple, nodding gravely. 'The War Owl computed the various reports that we've received and forecast that the monster would come in through the lost domain.'

'Yes, but are we going to fight?' asked Quaver, eagerly. 'For the Great God Bird's sake, tell us what has been decided.'

'Nothing, yet,' said Steeple, looking solemnly at each of them in turn. 'There will be a show of wings immediately after this recess.'

'Go and eat something, Steeple,' said Hunter's mother, looking sad, though calm, and speaking very softly. 'You haven't had a bite all night and who knows when you'll get another opportunity?'

'I can wait,' replied Steeple, patiently. 'It's only right that my family should know the situation as it stands.'

'What are the motions that you vote on?' asked Dawn Raptor, in a detached, almost disinterested manner that made her seem mature beyond her years. 'To fight, or not to fight? Surely it can't be as simple as all that?'

'No, not quite,' said Steeple, with the trace of an ironic smile that suddenly made him seem less old and tired. 'Basically, there are three alternatives. The first is to evacuate, or go into hiding. The second is to join forces with the Tawnies and the third to mobilize an air force and offer resistance of our own.'

'Which will the council vote for, do you think?' Dawn Raptor asked, with her eyebrows quizzically raised.

'It's hard to say,' answered Steeple, the feathers on his forehead rumpled by a frown. 'Your future tutor, the new Owl Owl, is all for evacuation. He says neither the Tawnies nor ourselves have any hope of victory. In his opinion, the only help we can expect is from the giant Snowy in the north.'

'Winger is against any form of cooperation with the Tawnies,' said Dawn Raptor, with the smug complacency of one who knows. 'He calls them our once and future enemies, or sometimes "the enemy within". He says it would be a good thing for us if they were to be exterminated, or at least to suffer very heavy losses.'

'What arrant nonsense!' exclaimed Hunter angrily. 'I've never heard such a load of crow dung in my life! They are our neighbours, they share this territory with us and we've managed to live side by side in peaceful co-existence for the past three hundred springs. At this very moment they are preparing to fight and die for the territory we share. "The enemy within", what a heap of sparrow shit!'

'That's enough, Hunter,' his father said, reproaching him mildly with raised eyebrows. 'Each council member is entitled to his view and Winger is the incumbent Owl Owl now. The Man Owl agrees with him, but for a different reason. He says our only real hope against this monster is man and his firesticks. Because of the recent changes in their be-haviour patterns, he believes that the men are having some kind of war among themselves. There are some signs that this may be drawing to an end and when it's over the Man Owl believes that they will turn their attention to the monster and destroy him to prevent the killing of their hens, their lambs, their pheasants and their human fledglings. He thinks that we should evacuate and wait till then.'

'What about the War Owl?' Quaver asked. 'Surely his is the view that matters most at a time like this?'

'He believes that we should organize our own defence and fight the monster now,' said Steeple, speaking slowly and carefully, as if he were still summing up the evidence before casting his own vote when the council reassembled. 'He does not believe that man and his firesticks can destroy the Eagle owl and considers the Tawny battle plan too sudden and too rash.'

'How can he, when he doesn't even know it?' Hunter asked.

'If we fought with the Tawnies, he'd be subordinate to their commander-in-chief,' said Dawn Raptor, cynically. 'He probably wants the sole glory of leading the Barn owl forces to their defeat and death.'

'Is no one in favour of joining forces with the Tawnies?' asked Hunter, who could hardly believe his ears, or credit that any owl could value his own opinion or career above the collective chances of survival.

'Oh, yes,' Steeple said. 'Quite a strong faction agrees with fighting alongside our proud and ancient neighbours. The History Owl, the Language Owl and the Geography Owl are all in favour. And incidentally, so am I.' Steeple paused and looked at each of them in turn. 'It only grieves me that our constitution prevents me, as member for religion, from doing violence to another owl of any species whatsoever.'

'Even the monster?' asked Hunter in amazement.

'I'm afraid so,' answered Steeple, with a sad shake of his head. 'Otherwise I'd be the first to volunteer.'

'Does the council really know the Tawny plan?' asked Hunter, desperate for action now as the members began to fly back for the final vote. 'And do they know what the monster did to Melody and Brook? Have they seen any of his victims yet?'

'I must go now,' said Steeple, as a large, middle-aged Barn owl flew somewhat ponderously back into the barn below them. 'Our leader has returned. In a few moments the votes will be cast and we shall know.'

'What does the leader think?' demanded Quaver, sounding as impatient as his brother. 'And my tutor, Bardic? Which way will he vote?'

'Wait, Quaver,' said Steeple, who was obviously impatient to return to the assembly. 'In a moment, you will know.'

'Father, before you go,' said Hunter, interrupting quickly as Steeple prepared to leave them, 'I have to tell you that I've volunteered to fight with the Tawnies, at dawn in Ripper's wood. I've also promised to take a contingent of Barn owl volunteers. There's not much time.'

'I know,' said Steeple, nodding, though showing no emotion. 'I'll tell the council now, before the final vote.' With that Steeple took off and flew back into the barn, pausing to let the last returning member of the council flap in through the aperture before him.

'I bet Bardic votes in favour of fighting with the Tawnies and also for raising an army of our own,' said Quaver, with a cynicism that almost matched his sister's. 'That way I shall be exposed to both battles and he'll get to compose two separate epics for posterity.'

'Honestly, Hunter, what chances do you think the Tawnies have?' asked Dapple. 'You know their plans and you know the mettle of their forces. Is there any chance at all, or will all those present be wiped out?'

Hunter paused before replying. He looked at his mother and saw in her eyes the dreadful anxiety that her outward composure could not hide. Dawn Raptor's expression told him nothing. It was as enigmatic as ever, as if the whole business of the invasion and the impending battle had been blown up out of all proportion and did not really merit her attention. For a moment or two, he almost hated her for that. 'I think they stand a chance,' he said. 'Not much of a one, I admit, not even with our help – and without it, even less.'

'Go and eat now, both of you,' his mother said. 'Only the Great God Bird knows when you may get the chance again.'

'No,' said Hunter, gently, feeling surprisingly protective towards his mother. 'I'll wait for the vote and for the volunteers. Directly after, we must leave.'

At that moment there was a general stirring in the barn beneath them and almost immediately afterwards the council members began to reappear, one by one, and fly off purposefully in their different directions. Quite soon Steeple appeared beside them on the roof. He looked tired but satisfied and much happier than might have been expected. 'Come on, Quaver,' he said. 'Bardic is waiting for you in the barn. And you, too, Hunter. I'll introduce you to your volunteers.'

'Volunteers!' Hunter exclaimed. 'Surely you don't mean members of the council?'

'Of course,' said Steeple. 'If we're to fight in Ripper's wood at dawn, it's much too late to summon anybody else.'

'How did the vote go, father?' asked Quaver, bouncing up and down with excitement now that the moment of truth had finally arrived.

'It was split, as I predicted,' answered Steeple. 'Three voted for hiding or evacuation, four voted in favour of raising our own forces and four decided that our only chance of survival lay in joining forces with the Tawnies. Each member has flown back to his own district to raise what troops he can, except for the volunteers, of course.'

'Who are they?' asked Hunter, whose heart was racing with excitement at the thought of leading such an important contingent to the battle zone.

'History, Language and Geography,' said Steeple. 'The History Owl is still young, fit, strong and exceptionally brave. As fighters, I'm not so sure about the other two, but at least we shall be honourably represented. But come now, no more talking. Time presses and the battle calls.'

With these brave words Steeple took off, flew back into the barn and introduced his sons to the three most eminent volunteers. The Language Owl was a small, wiry, alert bird approaching middle age, the

Geography Owl, though larger, appeared to be somewhat disjointed and rather dowdy, while the History Owl was lithe, bright-eyed and positively shining with good humour, health and strength.

'Right, Hunter,' he said, as soon as the brief introductions had been made. 'You're the one that knows the drill. Brief us as quickly as you can so that we have at least some idea what to expect when we reach the battle zone.'

So Hunter told them everything he knew, concluding with the role that had been chosen for the Barn owl troops in the forthcoming battle.

'Well, that sounds most encouraging,' said the History Owl. 'It shows that the Tawnies have retained most of their ancient battle skills, though I must say I can't see why we've been chosen for the close in-fighting among the trees. With their shorter, blunter wings, the Tawnies are much better equipped than we are for that kind of thing. It is their natural habitat, after all. We'd probably do better in the open sky, as one of the first assault waves, and we'd certainly make much swifter decoys over open country.'

'I see that the History expert wants to get us killed at once,' said the Language Owl, with a little twinkle in his eye. 'For my part, I think the Tawny plan is admirable. They provide the decoys and the early suicide squadrons, so to speak, and leave us to be slaughtered with their weaker troops among the trees.'

'The learned member for History is quite right,' said the Geography Owl, lugubriously. 'He and the admirable Hunter here would make faster, more efficient decoys than any blunt-winged Tawny. But fortunately for us, our neighbours clearly require the glory of dying first themselves.'

'Speak to Yoller when we get there,' said Hunter, turning eagerly to the History Owl. 'I'm sure he'll accept any suggestion that will help us win the battle and the war. It's not glory that he's after, but survival.'

'Congratulations, Steeple,' said the Language Owl, turning to Hunter's father with a solemn expression that was tempered by the constant twinkle in his eyes. 'I do declare that you've bred up this young fledgling to be a veritable fount of wisdom and of common sense, and the latter, you must agree is an exceedingly rare quality among owls of any kind.'

'Enough of this idle chatter,' replied Steeple. 'Duty and honour call. We are no longer strong with the first flush of youth, but our courage still remains and some work of noble note may yet be done before the end. Let us away now to destiny and Ripper's wood, while darkness still holds the dawn at bay and we may fly in the safety of sacred owl light.'

'Are you coming, too, father?' asked Hunter in surprise. 'I thought you said you weren't allowed to fight.'

'Under martial law, a Religion Owl can defend himself if and when he is attacked,' said Steeple, who was not at all his usual, solemn self and seemed unnaturally elated at the prospect of battle and of almost certain death. 'And in any case,' he added, 'the Tawnies could use me as a decoy. That way I wouldn't be fighting, would I? Just merely flying, you might say.'

'If you stayed here, you wouldn't be attacked at all, old boy,' said Bardic, who in contrast to Steeple seemed very unhappy and subdued as they prepared to leave the safety of the barn and set out on their historic flight.

'Of course I should be attacked eventually,' said Steeple. 'So should we all. And I prefer to go forth and meet my destiny, not skulk at home in hiding waiting for fate to overtake me.'

'Bravely spoken, Steeple,' said the History Owl. 'Come on Bardic, do cheer up! Cometh the time, cometh the owl, isn't that what they say? And this time the owls to come are us, and you in particular to record this epic for all future time. Lead on, young Hunter. We will follow in formation. And while we fly, think of the great victory that lies ahead. Some of us may die, but others will survive to enjoy the freedom of the skies. Think only of liberty and freedom while we fly, not death. And remember the words: "With us still you will survive for all eternity and beyond the boundless limits of all wisdom and all time."'

They left the barn then and after a brief, highly charged goodbye to Dapple and Dawn Raptor, Hunter led them across field, copse, meadow and no man's land towards Ferocity and Ripper's wood. Flying at the head of the formation, with his brave brother, his father and the four council members close behind him, and with the History Owl's strong words still ringing in his ears, Hunter nonetheless found it impossible to forget that many of them would not live to see another moonrise.

As they flew on towards the slow break of day, the two burning questions in his mind were whether any of them would survive at all, and if they did, would he himself be numbered among the living or the dead?

Soon after they had entered Ripper's territory, a call from Yoller led them on and right across the woods to the small clearing about a meadow's length from where the trees began to thin and give way to the no man's land of copse and spinney that led down the valley to Brook's Barn owl territory beyond.

Yoller met them as they flew in and guided them down into the branches of a mighty beech tree on the near side of the little clearing. 'These are your quarters,' he said, once they had settled in separate ranks on the sturdy centre branches of the beech. 'You will be stationed here until the battle starts. The first assault squadron is already in position, half a meadow's distance nearer to the edge of the wood, but still deep enough among the trees for the monster to be at a disadvantage when we bring him down. When the first wave of three rises to attack, you will proceed to the battle zone and await instructions. Is that clear?'

'What about your brother?' Hunter asked, before any of the others had a chance to speak. 'Did he get here in the end?'

'He did,' said Yoller, looking very drawn and tense, although his outward manner was still calm. 'He got here, but he brought bad news with him, I'm afraid. It seems the Eagle owl can fly much faster than we thought. My brother saw him catch and kill our second refugee over the parkland in the lost domain. He says the monster is so fast over open country that it was like watching a peregrine falcon overhaul a geriatric sparrow.'

'Have you changed your plans accordingly?' asked the History Owl, who was perched poised and erect on the branch above the one on which poor Bardic cowered, clutching at the tree trunk and looking quite unlike his florid, handsome self.

'I am reviewing the situation with my father and my brother now,' said Yoller, nodding towards an elm on the south side of the clearing. 'But it is already clear that one decoy will be insufficient. Somehow, we shall have to work a relay system.'

'Let us fly as decoys,' said the History Owl, in clear, decisive tones. 'We are faster over open country and less effective at fighting among the trees.'

'You don't know the territory,' said Yoller doubtfully. 'And in any case, the first decoy must start from the forest in the lost domain.'

'Then let the first one be a Tawny, as you'd planned,' said the History Owl. 'We can take over when your decoy emerges from the forest and hits the Barn owl country between here and the lost domain.'

Just then there was a call from across the woods to the east of them which was answered at once from the elm tree on the other side of the clearing. 'That's my uncle arriving with his two retainers,' said Yoller, looking visibly relieved. 'We are at full strength now and battle can commence as soon as I have briefed the new arrivals. In the meantime, discuss this decoy business among yourselves. I will consult with my father and my brother and give you our decision.'

Yoller was about to take off when he seemed to remember something, turned again and spoke privately to Hunter. 'Will you fly with me a little way?' he asked, reaffecting the old, casual drawl that Hunter knew so well. 'I want to have a word in private.'

'Of course,' said Hunter, and followed the young Tawny till he paused and hovered out of earshot in the centre of the clearing.

'There's someone here to see you,' Yoller said, sounding distant and embarrassed. 'A friend of yours, she says.'

'A friend of mine? Where?' asked Hunter in surprise.

'Over there,' answered Yoller, nodding at a partly hidden sycamore across the clearing. Hunter looked carefully at the tree in question and was amazed to see little Alba perched inconspicuously on one of the lower branches. He thought he saw her smile at him across the open space, but he was too astonished to respond and instead turned back to Yoller, who was hovering impatiently beside him.

'What on earth is she doing here?' he asked ungraciously. 'I didn't think you allowed little immigrants on Tawny land.'

'We don't normally, but this is wartime and the rules are different,' Yoller said, dropping his familiar drawl and reverting to the clipped, matter-of-fact tones of the military leader. 'She said she wanted to see you once more before the battle and I gave her permission to stay here, provided that she didn't make a nuisance of herself or get in anybody's way. She also volunteered to fight with us, but I said no, of course, unless we're running out of troops right at the end, when we've got the monster down among the trees.'

'I'll have a word with her when we've settled the business of the decoys,' said Hunter, attempting to sound as indifferent as he could, whereas in reality he was overjoyed and deeply moved by little Alba's presence. When Yoller left him and flew across to the southern side of the clearing to join his own contingent, Hunter stared back at the sycamore, trying to pick out the expression in the little immigrant's eyes. It seemed to him that she was smiling in that half-wistful, half-quizzical way that he had come to know so well, but he could not be sure because the distance was too great and in any case her face was partly veiled by the last of the sycamore's fast-fading autumn leaves. He half-lifted one wing in a perfunctory salute, to which Alba at once replied with a much firmer and more energetic wave. Resisting the temptation to go to her at once, Hunter turned and flew back to join his fellow Barn owls in the beech tree, where he found them engaged in heated debate about the strategy and tactics of the forthcoming battle.

'Tell us, Hunter,' said the History Owl, before he had had time to settle on his branch. 'You know the terrain between here and the lost domain. How many decoys do you think we'll need from there across the Barn owl country in between?'

'I don't know,' said Hunter, 'but from what Yoller tells us, I'd say two, at least.'

'I think three,' said Steeple, firmly. 'And I wish to be the first. Since our constitution forbids me to attack another owl, I'd be quite useless later on, in the battle here among the trees.'

'I know the territory, father,' Hunter said. 'It's obvious that I must be the first.'

'You can show me where to wait,' said Steeple. 'All I need to know is where the monster will emerge. From there any fool can fly a straight line due south-west to the point where number two takes over.'

'With respect, Religion,' said the History Owl, 'it doesn't matter much who goes first or last. What matters is how many of us go and above all how we organize the thing.'

'According to my information and to my calculations,' said the Geography Owl, calmly, slowly and with more authority than suggested by his rumpled, drab appearance, 'the decoys must fly a total of fourteen meadows' distance across Brook's territory from the lost domain to the battle zone among the trees. A fit Barn owl can sprint, or fly flat-out, for five meadows' distance at the most. Therefore three decoys must be used. Hunter first, because he knows the lost domain. There is no guarantee that the Tawny decoy will succeed in leading the monster right to the edge of the forest. He may be caught and killed first.

'In that case, our first decoy will have to penetrate the forest, take his place and lure the monster into open country. The second decoy, History or Religion, it doesn't matter which, must take over four meadows' length inside Brook's territory, near the abandoned cowshed where he lived. He flies full five meadows' length and then the final decoy takes over and brings the monster to the battle zone.'

'Very logical, Geography,' said the History Owl approvingly.

'I don't agree,' said Steeple. 'I still think I should go first.'

'It's too late to argue now,' said Hunter. 'Look, Yoller's on his way back across the clearing.'

'History, Geography, Youth and Religion shall combine to lure this monster to his death,' said the Language Owl, enthusiastically. 'I like it. It has a fine irony and augurs well for the death of any tyrant.'

Yoller landed in the beech tree, glanced briefly round at the Barn owl contingent and then came straight to the point. 'Our council of war has discussed the matter and we agree that you should act as decoys,' he said, using the clipped tones he adopted as a military leader. 'My brother Forster has already left for the lost domain to locate the monster and lure him through the secret forest. Your first decoy should leave now.'

'I'm ready,' said Hunter, boldly, though he felt his heart first skip a beat and then sink slowly downwards towards his belly.

'We all three fly together,' added History at once. 'Hunter must show us exactly where to take up our positions.'

'I'll be back with you in a moment,' Hunter said. 'First I must say goodbye to a friend of mine.'

'May the Great God Bird go with you all,' said Yoller, casting a brief but solemn glance at Hunter, Steeple and the History Owl in turn. 'You will find your comrades and my squadrons waiting to destroy the monster when you bring him in.' With that he flew back to join his own troops, while Hunter took off and flew across the clearing to the spot where little Alba waited, half-hidden amongst the fading foliage of the sycamore.

'Hi, Hunter!' she said, as he alighted on the branch beside her. 'I hope you're not mad at me for coming?'

'Of course I'm not,' said Hunter, looking at her very hard and remembering that he might never, ever see her smiling face again. 'I'm glad you came and I'm glad that Yoller let you stay.'

'He was kind,' said little Alba. 'I'd never have expected that from a Tawny, especially on his own territory.'

'It's not his,' said Hunter automatically. 'And if we fail today, the whole question of territories won't matter any more. Wood, forest, fields, meadow and even no man's land will all belong to the monster.'

'I guessed you'd be going as a decoy, Hunter,' said Alba, her voice trembling as she looked at him with big, wide-open eyes. 'For my sake, please take care. I'll stay near to you when you get back and I promise that I'll help you all I can.'

'No, Alba,' Hunter said, shaking his head and attempting to control the emotion that was welling up inside him. 'Take my advice and leave this very moment. Fly east before the battle starts. Win or lose, the monster will have his talons full until the sun is high. Fly east and you might still survive.'

'I'll be waiting here,' said Alba, leaning sideways on the branch and resting her head against his shoulder. 'Fly hard, Hunter, fly fast and above all, fly back here to me. Even if we both die in the battle, promise that we'll meet one more time before the end.'

'I'll do my best,' said Hunter, putting his wing around her and hugging her close to him. 'Believe you me, I'll do my best, for both our sakes.'

He took his wing away from around her shoulders, rubbed his bill quickly and gently on the top of her head and then took off and flew to join his comrades, not once daring to look back.

CHAPTER

 18

The three decoys did not pause or speak until they had flown five meadows' distance out of Ripper's wood, when the History Owl peeled off from the formation and took up his position in a solitary elm. Hunter and Steeple then flew on swiftly to the deserted cowshed where Brook and Melody had once lived. Here Steeple waited, facing the dark and distant outline of the secret forest towards which Hunter flew on alone as dawn began to lighten the blackness of the autumn night. As the forest loomed towards him in the lifting darkness, an uncanny stillness filled those moments before daybreak with a tension that seemed to hold every creature, every tree and every blade of grass in its icy, all-pervading grip.

Hunter stopped at the edge of the forest and perched high in a tall and ancient oak tree just inside the first line of trees. From his vantage point in the upper branches of the lofty oak, Hunter could see far across the secret forest, which was immersed now in an even deeper, more sinister silence than when he had crossed the lost domain at dead of night. Soon, much sooner than he had expected, Hunter picked up a gigantic predator, something so huge and powerful that it blotted out all other living creatures from his scanner, which told him that the monster was only five meadows' distance deeper in the wood and moving very fast in his direction. Soon his equipment picked up a Tawny on the same flight path as the monster, but travelling lower on a hell-bent zigzag through the upper branches of the trees.

Icy fear gripped Hunter, but he stood his ground and strained his eyes into the lightening darkness above the sea of trees that stretched ahead of him. Then the monster came in sight and the sheer size of it took Hunter's breath away. With fear threatening to choke him, Hunter fought hard to regain control of his breathing and forced himself to watch the invader's fast but leisurely approach. To keep pace with Yoller's brother, flying flat out beneath him, it seemed that the Eagle owl needed only half the power of those broad, enormous wings which moved with a majestic, slow and savage sort of grace.

'Now!' Hunter told himself, as the giant loomed to within half a meadow's distance from his perch. 'Attract his attention and fly now, or the monster will drop and kill poor Forster as soon as he emerges from the trees.'

With a supreme effort of will, Hunter rose above the branches of the oak, screaming and hissing his defiance at the fast approaching giant. Then he turned and fled, that one close glimpse of the monster's massive head prompting him to accelerate more quickly than he had ever done before. The Eagle owl made a slight change in his direction and put on a surge of power in pursuit of his latest prey.

Then, suddenly, as Hunter strained wing and sinew to stay ahead of death, the monster paused in mid-flight, hovered for a moment above the confines of the forest and then crashed down among the trees with a mighty howl of triumph – a howl so bloodcurdling and so shatteringly loud that it must have carried full fourteen meadows' distance to where Yoller and his troops were waiting among the trees in Ripper's wood. The monster's howl was followed by a short, sharp scream of pain, and as Hunter turned and glanced back fearfully in flight he saw the Eagle owl rise up from the edge of the forest with Forster's body dangling like a lifeless toy from the talons of one giant claw. Though Forster had been bigger and stronger than the average Tawny, his broken body seemed smaller than a newborn fledgling's as the monster trailed the crumpled carcass contemptuously beneath him.

In spite of this tragedy and even in the midst of all his panic and his fear, Hunter knew that the mission must continue, so he summoned all his strength and all the remnants of his failing courage and raised one weak yell of challenge and defiance to lead the monster on. The Eagle owl loosened its grip on the torn and crumpled body, allowing it to fall with fluttering, lifeless wings and crash down to its last resting place on the confines of the secret forest. Then the Eagle owl let out another dreadful howl and set off across the open country in hot pursuit of Hunter, closing the gap between them with each beat of those broad, gigantic wings. There was no cover anywhere on the ground ahead of Hunter and no shelter till he reached the deserted cowshed where his father was waiting to take over. At half a meadow's distance from the isolated building, the monster had gained ground to within a dozen lengths of his quarry's tail and at the quarter-meadow mark Hunter felt the monster rise above him, ready to drop and pluck him in full flight. Though panic-stricken, Hunter did not flag or falter but strained every breath and every muscle in the flight ahead.

Then, as the monster blotted out the sky above him, he saw his father rise from Brook's abandoned cowshed and launch himself upwards like a rocket in the monster's path. As Steeple soared into the attack, the monster seemed to hesitate, uncertain whether to drop on Hunter or to deal first with this unexpected, suicide assault. 'Fly on, Hunter!' were the first and last words Steeple shouted as he rose above his fledgling's flight path and hurled himself with talons bared at the monster's mighty head.

Gasping with exhaustion and distress, Hunter heard the monster's howl of rage and then the thud of impact as he and Steeple met. Then, flying blindly onwards, he heard the sickening sound of tearing wing and limb and knew for certain that his father must be dead. Soon after, his senses told him that the Eagle owl was on the move again, but had now fallen back to a full half-meadow's length behind him.

'Forster and my father dead,' thought Hunter, straining every ounce of energy to maintain the precious distance. 'Forster and my father torn to shreds to gain me half a meadow's length.' That was the one recurring thought in Hunter's head as he flew onwards for his mission and his life. 'Both dead for half a meadow's length,' he whispered, his heart near to bursting as he sped on through fatigue and pain and beyond the limits of his body's strength.

With the tree where the History Owl waited to take over now in sight, Hunter realized that he was still a quarter-meadow's length ahead. 'Perhaps Steeple wounded him before he died,' thought Hunter, with a thrill of hope and pride. But then the giant wing beats in the sky behind him suddenly stepped up their tempo, as if the monster were merely playing cat and mouse. Hunter drove his bursting lungs and aching muscles onwards and as the isolated elm tree drew nearer, and through the mists of pain he thought he could see the History Owl sitting there bravely, waiting for his hour to come. 'Cometh the time, cometh the owl,' thought Hunter, very near to hysteria as he sensed the monster closing in and beginning to rise above him for the kill.

Then for the second time that early dawn a seeming miracle saved Hunter's life. As the Eagle owl prepared to drop on him, the History Owl rose prematurely from his tree and called out his challenge, just as Hunter had done earlier in his attempt to save Forster on the edges of the secret forest. This time the monster did not hesitate but bellowed in his rage and flew on high over Hunter's head, while the History Owl turned and propelled himself full speed towards Ripper's wood.

Hunter slowed down gratefully and then drifted on behind them, watching in awe as the giant effortlessly closed the gap on his speeding quarry. 'I must stay with them,' he told himself. 'I must take over as decoy again if History is caught and killed before our mission is complete.'

So Hunter accelerated again as Ripper's wood came into sight a meadow's length, then half a meadow's length ahead. He saw the monster rise above History for the kill as both the invader and his quarry crossed the first line of trees and flew on high above the wood. Just as the monster prepared to fall upon his victim, the early dawn air was rent by three bloodcurdling battle cries as Ferocity, Stoop and Ripper rose from the tree tops and flew straight at the monster in assault formation, while the exhausted decoy owl dived gratefully down into the cover of the wood.

The monster howled with rage and rose higher in the sky in an attempt to stay above his three attackers, but Stoop and Ripper hurled themselves at his massive head and chest while Ferocity climbed above him and then dived into his back and tore at him with beak and talons. The monster screamed again in pain and rage as the three Tawnies clung on and ripped away at his chest, belly, back and neck in an attempt to bring him down among the trees.

As Hunter drew closer it seemed for a while as if they might succeed, but then the monster recovered from the surprise of the sudden, brave attack, summoned all his mighty strength and ripped first Stoop and then Ripper from his chest and belly with one dreadful, giant claw. Still they fought on, even as his deadly talons hacked them into pieces, while Ferocity tore whole chunks from the monster's back and neck.

First Stoop fell, with one wing almost severed and a wide, gaping wound across his chest. Then, as Hunter dived to join the Barn owl squadron in the clearing, Ripper's mangled body crashed down into the woods behind him, half-decapitated, with the head lolling grotesquely from the neck. But in the sky above the tree tops Ferocity still clung on and wrought her dreadful vengeance on the monster's back, and as he struggled to free himself the second assault wave flew into the attack. Yoller's uncle rose above the monster and then crashed down on him as Ferocity had done, while his two retainers flew straight at the monster's head and chest. The first was clawed and killed outright but the second crashed into the monster's damaged chest and clung there while Ferocity and Yoller's uncle fought to bring the huge owl down.

While the three of them were locked in deadly combat, a call from Yoller summoned the Barn owl contingent from the clearing to the battle zone.

'I'm next,' he said, keeping his eyes on the airborne conflict as he spoke. 'I need two of you with me. Decide now!'

'You and me?' asked the Geography Owl, with an enquiring glance at Hunter.

'Right,' said Hunter, nodding and knowing that this time his hour had really come.

'We'll take the front,' said Yoller to the Geography Owl. 'You take the back, Hunter, with Ferocity or my uncle, if either one survives.' Hunter nodded again and gazed upwards in fear and fascination as the monster writhed and heaved to free himself from the three Tawnies who were slowly but surely forcing the huge bird downwards to the tree tops.

But then, just as it seemed they would succeed, the mangled mass of blood and feathers gave a huge convulsion as the wounded monster found a final spasm of enormous strength, ripped Ferocity from his back and killed her with one dreadful blow of his lethal talons. At the same time, the other Tawny let go and drifted downwards, not dead, but very badly wounded and faint with loss of blood, leaving only Yoller's uncle still clinging to the massive creature's back.

'Now!' cried Yoller, and took off with a bloodcurdling battle cry, while Hunter and the Geography Owl shot up immediately behind him.

Those few moments before contact with the monster seemed in Hunter's mind to last for all eternity. As they rocketed skywards in the few seconds before impact, it seemed as if the whole of his past life rolled by him in slow motion. He saw his mother and that first shaft of sunlight filtering through the rafters in the barn, he smelled the bee-sucked linden and wild thyme and saw the burnished copper cornfields glowing in the light of the blood-red harvest moon. He saw the lake, the parkland and the secret forest of the lost domain and heard the vixen's futile baying at the moon as he and Steeple disappeared into a dimension that she did not understand. But most vividly of all he saw Beak Poke's abandoned farmhouse and the fields and meadows of the humble, run-down territory that was now his own.

These and many other things he perceived in the slow motion of his mind's all-seeing eye, and in his sudden glimpse of vision he wished the world would roll on by, with all its tumult, violence and adventure, leaving him to live in safety and in peace at home with little Alba.

Then Yoller and the Geography Owl hit the monster head-on, while Hunter climbed higher, dived and drove his talons into the giant, lacerated back. The Geography Owl was hit and badly wounded as they went into the attack, but this let Yoller through to score the most decisive hit of the battle as he ripped the monster's right eye from its socket. The Eagle owl's howl of agony and his one giant convulsion shook the dawn sky and was heard in all corners of the territory, way beyond the lost domain and as far away as Bardic's unusual seat of learning beside the iron tracks, and not one of the many scattered owls who heard that dreadful cry would forget it till the day they died.

The monster's great convulsion shook Yoller's uncle off his back, and though Hunter clung on tenaciously, his talons embedded deeply in the torn and bleeding body, neither he nor Yoller could prevent the beast from killing the brave Tawny as he was flung loose and came briefly within vision of the one remaining eye. But the monster's strength was ebbing fast as the blood flowed profusely from his many wounds. His giant wings no longer had the strength to bear him aloft and as little Alba appeared from nowhere and took the place of Yoller's uncle on the monster's back, the great beast began to drift down slowly towards the tree tops. Yet even as Hunter tore away at the muscle and bone beneath him, he was still conscious of the crippled monster's mighty strength and knew that even though the tide had turned at last and the allies were now winning, much danger still remained before the end. The monster heaved and struggled, but to no avail and soon his great wings began to brush against the upper branches of the trees. Sensing the danger in his pain and rage, and knowing that his end was near, the Eagle owl summoned up the remnants of its dreadful strength and threw everything into one last effort to free himself of the three owls who were now so close to grounding him.

In the monster's final burst of fury, Yoller was flung free and clawed just once by those dreadful talons. As the Tawny fell, the same claw ripped Hunter from the Monster's tortured back and flung him hard against the top of an elder trunk, just as the last assault wave tore in for the final kill.

CHAPTER 19

When Hunter regained consciousness it was broad daylight and the war was over. The monster was dead, its giant wings and bloody corpse marooned and grotesquely spread among the middle branches of a chestnut tree. 'What a pity his carcass is too big to slip down to the ground,' thought Hunter, half-deliriously. 'He fought well, after all, and a fitter resting place would be on the woodland's mossy floor, where I am lying now.'

After the monster, the second owl that Hunter saw was little Alba, who had been standing beside him, waiting protectively and patiently for him to wake. A little farther away, he caught sight of Yoller, leaning unsteadily against the trunk of a small sycamore. He was bleeding and looked very ill, but his father and the Language Owl were standing beside the wounded hero and both of these two were apparently unhurt.

The rest of the surviving Barn owl contingent had assembled in the branches of a larger sycamore, almost directly above the place where Hunter lay.

'Lie still,' said little Alba, as Hunter's head moved on the mossy woodland floor in an attempt to identify some of the mangled bodies that he could see lying around him on the ground. 'You are badly hurt, Hunter, but you will recover. Lie still until the shock is over and some of your strength comes back.'

Alba moved closer to him as she spoke and stroked his head gently with one of her rounded little wings. Hunter looked up at her and smiled weakly. He knew that he was badly hurt and yet he felt no pain. 'The pain will come later,' he thought. 'The pain and the sorrow for the dead.'

Just then Yoller's father took off from the ground and flew up into the bigger sycamore to confer briefly with the Barn owl contingent. He flew tipsily, as Tawnies do by daylight, but as soon as he landed on the branch, he regained the posture and control of an old, experienced commander. After a short conference, during which Hunter sometimes closed his eyes and sometimes looked up trustingly at little Alba, Yoller's father flew down again and landed at Hunter's side, together with Bardic, Quaver and the History Owl. Little Alba moved aside and allowed the four owls to form a semicircle around Hunter's wounded, bleeding body.

'I bring greetings from my son,' said Yoller's father. 'He is badly injured, but he will definitely live. He salutes you as a brave warrior and a friend.' Hunter smiled and nodded, but still felt too weak to speak. 'We won a great victory here today,' said Yoller's father, glancing up at the enormous carcass hanging in the trees. 'The war is over, the monster is dead, but our losses have been tragically high. Both our refugees were murdered in the lost domain, my son Forster died on his decoy mission, and Ferocity, Stoop, Ripper, my brother and one of his retainers were all killed here in the decisive battle. It is a high price to pay, but we have paid it and with our blood we have bought freedom for the survivors of this battle and liberty for all the other owls that dwell here in these territories but did not choose to fight today.'

'You will be remembered,' Bardic said, making a rather pompous, all-embracing gesture with one well-groomed wing. 'You will be immortalized in our epic Barn owl ballad and your dead will be hallowed and remembered at moonrise and at dawn from this day forth for evermore.'

'I hope so,' said Quaver, glancing at the bodies scattered round them on the woodland floor. 'Otherwise, what a waste all this would have been.'

'We Barn owls have also had our losses,' said the History Owl. 'Religion is dead, and though Geography will live, his face will never be the same again. Our young hero Hunter will survive, but he will bear the scars of today's battle with him till the day he dies. For all that, he will be glad he was present and among us on this day, for history is a harsh judge and the many who stayed away will be weighed in the balance and found wanting, while, as Bardic says, those who fought with us here will be honoured and remembered for as long as Barn owls and Tawnies survive in liberty to fly in the night skies.'

'Do not delude yourselves,' said Yoller's father. 'A thousand winters hence, the things your Bard Owl sings of will be treated as mere myth or legend. They will become a sometime thing, a mere hint or stirring from some long forgotten yesterday, changed and perverted by future owls and by the ebb and flow of time. For those of us who shared this dawn of glory, let it suffice that we fought for freedom and we won, even though our deeds will soon be forgotten as a dream that fades and dies at twilight when we wake.'

On this realistic note, as the evening shadows lengthened, Yoller's father bowed a grave farewell to each of the Barn owl contingent and made history by nodding once to little Alba, since there was no previous record of any Little owl being acknowledged or made welcome on traditional Tawny land. The old leader then flew off to rejoin his wounded son, leaving the rest of the assembly to turn their attention back to Hunter.

'You must try to move soon,' said the History Owl, as the sun sank still further in the west. 'You must try to make it to your mother's home tonight, before your injuries stiffen up and you find it hard to fly.'

'The words,' said Hunter, weakly. 'Who will say the last words for my father's body?'

'Never fear, dear boy,' said Bardic. 'Your brother and I will fly there as soon as twilight falls. Then we will return at once and escort you very slowly to your mother's home, where you can rest and convalesce till winter's over and your wounds are fully healed.'

Hunter sat up groggily and shook his head. 'My sister is still there,' he said. 'I sense a bitter winter coming and food will be scarce for three. In any case, I'm not strong enough to bear my mother's grief. You fly home and tell her, Quaver. Then bring me word of them on your way back to Bardic's seat of learning.'

'Don't be silly, Hunter,' said his brother, crossly. 'Look at the state you're in! You may be a hero now, but you heard what Bardic said. You won't be able to feed or protect yourself until the early spring. Who on earth will look after you till then?'

'I'm going back to my abandoned farmhouse,' said Hunter, for the first time feeling a great wave of pain where the monster's talons had slashed his head and chest. 'Alba will take care of me,' he added, as her eyes gave him the message. 'There's food there and room enough for two. Remember the hardest lesson, Quaver. You can't go home again.'

Bardic, the History owl and Quaver looked at each other in consternation and surprise. Then the History Owl turned to Alba, coughed nervously, cleared his throat and spoke. 'Do you think you're capable of looking after him?' he asked, sounding unusually embarrassed for an owl of his experience and standing.

'Sure,' said little Alba, nodding and giving the three worried Barn owls one of her harder, brighter smiles. 'He'll make a lousy patient, but I guess the two of us will manage.'

The History Owl looked at Bardic and Quaver again and then turned back to Hunter. 'Frankly, I think this is unwise,' he said, with a worldly little sigh. 'But since you are the hero of the day, we will respect your wishes. Quaver will bring you news of your mother and your sister on his way back to Bardic's place.' He paused, stretched out a wing and patted Hunter gently on the shoulder. 'Get well soon,' he said. 'We'll meet again in spring.' Then Bardic and Quaver said goodbye and the three of them flew back into the sycamore tree to prepare the wounded Geography Owl for his departure.

'Are you ready?' Alba asked him, very gently. Hunter looked up at her gratefully, nodded and then winced with pain. 'Come on then, my hero,' she said, softly. 'Fly with me, very slowly, and I'll take you home again.'

CHAPTER 20

Winter came quickly after the war and bandaged the battlefield in Ripper's wood with a smooth white sheet of late November snow. More snow came and a thick white blanket soon covered what was left of the bodies scattered beneath the trees. It froze then and more snow fell until the whole of the abandoned battle zone took on a silent, ghostly stillness, waiting for new life and new hope to flourish with the coming spring.

Back home in Beak Poke's abandoned farmhouse, Hunter slept, suffered and recovered very slowly. His wounds healed a little day by day and his strength began to return as soon as he was able to swallow whole again and Alba no longer had to cut up the food she brought for him two or three times between each early twilight and each bitter winter dawn.

Though winter fell both hard and early, Hunter's fears of a food shortage proved to be unfounded, for the war against the Eagle owl had reduced the feathered raptors in the district to less than half their former population. On the few occasions when Beak Poke's territory provided insufficient food for both Hunter and herself, little Alba flew over the white, snow-covered fields and meadows to the lost domain, where the lake lay frozen like a stone, where the parkland stretched hard as iron under its wide, white blanket and bitter winds howled through the bare branches in the bleak darkness of the secret forest.

Of his brother's first visit, Hunter remembered very little, save the moaning of the wind in the first snowstorm of the winter and the throbbing pain that lay always with him in the shelter of his farmhouse den. But by the time of Quaver's second visit, he was eager for news and strong enough to entertain his brother while Alba flew off to the lost domain, leaving the two of them to talk in private.

'Dapple still shows no signs of recovering from father's death,' said Quaver. 'The shock of it has aged her and I fear that she may lose the will to live.'

'I'll go and see her as soon as I'm strong enough to travel on my own,' said Hunter, experiencing a twinge of guilt at the fear he still felt for his mother's grief.

'I think you should,' said Quaver, pensively. 'She's very concerned about you, you know. I think it might help her to see you strong and well again.'

'She shouldn't worry so much,' said Hunter, guilt making him sound intolerant and irritable. 'Presumably you've told her that I'm expected to make a full recovery before the spring?'

'You know what mothers are,' said Quaver, with an uncomfortable little shrug. 'And then, of course, she's quite upset about the fact that you're convalescing here instead of at home with Dawn Raptor and herself.'

'I told you, I didn't think there'd be enough to eat for three,' said Hunter, churlishly wishing that his brother would either go away or change the subject. Somehow, Quaver seemed to get the message and squirmed a little on top of the chair back he was using as a perch.

'That reminds me,' he said quickly. 'Dawn Raptor's going to Winger's seat of learning in the spring, and if you ask me, she'll be getting higher education in much more than owlology.'

'What do you mean?' asked Hunter.

'You know what I mean. The urge, of course,' said Quaver.

'The urge? What urge?' asked Hunter, feeling uncomfortably ignorant and out of his depth.

'Why, sex, of course,' said Quaver. 'Don't tell me you haven't had it yet? The urge, I mean, not sex itself. Under the present circumstances I wouldn't be so indiscreet as to ask you that. But that's something else that must worry Dapple, your living here with a little immigrant like this. You might have got away with it before the war. Then you were just an unknown young owl like any other. But now, of course, it's all over everywhere.'

'What's wrong with Alba staying here?' Hunter asked assertively.

'She's one of my best friends, she practically saved my life and now she's looking after me and nursing me back to health. What could be more natural than that?'

'Oh, nothing, dear boy,' said Quaver, all of a sudden sounding very like his tutor Bardic. 'Absolutely nothing could be more natural, if she were another Barn owl, or if you were a Little owl like her. But please don't think I disapprove. I'm broad-minded, so it doesn't bother me. Generally most poets and musicians are broad-minded, and if you study under Bardic, then you have to be. But you can't expect a mother to be so easy-going, can you? Especially when your father was Religion Owl.'

'Has Dapple mentioned anything to you?' asked Hunter, staring out at the midwinter night through the gap in the wall where the window had once been and trying to come to terms with what his brother had been saying.

'No,' said Quaver, shaking his head. 'She hasn't actually said anything, but I know what she's been thinking. And, of course, other owls have said things, though more to Bardic than to me. But I've overheard them, and you might almost say that in your own small way you were becoming a subject of scandal and concern.'

'And what does Bardic say about it?' asked Hunter, trying to keep calm, though his first experience of unwanted notoriety provoked anger and rebellion at the interference of others and at the same time a sickening, sinking feeling in his stomach.

'Oh, you know what Bardic's like,' said Quaver, with a histrionic wave of his wing that looked as if it had been directly copied from his tutor. 'He doesn't disapprove at all. In fact, he says he'll compose an epic love ballad about it if you and Alba should stay together for much longer. For an artist, you know, things of that kind are simply good material and nothing more.'

Shocked, Hunter turned back from his contemplation of the winter night and gazed steadily at his younger brother. While listening to Quaver, he had been trying to work out whether what he felt for little Alba was the urge, come upon him unawares, and decided that it was not. He told his brother so, in no uncertain terms, and added at the end, 'and I'm quite sure that for her it's exactly the same thing.'

'Oh well, look here,' said Quaver, for once sounding embarrassed and confused. 'You don't have to justify yourself, at least not to me, you don't. Remember, I'm your brother. And of course, it is quite possible that you haven't felt the urge for Alba yet. Sexually, you may be a late developer. And in any case, it's the middle of winter and you've been very badly injured. But what will happen in the spring? You'll feel it then, and so will she. That is, if she hasn't done already.'

'Please go now,' said Hunter. 'I'm tired, and all this has upset me. I need time to digest it all and think in peace. I'd no idea that other owls could be so interfering and so bloody minded.'

'You've brought it on yourself, in part, by being such a hero,' Quaver said. 'Great things are expected of you now, and of course that causes gossip and a fair amount of envy.'

'Don't mention it to little Alba, if you meet her on the way,' said Hunter, as his young brother prepared to fly away. 'She's my best friend and I don't want her upset. I don't want her to hear the things that you've just told me.'

Quaver glanced sharply at his brother and then turned away. 'I guess that she has a fair idea already,' he said, looking out into the cold winter night that waited for his journey. 'Remember that the females of all owl species mature sooner than the males, and she's older than you are, anyway. Goodbye, Hunter. Rest now, and visit Dapple when you're strong again. And visit Bardic, too. He wants to talk to you about the ballad. He also says that an epic of this kind requires a very long period of gestation to do full justice to the subject. He keeps going over the battle from the beginning to the end, and his own role seems to get a little bigger every time. In fact, if he carries on that way, in the course of time he'll come to believe that he won the war all by himself!'

'I don't remember him as being active in the battle,' Hunter said, still thinking of little Alba, though the subject had now been dropped. 'I thought he stayed behind in the clearing, awaiting your despatches.'

'He did join in at the very end, after you were wounded and unconscious,' said Quaver in the ironic manner he was rapidly acquiring. 'He may even have pecked at the monster once or twice, though by that time I believe it was already dead.'

'Do give him my regards,' said Hunter, picking up his brother's derisory tone. 'And tell him that I'm most flattered to be thought of as possible material. I know there are some owls who believe that any kind of publicity is preferable to none.'

Quaver grinned and patted his brother with one wing. 'Get well soon, Hunter,' he said. 'And stay cheerful. There are much worse things in life than being the centre of attention. That's something that I'm sure you'll learn to live with.'

Hunter sat still and brooded for a long time after Quaver had left him and set off on the long winter journey to his seat of learning. He said nothing to little Alba when she returned from the lost domain, bringing him a short-tailed vole that she had taken on the way. For several nights after that he mulled things over in his mind, but kept silent and still had not broached the subject some time later when the first snowdrops and winter aconite appeared and he knew that he was ready to make his first, short solo flight since he had been wounded in the war. 'I'll try to get as far as my former meeting place with Yoller in the spinney,' he said to little Alba, late one freezing twilight after a light snowfall had freshened the whiteness of the countryside around them. 'Of course,' he added, unenthusiastically, 'you're quite welcome to come with me if you want to.'

'No thanks, Hunter,' Alba replied, with one of her wistful little smiles. 'It's sweet of you to ask, but I guess it's better if you go alone. Your friend Yoller is very kind, as Tawnies go, but you know the way the woodland owls really feel about us immigrants. Sure, he puts up with me for your sake and to get news of you, but I'm no longer needed now you're strong enough to fly alone.'

'You will always be needed.' Hunter wanted to say, but did not. He wanted to put his wing around her and cuddle all their worldly cares away, but he was still confused by what Quaver had told him and he still needed time to think. 'All right, then,' he said. 'I'll go now and I'll get my own food on the way.'

'Take care, my hero,' Alba said, looking at him with a kind of tender resignation in her eyes. 'And don't get into any kind of trouble. Remember, you're still not strong enough to fight. Give Yoller my best greetings. I'll be waiting here when you get back.'

Hunter looked at her in an agony of indecision. From the expression in her eyes, it seemed that she could read his mind and though he knew it was impossible, he could have sworn that she had heard every word that Quaver said. In spite of the friendship and the tenderness they shared, it seemed as if a barrier had been growing up between them since his brother's second visit. Though Hunter's instinct was to break through that fragile barrier and pour forth his heart and soul, he refrained, held back by inexperience, inhibition and by the powerful forces of his Barn owl education. 'I'm sorry you won't come,' he said. 'The three of us fought together in the war, you know. We were on the same side then.'

'Go on your own,' said Alba, gently. 'It will do you good. You two wounded heroes wouldn't want a female present at your big reunion, not even if she were a Barn owl or a Tawny.'

'See you later, then,' said Hunter, and leaning forward he brushed his cheek against her own. She nuzzled him gently back, just once, and then watched him fly out of their farmhouse den into the cold winter night for his first solo outing since the war.

CHAPTER 21

When Hunter returned from his reunion with Yoller, his attitude to little Alba and to the world in general had undergone a change. The information his war comrade had let slip, perhaps deliberately and perhaps quite innocently, imagining that his friend already knew, made it all the more difficult for Hunter to open up his heart, or even to ask Alba whether what he had heard was true.

Now that he could hunt alone, they spent fewer of their waking hours together, and though they talked a lot at dawn and dusk, deep inside himself Hunter felt that their idyll was drawing to an end. Though he said nothing, and outwardly most things remained the same, the intimacy they had shared in war time seemed to be slipping imperceptibly away. Sometimes he felt that their estrangement was merely a figment of his tortured imagination, brought on by what Quaver had told him and made infinitely worse by what he had heard from Yoller. At other times the growing barrier was real enough for him to bang against, so that it hurt and made him miserably unhappy.

At last, when the frost let go its iron grip and primrose and celandine began to stir beneath the melting snow, Hunter could hold his peace no longer and confronted little Alba one day when twilight deepened and she prepared to set out on yet another journey to the lost domain.

'Why don't you stay here and hunt with me?' he asked her suddenly, no longer able to hold back the question that had been tormenting him since his long talk with Yoller in the spinney. 'There's plenty of food here. There's always been enough and there'll be more now that the thaw has finally set in.'

Alba turned her head and gave him a shy and rather wistful smile. Hunter felt his heart beat faster, for something in her look told him that his worst fears had been well-founded and the moment of truth was very near at hand.

'There's a kestrel,' she said, still looking him in the eyes with that crooked, wistful little smile. 'A rogue kestrel has been hunting here right through the cold spell we've been having. It hunts at dawn and twilight, too. While he's been around there's only been enough food left for you.'

'That's not true,' said Hunter, flatly. 'And what's more, you know it isn't!'

'It is true, I swear it,' said little Alba, while her eyes pleaded with him for gentleness and understanding. There was a long pause while they looked at each other, each slowly accepting that the time had come to stop pretending and cross the great divide between formality and truth. 'Leastways,' said Alba, eventually, with a wry, lopsided grin, 'it's true about the kestrel and the food.'

'Then why didn't you tell me before?' asked Hunter, harshly.

'Because you're still not strong enough to fight,' said Alba. 'If I'd told you, then you'd have gone out there to look for him and got yourself killed or badly mauled again.'

'Why didn't you tell me that your cousin and his friend had come back to the lost domain?' asked Hunter, half-relieved and half-frightened now that at last he had got the burning question out.

As Alba looked back at him her eyes pleaded for tolerance and understanding and her feathers seemed to shrink and crumple as though they were telling him that deep inside she knew she had done him wrong. After what seemed like a very long time, she turned her head aside and glanced at the night outside the gaping window. 'I guess Yoller must have told you,' she said eventually, not asking him but merely confirming for herself that the inevitable had happened.

'Why did you tell me you were going there to hunt alone when in fact you've been spending all your time with them?'

'Oh, Hunter, don't!' said Alba, with an unhappy little cry. 'Don't torment yourself that way. Don't you see that the whole thing can't be helped?'

'Don't you like it here with me?' asked Hunter, staring angrily at her pretty face and the hurt in her wide, expressive eyes. 'Is this place too small for you, or is it the company that you don't like?'

'Hunter, sweetie, don't!' Alba said imploringly. 'You know it had to happen someday. You know we can't go on like this.'

'Why not?' asked Hunter bluntly. 'It was good enough for you before the war. In fact, you begged me to let you stay.'

'I only asked permission to hunt here on your territory,' Alba said. 'I never asked you to let me share your home.'

'Are you worried about what other owls will think?' asked Hunter, his voice hard and strident with the hurt he felt. 'Is that the problem? Have you suddenly decided that your reputation is at stake?'

'It's your reputation that worries me, not mine,' said Alba. 'Surely you can see that your whole future will be damaged if I stay around once you are well again?'

'My career, you mean,' said Hunter. 'My future will be damaged if you go. I'm not ambitious. To me, the idea of a career is just a heap of sparrow shit. All I want to do is to live in peace here on my territory with you. For always. I realized that in a sudden flash when I was flying into battle. When death stares you in the face like that, you realize how futile most ambitions really are. At a time like that you'd give everything just to settle down and live your life in peace, enjoying the countryside and the pleasures of each season. After all that carnage, it's enough to be alive and well with someone that you love and trust. For always.'

'Oh, Hunter,' little Alba said, with tears welling up in her big, wide-open eyes, 'knowing you and taking care of you has been a wonderful experience, but always is not a word for us. Always is a word for sunset, for moonrise and for green grass growing every spring.'

'We can make it a word for you and me, if both of us decide,' said Hunter stubbornly. 'No one can divide us if we both make up our minds.'

'Can't you see the odds against us are too great?' asked Alba, wiping away a tear with the tip of one stubby little wing. 'Can't you see that if I stayed here you would eventually be ostracized?'

'What does that mean?' asked Hunter, who had never heard the word before.

'It means that none of your own kind would come near you any more,' said Alba. 'It means that you would become an outcast among others of your species. They wouldn't understand the feelings we have for each other, and what owls don't understand they fear and shun.'

'Would the same thing apply to you?' asked Hunter, whose anger had been washed clean away by little Alba's tears. 'Would owls of your own kind shun you, too?'

'I guess so,' replied Alba. 'I guess all of them would, or all but a very few.'

'Does it matter what the others think?' asked Hunter. 'As long as they don't hurt you? And I won't let them hurt you, Alba. I'll protect you, I can promise that.'

'Oh, Hunter, you know that's not all there is against us. I love you, too, but we can't mate. We can't have chicks. You know that as well as I do.'

'I don't care,' said Hunter, calmly. 'We can live without them. Some owls of the same species do, especially when they're old. So why can't we?'

'No!' said Alba, shaking her head with exasperation and willing him to understand. 'Some day you'll meet a female of your own species and fall in love with her. She'll want fledglings sure enough, and so will you. Then little by little you'll come to hate me and hold me in contempt. I would stand in the way of the normal life you could have had. Because one day you'll get over your injuries, Hunter, and you'll recover from the shock of the war and of your father's death. Then you'll want what others want and you'll be ashamed to be seen with me.'

As Alba poured out these words with passionate conviction, Hunter remembered how scruffy and ragged she had seemed on the first occasion when they had met, and how loath he had been for Yoller or for any other owl to know that they were becoming friends. Perhaps it was true that one day he might feel the same again. 'We don't have to go anywhere or meet anyone,' he said, inadvertently confessing that he had already felt ashamed of her in public. 'We can stay here and live happily, just the two of us, the way we have done up to now.'

'Listen, Hunter,' said the little immigrant, leaning forward on her perch, determined to exploit the first sign of hesitation that he had shown, 'if I leave you soon enough, the others will forget, or else they will remember the extenuating circumstances and pretend they understand. They will put it all down to the stress of battle, your war wounds, to the shock of your father's death and even to the disappointment you must have felt at your sister's being chosen to study owlology instead of you. They'll understand that you felt hard done by and think that you were trying to follow in your dead tutor's footsteps.'

'What do you mean?' asked Hunter. 'You didn't live with Beak Poke, did you?'

'Don't be silly,' Alba said. 'What I mean is that they'll think you were trying to be a pragmatist like him. After all, he was well known for his empirical approach and he once told me that he'd learned more in the field, from talking to Little owls and Tawnies, than when he was your age and studied theory with his tutor. Remember, Hunter, most owls look for motive and self-interest in any kind of action. "He's clever, that one is," they'll say, if we split up in time. "He got himself looked after, learned more about the immigrants than his sister ever will from Winger, and then kicked her off his land." Then there's your relationship with Yoller and your record as a war hero. "Oh, you wait and see," they'll all say, nodding wisely. "He's one on his own, that Hunter is. You mark my words, one day he'll be a leader."'

'I don't want to be a leader,' said Hunter, firmly. 'I want to stay here and live in peace and privacy with you. I've made up my mind, but it's obvious that you need more time to think, and for that you need to be alone. I understand that and I don't want to put you under any pressure. Also, I don't want you to feel obliged to go back to the lost domain. I know you came in the first place to avoid the unwelcome attentions of your cousin and his friend. So you stay here and I'll go home and pay an overdue visit to my mother. You'll be safe here till I get back and then we can decide.'

They looked at each other for quite some time when Hunter had stopped talking and in Alba's eyes there was a whimsical mixture of resignation, love and pain. 'All right, Hunter,' she said, eventually. 'We'll do it your way. Go and see your mother and when you get back, I'll let you know what I've decided. But spring will be here soon and my decision will be final, either way. Is that OK?'

'Of course,' said Hunter. 'It's the only way.'

'Then go now,' Alba said, 'and watch out for the kestrel. I couldn't bear to see you badly mauled again.'

'You take care as well,' said Hunter. 'I shall miss you while I'm gone.'

He flew off then through the gap in the wall that had once been a window and set out on the first stage of a journey that would take him across the lost domain and on to the place where his father had been killed and to the battlefield where he himself had so very nearly died. As he flew through the milder weather and the melting snow, he thought long and hard about himself and little Alba, but try as he might, he could no longer imagine life without her. If they should part, he decided that he would worry every day for the rest of his life about what had become of her. 'I would get no peace from here to all eternity,' he thought. 'If she won't share the farmhouse with me, then she could go back to her funk hole in the hollow tree. That way, even though we lived apart, I could still protect her and we would both be hunting and sleeping close to each other under the same small patch of sky.'

Hunter was so deep in thought that the first part of his journey passed very quickly and to his surprise he soon found himself emerging from the outer woodland of the lost domain and approaching the great house, the gardens and the lake, all of which were blurred and changed by the whiteness of the melting snow. He flew on towards the centre of the parkland, wondering whether to pause there for a snack, when suddenly three Little owls rose from the solitary oak in which he and Alba had banqueted on vole and mole before the war in that early dawn that now seemed so very long ago. Hunter steeled himself and flew onwards, while the three immigrants climbed higher in formation and hovered menacingly ahead of him, setting up a three-pronged barrier in his flight path.

For a brief moment, Hunter wondered whether to veer west and outfly them, a thing he knew that he could do with ease, in spite of not yet being fully fit. But courage and curiosity got the better of him and he flew on to confront them. After all, he thought, it might be enlightening to meet some of Alba's kinsfolk face to face. He slowed down as he approached them and then stopped and hovered a few lengths' distance from the owl in the centre of the three-pronged barrier in front of him. 'Going somewhere, big white owl?' asked the middle immigrant, with a queer half-smile playing on what looked to Hunter like a sly and cruel face.

'Naturally,' Hunter replied, upset by the unfriendly reception. 'I'm not in the habit of flying without a destination.'

'And where would you be going, big white bird, if I might make so bold?' enquired the same owl, still with that sarcastic little smirk that Hunter longed to ram right down his ugly little throat.

'That's my business, don't you think,' replied Hunter, in tones of icy calm. 'This is no man's land and I have as much right here as you.'

'Not from today you don't,' said the immigrant hovering to the left of the one who had challenged him. 'From today on the lost domain is no longer no man's land. It has been found and colonized by us.'

Hunter looked at the second Little owl in anger and amazement. He was a strong, brawny little brute with a truculent, unsubtle manner that made Hunter seethe with indignation.

'You look surprised,' the first immigrant said, 'but my friend Falco here is right. This territory now belongs to the first Little owl collective, and from this day on you need a permit to pass through.'

'And what if I come here for food?' asked Hunter, who had forgotten all about his war wounds and was ready for a fight.

'You can never hunt on this land again,' said the first owl, with that infuriating smirk still flickering on his face. 'From now on all the game in the lost domain belongs to the Little owl cooperative and all trespassers will be escorted off our land, or killed if they refuse to go in peace. That's final, big white owl, so get out now or we'll tear you into pieces!'

'Wait,' said the third immigrant, looking at Hunter with a worried expression on his face. 'You've handled this badly, Primo,' he said, turning to the owl in the centre of the barrier. 'We don't want to kill you, white owl. We want you to understand. You must forgive my friends. They get very nervous when they think there's going to be a fight. If you have a reason for your journey, we will grant you free passage, now and at any future time. But if you come here to hunt, then we shall have to kill you, and I'm going to tell you why.'

Hunter stared back at the third immigrant who was better-looking and better-spoken than the other two, though just as hard and steely and possibly the strongest of the three.

'As a matter of fact, I didn't come here for food,' said Hunter, rather haughtily. 'I have my own territory near here and that provides me with more than sufficient for my needs. I am flying south-west to my mother's home and the lost domain lies directly on my route. It would take me far too long to make a detour of this place, and since I have often flown and hunted here before, I have no intention of relinquishing my right to do so in the future.'

'Then you will die, white owl,' snapped Falco. 'If you steal one morsel of food from our territory, we will rip you into pieces.'

'Wait,' the third owl said again, while Hunter seethed with rage and prepared to sell his life as dearly as he could. 'Listen, this must be the Barn owl that gave shelter to your cousin. You remember? The one who fought with the Wood owls in the war.'

'Is that true?' asked Falco. 'Are you the owl who took over from old Beak Poke? The one who allows my cousin Alba to occupy a hollow tree of yours and hunt freely on your land?'

'I am,' said Hunter, watching the hostile expression on the faces of the three male immigrants change into reluctant recognition and acceptance.

'In that case, things are not the same,' the third owl said, fixing Hunter with his firm and steely gaze. 'We are grateful to you for the hospitality you offered to Falco's cousin, Alba. She is one of the dozen Little owls who have been chosen to settle with us here and turn this place into our promised land. You are a neighbour and a friend – a friend because you fought against our common enemy and because you helped a fellow immigrant of ours when she was in distress.' The third owl paused at this point and glanced at his companions as if to gain consent for what he was about to say. 'Because of this, you may have free passage across our territory whenever you require it,' he continued. 'And you can help us still further if you take news of this to your Barn owl parliament, council, or whatever it is you call it.'

'What if the men with firesticks should return?' asked Hunter, playing for time as his mind raced with the shattering news that little Alba intended to leave him, and settle with her kinsfolk in the lost domain.

'We have to take that risk,' the third owl said. 'They have been absent for some time and in any case we have nowhere else to go.'

'And the Tawnies?' Hunter asked. 'You know that they intend to reclaim the secret forest once the last of the man-made paths are finally engulfed and overgrown?'

'You can also help us there,' the third owl said. 'You fought with the big brown owls and know them well. Tell them that we have claimed this place to be our promised land and that we intend to keep it for our own. If they try to take it from us, there will be a bloody war, for you can be certain that we shall defend it to the death. That must be the last thing the Tawnies want, after the bitter losses they suffered in repelling the invasion. And tell both the Tawnies and the owls of your own race that as long as we have a territory of our own, there will no longer be any danger of squatting, trespassing or poaching in their precious woods or on your open farmland. For the first time in history we shall be self-sufficient, and that should more than compensate the Tawnies for the loss of the secret forest that they no longer use or need.'

'What is your name?' asked Hunter, boldly, for it now seemed obvious to him that this least unattractive of the Little owls would become the leader of their new collective.

'Renato,' the third owl replied. 'In your language that means Born Again.'

'Do you wish me to return here and tell you what the Tawnies say?' asked Hunter, holding the future leader's firm and steely gaze.

'We should be grateful for your mediation in these matters,' Renato replied. 'Though young, you are a reasonable, objective sort of owl. You will put our case fairly, without prejudice, and that is all we ask.' Hunter nodded and looked at Falco and Primo who were both still hovering in his path, though neither of them looked quite so fierce and unfriendly as before.

'Go now,' said their leader. 'Go in peace, and when you cross the battle zone in Ripper's wood, pay homage for us to those who fought and died that we might live.'

Having spoken, he flapped his short, blunt wings and rose higher in the sky. Primo and Falco followed his example, leaving Hunter space to pass beneath them and continue his journey across a territory that was still to be forbidden, but no longer secret and no longer called the lost domain.

He flew rapidly on across the remaining parkland and then entered the secret forest, where the paths made by man had been virtually obliterated as the ancient woodland devoured their traces and proliferated to reclaim its own. By the time he had flown halfway across the broad sea of tree tops, Hunter's racing thoughts had slowed down sufficiently for him to absorb the shock of hearing that little Alba intended to join the immigrant cooperative and settle in the lost domain. 'If she really intended to leave me, for the sake of my reputation, where else would she go?' he asked himself, as he approached the edge of the forest and the place where the monster had crashed down from the sky and murdered Yoller's brother. 'If she does decide to leave me, where else would she go but to what they now believe to be their promised land? Though I must say I don't think much of Primo, Falco and Renato, the founding fathers of this new collective. Born again, indeed! Do these Little owls believe in reincarnation, then? I must ask little Alba when I get home again. And if that arrogant trio do take another form of life the next time round, I hope they come as worms or slugs, or perhaps as three stinking deathwatch beetles. That way perhaps they'd learn some manners and some much needed humility.'

Pondering on the night's events, Hunter soon found himself flying over open country, close to the spot where Brook and Steeple had both died. With a great effort of will he forced himself to land on the place where Steeple had fallen, but no trace of his father's body was to be found among the melting snow that lay soggy and glutinous upon the ground. Hunter perched in the cold, wet snow by the place where Steeple's body had vanished so completely and said the last words slowly and with great feeling. At the end, he added a homage from the three fierce Little owls and then flew onwards to the scene of the battle in Ferocity and Ripper's wood.

To his amazement, the only sign that remained of the dreadful carnage was the monster's skeleton, parts of which still hung suspended in the branches of the chestnut tree where he had met his end. The length and breadth of the skeleton and thickness of the snow-wet bones filled Hunter with a kind of reverence and dread. 'How did we do it?' he asked himself as he flew onwards. 'How did we overcome a giant of that size and strength?'

Hunter felt sadder and sadder as he travelled onwards through the silent and empty Tawny woods, remembering the many who had fallen and wondering for the first time since the war whether all the bloodshed and loss of life had been worthwhile, especially now that a new conflict threatened to smoulder into flame from the snow-drenched embers of the old. If a civil war should break out over the right to colonize the lost domain, would his own suffering and the death of so many comrades have proved to be in vain?

Pondering on these things and longing to return to little Alba and the comfort of his farmhouse den, Hunter flew out of Ripper's wood, crossed no man's land and entered the fertile territory where he had been born and enjoyed those stirring hopes of early youth that now seemed to have vanished more quickly than snow melts in the first warm sun of early spring.

'He would have wanted it that way,' said Dapple, peering sadly into the night through a chink in the rafters of the barn. 'Although it's a tragedy for me, I have a notion it's the exit your father would have chosen, rather than a long, lingering decline with a slow fading of the senses one by one.'

'He saved my life,' said Hunter, who found his mother much older than he remembered, almost too old to have mated once with Steeple, who had still been swift, strong and vigorous on the day he died. 'He attacked the monster head-on,' Hunter continued. 'He was alone, it was against his religion and he must have known that he would die, yet he attacked head-on, without a moment's hesitation.'

'I'll tell you a secret, now that he has gone,' said Dapple, turning back from her contemplation of the midnight sky. 'He never really wanted to be Religion Owl at all. But in those days there were fewer opportunities for further education, so when his father found him a place under their neighbour, the Religion Owl, he was only too happy to accept.'

'What did he really want to be?' asked Hunter, to whom this was a most surprising revelation.

'Oh, I don't think he really knew,' said Dapple, sighing as she remembered her lost youth with a blend of sadness and nostalgia. 'I think he wanted to know everything, when he was young. At different times he spoke of studying owlology, history, geography and even man.'

'Why didn't he?' asked Hunter. 'Surely he could have gone on and specialized in a second subject as soon as he'd finished with religion?'

'I've told you, times were harder then,' said Dapple. 'And soon after we met, I wanted to mate and start a family. Perhaps I should have waited. But anyway, as soon as he'd finished, his tutor died and your father got the chance to take his place. He said he was too young and in any case, as I've already told you, he wanted to continue with his education and study something else. But the main advantage was that this territory and our home here went with the position he'd been offered on the council, so I persuaded him to take it. He never reproached me for it, but I've often thought that I was wrong.'

Silence fell in the barn and Dapple turned back to the chink in the rafters to gaze at the night outside and beyond it back into her past. Hunter watched her, not knowing what to say and wondering how much longer it would be before Dawn Raptor returned with the History Owl. She had left to fetch him soon after twilight, so that Hunter could report on the latest developments in the lost domain. 'You shouldn't blame yourself,' he said eventually. 'He had a good life, he died a young owl's death, and while he lived he was an example to us all.'

'Oh, he was,' said Dapple, turning round and clutching gratefully at the comfort Hunter gave her. 'He never stopped learning, about all sorts of things, and he always saw religion as ethics more than dogma. He was never strict and narrow, like his tutor and predecessor on the council, though he had to be firm with the three of you when you were fledglings, as any decent father must.'

'Would you like to see the place where he was killed?' asked Hunter, feeling a sudden flood of pity for his mother. 'It's on my way back to Beak Poke's, as you know. I could take you there tomorrow night and you would easily find your own way back home.'

'No, I couldn't bear it,' said Dapple, with a vehemence that Hunter had not expected. 'I prefer to remember him alive. And why must you go back to Beak Poke's place? Why can't you stay here with me? Dawn Raptor's leaving soon to start her studies under Winger and even as things are there's room and food enough for three.'

'The hardest lesson,' said Hunter, who was surprised and shocked by this suggestion. 'You remember? You taught it me. You can't go home again.'

'I hated teaching you that lesson,' Dapple said. 'I always felt that it was wrong and unnatural to harden a young owl's heart to reality too soon. But it was my duty, so I did it. Even so, I'm sure there must be some exceptions to the rule, especially at a time like this, after a war in which your father was killed and you were badly wounded. Surely the rules must be different at a time like this?'

'I can't come back now,' said Hunter, resenting the emotional blackmail his mother was applying. 'Not after the initial wrench. In any case, I have my own territory to consider.'

'You won't be there for long,' his mother said. 'You know you'll have to leave as soon as a place is found for your higher education. You could come and stay here in the meantime.'

'Who says there'll be a place for me?' asked Hunter, deciding that attack would be the best form of defence. 'I had a place, but Beak Poke died and afterwards came the invasion and the war. Then Winger chose my sister to study owlology instead of me. I might not get another place, and even if I did, I'm not sure I would take it. I'm not ambitious. The war taught me that. A quiet life will do for me.'

'But you're so young,' his mother pleaded. 'And of course you'll get a place! The History Owl thinks very well of you and so do all the others on the council, especially those who fought beside you in the war. Mark my words, you'll get offers from more than one seat of learning in the spring.'

'Well, I shall stay at home till then,' said Hunter doggedly. 'I have a territory of my own and the war has taught me how important that can be. I'm keen to learn everything I can, but if I had to choose between formal education and a territory that belongs to me, I'd choose to own the land I live on and sacrifice the theory for the facts.'

'You don't mean that,' Dapple said. 'And as far as a home of your own is concerned, you can inherit this barn and land from me. I am too old now for a future of my own, and much too sad. Rest assured, my son, I shall not mate again.'

Hunter was too surprised to make any immediate reply. At her age, he would have taken it for granted that she would not wish to mate again. The very thought of it seemed almost indecent to one as young as he was, though he supposed that it was companionship she wanted – companionship that she was offering him and which he knew he would reject now that he had earned his independence, and still had a chance to share his home and his life with little Alba.

'You say you think a home of your own is more important than an education,' continued Dapple, willing him to listen to her reason with the same passionate conviction that Alba had used in their discussion on the previous night. 'Well, by all accounts this one is both bigger and more fertile than the place you have at present. From what I gather, Beak Poke's land will barely feed two adults, let alone a family. And you'll want a family one day, won't you?'

'I don't know,' said Hunter, lying carefully. 'I haven't thought about it yet.'

'Of course you will,' said Dapple. 'And this place can be yours one day, if you want it. All you have to do is move back here and live with me. That way, it will be yours by right the day I die.'

'I don't know,' said Hunter, who was confused and resentful but still did not want to hurt his mother's feelings. 'I'll have to think about it carefully. It does seem to go against the theory that you taught us.'

'So does living with a little immigrant!' said his mother, sharply. 'Please don't misunderstand me, Hunter,' she added quickly as he opened his bill to answer back. 'Now that you're an adult, you'll find me more broad-minded than you think. I'm pleased you gave the little creature shelter on your land and I'm very glad that she's looked after you so well and nursed you back to health. But it can't go on indefinitely, you must both know that already. Coming back here would be a way out of your commitment to her. You could tell her I was old and grief-stricken and needed looking after. I believe Little owls attach even more importance to the family than we do, so I'm sure she'd under-stand.'

'I've asked her to stay on and share my territory,' said Hunter, stubbornly. 'She's saved my life and she's the best friend I've ever had. So I want her to go on living with me, or at least to stay and share my land.'

Dapple did not answer at once, but gave Hunter a long look of bitter reproach. He winced and wilted inwardly but held his head high and returned her stare to show that his mind was made up and that he would not weaken under pressure.

'My poor, misguided fledgling,' his mother said at last, turning her head to one side and sighing deeply. 'And what does your best friend the immigrant have to say?' she asked, fixing her eyes on him again. 'Has she accepted your proposal?'

'Not yet,' said Hunter, wishing he were somewhere else. 'She says she'll give me an answer when I come back from this visit.'

'I see,' said Dapple, nodding slowly. 'Well, if she's as shrewd and experienced as I imagine, then she'll know exactly what she has to do. It won't be easy for either of you, but you'll get over it in time.'

'What do you mean?' asked Hunter, with a sudden stab of fear. 'What is it that she has to do?'

'Never you mind,' his mother replied, looking at him less resentfully and with something like compassion. 'You'll find out soon enough, unless, of course, she accepts your proposal and ruins both your lives. But fortunately for both of you, I don't suppose she will.' Hunter was about to reply when he picked up the rapid approach of two Barn owls and his mother leaned forward and spoke to him in urgent undertones. 'That will be Dawn Raptor with Rivers, the History Owl,' she said. 'We won't discuss these things in front of them.'

'Of course not,' Hunter answered gruffly, glancing at the gap in the roof of the barn through which his sister and his ex-comrade at arms would presently appear.

'But remember what I said,' his mother added quickly. 'You can give me your answer after you've been back to Beak Poke's territory and spoken to your friend.'

Hunter merely nodded, said nothing and puffed himself up a little to greet Rivers and Dawn Raptor as they flew in and perched beside him on the rafters. At least, the History Owl perched beside him and gave him a broad smile and a warm hug of greeting, while Dawn Raptor settled in her usual place and observed the others with her special, supercilious little smile. 'You look marvellous, Hunter,' Rivers exclaimed, raising one wing in jubilation. 'What a wonderful recovery! The last time I saw you, you were on the verge of becoming past history rather than a subject for contemporary studies. Tell me, how do you feel?'

'All right, thank you,' said Hunter, smiling as he remembered his senior comrade's wit and courage in the battle. 'And how are you, History Owl? Have you recovered fully from your wounds?'

'Oh, long since,' laughed Rivers. 'They were only scratches as compared to yours. And tell me, how is our Tawny friend, young Yoller? My goodness me, what a hero that owl turned out to be!'

'He is well and sends his greetings,' said Hunter, feeling certain that Yoller would wish to be remembered to one of the bravest birds to have fought beside them on that famous day.

'And what is this message that you bring us from the immigrants?'

asked Rivers. 'Is it connected with your little friend who was with us in the battle?'

'Only indirectly,' Hunter said. 'The important information is that the Little owls intend to colonize the lost domain. They already look upon it as their promised land and intend to turn it into a territory all their own.'

'That is news indeed,' said Rivers, looking at Dapple and Dawn Raptor with his eyebrows raised. 'That is news to make the rafters ring. If the Little owls do settle there, it will be the first time in recorded history that they have a place that they can truly call their own.'

'What about the old country?' Hunter asked. 'I've heard them mention it. The place they came from about a hundred springs ago.'

'They were squatters there as well,' said Rivers. 'Or so I've heard it told. History has it that they've always lived in no man's land, since time itself began. They are an older race than we are, as you know, and some say they are even older than the Tawnies, though no one really knows how far back their history stretches before the beginning of recorded time.'

'It will lead to trouble in the end,' said Dapple, brooding darkly. 'Our tradition and religion have both taught us that the immigrants will never have a home to call their own. We were taught that they were born to suffer ceaseless troubles and condemned to live in no man's land until the end of time. One day the Tawnies or the men will drive them from their so-called promised land, of that you can be certain.'

'That's just superstition,' said Dawn Raptor, 'Like so many of the other things we've been brought up to believe.'

'It's not entirely superstition,' said Rivers, smiling quickly from mother to daughter in an attempt to keep the peace. 'And in any case, there is a very thin dividing line between superstition and religion, as there is between legend, myth and history itself, though in my official capacity it pains me to have to say so.'

'It will lead to strife,' said Dapple stubbornly. 'If the immigrants settle together in one place, sooner or later there will be a war.'

'That is a future possibility,' admitted Rivers, 'but the main thing at the moment is to maintain stability, to establish and maintain some sort of *status quo*. The war has created a kind of unity, for once, and we must strive to see that some sort of coalition or three-way alliance is kept up in case of any future outside threat. The monster is defeated now, and dead, but he may have offspring somewhere across the salty waters who may one day wish to crush us and avenge his death. We were complacent to imagine that the monster was extinct. In future, we must be wary, ever ready and prepared.'

'Isn't it strange that it took the invasion to create an alliance with the Tawnies?' Hunter asked. 'Surely we'll all work together in the future to protect our territories, as you said?'

'That's by no means certain,' said Rivers, with a rueful little smile. 'History shows us that it always takes an outside threat to create unity among those of the same race and religion, let alone among those of different cultures, blood and creeds. It's a great shame, but memories are short and conflict of some kind is never far away.'

'Winger says that the Tawnies are our real enemies,' said Dawn Raptor, smiling provocatively. 'I've told Hunter that before, but of course he didn't listen. "The enemy within" is what Winger calls them. He says that in time some of them will come to regret the defeat of the monster, who was really only a bigger, more powerful version of themselves. In the course of time, he says they'll come to wish that they'd formed an alliance with the Eagle owl to rid the territory of immigrants and of Barn owls like ourselves. He also says that the monster's offspring will eventually return and kill us all next time unless we form an alliance with the great white owls who live in the far north and east. They are the only ones who are strong enough to defeat the monster, tame the Tawnies and maintain a state of universal peace.'

'What pigeon shit!' said Hunter, turning on his sister with fuming indignation for the brave owls who had fought and died so that Winger and Dawn Raptor might survive to enjoy the freedom of the skies. 'What a shower of rancid sparrow's piss!' he added, fumbling unsuccessfully for the right words to express his anger and frustration.

'Calm yourself, Hunter,' said the History Owl, looking severely at the smirking Dawn Raptor and her boiling, livid brother. 'My colleague Winger is entitled to his learned and informed opinion,' continued Rivers, politely but with a new steely coldness in his tone. 'On the other hand, there are those of us who believe that the giant white owl may one day prove as great a threat to our independence and survival as did the monster we have just defeated. Only time will tell. In the meantime, we must be prepared.' The History Owl smiled a tight, polite smile which he switched quickly from Hunter to Dawn Raptor as if to tell them that the argument was at an end. 'Will you be staying long?' he asked, turning back to Hunter with a more friendly expression on his face. 'The question of your further education will come up at the next council meeting and we should like to know where you can be located.'

Hunter glanced quickly at his mother, feeling the pressure and sensing that society, protocol and family were conspiring to clip the freedom of his young and independent wings. 'I don't know,' he muttered hesitantly, looking at the History Owl but still feeling his mother's eyes on his back, watching him closely and willing him to express his intention of returning home. 'First I have to return to my territory and tell Yoller about the little immigrants and the promised land.'

'And after that?' asked Rivers, with eyebrows raised and a faint smile playing on his face.

'I haven't yet decided,' Hunter said. 'I need some more time on my own.'

'That's very wise,' said Rivers. 'Many strange things happen in a war and it takes much time to adapt to a state of peace again. In any case, when the time comes, we will contact your mother and she will tell us where to find you.'

The History Owl then said goodbye to Dapple and Dawn Raptor and before take off turned one final time to Hunter and closed one eye in a brief and friendly wink, conveying that though much could not be spoken, much was understood and left unsaid. When he had gone, Hunter felt trapped and uneasy with two pairs of female eyes trained on him, both questioning in their separate ways, as if they expected him to declare himself or to make some further revelation.

'I must go now,' he said, fidgeting restlessly on his rafter perch. 'As you both know, I have a mission to accomplish.'

'You've become very hard and purposeful since your war experiences,' said Dawn Raptor, mockingly. 'Not at all like the nice, soft-hearted elder brother I once knew.'

'And you, Dawn Raptor, have remained exactly the same snide and enigmatic little sister I remembered,' riposted Hunter warmly. 'Perhaps your education in owlology will change you for the better, but I doubt it.'

'I shall certainly enjoy it,' said Dawn Raptor. 'It will be interesting to see how both of us develop, don't you think? You, with your famous empirical approach and your personal relationships with young and rather insignificant owls from other species, and me with Winger's superior knowledge, culled from centuries of science and analysis.'

'Science!' said Hunter, trying desperately to keep his fraying temper. 'If you ask me anything, owlology is mostly experience and common sense. And I can tell you one thing that Winger doesn't seem to know,' he added, remembering the words of little Alba. 'The joys and sorrows of all owl species are basically the same.'

'How very profound,' his sister said. 'And which of your foreign friends taught you that little masterpiece of homespun philosophy? The big hero Yoller, or the little squatter to whom you seem so morbidly attached?'

'I'm going now,' said Hunter, turning to his mother and suppressing a tremendous urge to rip his sister's eyes out. 'I'll either return in person, or send you word of my decision. Once more, I wish you well.' And with that he flew out of the barn into the last of the darkness that would soon be banished by the rising dawn.

Seething with rage, indignation and sorrow, he winged his way low and uncaring of danger across the meadows, fields and spinneys where as a clumsy fledgling he had learned to fly. 'Alone again,' he muttered to himself, as he sped past the deserted church and onwards towards Ferocity and Ripper's wood. 'A loner, that's the way I like it best. Or, better still, in the company of one single, trusted friend. Politics, society and family bitchiness, they all make me sick! I'll sleep this first day of spring by the battlefield in Ripper's wood, or else in the middle of Brook's meadow, where my father fought and died to save my life. Winger, Dapple and Dawn Raptor didn't fight as Steeple, Rivers, Yoller and the others did. They'll never know the true meaning of loyalty and comradeship that flowers in times of trouble. And tomorrow night I'll make Alba promise to share my land and stay with me forever. She and Yoller are true friends, each worth a thousand families and Barn owl councils put together. They can keep their careers, their ambitions, their ingratitude and their hypocrisy. All I need is my den, one or two friends and above all the freedom of the sky.'

Thus soothed by the love and friendship that had sustained him in the heart of danger and despair, Hunter flew on towards his destination as the first spring break of day began to stir and soften the long darkness of the winter night.

CHAPTER 23

After sleeping near the battlefield in Ripper's now deserted wood, Hunter took off again as soon as twilight fell and flew across Brook's empty Barn owl territory and then high and fast across the lost domain – as high and fast as he had flown on his first solo journey that now seemed so long ago, when he had left his fledgling home and travelled hopefully to study under Beak Poke, who died before he and his new acolyte had had a chance to meet.

He flew high and fast to avoid the new immigrant masters of the lost domain, not because he feared them but because he could not wait to return to little Alba and begin the long, peaceful life with her of which he had dreamed since his glimpse of vision in the heat of battle, the dream of a free life safe and hidden inside his territory from the rack of ambition, strife and war. 'Self-study and contemplation are the things,' he said to himself as he flew swiftly on above the secret forest and saw the first immigrant sentinel rise up and follow in his wake. 'I can learn much about nature and the true meaning of life by myself, as Beak Poke and my father did before me.'

As Hunter left the secret forest behind him and flew across the vast expanse of parkland, a second sentinel rose from a solitary beech tree far below him. Hunter did not hesitate but dipped a wing and called out to identify himself without once slowing in his sure, swift homeward flight. Soon he had cleared the gardens, the lake and the great house itself and was heading fast across the final belt of woodland that separated the lost domain from the village and then from the fields and meadows of his home.

He arrived almost breathless with anticipation, hovered briefly outside to compose himself and then flew through the windowless gap into the place where he had first found independence, where he had recovered from his war wounds and which he had now come to cherish as his own.

The den was empty. There was no one there. Hunter hovered for a while inside the abandoned bedroom, then flew to his headboard, perched and began to breathe deeply in order to control himself and to contain the bitter disappointment that he felt. 'I'm back early,' he told himself. 'And in any case, she has to go out for her food. She can't sit here waiting all the time. She might even have gone hunting in the lost domain and I might have missed her there. But it doesn't matter. She'll be back, so you just sit here quietly, compose yourself and wait.'

This reasoning was all very well and it worked for a while, but as midnight came and went Hunter began to feel both resentful and uneasy. 'This is all very well,' he muttered to himself, 'but what about my dinner? I have to eat as well. Yet if I go out now, she might return in the meantime and I might miss her once again. She could have been a little more considerate.

'Unless something has happened to her while I've been away! She told me that a rogue kestrel had taken to hunting here at twilight and at dawn. What if she surprised him and there was a conflict? What if she's lying wounded and alone in some distant corner of the territory? I'd better go and look.'

But still he hesitated and stayed where he was while the night wore on and his hunger and resentment grew. He could feel the strong fragrance of the early spring in the mild darkness of the night outside, and this made him restless and uneasy, affecting him physically in a manner that he had never known before. At last he could stand it no longer, flew outside and began to circle his territory in the heady freshness of the night. There was an abundance of food now, as voles, field mice and even moles exposed themselves to danger with the coming spring. Hunter killed and ate with careless, unthinking ease, for his real quest was for little Alba, not for the nourishment his body needed. He could find no trace of her in any corner of his land and the abundance of defenceless, unwary game suggested that she had not hunted there for quite some time. With growing anxiety, Hunter eventually headed back to the farmhouse, uncertain of what to do next if he did not find her there.

Again, there was no sign of her and as Hunter sat on his perch, his heart beat faster than it should and his brain and body both seemed strangely intoxicated by worry and by his longing for little Alba's presence. Shortly before dawn she came and such was Hunter's state of agitation that he trembled on his perch and could not speak.

'Hi, Hunter!' she cried, flew to him briefly, touched his cheek with hers and then took off at once and landed on her perch before he had had time to enfold her in his strong but trembling wings. As he stared across the room at her she gave him a bright, determined smile which seemed unnatural to Hunter and not at all like the quizzical and tender glances that he had come to know and love so well. 'I sure am sorry that I missed you,' Alba said. 'I guess I didn't expect you back so soon. I was hunting in the lost domain and it wasn't until well after midnight that they told me they'd seen you passing through.'

'It doesn't matter,' said Hunter, half-choking on the words. 'You're safe and well and to me that's all that matters. But please don't go back there, Alba. Don't go back to the lost domain again. Now that I'm home again, you can stay here and live with me.'

As Hunter gazed at little Alba her bright smile faded and an expression of pain and worry took its place. 'Oh well, I guess I'd better tell you now,' she said, shrugging to harden herself for the devastating announcement she was about to make. 'I'm leaving, Hunter. I'm going to live in the Little owl collective in the lost domain. And what's more,' she said, pausing and wilting from the cruel words she had to say, 'and what's more, I'm about to mate.'

Hunter could not believe his ears. He sat on his perch and stared at her, numbed by the shock, while the pain and worry in Alba's eyes intensified as she leaned forward to explain. 'You knew that it was hopeless,' she said pleadingly. 'For your sake, as well as mine, you know I can't stay here. Now that the lost domain has been colonized by Little owls, it seemed the best way out for both of us. I didn't want to do it, Hunter, but I had to. One of us had to make the decision before it was too late.'

'Which one are you going to mate with?' asked Hunter, who was still stunned by the shock and could scarcely take it in. 'I thought you didn't like your cousin and his friend. I thought you came here to escape them.'

'It's an owl I didn't know before,' said little Alba, averting her eyes from Hunter and looking downwards in acute embarrassment. 'His name is Renato.'

'I met him on my last but one trip through the lost domain,' said Hunter, whose feelings were just beginning to return as the anaesthetic of the shock wore off. 'He's not quite so ill-mannered or so ugly as the other two, I'll give you that.'

'Don't, Hunter,' little Alba pleaded, looking up at him with tears of chagrin in her big round eyes. 'Please don't make it hard for me. I don't want to do it, but we both know it's for the best.'

'Don't do it, then!' said Hunter, as a powerful new sensation welled up inside him and filled him with a new, reckless strength and passion that he did not at once identify. 'I forbid you to go,' he said, springing from his perch and landing by little Alba's side. 'They'll take away your freedom,' he said, with his face very close to hers and his eyes full of passionate conviction. 'They'll make you unhappy. Alba, I want you here with me, for always!'

Then Hunter put his wings around her and as he did so he realized that this new overpowering sensation was what his brother called the urge. He rubbed his cheek hard against hers, muttering a string of half-choked endearments as he pulled her close to him and held her very tight. All at once he felt as strong as a giant and as tender as a summer breeze caressing ears of corn.

'No, Hunter, don't,' she begged him. 'Can't you see that it would only make things worse?' Hunter felt her trembling gently against him and the softness of her small body made him groan aloud in ecstasy and pain. 'Don't!' Alba repeated, gently trying to wriggle free as he pressed her to him and rubbed her soft cheek with his own. 'Don't! We mustn't do it. I love you, Hunter, but not this way. Please, I can never love you in this way. With you, I can never have the urge.'

Hunter loosened his grip momentarily and Alba wriggled free. He stared into her frightened, loving eyes and realized with dreadful certainty that she meant every word of what she said, but the urge was so strong that Hunter longed to fling himself upon her and mingle the whole of his body and his being with her own. He could not bear to think that Renato or any other owl should share the tenderness and passion that she now denied him, and he found himself moving compulsively towards her to take possession of what both soul and body told him was his own.

As he thrust himself upon her, Alba did not resist but uttered one cry of anguish so pure and poignant that it struck a chord in Hunter's heart. As he tore himself away from her before it was too late, her moan of sorrow called forth a wild, wounded howl of pain and frustration from the depths of Hunter's being. Sobbing, he hurled himself blindly across the room, flew out into the first spring night and sped desperately away from all that he desired. He knew not why nor where he went but flew on hard and fast as if bent on placing an irrevocable distance between himself and the excruciating torment that possessed him.

As dawn lingered in the darkness, only a creature of the night could have sensed the presence of the kestrel hunting before daybreak and daring to usurp the sanctity of owl light. Hunter's inner vision located the falcon hovering above the five-barred gate near the place where Beak Poke had died and the scene of his first encounter with little Alba. Unhesitating, Hunter changed direction, climbed higher in the sky and then dived in deadly silence before the kestrel had sensed the danger or had a chance to prepare himself for the attack.

Hunter did not think as he fell like lightning from the sky, but felt the pure killer instinct soothe and absorb his raging torment, adding still more strength and purpose to his deadly task. Shocked by Hunter's sudden, suicide attack, the rogue kestrel turned and tried to flee, but Hunter's talons took him in the neck and tore with such force and perfect timing that the falcon's head was almost severed from his neck. The kestrel twitched, Hunter slashed once more and then the daytime killer dropped like a stone from the sky, landed on the hedge below and lay there headless and spreadeagled as a hideous warning to others who might dare to trespass on his land.

For some moments after he had done it, Hunter hovered high above the headless body in the hedge, feeling quite limp and numb. But when the shock wore off and he began to feel again, his immediate reaction was one of great remorse. 'I should have warned him,' he thought, beginning to tremble a little at the thought of what he had just accomplished through pure instinct and not as a result of education, thought and planning. 'All right,' thought Hunter, trying to justify himself, 'it's still not fully light and he had no right to be hunting at this hour, but I should have warned him. I might have scared him off without a fight.'

Hunter hovered still above the hedge, quite overcome by what he had done. Though the shock of the killing had purged him temporarily of his agony and longing for little Alba, he knew that his present numbness would soon wear off and the torment would return. Shivering with delayed shock, he decided to seek out Yoller and deliver his message about the little immigrants and the lost domain. Though the darkness was receding quickly now, their habitual trysting place in the spinney was less than two meadows' length away and Hunter set off in the hope of catching his Tawny friend before the day advanced still further and it became too bright and dangerous to fly.

There was no sign of Yoller in the spinney, but Hunter registered the presence of a large owl some distance deeper in the woods. He called and then waited hopefully on the willow branch as he had so often done before. To his immense relief, an answer came at once and Hunter's shivering abated at the thought of seeing the one true friend that he could still call his own now that little Alba had deserted him. He took care to perch in exactly the same place and in the same position as he had sat on all their previous meetings in the spinney and was gratified and reassured when Yoller landed beside him and greeted him in the same casual manner that he had always used before the war. So much had happened in Hunter's short, eventful life and so much had been swept away that he found strength and consolation in old habits and in the knowledge that certain things at least remained the same.

'I say, old chap, are you all right?' asked Yoller, cocking his handsome head a little to one side and with a crisper note of concern now underlying the usual, aristocratic drawl. 'You don't look half so well as the last time that we met.'

'I'm all right,' replied Hunter. 'I've had a shock, that's all.'

'It must have been a bad one,' said Yoller, leaning his head the other way and looking at Hunter with his eyebrows raised. 'What happened, if you don't mind my asking?'

'Oh, nothing much,' said Hunter. 'There was a kestrel hunting on my land and so I killed him.'

'You killed him?' Yoller said in great surprise. 'How amazing! When exactly did it happen?'

'Not long ago, only a few moments ago, in actual fact. It was just before the first light of dawn, so I'm well within my rights, but I wish I hadn't done it.'

'Did you eat him afterwards?' asked Yoller, still gazing at his friend in great surprise.

'No,' said Hunter, shaking his head vigorously and shivering a little. 'I couldn't possibly do that. He's far too much like one of us.'

'Ferocity ate one of hers,' said Yoller. 'Though she said it was delicious, I didn't really believe her. I'm afraid I couldn't bring myself to eat one either.'

'I wasn't hungry,' Hunter said. 'And that's another thing that worries me. You know that our religion does not permit Barn owls to take life unless it is for food or self-defence?'

'Or in defence of your territory,' added Yoller, scrutinizing his friend carefully, as if he were trying to see through to something way behind the words that Hunter spoke.

'Or in defence of our territory,' agreed Hunter. 'But in that case we're supposed to give a warning first. I didn't, and now it's on my conscience.'

'Your Barn owl conscience is a curse,' said Yoller with airy nonchalance. 'And yours, in particular, is developed out of all proportion, even for a member of your hung-up, complex-ridden species.'

'You may be right,' admitted Hunter. 'I suppose it comes from being brought up by a father who was the Religion Owl. I don't know, but in any case, it doesn't ease the pain.'

'You would have felt much more pain if the kestrel had killed you,' said Yoller, with a sarcastic little snort.

'I wouldn't, I'd be dead, and dead owls don't feel a thing,' said Hunter, whose inner eye had just seen little Alba smiling at him, as she used to do. The vision caused him so much acute pain that at the time he would not at all have minded lying headless in the kestrel's place.

'Nonsense,' Yoller drawled. 'You wouldn't have died cleanly. Your wounds would have caused you agony and your death would have taken many days.'

'Perhaps,' said Hunter. 'Anyway, it's over now, and I suppose it's just one more thing I'll have to live with.'

Yoller's eyes widened once more in surprise and again he studied Hunter closely. 'Are you sure the kestrel is your only problem?' he asked carefully.

'At least I did it cleanly,' Hunter said, ignoring Yoller's question. 'Would you like to see him? His body's lying on a hedge near here, close to the place where Beak Poke died.'

'Yes, I'd like to,' Yoller said, after a quick glance upwards at the brightening sky. 'Let's go now, before daylight comes and finds us in the open.'

So they flew off together, silently and swiftly, and Hunter led Yoller to the spot that many later considered to have marked his second claim to fame, but which Hunter henceforth tended to avoid, for he was one of the few who never came to believe in the legend that grew up around him and forever after in his own mind was to associate the place with secret guilt and shame.

As they circled above the kestrel's headless body, Yoller emitted a melodious whistle of amazement and for the third or fourth time that morning glanced sideways and studied Hunter in surprise. 'Good grief,' he whispered softly, half to Hunter and half to himself. 'Killed him cleanly, did you say? My guess is that he didn't know a single thing about it. Big, fierce brute he was, too, by the look of his ugly carcass, yet you did such a perfect job on him that anyone who saw his body would think the monster had come back.'

'Don't mention it to anyone,' said Hunter, as they ceased their circling above the gruesome sight and winged their way back to the spinney side by side. 'It was just something that I had to do, that's all. I'm not proud of it and I don't want the word to get around.'

'Don't be ridiculous, old boy,' said Yoller. 'The night has a thousand eyes, you know that as well as I do. By midnight tomorrow, most of the owls in the territory will know and so will the daytime raptors, so I don't suppose you'll have trouble with any more of them.'

'I know it's nearly daylight,' said Hunter, as they glided silently back into the cover of the spinney, 'but I have something else to tell you, something I don't think can wait.'

'I'm all ears,' said Yoller, as they settled in their former perches on the willow branch. 'You won't mind my saying so, old boy, but I guessed you were holding something back.'

'The Little owls have colonized the lost domain,' said Hunter, once again ignoring Yoller's cue. 'They intend to settle there and turn it into what they call their promised land.'

'I know,' said Yoller, sounding a trifle disappointed.

'How so?' asked Hunter, leaning backwards on the branch, for it was his turn now to be surprised. 'It was only the night before last that they asked me to tell you, when I flew across the lost domain on my way to see my mother.'

'Bad news travels fast,' said Yoller, refusing to be drawn. 'And our intelligence service still functions pretty well, in spite of the war damage and our depleted numbers.'

'What are you going to do about it?' Hunter asked. 'Are you going to drive them out or let them stay?'

'What are your lot going to do about it?' asked Yoller, once more avoiding a direct reply to Hunter's question. 'What action are they going to take?'

'I don't know yet. I've only told the History Owl so far, and I don't suppose any official decision will be taken until he reports it to the next meeting of the Barn owl council.'

'A wise young bird, your History Owl,' said Yoller, with a faint smile playing on his handsome face. 'What was his reaction when you told him what the immigrants had done?'

'He thinks it's a good thing,' said Hunter, 'providing they grant rights of passage. He thinks they're more likely to help repel any future invasion if they have a territory of their own. Above all, he wants to maintain the alliance between you Tawnies and ourselves and to extend the agreement to the Little owls as well.'

'We don't intend to touch the lost domain,' said Yoller. 'At least, not until the last trace of man has vanished from the secret forest, which is ours by right. For the time being, the immigrants can have their promised land. For the moment, your History Owl is right. It will also help to solve the squatter problem. I suppose you've thought of that?'

'Yes,' said Hunter, guardedly. 'The immigrants asked me to tell you that they wouldn't squat or trespass any more if you promised not to attempt an invasion of the lost domain.'

'Of course, it's particularly convenient for you,' said Yoller, in a casual yet somehow questioning tone. 'Your own immigration problem should reach an honourable conclusion, at long last.'

'I'd rather not discuss it,' Hunter said, blurting out the words as the pain and misery welled up inside him.

'Sorry, old boy,' said Yoller calmly. 'It's your business entirely. It's entirely up to you. I just imagined that for you and little Alba, the new colony would be a great relief.'

'She's going there to mate,' said Hunter, half-choking on the words and making a brave but unsuccessful effort to control the trembling in his limbs. 'As far as I know, she's already left and gone for ever.'

'I thought there was something wrong,' said Yoller, nodding sadly to himself, as if he now understood many things that had not been made plain to him before. 'I know it's no good saying so, old boy, but in the future you may come to realize that all this has happened for the best.'

'Don't, Yoller,' said Hunter, whose pain had now brought him to the verge of tears. 'Leave me now. It's daylight. And I beg you, please don't mention little Alba's name again!'

'Sometimes it helps to talk,' said Yoller, as concern and compassion sharpened his studied, casual tones. 'At certain times in one's life, one simply has to talk to someone, but it's entirely up to you. And listen, Hunter, I have a proposition that I want to put to you. There is a dangerous mission I must undertake, involving a long, exciting journey. I wondered if you'd care to join me?'

'Where are you going?' Hunter asked, clutching gratefully at the chance of companionship and at some way of filling his now bleak and empty future life.

'To the city,' Yoller said. 'I have to go and tell my cousin and her mate that they can come home and repopulate Ferocity and Ripper's wood.'

'What is a city?' asked Hunter, who had never heard the word before.

'The city? It's a huge place where countless thousands of men all herd together, like mindless starlings or peewits on a single patch of meadow. The city is like ten thousand villages all lumped together, all full of noise and lights and other things that neither of us could possibly imagine.'

'We call that a town,' said Hunter. 'I heard about them in my basic human studies.'

'Well, it's the biggest one of all I have to go to,' Yoller said. 'It seems that the journey will take me six whole nights and that the dangers when you get there are appalling. But I have to go. Our intelligence service tells us that things have changed, making it even more difficult for our Tawnies who had to settle there when there was no more woodland left.'

'How do they manage?' Hunter asked. 'I was taught that no Barn owl could survive in such a place, not even on a visit.'

'There was a plague of rats,' said Yoller. 'Four or five winters since, fire began to fall from the sky, or rather from those enormous artificial birds men fly in. Parts of the city burned, many men were killed and the rats provided abundant nourishment for my cousins and the other Tawnies who had settled there. But as I said, it seems that things have changed, the burning has stopped and the rats have gone away.'

'What do they live on now?' asked Hunter, who was trying to visualize a town or city, but found that his imagination simply could not stretch that far.

'Pigeons mainly, but also starlings, sparrows and the like. Apparently there are millions of silly pigeons in the city and killing them is easy.'

'But how awful,' Hunter said. 'Think of it, all those men, all those buildings and all that dreadful noise. Even a small village makes me feel afraid.'

'I know,' said Yoller, with a heartfelt little sigh. 'It's all most dangerous and unnatural, but I have to go. I wouldn't have mentioned it, only you seemed so upset over losing little Alba.'

'Oh, I'll come with you,' Hunter said. 'I've made up my mind. I've already quite decided.'

'Think about it carefully,' Yoller said. 'It's a long journey from which neither of us may return again. For me it's duty, for you it would be pure, unadulterated folly.'

'Folly is the best antidote for pain,' said Hunter, smiling bravely. 'When do you want to leave?'

'Let's say in seven nights' time?' suggested Yoller. 'I'll meet you here at twilight. And remember, I shan't be offended if you change your mind. If you do come, I suppose you'd be the first Barn owl ever to set out on such a journey, and I suppose that in the city you'd learn a lot about the men that your species live so close to on the land. Incidentally, did you know they had been killing one another with their firesticks?'

'We had heard they might be having some kind of war. Why would that be, do you think?'

'I don't know,' Yoller said. 'Maybe there are different species of men and they have their territorial conflicts just the same as owls.'

'Where did you hear it?' Hunter asked. 'Who told you they'd been killing one another?'

'A nomad Short-eared owl who flew across the salty waters,' Yoller said. 'He told a distant cousin of ours that they'd been killing one another for several winters past, but recently it appears that they have stopped.'

'There's been no fighting in these territories then?' asked Hunter to whom the whole new concept was beyond his ability to imagine, in the same way as he had found it impossible to visualize a town.

'No, not here,' said Yoller. 'Except for fire falling from the sky, there's been no fighting here.'

They said goodbye then and Hunter watched as Yoller flew away, staggering drunkenly in flight the way all Tawnies do once the sun has risen high. He sat alone on the willow branch for quite some time, having no desire to return to the lonely farmhouse, but eventually he pulled himself together and flew back across the sunlit fields and meadows, uncaring of the daytime dangers all around him.

As he expected, there was no trace of little Alba in the home they had shared happily in times of trouble and through the long winter of his convalescence. Heartbroken, Hunter could not rest, but hopped disconsolately from one corner to another, trapped in his misery like a wild, caged bird with both wings cruelly clipped. After fidgeting for a long time, he found one small downy feather on the chest of drawers that had once been Alba's perch. He stared at it, remembering the single feather Steeple had left behind him to torment the earthbound vixen, while he and Hunter regained their liberty in flight. More than anything little Alba had said and more even than her absence from the den, this single feather she had left behind finally convinced Hunter that she had gone forever, and for the first time in his life, he broke down and wept.

CHAPTER

 24

After two days and nights in the lonely farmhouse, Hunter could stand the agony no longer. 'I must see her,' he decided soon after twilight on the second day. 'Supposing she really did it all for my sake, to save my reputation? Supposing she couldn't stand the thought of mating with this Renato and changed her mind at the last moment? I must go there and find out, and if she hasn't mated yet, I will beg her to come back.'

Having made the decision, Hunter felt his strength and confidence surge back for the first time since he had killed the kestrel. Filled with his new sense of purpose, he glided out in the deepening twilight, killed and ate a whole mole and two field voles for his breakfast and then flew to the farmhouse to make a plan of action. 'I have two legitimate excuses for flying to the lost domain,' he told himself as he rocked backwards and forwards on his headboard perch, staring across at the chest of drawers from which Alba had watched over him all winter long. 'First I have to tell them that the Tawnies don't intend to reclaim the secret forest, at least not for the moment. Second, I have to report on the History Owl's reaction to their settling in what they call the promised land. I can't wait for the official decision at the next council meeting. If Alba hasn't already mated with Renato, she will have done by then. Third, the immigrants have granted me free passage any time I choose, and whatever happens I must see her again at least one more time.'

So Hunter spread his wings, flew out into the darkness and headed for the lost domain, warmed and thrilled by the prospect of his mission and spurred on by the faint, unfounded hope of persuading Alba to return and live with him again. Though night masked the flowering of violet, primrose and celandine and hid the first budding daffodils that now carpeted the spread of copse and meadowland beneath his whispering wings, Hunter sensed their presence and sensed a renewed seething of activity among the thousand creatures of the night, as they, too, prepared for the creation of new life.

His hopes rose still higher as he glided through the moonlight and across the belt of woodland that protected the great house and gardens at the beginning of the lost domain. To his surprise, the moonlight seemed strangely brighter as it filtered through the dense, budding branches and brighter still as he approached the edge of the wood.

As he reached the last line of trees and caught his first glimpse of the great house, he gasped and then dived for cover among the evergreen foliage of a mighty cedar. Till now he had only seen two lights at most glowing dimly on the lower floor, but now at least half the many windows were blazing with a brighter man-made light than he had ever dreamed of.

For some time, Hunter cowered in the darkness, hugging close to the cedar's mighty trunk and watching the uncanny light as it glared through the branches ahead of him. 'I'll skirt round inside the wood,' he told himself eventually, after resisting a natural impulse to flee back the way he had come. 'That man-made light doesn't shed its brightness very far. Not even halfway across the gardens and nowhere near the lake.' So he took a deep breath and then set off, weaving slowly and silently through the trunks and crisscrossed upper branches until the garden beyond the wood lay once again enveloped in familiar darkness, though the lights from the house still blazed like a great beacon in the night behind him.

Right on the edge of the wood Hunter paused, plucked up courage and was about to strike out across the gardens towards the lake that lay glistening silver in the moonlight, when he picked up two men still and silent in the parkland far beyond. A little farther still, almost halfway to the secret forest, he sensed the presence of two more men and then picked up the stealthy movements of a dog fox not far from where the second pair of humans stood. Suddenly, a blaze of man-made light flooded the great oak in the centre of the park and immediately afterwards four deafening explosions shattered the stillness of the night air.

As if the first explosion had been a signal, a second man-made ray shone out and mingled with the distant moonlight. Then four more deafening explosions rang out in quick succession. Hunter hugged his tree trunk in terror and waited till the last echoes of the shots had died away. He heard men shouting in the distance and then the two separate beams of light began to move and converge on each other in the centre of the park. Soon after, bobbing in the darkness, they began to move slowly back across the parkland towards the gardens and the house.

Trapped and exposed on the bare branch of his black poplar tree, Hunter watched the two bobbing lights as they came towards him from far across the park, entered the gardens and lurched closer until he was well within their range. He held his breath and stared in horrified fascination as the four men appeared below him on their way to the great house. Each carried a firestick slung across his shoulder, but to Hunter far more terrifying than the firesticks themselves was the sight of two Little owls swinging lifeless from the first man's waist. The immigrants' legs had been tied to a special belt around his middle and their round bodies, blunt wings and lolling heads bounced grotesquely against the man's buttocks and the back of his thighs as he strode purposefully towards the blazing pool of light around the house.

Hunter watched in mounting horror as he saw a third owl dangling from the waist of the man who was bringing up the rear. The distance was too great for him to guess the identity of the murdered immigrants, but the thought that little Alba might be among them petrified Hunter and froze him to the tree trunk where he stayed motionless and scarcely breathing long after the four men, their bobbing flashlights and the bodies of the three dead owls had been swallowed up inside the massive house.

As the night wore on there was no sound from the gardens or the park. One by one the lights in the mansion ceased to blaze, darkness reigned again and for a long time nothing stirred to break the deadly silence of the night. It was as if all creatures living in the lost domain had gone to ground, or else clung still and petrified to some hidden perch, paralysed like Hunter by the man-made devastation.

Only the dog fox flickered still in Hunter's perception, blotting out another faint and muffled signal from a point halfway across the park, near the oak tree where Alba and Hunter had banqueted on mole and vole before the war. The dog fox had not moved since the second volley from the firesticks and his signals faded and grew fainter as the night slipped by. Eventually, they flickered and then ceased altogether and Hunter guessed that the arch-killer had himself fallen victim to the firesticks and then been left to die slowly in the darkness where he lay.

Without this masking interference from the dying fox, the second set of muffled signals came through much more clearly and Hunter's heart leapt as he located the presence of a Little owl close to the oak tree that he and Alba had once used as their hunting lodge. Hunter dared not call out to announce his presence, but took off at once and headed out across the lake and parkland, his fear quite vanquished by the wild hope that he might be within one meadow's length of the longed-for reunion with his loved one.

Hunter's flight path took him above the dog fox, whose rank smell still emanated after death, and then on to the great oak tree which the men had flooded with their instant light. To his dismay, Hunter saw the body of a dead male immigrant lying on the grass a mere ten lengths from the tree. He did not stop to identify the corpse but flew on to the point in the parkland from which the faint signals of a living owl still came. With a terrible fear in his heart, Hunter paused, fluttering for a moment in the air, and then swooped down beside the prostrate creature and saw that it was little Alba.

One wing was broken, there were holes in the side of her body and half of her face had been so badly damaged that it was almost shot away. She was unconscious as Hunter bent over her and he knew without the slightest shadow of a doubt that she was dying.

He sat beside her for some time, until the shock wore off, his feelings returned and his heart began to break. It seemed so wrong that there was nothing he could do to comfort her in the last few moments of misery and pain that might be left to her from all eternity. It was beyond his power to help her, and as he looked down at the broken body there welled up inside him the most heart-rending blend of love, sadness and compassion. 'If the world had been a better place,' he thought, fully conscious for the first time in his life of the chasm that divided individuals from one another and, however hard they tried, kept them always just a little distance from a living state of grace. 'If the world had been a slightly better place, or if its pressures and prejudices had not driven us apart, she might not be lying here now in such dreadful suffering, with her face and body torn asunder by the firestick's devastation.'

Alba opened her eyes then and recognized him through the mists of pain. For a time, a hard, cynical expression mingled with the agony that now glazed her once lovely eyes. Then the hardness faded to be replaced in slow degrees by a softer, shyer smile, like the ones he remembered from the time of their first meeting and early days together in the strangely idyllic surroundings of the lost domain. 'Hi Hunter,' she said, in a voice so faint and husky that he could hardly hear it. 'I guess I knew you'd come and get me. I love you, too. You know that, don't you? I love you and I always will.'

'Hush,' said Hunter, stroking her one unhurt wing with his. 'Hush now. Don't tire yourself. Keep all your strength for getting well.'

'I mated with Renato,' Alba said, her eyes glazing over once again with pain. 'I knew you'd want to come and get me, so I did it for your sake. I mated with Renato and I would have had his fledglings when the oak and maple blossomed in late spring. I did it for you, Hunter, to make it easy for you to be free. Now I'm dying, poor Born Again is already dead and no fledglings of mine will ever see the sunrise or the silver moonlight on the lake.'

'Don't,' said Hunter. 'Don't talk now, just rest.'

'Promise me one thing,' she whispered huskily as the last light in her eyes began to fade. 'You are the nicest owl I ever met. Don't change. For my sake, please try to stay the same.'

'I'll try,' said Hunter, choking on the words as little Alba's eyes closed once again, her breast heaved convulsively and he knew that the end was drawing near. In desperation, he bent his head and rubbed one cheek very softly against her face on the side where the firestick had not hurt it. She stirred a little, opened her eyes and smiled at him with the saddest, sweetest tenderness that he had ever seen. After that her eyes closed, her breast heaved for the final time and the life left her body on its journey to the great beyond.

In his utter chagrin and despair, Hunter remembered that the last words had not been spoken. Alba was an immigrant and another kind of owl, but at that excruciating moment Hunter no longer considered the protocol nor cared. 'If the last words are true, they must be true for everyone,' he thought. 'They must be true for Tawnies, immigrants, and indeed for all the owls that live and breathe upon this earth.'

'As you depart this earth and sky and go at last to rest, know that you are not alone,' he said and then paused, realizing that 'our species' in the next line would exclude an immigrant like little Alba. So Hunter looked up into the night sky and risked the wrath of the Great Barn Owl God Bird by changing the words to suit the compassion of his purpose.

'Know that your species will survive for all eternity, beyond the barnyards, fields and meadows where we live – and no man's land,' he added hastily, determined to make this a special prayer for little Alba – 'beyond the twilight and the dawn, beyond the pale moon that glimmers and the stars that shine forever in the black and vibrant night.

'Through knowledge and self-sacrifice you will survive until the sun no longer sets and until the moon fails to rise and give us light. Know that with us and among us still you will survive for all eternity and beyond the boundless limits of all wisdom and all time.'

Distraught and filled with the mystery of death, he sat beside little Alba's body until dawn had filled the sky with deep, red streaks and the acrid richness of the fertile earth rose up around him with the morning light.

Slowly, and with infinite sadness, he turned from her body and began his flight back to the farmhouse they had shared. 'One day the world will be a better place,' he thought, forcing himself to believe that there must be something an owl might achieve beyond mere breeding and survival. 'The world will be a better place some day,' he forced himself to say, in spite of all the misery and all the troubles he had seen. 'Some day owls will be more enlightened. There will be more knowledge, and out of greater knowledge, greater kindness and tolerance will grow. And I shall devote my life's purpose to that end.'

So Hunter flew on into the rising sun, above the blossoming of wood anemone and early purple orchis, convinced that at some time in the future the world would be a better place. He was still a very young owl, and at that time it was only right and proper he should think so.

Part Two

Learn, learn of the corn
Of things coming to pass...

Vernon Watkins
Cornfields

I returned and saw under the sun, that the
race is not to the swift, nor battle to the strong,
neither yet bread to the wise, nor yet riches to
men of understanding, nor yet
favour to men of skill; but time and chance
happeneth to them all.

Ecclesiastes, IX, XI

CHAPTER

1

In the second spring after Hunter's disappearance Quaver flew out of Ripper's wood and winged his way across no man's land on the last stage of his journey home.

As he reached Dapple's territory and glided on above the undulating fields and meadows of his youth, the sun rose in a blood-red ball of fire, shedding its first light on the corn that still blew green and rippled in the wind beneath his wings. 'Learn of the corn of things coming to pass,' Quaver quoted to himself, remembering the line from a ballad that he had learned from his tutor Bardic, from whose seat of learning he had been summoned on this unexpected mission home.

'Oh, green and rippling corn what can you teach us now?' he wondered, as he approached the ancient barn where he had first seen the light of day. 'What happiness can you foretell, with our old world torn apart by war and our future marred and made uncertain by too many sudden changes?'

Quaver paused and hovered for a while above the roof, uncertain as to what awaited him inside. Then he gave a fatalistic little shrug and dropped through the gap in the rafters back into the barn where he had been born. His sister Dawn Raptor was already there, perched on the same beam she had always sat on as a fledgling, with the same supercilious smile still playing on her fully adult face.

After greeting his mother and his sister, Quaver, too, sat on the old beam where he had first learned the words and received most of his basic education. Though in some ways the barn seemed smaller than Quaver had remembered, for one sudden moment it seemed vast and bare because of the two gaps left where his father and his brother had once perched. 'One dead, one missing,' thought Quaver sadly, as the first rays of sunlight filtered through the broad chinks in the roof, causing his mother's sad eyes to blink and making her look old and weary in the morning light.

'Well, now that Quaver's finally arrived, may I ask what all this is about?' said Dawn Raptor, looking impatiently from Dapple to her brother and then back again. 'I've come a long way tonight and at dusk I must start the return journey to my seat of learning.'

'So soon?' asked Dapple, sadly. 'Surely Dirge won't miss you for just one more night?'

'No, sorry,' said Dawn Raptor, with a sharp shake of her head. 'We're expecting a visit from our leader and it's important that I should be there.'

'I can't stay either,' Quaver said, speaking more gently than his sister and with genuine regret. 'Bardic and I are expecting him as well, either just before or just after his visit to Dawn Raptor and to Dirge.'

'I see,' said Dapple, turning her eyes sadly from her daughter to her son. 'Well, I suppose it can't be helped. In fact, under the circumstances it may be for the best.'

'What circumstances?' asked Dawn Raptor irritably. 'Listen, mother, the sun has already risen. Will you kindly tell us why we're here?' Quaver turned to his sister, but Dapple spoke first, before he had a chance to rebuke Dawn Raptor for her lack of tact and sensitivity.

'You will know the purpose of our meeting soon enough,' said Dapple, speaking with quiet dignity. 'But to begin with, I want us all to say the words. The first words for all other Barn owls in these uncertain, troubled times, and for your father, who is dead.'

'Oh mother, no!' Dawn Raptor said. 'It's too old-fashioned. Here we are with a new leader, a new council, a brave new world to build, and all you can do is hark back to the past. In any case, no one says the old words any more. They are in the process of being changed.'

'Not for me, they're not!' said Dapple firmly. 'This is my home, and while I'm still alive we'll do it my way.' Dapple then bowed her head and closed her eyes while Quaver stared at his irate sister, desperately willing her to stop contesting everything and do the same.

'Hoard and covet not,'

Dapple began, with Quaver joining in the second line,

> 'But be brave and free,
> Quest always after knowledge
> And slowly learn to know
> What science cannot see.
> Seek and strive for learning,
> Be temperate and wise,
> For skill and wisdom only
> Will help us to survive.'

There was a brief, pregnant pause when they had finished and Quaver sat still with his eyes closed for a moment or two longer, remembering his secure infancy and happy adolescence before the shadow of the invasion and all the dreadful carnage and the killing of the war. Then Dapple drew herself up and leaned forward to address them, blinking vulnerably as the shafts of morning sunlight streamed in through the rafters and mulled the weary sadness in her eyes.

'I have called you here,' she said, speaking in slow, deliberate tones, 'because something must be done about your brother. It is five seasons since he left these territories and disappeared with Yoller towards the enormous town they say lies ten thousand meadows' distance to the south of here. Spring has come again, the corn will soon turn golden and still we have no word from him. It is clear that something must be done.'

Quaver glanced quickly at Dawn Raptor and saw from the expression in her eyes that she, too, had both dreaded and expected that Dapple might drag up the question of Hunter's disappearance once again. 'What can we do, mother?' he asked, as gently as he could. 'What can we do, from this great distance and after so much time?'

'He must be searched for,' Dapple said, with quiet determination. 'He must be searched for, and what's more, he must be found.'

Quaver glanced at his sister again and saw that though saddened by her mother's grief, she was finding it difficult to hold back her impatience, so he cut in quickly, before Dawn Raptor had a chance to speak the brutal truth. 'We're both very busy, mother,' he said patiently. 'Dawn

Raptor is helping Dirge to develop the new dogma and dialectic and I am working with Bardic on the long overdue epic to commemorate our victory in the war. Neither of us would get permission to set out on a journey of that kind.'

'Permission?' Dapple said, with her eyebrows raised and her mouth turned down in scorn. 'Who needs permission to fly the freedom of the skies? All owls are individuals, each responsible for his or her own destiny. That is an eternal truth and cannot be denied.'

'The new code states that we must put our species first,' Dawn Raptor said. 'It says that we must sacrifice both self and family for the future of our kind.'

'So does the old credo, in a way,' said Quaver reluctantly. 'You and Steeple taught us that, here in this very place, when we were fledglings.'

'The words say be brave and free!' retorted Dapple. 'And that, at least, your brother is, wherever he may be. Your father was as well. Steeple gave his life for our species and Hunter almost died in the battle that was fought to set you free. I'd fly in search of him myself if I only had enough strength left to make the journey.'

'There's no point, mother, in searching for the dead,' said Dawn Raptor, as her patience snapped. 'Do not pine for Hunter, he is dead. Grieve for him, as you grieve for Steeple, but do not delude yourself. Hunter is dead and his remains have long since returned to the pungent earth from whence they came. Console yourself, if you will, with your old belief that his soul is somewhere with the God Bird in the sky.'

'I must admit it's unlikely that he's still alive,' said Quaver, inwardly cursing his sister's gross insensitivity. 'And even if he were, we'd never find him now. The world beyond our borders is much too big a place.'

'I want you to go in search of him,' said Dapple, looking sternly at her younger son. 'I want word from him, if he still lives, and failing that, I want the certain knowledge of how and when he died. And as for you, Dawn Raptor, I want you to use your influence with Winger. Ask him to let Bardic release your brother from his duties so that he may fly and find out the truth.'

'He won't do it,' said Dawn Raptor, shaking her head emphatically. 'He won't put pressure on Bardic or on Dirge to let us go. He'll say there can be no possible justification for a journey of that kind.'

'You owe it to your brother,' Dapple said. 'But for you, he would never have left with Yoller on that suicidal mission to the town.'

'It wasn't my fault,' said Dawn Raptor, though a guilty pout had now replaced the disdainful expression on her face. 'I couldn't help it if Winger chose me and not Hunter to study under him.'

'It was your brother's place by merit and by right,' said Dapple firmly.

'It wasn't my fault,' Dawn Raptor repeated, still pouting furiously at her mother's accusation. 'How could I help it if Hunter was old-fashioned, just like you and Steeple? Winger needed new owls. Owls with an open mind, who would help him to create the New Apostasy.'

'Theories!' snapped Dapple contemptuously. 'Theories that take no account of instinct, true learning or twelve million years of Barn owl history and lore.'

'Careful mother, that's subversive!' said Dawn Raptor. 'Remember that the ancient reign is dying and Winger is our leader now.'

'No continuity!' retorted Dapple. 'No respect for nature or for anything that's gone before. Just look at the way Winger dumped you the moment he was elected leader. Dumped you and then sent you off to Dirge. I ask you, Dirge! The so-called Owl for Dogma and Diatribe.'

'Dogma and Dialectic, mother!' said Dawn Raptor in a rage. 'Not Dogma and Diatribe.'

'I know the difference,' said Dapple sarcastically. 'The question is, does he? When I think of the uncouth, uncultured council members Winger has appointed, it makes me want to weep.'

'Mother, that's enough!' said Quaver, casting a worried glance at the angry faces of his mother and his sister. 'This sort of thing will get us nowhere,' he continued. 'Dawn Raptor, you are as impossible as ever and you, Dapple, must realize that things have changed. There is no Religion Owl on the council, as there always used to be. Instead, there is the Owl for Dogma and Dialectic. It may not be a change for the better, but we must accept it in the interests of democracy.'

'Change!' said Dapple, with withering contempt. 'I've seen some changes in my time, and I can tell you this. Leaders, philosophies and councils come and go like the winter frost and snow. Only the eternal truths remain. Winger and his doctrine will be swept away one day, as surely as the Eagle owl was finally brought down in Ferocity and Ripper's wood.'

'Maybe, but the monster did a lot of damage on his way,' said Quaver, interrupting quickly as Dawn Raptor twitched and seethed with anger on her perch.

'So will Yoller and his mate May Blossom be swept away one day,' continued Dapple in full flow. 'May Blossom, this new Tawny tyrant with the manners of a falcon and the morals of a crow! So shall we all be swept away one day, by time and chance that happen to us all. But in the meantime, the dead must be respected and the all-time truths must still be known. Find your brother for me, Quaver, or otherwise discover the time, place and manner of his death. Do it with or without permission, and with or without your sister's help. Only do it, or else count yourself no more a son of mine!'

'But I'm no hero, mother,' protested Quaver, mildly. 'I've never had my brother's brains or strength. I have some talent as a minstrel and a poet, and though I don't care much for Bardic I am reasonably content. I am one born to be attendant on the course of history, not a prime mover in its cause. Don't ask me to undertake a fatal quest that lies beyond my powers.'

'Your brother was a legend in his time,' said Dapple, who seemed suddenly overcome by fatigue from the conflict with her daughter. 'I warn you, if one of his mettle and his fibre is not found again, there will be a war against the Tawnies, a war that will prove bloodier still than the one the ballads speak of, the war fought three hundred springs ago when that bigot Grumwell was our leader.'

'Nonsense!' said Dawn Raptor. 'The Tawnies were decimated in Ferocity and Ripper's wood. Yoller is a shadow of his former strength and May Blossom, their new leader, is ridiculous in the extreme. Whoever heard of the Tawnies being governed by a female anyway?'

'It has been known before,' sighed Dapple, wearily. 'Rivers, the History Owl, has told me that twice in the past they were led by a female and during each reign they flourished and were rampant, both in their ancient woodlands and beyond.'

'Rivers has been discredited,' snapped Dawn Raptor. 'His word counts for nothing any more. Winger is right. We must strike now and appropriate the woodland that once belonged to Ferocity and Ripper. We must do it now, before the Tawnies repopulate the zone.'

'We can't do that,' protested Quaver. 'The ancient woodlands have belonged to them for forty million springs.'

'According to the new dogma, the land belongs to no one,' said Dawn Raptor. 'From now on it will be divided and apportioned to each owl according to his needs. In any case,' she added, changing from her high-handed, didactic tone of voice to a manner that was much more down to earth, 'men are building a new town around the village to the west of here. Where shall we expand, if not north-east into the sometime Tawny woods?'

'I fear the worst,' said Dapple, 'and so do History, Language and Geography. Thanks be to the God Bird that they're still on the council and can make their warning heard!'

'The minority of three,' Dawn Raptor said sarcastically. 'They're just a nuisance and they count for nothing any more.'

'That may be so, but I agree with them,' said Quaver angrily. 'I saw the Tawnies fight against the monster and I tell you that, depleted as they are, they'd tear us limb from limb.'

'That's defeatist talk,' Dawn Raptor said. 'This is about survival. Survival of our species, and our new doctrine is the only way.'

'Your new doctrine will mean war,' said Dapple, bluntly. 'Just tell your precious leader that! And you, Quaver, tell Bardic you can't return to work on his epic ballad until you've found out what happened to your brother. If he's still alive, we need him here. There may be something he can do to help. Much is taken from me. First your father, then Hunter and now much of the ancient reign as we once knew it. But something still remains before the end and in such time as I have left to me I shall make every effort to avert what could well prove to be a worse holocaust than the one Quaver witnessed in Ferocity and Ripper's wood. That is all,' she said, looking long and hard at each of them in turn. 'The sun is high and I am tired. Sleep now, till twilight. Then go your separate ways and do my bidding, before it is too late.'

CHAPTER 2

'She's gone senile,' said Dawn Raptor as she and her brother flew north-east through the twilight towards Ferocity and Ripper's wood, while the dull red sun sank slowly behind them in the west. 'The loss of Steeple and then Hunter has addled her old brain.'

'I'm not so sure,' said Quaver, regretting that their paths would not divide until they had crossed the sometime Tawny woods. 'She has a point about the changes Winger's making. Some of them seem to ignore the very nature and instinct of our species.'

'Conditioning!' snapped Dawn Raptor, as they left the last of the waving corn beneath their wings and headed towards the darkly wooded hills. 'I always told you that when we were fledglings. Twelve million springs of superstition, religion and conditioning and now, at last, we have the chance to make a new beginning. To sweep away all the old miasmal myth and remould history right from the beginning.'

'Tricky, that,' said Quaver, surprised at how eloquent his sister had become since she first went to study under Winger. 'You can't abolish all that history and tradition between the dawn and twilight of one day. However hard you try, old ballads, old myths and much primeval culture will remain.'

'That reminds me,' said Dawn Raptor, as they entered Ripper's wood. 'How is your own epic ballad going?'

'Slowly,' Quaver said. 'As we all know, Bardic is somewhat pompous and long-winded. Also, the more he works on the ballad, the more it seems he won the war all by himself, whilst in reality all he did was skulk and cower in a hollow tree not far from here while I flew backwards and forwards from the front with a blow-by-blow account of the proceedings.'

'Bardic is verbose,' said Dawn Ratpor, seeming less sure of herself now that they found themselves flying through the black heart of the wood and on towards the place at its outer limits where so many had bled and died to save the lives of those who had fled or hidden craven in their homes. 'Winger says that Bardic is verbose, obese and decadent,' she continued, slowing down a little and missing the occasional wing beat in nervous apprehension as they neared the scene of all the slaughter and began to sense the ghostly presence of the dead. 'He says your tutor is too temperamental and too decadent to give voice to the rational, egalitarian ethos of the New Apostasy.'

'I should have thought verbosity was more in Winger's line,' retorted Quaver sharply as they neared the battle zone and his sister wavered further in her flight. 'He seems to have imported or invented a thousand words that have very little meaning for a minstrel or a poet. Dogma, dialectic, collective and the like are hardly sounds to sing with or symbols you can use to touch the heart and stir the soul.'

Dawn Raptor was about to reply in anger but just then they came upon the clearing below the battlefield where the bursting profusion of spring and summer growth had once more buried all that remained of the many dead, save for great splinters of the monster's skeleton that still lay blanched and glowing in the ghostly light as a lasting testament to his enormous power and strength. To his grim satisfaction, Quaver saw his sister miss several wing beats more before they finally emerged from the wood and flew on towards the place where Steeple had died to save Hunter as they lured the monster into ambush from the lost domain.

'I shall pause a while where father fell,' said Quaver. 'Do you want to join me, or will you travel on?'

'I'm sorry,' said Dawn Raptor, curtly. 'I'm in a hurry. Dirge and I have work to do.'

'Tell me,' said Quaver, slowing as they reached the place where his father had fallen, torn and dismembered after his brief battle in the sky. 'Are you happy with Dirge and his daughter Ivy Perch, or do you wish you were still studying under Winger?'

'The leader of the council never teaches,' said Dawn Raptor. 'You know that as well as I do.'

'Before he was elected leader, mother thought that Winger might intend to mate with you,' said Quaver, as they hovered over the place where the earth had reclaimed Steeple's bones. 'Are you disappointed that he didn't? Or is there still some chance of that happening, do you think?'

'That's not your business,' said Dawn Raptor, shortly. 'And in any case, it's not for me to say. If we are to build a New Apostasy, each of us must make sacrifices and serve the community as best he may.'

'Oh, quite,' said Quaver, rather sceptically. 'I only wondered how you felt.'

'Of course it isn't easy,' said Dawn Raptor, relenting a little as they hovered briefly before parting. 'I mean, Dirge didn't have the advantage of a further education, or indeed of any education worth the name. But that's what Winger wants. He wants new owls who can grasp the dogma quickly. Owls who are untrammelled by centuries of myth and superstition.'

'You mean he wants acolytes with no intellect?' asked Quaver. 'Owls who will follow and won't ask the reason why?'

'Of course not!' said Dawn Raptor. 'In the interests of equality, the common owl must rule. Or he must be represented on the council, anyway.'

'By the way,' said Quaver, taking advantage of the fact that his sister seemed slightly less than her usual, assertive self, 'what does dialectic mean? I've asked Bardic and several other owls, but no one seems to know. Does Dirge know? Do you?'

'Of course I know,' replied Dawn Raptor angrily. 'Dialectic is the art of investigating the truth by logical discussion.'

'I see,' said Quaver, doubtfully. 'But doesn't that mean that one has to study logic first? Naturally, I don't know about these things, so do correct me if I'm wrong.'

'I've no time at the moment,' said Dawn Raptor, who seemed embarrassed by the question. 'But Quaver, let me tell you this: there are more things happening at the moment than you would ever dream of, including the reason why I cannot mate. You wouldn't know about these major happenings because you're not privy to a council member and you're not close enough to Winger anyway.'

'Bardic is a council member,' Quaver said. 'And frankly I'm more privy to his thoughts than I would care to be.'

'Bardic doesn't count,' Dawn Raptor said. 'He counts no more than the minority of three.'

'Why not?' asked Quaver. 'He voted for Winger, didn't he?'

'To save his position on the council,' Dawn Raptor said. 'Not because he cared. Remember, Quaver, you may be Bard Owl yourself one day. Maybe even sooner than you think.'

'If I am committed to the New Apostasy?' asked Quaver. 'If I compose and sing what Winger thinks?'

'If you help us shape the future, yes.' Dawn Raptor said. 'At this time in history there is no time for subtlety or for sitting on the fence. From now on, you're either with us or against us, that's what Winger says.'

'Winger says, Winger says,' Quaver muttered to himself, but then turned quickly to his sister and said out loud before she left, 'Tell me, Dawn Raptor, we both know that Hunter's dead. How can I find out what happened without going on this dangerous quest?'

'Surely that's obvious,' his sister said. 'Ask Yoller. He's the only one who knows.'

'But he's told us,' Quaver said. 'He told us all he knew when he came back from his mission to the town.'

'Did he?' asked Dawn Raptor, narrowing her expressive eyes and staring at Quaver with suspicious intensity. 'He told us he lost Hunter in the town, but who knows what reasons he might have for concealing the manner of his death? Yoller is a Tawny, don't forget!'

'Oh, what rubbish!' Quaver said. 'Yoller is an honourable bird. As honest an owl as I have ever met. And after all, Hunter was his best friend.'

'Was he?' asked Dawn Raptor, with an enigmatic widening of her eyes. 'Who knows what really happened on that long and dangerous journey? Supposing Hunter had been set upon and murdered by another Tawny, do you think Yoller would have dared to tell us so himself? Even if he couldn't help it, even if he did everything he could to prevent Hunter's death, his pride would stop him from confessing that it had happened under his protection. The word would spread, and where would be his honour and his reputation then?'

'Have you any reason for suspecting this?' asked Quaver. 'It all sounds most peculiar to me.'

'The only good Tawny is a dead one!' said Dawn Raptor. 'Or at least, that's what my tutor says.'

'Dirge would,' Quaver said. 'And for the God Bird's sake, don't let's start all that again. We all know that for any acolyte of Winger's, the Tawnies are the enemy within.'

'Blood is thicker than water,' warned Dawn Raptor. 'But it's your problem. You must do as you think fit.'

'I think I'll go and ask, in any case,' said Quaver. 'I must confess I did feel that Yoller might be holding something back. It could be that Hunter died some truly awful death and he doesn't want to cause us grief. I'll do as you suggest.'

'Please yourself,' said Dawn Raptor, shrugging to show her indifference. 'The fact is Hunter's dead and it's high time Dapple came to terms with it. I can't bear this morbid fixation that he might still be alive.'

'I'll ask for my own satisfaction,' Quaver said. 'Like Dapple, I want to know the truth about my brother's death.'

'You mean you don't want to undertake a foolish, fruitless mission like the one that killed him. That's the real reason, but at least it's one I understand. Goodbye, Quaver. I must get back to Dirge and prepare for Winger's visit.'

'Goodbye, Dawn Raptor,' Quaver said, and then watched with feelings strangely mixed between anger and relief as his sister flew off across the moonlit cornfields towards the ruined cowshed that had once been Brook's and was now inhabited by Dirge and his daughter, Ivy Perch. He dropped from the sky then and landed in a tiny clearing among the gently waving corn next to the spot where his father had fallen in the war. Through the darkness to the east of him he heard his sister call to announce her coming and then winced as Dirge's harsh response rent the night air and grated on the finer tuning of his minstrel's ear.

'I wish you were alive now, to advise me,' he whispered earthwards in the eerie silence that followed Dirge's dying call. 'You were wiser than we thought. You would tell me whether to keep Dapple happy by going on this hopeless quest, or whether to travel farther and more safely in my mind, the way all true dreamers do.'

Quaver raised his head and gazed around him at the waving corn, as if seeking inspiration in the ripple of the night-time breeze. Finding none, he took off, flew north to the confines of the lost domain and then westwards all around the long perimeter, never daring once to penetrate the secret forest which belonged to the Tawnies by right, had been usurped by man and was now populated by the little immigrants who had formed their first collective there and called the place their promised land. Quaver wondered at their courage as he flew. Perhaps having no home of their own had made them brave enough to stay on in the lost domain, even after the men had returned and murdered so many of their number with the firestick. 'If the alternative was no man's land, perhaps I'd have their courage, too,' thought Quaver. 'Perhaps their kind of courage is closer to despair.'

But then he remembered how his missing brother had explored the lost domain and hunted there even before the Little owls had claimed it for their own. He remembered, too, how Hunter had returned in search of little Alba on that fatal night when the men had murdered so many of the immigrants and how he had braved the firestick to sit beside her till she died, and then stayed to watch over her broken body until the red sun rose above the lost domain and looked down upon the mystery of death.

'What kind of courage had that been?' Quaver wondered. Like Hunter's courage in the war, it had not been born of hunger or despair. Out of need, perhaps, but a need for liberty and love that Quaver himself aspired to but did not dare pursue, save in his inner land of dreams.

'Perhaps it's a good thing he never did come back,' thought Quaver, sadly, as he skirted the western borders of the lost domain and headed north again across open Barn owl country towards the long abandoned farmhouse which had once been Hunter's home. 'He'd have found too many changes, and worst of all, he'd have found me and Bardic cramped up together in the place where he lived with little Alba.'

Quaver flew on over hedgerow, copse and meadow till at last the ruined farmhouse loomed up ahead of him. He flew in through the gap in the wall that had once been a window and found Bardic sitting moodily on the wooden headboard that had once been Hunter's favourite perch.

'You're back at last,' the Bard Owl said with an irritated wave of one large, flamboyant wing. 'Listen to this, dear boy, and tell me what you think.' Quaver perched wearily on the broken chest of drawers and watched while Bardic cleared his throat and then began to declaim from his latest revision of their epic ballad for posterity. As usual, he was embarrassed by the slightly effeminate way in which his portly, well-groomed tutor rolled his eyes and flapped his wings in time to the music of the words. In fact, the Bard Owl's florid, histrionic manner made it hard to concentrate on the verses he was speaking, but as he listened

Quaver was once more filled with misgivings about Winger's reaction to their work, and especially to passages like the one that Bardic was currently declaiming.

> 'He tore his breast the Bard Owl then,
> Great God Bird, set me free!
> How shall I sing while others fight?
> Oh, not for me a coward's plight,
> Take my soul and life for liberty!
> You are the voice of the future,
> The God Bird's answer came
> Your path leads to posterity
> And not to a martyr's fame . . .'

And so it went on, endlessly, telling of the poet's inner conflict at the choice between going into battle or else filling his appointed role as a chronicler for future generations. To Quaver, listening, it seemed as if the ballad had got stuck on Bardic's inner struggle the way that wet November weather sometimes sets in for what seems an eternity of dreary nights and days. Numbed by Bardic's bombast, pomp and rhetoric, he was on the point of nodding off to sleep when his tutor suddenly ended with a flourish and asked him what he thought.

'It's all about you again,' said Quaver. 'We've been working on the ballad for almost six seasons now and we haven't even got to the start of the battle yet!'

'But don't you see?' cried Bardic, with another flamboyant wave of his left wing. 'The background is vitally important in an epic of this kind. It's not just the fighting, you know. It's also the build-up and all the conflicting emotions of those who knew they were about to die.'

'And there's another thing,' said Quaver, speaking frankly for the first time since the beginning of his long apprenticeship. 'That bit about your conversation with the God Bird. For me, it doesn't work.'

'Why not?' asked Bardic, sitting upright on his perch and ruffling his feathers with offended dignity.

'Well, it's all right invoking the deity,' said Quaver. 'But does the God Bird ever answer back? I mean, did he really speak to you that way?'

'Of course not!' said Bardic, in tones that displayed a lofty contempt for the ignorance of his apprentice. 'That's what we call poetic licence.

The conversation is a symbol of my inner conflict, not a literal rendition of what the God Bird said.'

'You mustn't be offended,' answered Quaver. 'I'm only worried about what Winger might have to say. You know he doesn't care for any mention of the God Bird whatsoever.'

'You're right. I should have thought of that,' admitted Bardic, as his haughty posture crumpled and his plumage drooped making him look suddenly forlorn and rather helpless. 'We'll change it,' he added quickly. 'But we'll have to start at once. It's the last chance we've got before he comes.'

'Sorry,' Quaver said. 'I'm going out. I haven't eaten yet.'

'Oh, all right then,' said Bardic, sulkily. 'I'll do it on my own. But make sure you get back here in time for the recital. Remember, your future reputation rests on this as well.'

Groaning inwardly, Quaver nodded his assent and then flew out of the window and across the fields and meadows towards the copse, wondering if perhaps Dawn Raptor had been right. Perhaps the fact that Winger had taken over without incurring any kind of heavenly retribution was conclusive proof that the Barn owl God Bird was a myth. 'Perhaps the Tawnies' God Bird is a myth as well,' he speculated idly as he entered the copse, perched on the willow branch and stared up at the secret, wooded hills. Then he took a deep breath and called out loud for Yoller, his mind turning from mythology and comparative religion to the more pressing question of the truth about his missing brother.

CHAPTER

3

'So you think I ought to go?' asked Quaver. 'You're saying there's a chance that he might still be alive?'

'I last saw him in the city,' Yoller said. 'It's a long, long way from here. I doubt if you'd make it on your own, and even if you did get there, you wouldn't survive in that asphalt jungle long enough to find him. It's dangerous enough, even for our town-bred Tawnies, and no Barn owl in living memory has come back from that place alive.'

'Then my brother must be dead,' said Quaver, who now shared his sister's feeling that Yoller knew much more than he dared tell. 'What was he doing when you last set eyes on him? You've never said. All you've ever told us is that you lost each other in the city. For the Great God Bird's sake, if you know more, then tell me now! My whole future is at stake. Even my life itself, if I have to set out on this blind and endless quest for my brother's bones.'

Yoller turned and looked hard at Quaver for a long time before he spoke. His great Tawny eyes were troubled with some inner conflict, and with a little thrill of fear Quaver sensed that at long last he was about to learn the truth. After what seemed an eternity, Yoller turned away and stared through the darkness at the sweeping, wooded hills of his ancestral home. He stared hard and long as if seeking strength from those massive, darkened ranks of ash, sycamore and oak within whose secret depths his ancestors had reigned for centuries, unthreatened by the thousand dangers of the outside world.

'All right, I'll tell you!' he said, turning suddenly back to Quaver. 'But there are two conditions that you must accept before you know the truth.'

'What are they?' Quaver asked, as a twinge of apprehension chilled his stomach and froze his talons tighter to the willow branch.

'First, you must tell no one. Not a living soul!' said Yoller, glaring at him fiercely. 'And second, you must invent some other story for your mother. You must tell her something that will give her hope.'

'All right,' said Quaver, attempting to sound composed and in control. 'I don't want her to die of grief, and I promise that no other owl shall ever know.'

The Barn owl and the Tawny stared at each other in solemn silence for a moment. Then Yoller looked back towards the sweeping forest hills and sighed, as if a great weight was about to be lifted from his mind. 'The truth is, your brother must be dead,' he said, turning back to Quaver. 'And it was my fault. He died to save my life.'

'In the city?' Quaver asked, surprised at how numbed he felt at the certain knowledge Hunter was no more. Though he thought he had long since accepted the inevitable, he now realized that somewhere deep inside he had still been cherishing a secret hope that Hunter might be out there somewhere, still alive and now more than ever a legend in his time.

'It happened in the city,' Yoller nodded. 'Deep in the smoky bowels of that stinking, man-made hell.'

'How?' asked Quaver.

'I'll tell you,' Yoller said. 'But it's a painful story. I don't know where I should begin.'

'At the beginning,' Quaver said. 'You tell me I must invent something I can tell my mother. If I base it on the facts I get from you, I can create something that's partly true and therefore more convincing.'

'Well, we got there,' Yoller said. 'And when I saw the city limits sprawling out below us, I told him to go back. It was an awful sight,' he added, with a little shudder. 'Ahead of us, the night sky glowed in a boundless, uncharted lake of yellow light. You could hear a distant rumble and you could tell that ahead of you the buildings would thicken like the corn in spring, rising ever higher in the sky and clogging together until they congealed into a massive, asphalt pile where the distant rumble would swell into a deafening roar and either burst the eardrums of a country Barn owl like your brother or else drive him hopelessly and irredeemably insane. "Go back!" I said, seeing he shared my instinctive desire to turn and escape into the wild. "It was good of you to come so far. From now on, I can manage on my own."

'I saw him turn and look back in longing at the last of the countryside that stretched into the distance far behind us. He took a deep breath as if he knew it was the last time he would inhale the fragrance of honeysuckle or wild thyme and the last glimpse he would ever get of pear blossom or white hawthorn in the hedge. Then he turned to me and shook his head.

'"I won't leave you now," he said. "And in any case, I've got nothing to go back to now that little Alba's dead."

'"Go back to the young female that you met," I said. "The one who lives in the secluded valley not far north of here. Wait there till I return with May Blossom and we'll fly back home together."'

'Female?' Quaver asked, pricking up his ears at the sound of something he might tell his mother. 'Was she a Barn owl, or another immigrant like little Alba?'

'She was one of your species,' Yoller said. 'She lived alone in that hidden valley with her old and ailing mother. All the other owls had either fled or been killed in the invasion.'

'And Hunter liked her?'

'I think so,' Yoller said. 'She certainly liked him. She seemed a brave and gentle creature and they agreed to meet again on Hunter's journey home.'

'And did you tell her he was dead?' asked Quaver.

'No, old boy, I'm ashamed to say I didn't. I just couldn't face it, so on my way back with May Blossom I made a detour round the place.'

'And so Hunter flew on to the city with you?'

'He did, but not before I'd tried again. I told him that for me this dangerous mission was a duty. "On the other hand," I said, "for you there will be no glory, praise or gain. For you to go any further would amount to pure recklessness and folly."

'"Lead on," your brother said. "I told you when I agreed to come that folly is the best antidote to pain." So we took off and flew south above the two iron tracks which soon widened into four, six, eight and then ten as the buildings on either side closed in on us and rose higher in the sky, while the man-made lights grew so many and so close that they suffused into one single, artificial moon that lit up the late night sky with an eerie yellow glow. At last we came to the great iron barn in the centre of the city, the end of the tracks and the place where I had been told to hoot and wait.

'The great barn was full of what you call zoomerangs, the things that dash up and down the iron tracks and drove you and Bardic from your previous home. We perched on the roof of this foul, polluted place and gazed around us at the wilderness of buildings, watching the million man-made lights fade one by one until the eerie yellow light dimmed down at last into something like the darkness that we knew. At last a town owl called Welkin came to fetch us and we flew across the wilderness of buildings to a great park where he and May Blossom lived. It was almost as big as the parkland in the lost domain and at that late night hour there were no humans to be seen.'

'A green haven in the centre of the city,' Quaver said. 'It must have been pure bliss!'

'Not really,' Yoller said. 'You see, within the limits of the park, there is the prison.'

'Prison?' Quaver asked. 'What's that?'

'It's a place where men keep owls and all kinds of wild animals and birds locked up in cages, pens and little tiny cells.'

'What for?' asked Quaver, who found this frightening concept very hard to grasp.

'May Blossom says it may be to observe their habits and behaviour patterns,' Yoller said. 'She went to the city to get knowledge, so she ought to know.'

'You said owls?' asked Quaver. 'Do you mean Barn owls and Tawnies like ourselves?'

'I mean all sorts of owls,' said Yoller. 'More species than we ever dreamed existed, including giant Snowies from the north and even an Eagle owl like the one we defeated in the war.'

'And you slept beside them in the park?' asked Quaver. 'Weren't you terrified they might escape?'

'I was,' admitted Yoller, 'even though May Blossom said they couldn't. And so was your brother. After the first night, he wanted to go home. For him, worse than the cries of the owls and the other animals in prison was the ceaseless thunder of the city and the foul grime in the polluted air. And the food, of course. No mammals, only birds.'

'So why didn't you?' asked Quaver. 'Leave at once, I mean. Surely May

Blossom and this Welkin could have conveyed your message to the other Tawnies in the city?'

'I know,' said Yoller. 'I should have left at once, but I wanted to fly back with May Blossom and she wanted me to stay. She said it would be a shame for me to travel all that way and then not take advantage of the city to get knowledge.'

'What did my brother say?' asked Quaver, who could imagine the disappointment Hunter must have felt at being let down so far from home by his oldest comrade and best friend.

'He asked me why in the name of crow dung it depended on May Blossom, so I confessed that she'd been my ulterior motive for coming to the city. I told him her knowledge would be invaluable to me in the hard times that lay ahead. I said I'd asked her to mate with me and she'd accepted, so then he understood.'

'And he decided to go home alone?'

'Yes. He asked me when May Blossom would be ready and I said not until the next full moon.'

'So that was the last time you saw him, when he left?'

'No, I told you he was sick of eating pigeon, starling and sparrow, the staple diet of a Tawny in the town, so we decided to have a mammal banquet on the night before he left.'

'Fire falling from the sky and the plague of rats,' said Quaver. 'I've heard of that before.'

'Yes,' said Yoller, 'but men rebuild quickly and there weren't many ruined houses left. However, Welkin knew a place not far from the park so the three of us flew there together and that's how your brother met his end.'

'No!' said Quaver, shocked by this sudden revelation. 'Don't tell me Hunter was beaten by a rat!'

'Of course not,' Yoller said. 'Though some of them are giants compared with the kind we get up here. No, in the middle of the hunting I got trapped down on the ground and attacked by feral cats.'

'Feral?' asked Quaver, who was quite bewildered. 'What does feral mean?'

'Wild,' said Yoller. 'I learned that in the city. They are cats that for some reason men don't castrate, domesticate and keep. They're much hungrier and tougher than the tame ones and not having had their balls off, so to speak, they're also much fiercer and more aggressive.'

'So the wild cats killed my brother,' said Quaver, overcome with horror as he remembered the cruelty of the tame cats he had seen playing with their feathered victims for what seemed like an age before the final kill.

'Wait,' Yoller said. 'Let me tell you exactly how it happened. We flew out of the park and across the brightly lit roads and houses till we came to this dark, devastated area covered with ruined buildings whose entrails spilled out over what had once been gardens and where wild grass now sprang up tall among the twisted rubble on the ground. As we circled above this dark patch of wasteland we could hear the scurrying of claws below and I was the first to swoop down and catch an enormous rat as it scuttled across what must once have been a garden. I killed the thing outright, but as I drove my talons through its neck I felt those on my right claw catch and twist themselves round something on the ground. I tried to pull them free, gently at first, then harder, but nothing happened. All three were embedded in this wire mesh that had been half-buried in the ground and covered by the grass.'

'How dreadful!' said Quaver, who had always dreaded being trapped down on the ground. 'How did you get them out?'

'I couldn't,' Yoller said. 'While I was trying to work them free, I heard Hunter and Welkin drop down, catch their food, swallow it and then take off and circle above me once again. So I ate my meal and waited for one of them to come down and find out what was wrong. But then I sensed the cat and saw it sneaking stealthily across the wasteland to the place where I was trapped. It was a mangy, hungry female and I saw her yellow eyes gleaming bigger and brighter as she stole closer to me, lusting for my flesh and blood.'

'Why didn't you call out for help?' asked Quaver.

'I didn't need to,' Yoller said. 'Just before the thing got within pouncing distance of me, your brother dived down from the sky with his talons aimed directly at her neck. She sensed him coming though, and turned at the last moment, so that he missed his target and ripped a great gaping hole in her back instead. The wild cat howled and ran for cover as the blood spurted from her back and dripped in the darkness on the rubble and the unkempt grass.

'Hunter hovered for a little while and then landed beside me when he was certain that the killer wasn't coming back. I told him what the trouble was and he did his best to help. We got two talons free but the centre one had got enmeshed and twisted right round in the thin wire net, and while we were still trying to work it loose we saw two more wild cats creeping towards us in the darkness. Both of them were males and much bigger than the she-cat Hunter had very nearly killed. "Go now, Hunter," I said, as they crept closer towards us on those cruel, feline haunches. "Take off while you've still got time."

'But your brother wouldn't move. He stood his ground in front of me and we both watched as the first of the two scrawny killers moved to within striking distance of him. Then Hunter used his static defence technique, flared his plumage till he looked nearly twice his size, clappered his bill ferociously and rotated both wings forward like a giant fan. The wild cat sprang back in alarm, hissed and then crouched down on its haunches. The second one stole up to join him and they both sat there with their necks stretched forward watching us and waiting to attack again.'

'Where was your town owl all this time?' asked Quaver. 'Didn't he fly down to help?'

'Not Welkin!' Yoller said. 'And frankly, old boy, one wouldn't have expected it of him. He's a plebeian, opportunist owl, like many of our species in the town. They tend to be quicker and more devious than we are, but nothing like so bold. We found out later that he'd gone off to fetch May Blossom. If he'd stayed and attacked the cats, even if only to distract them, it might have saved your brother's life.'

'What happened next?' asked Quaver, who did not really want to hear the gory details but knew it was his duty to sit and listen till the bitter end.

'The two cats closed in again,' said Yoller. 'They crept forward to within pouncing distance and Hunter puffed himself up again, howled at them and whirled his wings round even more wildly than before. They sprang back a bit and crouched among the rubble but you could tell that next time, or the time after that, they'd spring in for the kill. "Go now!" I begged your brother. "I've got one free claw and my bill to fight with. I know that I can't win, but I promise I'll take at least one of those killers with me to the Great Beyond." But Hunter wouldn't listen. He just sat there, looking at the cats and waiting for them to move in again. There was no sign of Welkin or May Blossom, so when they began to creep to within striking distance, I made my big decision.'

'What decision?' asked Quaver, wishing Yoller would get on with it and tell the story to the end.

'Oh, hadn't you noticed,' said Yoller, reverting to his usual, casual drawl. 'That was when I lost my talon. Look!'

He held up his right claw then and to Quaver's astonishment he saw a great gap where the middle one of his three talons had been ripped clean from its socket in the centre of the Tawny's claw.

'You did that?' gasped Quaver. 'You ripped it out yourself?'

'I had to,' said Yoller, glancing ruefully downwards at the yawning gap which had so cruelly reduced his powers as a warrior and a hunter. 'I knew I had to do it when I saw the wild cats moving in. It took me all my strength and courage and as I finally tore it from its socket, I must confess that I howled out in pain and very nearly fainted. But maybe that was just as well. It shocked the cats and stopped them at the very moment when they were poised to spring on Hunter for the kill. Blinded by pain, I took off and flew low across the wasteland, expecting him to follow. I gained height, crossed the dimly lit road beyond the wilderness of burnt-out houses and then looked back to see if he was coming. He was. To my great relief I saw his white shadow flying fast and low across the wasteland towards the road. And then, to my eternal sorrow, I saw the dreadful thing that happened.'

'What was that?' asked Quaver, who was utterly bewildered.

'The blazing lights!' said Yoller. 'As Hunter was about to gain height to fly across the road, a machine swept fast round the hidden bend and blinded him in its blazing beams of light. It was horrible to watch. He simply hovered there, quite mesmerized, and though the machine slowed down a little, it struck him in mid-air and flung him sideways to the ground. I saw the machine slow down and stop, and so I waited. Two men got out, walked back, bent over your brother and then picked his body up.'

'No!' said Quaver, shuddering at the thought of such desecration. 'Not humans! Not touching and defiling the body of an owl?'

Yoller nodded and for a moment or two seemed too overcome by emotion to continue with his gruesome tale. 'They picked his body up,' he repeated with an effort. 'They walked back down the road with it and put it inside their machine. Then they got inside themselves and immediately the machine started up and moved away. I suppose I should have followed, but I was still in too much pain to think and also half-stunned by what I'd seen. In any case, it would soon have disappeared among all those other man-made lights. Just one machine among so very many.'

'Why did the humans take his body?' asked Quaver, after giving himself time to let all of this sink in. 'To eat it, do you think?'

'No,' said Yoller, shaking his head vaguely and seeming quite drained by the effort of the story he had just told. 'I've never heard of humans eating any kind of owl, have you?'

'Not here in the country,' Quaver said. 'Yet you tell me you ate sparrows and pigeons in the city, a thing you seldom do here in your ancient Tawny woods. So perhaps town men have a different diet, too?'

'I never thought of that,' said Yoller. 'And you may very well be right. I never saw any cows, pigs or chickens in the city, not even in the parkland, so they must eat something different from the ones in the rustic territories here.'

'They ate the dead body of my brother,' Quaver said, nodding slowly as he forced himself to face up to the final, dreadful end his brother must have met. 'What else would humans want with the carcass of an owl?'

'I don't know, old boy,' said Yoller gravely. 'It's too terrible to contemplate.'

'Can you imagine it?' asked Quaver, still struggling to recover from the shock. 'An owl being eaten by a man? It's not natural. To my knowledge, no owl has ever eaten one of them.'

'We don't know for certain,' Yoller said. 'For the Great God Bird's sake don't let your mother think a thing like that!'

'It would kill her,' agreed Quaver, nodding once again. 'I suppose that's why you've said nothing until now?'

'I couldn't,' Yoller said. 'I felt responsible. If he hadn't come with me on my mission, he'd never have been killed. And then he saved my life. Somehow, I should have managed to save his.'

'You're quite wrong,' Quaver said. 'It was always his decision. But of course, I understand your feelings. What I don't understand is what I'm going to tell my mother.'

'Just repeat the story that I've always told. That I lost him in the city. After all, in its own way it's true.'

'But then she'll expect me to go in search of him,' said Quaver. 'Steeple is dead, she's too old and Dawn Raptor didn't like him, so I am her only hope.'

'Add to the story,' Yoller urged him. 'Remember what you said? If I gave you the basic facts, you could invent something that would keep her hopes alive. After all, you're a minstrel and a poet, so it shouldn't be too hard.'

'Tell me more about that female that he met,' said Quaver, who knew that he would have to play for time and realized that Yoller's suggestion was probably the only way.

'I've told you most of what I can remember,' Yoller said. 'And I have an urgent message to give you before dawn. A message from May Blossom that may prove vital to the future of both our species.'

'Is the message for our leader?' Quaver asked. 'If so, he's coming here tomorrow night.'

'No, not for your leader,' Yoller said. 'Winger is mad. One can't negotiate with him. This message is for Rivers, the leader of your Barn owl opposition.'

'Why me?' asked Quaver.

'Because Hunter isn't here,' said Yoller. 'Who else would you suggest?'

'I'll take it for you,' Quaver said. 'But first, tell me more about this female Hunter met. Dapple is a shrewd old bird, and in any case, inventing a story to satisfy one's mother always takes much energy and time.'

'Her name was Holly,' Yoller said. 'I've already told you that she lived with her mother who was old and sick and that all the other owls in that secluded valley had been killed by the monster in the war. Except for one, whose father was the last of the aristocratic Barn owls, or so Hunter said. This son of his had wanted to mate with Holly when she was fully fledged, but he'd left and flown north some time before the invasion and the war.'

'And would she have accepted him, if he'd come back?' asked Quaver.

'I don't think so,' Yoller said. 'But her mother wanted it. He owned the whole valley, after all.'

'So she was waiting there for him to return and claim them both, the territory and her?'

'I suppose so, but after all that time, she thought he must be dead.'

'And now she waits for Hunter, who is dead as well?' said Quaver. 'Not a happy situation to be in. Perhaps she should be told.'

'I know,' said Yoller. 'But I've already told you, I couldn't bring myself to do it.'

'What did this Holly look like?' Quaver asked. 'You must understand, I need every detail I can get.'

'I don't remember,' said Yoller, who was anxious to deliver his important message from May Blossom before dawn. 'And in any case,' he added, 'all your female Barn owls look much the same to me.'

'But you must remember something!' Quaver said. 'Her accent, for example. Did she speak the same way as we do here?'

'No,' said Yoller. 'That I do remember because Hunter seemed enchanted by the way she spoke, or sang, he said, with a soft lilting cadence that soothed you like the song of a nightingale in some quiet glade, but at the same time laughed and bubbled with the clear sparkle of a mountain stream. He said it sang of woodsmoke and of summer flowers and he fell in love with it at once. Oh, and I remember something else. Hunter said you'd like her because she wanted to study poetry and singing. She wanted a higher education, but in her territory there were no owls left to teach her anything. Hunter said that if he survived his journey to the city, he'd bring her back with him to study under you and Bardic. Naturally, he thought Rivers would be the new leader and as a war hero he'd be able to do much as he pleased.'

'I see,' said Quaver, pensively. 'And would Hunter have mated with her, do you think?'

'I'm not sure,' said Yoller, shaking his head slowly. 'I've told you, he wanted to help her and he found her charming, but perhaps just a shade too ingenuous for him. And in any case, he was still much too overcome by grief. He really loved that little immigrant, you know. The God Bird alone knows what he saw in her, but he suffered really badly when she died.'

'It's nearly daybreak,' said Quaver, glancing upwards as the sky began to lighten overhead. 'I'm ready for your message now. I haven't much to work on, but my business is inventing stories, so I dare say I'll manage anyhow.'

But while Yoller delivered the Tawny ultimatum and told him what would happen if Winger should attempt to colonize Ferocity and Ripper's wood, Quaver listened with only one ear, for the other one was far away in a secluded valley, listening to an unknown voice that sang of summer flowers and sparkled like a mountain stream. As he listened to that distant, lilting song, he wished he had Hunter's courage so that he could undertake his mother's quest, even though he already knew the time, place and manner of his brother's death. If he flew far south, almost to the city, he could meet this Holly and settle in her sheltered valley, far from the internal strife that now threatened the peace and freedom for which both Barn owl and Tawny had paid such a bitter price. 'But I shall never do it,' he thought, knowing that the truth lay in the words he had spoken to his mother earlier that night. 'I am one born to be attendant on the course of history, not a prime mover in its cause. Let me survive in peace and hope for better times.'

And so in his mind's eye he saw Holly's lovely face and with his inner ear he listened to her lilting song. 'That is my fate,' he told himself as the dawn began to break and Yoller drew close to the ending of his ultimatum. 'To survive in my imagination, and in my mind's eye to travel far. Dreaming where learning hath no light and soaring with my song to heights no daytime eagle can attain. And for a coward's destiny, that can't be bad.'

But as the sun began to rise above the willow in the copse, Quaver had no inkling of how soon he, too, would be forced into action, find courage thrust upon him and in his own small way become a hero and a legend in his time.

CHAPTER

4

To Quaver the bedroom in the abandoned farmhouse felt both claustrophobic and overcrowded as Bardic began to declaim the opening stanzas of the ballad. He began by delivering the epic at full blast, as though he were reciting his work to vast hordes in a faceless arena instead of merely to an audience of two owls perched patiently in front of him.

As the performance continued, the source of Quaver's embarrassment shifted from the Bard Owl's histrionic manner to the content of the verse he was declaiming. The whole thing was even more long-winded and rhetorical than Quaver had remembered and he cast several apprehensive sideways glances to see how the leader of the Barn owl council was reacting, but apart from looking uncomfortable on his chair back perch Winger sat listening with impeccable restraint, allowing only the occasional flicker of an eyebrow to register surprise or perhaps disapproval of the singer or the song. As the whole thing dragged on and on, Winger's intense and bulging eyes glazed over, as Quaver's did, dulled by the pomp and bombast of Bardic's histrionics.

After the first hundred stanzas even Bardic began to suffer from fatigue and his dramatic rendering of the epic ballad slowly degenerated into a monotonous lament or dirge. At last he ceased declaiming, brushed his brow with one well-plumed wing and in a studied manner allowed the transported gaze of the great performer to fade slowly from his face. Then he smiled and bowed obsequiously to Winger. 'That's the first part finished,' he said proudly. 'It needs work, but I think you'll agree that it has the makings of an epic.'

Quaver glanced sideways at Winger who was sitting in stunned silence, his eyes still glazed over with the sheer weight and length of what he had heard. 'I'm partly responsible for this disaster,' thought Quaver with a shock. 'Why did I never realize just how bad it was before?'

'I see you're overcome,' said Bardic, when neither of them spoke. 'You're both experiencing an immediate, emotional response. In a moment or two your critical faculties will begin to function and you'll be ready for an intellectual appraisal of my work. But remember, it's the general owl public I'm concerned with. Let's call them the once and future masses. They are the great audience who will determine for all time the success or failure of my work.'

Bardic paused at this point but still no comment was forthcoming so he brushed a wing dramatically across his forehead and spoke again, this time with much less confidence, as though he had begun to suspect that their silence might not stem from unqualified admiration but from embarrassment and rejection of his work instead. 'My main aim here in this epic ballad is to portray squalor and death elevated to heroism and dignity through art,' he said. 'Words and music that will pluck the heartstrings of your normal, ordinary owl long after we are dead and – who knows? – perhaps for all future time to come. That is my objective. To create art out of passion, not merely to relate a dull chronicle of facts and statistics for the tedium of future generations. That is the task of the History Owl, not mine.'

'What do you think of it?' asked Winger, suddenly coming to life as he shifted his big, bony frame on the chair back perch and turned to Quaver with those bulging eyes and that slightly manic stare of his.

'Oh, I think it's very good,' replied Quaver in a panic, torn as he was between loyalty to Bardic and telling Winger what he really thought. 'At least, it has great potential, though in its present form it might be just a tiny bit too long.'

'Too long? Of course it's far too long,' said Winger in clipped and irritated tones. 'How can any normal owl be expected to remember an epic of that never-ending length?'

'My dear leader,' replied Bardic, raising one wing in a wounded attempt to stem this tide of disapproval. 'A great, epic work of art requires much time in its execution and much time for its subsequent performance. The story of how we repelled the invasion and killed the monster in the war is not a silly little jingle that can be tossed off in an afternoon. As I said before, it is history elevated by poetry and rendered into art.'

'It doesn't rhyme,' said Winger. 'At least, sometimes it does and sometimes it doesn't, and I'm afraid that rather puts me off.'

'Rhyme? Of course it doesn't rhyme,' said Bardic, looking aghast at their leader's ignorance.

'Why not?' asked Winger. 'Think of our oral tradition. How can you expect any owl to learn a thing of that length if it doesn't rhyme?'

'It's called blank verse,' said Quaver, welcoming this opportunity to soothe his tutor's wounded pride. 'It's considered the best medium for dramatic narrative and for noble emotion of this kind. Imagine four hundred stanzas of rhyming couplets. They would drive you mad.'

'I'll accept that explanation,' Winger said. 'Since I'm no expert, I won't argue with you about form. But what about the content? In your opinion, what is wrong with that?'

'Me?' asked Quaver, beginning to panic once again. 'I'm only an apprentice. I'm not qualified to say.'

'You've worked on this ballad, haven't you?' asked Winger. 'And you must know that unless the student constantly challenges his master, we shall continue to suffer from the prejudices of our reactionary past. I hold you responsible as well, so tell me what you think.'

Quaver glanced apprehensively at Bardic who was visibly shocked and obviously had not expected a critical inquisition of this nature. Then, for the first time, he decided to be absolutely frank, even if this should mean an untimely end to his apprenticeship and his career. 'I don't think our ballad tells the truth,' he said, trembling a little as he spoke. 'It makes it sound as though we Barn owls won the war all by ourselves and all the Tawnies did was lend a little help. Also, there's too much in it about Bardic and myself and not enough about the real Barn owl heroes like the History, Language and Geography Owls and my father and my brother. That's what I object to most about the ballad. It doesn't tell the truth.'

'The truth, he says!' cried Bardic, raising both wings high as if calling on the Great God Bird to come down and be his witness. 'The truth, dear boy, is relative. There's yours, there's mine, there's Yoller's and there'd even be the monster's if he were still alive to tell it. You must learn, Quaver, that truth is never absolute. It lies merely in the eye of the beholder. In this case, I am the Bard Owl by appointment and posterity shall learn the truth as I perceived it.'

'You are quite right, Bardic, about the subjectivity of truth,' said Winger, leaning his clumsy frame forwards and staring at them both with great intensity. 'And you, Quaver, are quite right when you say the ballad is too long. About everything else, it pains me to have to say, you are both completely wrong. In fact, you'll have to scrap the whole thing and start again from the beginning.'

'But why?' asked Bardic, as his plumage wilted with dejection and his expression changed from indignation to one of pain and shock. 'Perhaps you will tell us, Winger, exactly what is wrong with it?'

'The whole concept is wrong,' said Winger. 'You must start again from the beginning and tell how my strategy to avoid the war was overruled by the council, and how many subsequently died in a futile bloodbath that could have been avoided. You must show how this senseless carnage finally showed up the Tawnies as the reactionary warmongers they really are, paved the way for my election as leader and thus laid the foundations for our New Apostasy. And I want no reference whatsoever to our so-called Barn owl heroes. Instead, speak of pointless suffering and piles of unnecessary dead. This ballad must be a condemnation of the ancient reign, an indictment of the reactionary past and at the same time an anthem to the glorious future of our New Apostasy.'

Both Bardic and Quaver sat on their perches flabbergasted, both looking so obviously shocked that Winger toned down his burning intensity, changed to a lighter tone of voice and even coaxed a devious smile on to those lean and hungry features. 'Of course, you must mention yourselves in the ballad,' he said, in a casual, ingratiating sort of way. 'And naturally, if I approve of your new version, both of you will be numbered forever among the heroes of the New Apostasy. Think about it carefully. This is your chance to compose a hymn or anthem that will be the theme song of our species from now on. Think, and then begin. I want it short, I want it snappy and I want it finished by the next full moon.'

To Quaver's disgust he saw that his tutor's eyes were already lighting up again at this second chance of fame and a sponsored contribution to posterity. As for himself, he knew that he could never do it. He knew that he could never allow himself to be involved in a wilful distortion of history, let alone in the creation of propaganda that would tighten Winger's grip on those who knew no better, though naturally he dared not say so at the time.

'I have to take a break,' he blurted out instead, before his anger and determination were worn down by Winger's presence and implacable authority. 'My mother wants me to fly south to the place the Tawnies call the city to establish the time, place and manner of my brother's death.'

'That's impossible,' said Winger. 'This new version of the ballad is top priority and you must both start work on it at once. Tell your mother that I will go instead.'

'You?' asked Quaver, so amazed that his voice jumped up into the high squeak that had so amused Hunter and Dawn Raptor when the three of them were fledglings. 'But you are our leader. Surely you can't spare yourself for a private mission of this kind?'

'I have to travel to the south in any case,' said Winger, lifting up one claw and examining each of the three talons with calm and studied care. 'I have a secret council mission that will take me far south of here and almost to the city. It is a long and dangerous journey but I have flown that way before and I stand a better chance than you do of surviving such a mission. If I hear news of how your brother met his end, you and your mother shall hear of it as soon as I return.'

Quaver opened his mouth and then shut it again since there was nothing he could find to say. What could this mysterious expedition of Winger's mean and why should he suddenly concern himself with the fate of an owl that he had been long attempting to discredit?

'I leave tonight,' said Winger. 'In the meantime, get on with my new version of the ballad. And remember, it's your last chance. You've both wasted too much time already.'

With that Winger nodded curtly, subjected each of them to one last manic stare, then flew through the gap in the wall and disappeared into the eerie darkness that was now pregnant with the coming dawn.

The two owls did not speak for a long time after their leader had departed and it was not until the first rays of morning light stole in from where the window had once been that Quaver broke the silence that had hung between them for so long. 'What are you going to do?' he asked, as the Bard Owl began to preen his crumpled and dejected feathers back to something like their former glory.

'Do, dear boy?' asked Bardic with his bushy eyebrows raised. 'Why, do what he says, of course. What else do you suggest?'

'But we can't!' protested Quaver. 'We can't misrepresent the past like that. We can't perjure ourselves just to suit Winger and his so-called New Apostasy.'

'Can't we?' asked Bardic, still with his eyebrows raised. 'And what do you suppose will happen if we don't?'

'He'll get someone else to do it, I expect,' said Quaver, with an unhappy little shrug. 'After all, you can always find unscrupulous owls who are prepared to do anything for their own advancement.'

'Exactly! If we refuse, I'll lose my position as Bard Owl, and my place on the Barn owl council. You'll no longer be my apprentice and you'll find all other opportunities for further education barred to you.'

'I don't care!' said Quaver, who did in fact care enormously and found himself shaking with an odd mixture of fear, rage and frustration. 'I don't care what Winger does. I refuse to be involved in the wilful distortion of history or in creating false propaganda to strengthen Winger's grip on future generations. The truth does exist, in spite of what you and Winger say. I'm no hero, but there are some things that simply can't be done.'

'You won't have a place to live,' said Bardic, affecting a rather ostentatious yawn as he looked away from his apprentice and out into the rising dawn. 'We can't go back to our previous domain because that's infested now with men and zoomerangs that thunder up and down the iron tracks. Cramped as this place is, it's better than some stinking, ruined cowshed. And any upstart Bard Owl who's been used to nothing better might be very happy here. So might his apprentice.'

'It's no good, Bardic. I can't do it.'

'Think carefully,' said Bardic turning away from the window and looking hard at his apprentice. 'Before you make any decision fly down to the stream on the borders of the lost domain, perch on a willow branch beside the water's edge, look down at the dark, fast-flowing current and imagine you're a fish.'

'A fish? What for?'

'Imagine you're a fish,' repeated Bardic. 'And then decide which way you would swim if your aim was to survive and travel far.'

'With the current?' answered Quaver, after visualizing the swirling water for a while.

'Precisely, dear boy. Very strongly with the current. Not against it. Talk to your mother, to Rivers and to Quirk, the Language Owl, but remember that they have no power to help you. And remember that your brother and your father are both well and truly dead and soon to be forgotten. And finally, remember the words that Yoller's father spoke after the monster had been brought down in the battle.'

'You promised then you would immortalize the heroes of that day,' said Quaver. 'You said your ballad would ensure that both the Barn owl and the Tawny dead would be hallowed and remembered at moonrise and at dawn from that day forth for evermore.'

'And what did Yoller's father say? "Do not delude yourselves. A thousand winters hence, the great things of today will be treated as mere myth or legend. They will become a sometime thing, a mere hint or stirring from some long forgotten yesterday, changed and perverted by future owls and by the ebb and flow of time. It was ever thus," he said. "History is always reinvented to suit the mood and purpose of owls that are living at the time." Think carefully, Quaver, before you make a rash decision. Do not swim against the current and drown yourself in vain.'

With that Bardic took off and flew out into the dawn to get himself some food while Quaver remained seething on his perch for quite some time, certain that this time he would rebel and fight for truth and justice till the end. 'I'll join the resistance!' Quaver vowed, as broader, brighter beams of dawn sunlight poured into the abandoned bedroom and played on the headboard that had once been Hunter's favourite perch. 'At twilight, I'll fly south-west until I reach the History Owl's ancestral home and there I'll pledge my allegiance to the gang of three.'

And so it came to pass that shortly before midnight three owls perched and plotted in the depths of the countryside, hidden beneath the roof of the isolated ruin that had been the home of the History Owl and his ancestors for countless generations. The vast, crumbling edifice in which Rivers, Quirk and Quaver now conspired was so old, so broken-down and so far from the beaten track that not even the History Owl himself knew for what purpose the first men had built it or why it had slept forgotten for so many centuries, blending in with the wild landscape as naturally as the sloping meadowland that rolled down to the west or the wooded hills that hid it from the cold north wind.

'And so now you've decided?' Rivers said. 'You're quite prepared to risk losing everything, even your life, to bring down the New Apostasy and restore the ancient reign?'

'I am,' said Quaver firmly. 'I'm a poet, not a warrior, but I'll do everything I can to avoid a civil war against the Tawnies, especially if that means bringing Winger down.'

'It does,' said Rivers. 'According to the ultimatum you've just brought back from Yoller, if any Barn owl moves into Ferocity and Ripper's wood, the Tawnies will send a task force and the settlers will be slaughtered on the spot.'

'What message shall I take to Yoller?' Quaver asked. 'That we in the resistance movement intend to act now and take the leadership away from Winger?'

'No, it's much too soon for that,' said Rivers quickly. 'Tell him to bide his time while we try to stop Winger from colonizing Ferocity and Ripper's wood.'

'Also, explain to him why neither Rivers nor myself can meet with him in person,' put in Quirk. 'As council members, the History Owl and I must be very wary of any open collaboration or any hint of an alliance with the Tawnies. In the present climate, that might well be considered treason. If it were, we'd both lose our place on the council and our homes. On top of that, we'd probably be banished, and what would happen to the resistance movement then?'

'So what should I do?' asked Quaver, who was disappointed by the cautious attitude of these two war heroes who were supposed to stand for liberty and truth. 'Should I resign in protest, or should I stay on with Bardic, committed to an epic that will distort history and falsify the truth?'

'You must stay,' said the History Owl, without any hesitation. 'You must stay for the same reasons as Quirk and I retain our positions on the council. First of all, we need to know what's going on. We need information, and if we're banished none of us will get it. Second, when Winger is overthrown, it must be by a democratic process conducted from within.'

'Unless he dissolves the council and makes himself dictator,' put in Quirk. 'In that case, we would organize a counter-revolution.'

'But with outside help,' said Rivers. 'That's where your brother and the Tawnies would come in.'

'But my brother's dead!' said Quaver, momentarily forgetting the solemn promise that he had made to Yoller.

'We don't know that for sure,' said Rivers. 'Officially, we only know he's missing. And more important still, we know that Winger is afraid of him.'

'That's funny,' Quaver said. 'As far as I remember, they've never even met.'

'Afraid of his reputation, afraid of what he stands for,' Rivers said. 'And for that reason, you can be quite certain that when Winger returns from his secret mission, he will say that Hunter's dead. We, on the other hand, must spread the rumour that he's still alive. You see, we need an outside threat. We need a leader in exile, but a leader with charisma and one already well known to the population. Who could be better than your brother, who has already become a legend in his time?'

'It's quite true that Winger is afraid of him,' said Quirk. 'And until we find someone to take his place, we must keep his memory alive.'

'I see,' said Quaver, who was relieved that his promise to Yoller had not after all been broken, or at least had passed unnoticed. 'But have you an alternative in mind? Another owl who might one day lead the counter-revolution if Winger makes himself dictator?'

'Not at the moment,' Rivers said. 'But if we wait and bide our time, the right owl will appear. "Cometh the hour, cometh the owl!" That was true in the war, remember? Without Hunter and your father, we'd all of us be dead.'

'I don't understand how Winger ever got elected,' Quaver said. 'He didn't fight, and if the council had taken his advice, we'd all have been slaughtered in the barns or on the branches where we slept.'

'But that's just why he did get elected.' Rivers said. 'After a war, most owls always think it could have been avoided, and they always put part of the blame on those who planned ahead and made every sacrifice to save them. I suppose it's partly because they think it might be them next time. So they temporarily reject the heroes and vote for anyone who promises to make drastic changes and bring them peace at any price.'

'But there won't be peace if Winger has his way,' said Quaver. 'There'll be a bloody civil war against the Tawnies.'

'Precisely,' Rivers said. 'But if there is a civil war, or even the odd skirmish, they'll blame it all on Winger, just like the business of the broken eggs.'

'What broken eggs?' asked Quaver, who was becoming progressively more bewildered and confused by all these politics.

'We don't know exactly,' said the Language Owl. 'But we suspect it might have something to do with Winger's mission to the south. The point is, we know he's caught up in some secret crisis. Something so grave and confidential that he hasn't even told the council yet. With any luck, he'll fail to resolve the problem and the population will blame it all on him. With the fickle majority behind us, we'll outvote him on the council and put another leader in his place.'

'You'd best be going,' said the History Owl. 'Otherwise you won't make it back to Bardic's place before dawn. Keep in touch and find out all you can. Next time we'll meet in secret in the lost domain. It's not so far for you to fly, and with Winger's spies out everywhere, it's no longer safe to meet in our own territory.'

'All right,' said Quaver, doubtfully. 'But what if the Little owls won't let us in?'

'Oh, they'll let us in,' said Rivers. 'Unlike so many of our species, they remember the war and what we did for them.'

'I only hope you're right,' said Quaver, as he prepared for take off. 'Personally, I'm frightened of the place, but as Hunter's brother I suppose there's just a chance that they won't tear me limb from limb.'

'They don't trust Winger,' Rivers said. 'And he's scared to go in there himself, so at least we're safe from him.'

Quaver nodded reluctantly, smiled a wan, brave smile as he said goodbye to the two senior conspirators and flew out of the isolated ruin on his way back to the Bard Owl's seat of learning.

Not long before daybreak he reached the borders of the lost domain, landed on the willow branch beside the stream and gazed down into the swiftly flowing water, as Bardic had suggested. With his keen night eyes he saw the shoals of small fish surging swiftly and eagerly downstream, borne by the current towards some unknown and uncharted destination. Only the big, scaly pike lurked strong and stationary against the current, waiting hidden beneath the bank of the little river with his cruel jaws facing upstream to feed at will upon the passing innocents.

As he watched the lurking pike poised to pounce on those who swam so blithely with the current, Quaver saw the river running red, not only with the blood of Tawny and Barn owl warriors, but also with his own and that of the conspirators. At that moment his new-found courage drained away and he doubted once more whether he would ever have the courage or the strength to turn and swim upstream, away from the gaping jaws of history and fate.

CHAPTER
5

One warm May twilight six seasons after the invasion and the war, a lone Barn owl left the ruined church that was her home and headed east, while behind her the sun sank in a ball of fire and disappeared behind the deep green sea of wooded hills that marked the western boundaries of her land.

As the shadows lengthened, she flew swiftly over undulating field and meadow and then through her favourite copse, where even as night fell the trees continued to give birth, their buds bursting into the full-blown thickness of the coming summer.

Skirting well round the hamlet that was hidden from her by the copse itself, Holly reached the eastern border of her home territory, flew into a sycamore tree and perched there high above the embankment that sloped down to the iron tracks. She sat there for some time as gloaming hid the countryside in even deeper mystery and peace, waiting with the tender hope of one who is still young that something soon would happen to change the sadness of her story and to smoothe away all the trouble and grief she had seen.

As she stared at the dark expanse of gently rippling corn beyond the iron tracks, she remembered the same verses that had come into Quaver's mind only a few evenings before as he flew home so far to the north of her. 'Listen to the rippling corn, for it will tell you of your future,' was the way she remembered it and that captured the spirit of the verses, although the words were wrong. But though she listened hard as she stared eastwards, she heard nothing but the gentle sighing of the evening breeze. In the deep peace of the gloaming, she looked first south towards the distant, ever-spreading city and then north along the iron tracks. No owl had passed that way since Hunter and Yoller had flown by on their way to the forbidden city, bringing news of the great battle and the final defeat of the monster in the rustic territory from whence they came.

Then suddenly her heart leapt and she stared harder into the northern darkness, for in the distance she had picked up the signals of a powerful Barn owl moving fast in her direction. At first her heart almost stood still with the surprise and shock of it. Could this be Hunter, who had somehow survived his first ill-fated trip and was now returning on a second mission to the city? Hunter, whom she had known but briefly, yet whose image remained fresh and vivid in her mind and whose courage had come to symbolize all her dreams of a richer, fuller life.

Or was it Westwood, who had fled the secluded valley well before the invasion and the war? Was it the last of the Barn owl aristocrats, returning to claim his ancestral territory now that his father, his mother and his brother had been wiped out in the war? Westwood, who had always said he would never claim the land his father left and had wanted to mate with Holly in the springtime of her days. And if it was Westwood, should she mate with him now, for her ailing mother's sake, or should she cling still to her now fading dreams of independence and an education and most of all to her great hope of meeting Hunter once again? As the owl sped closer through the darkness and came almost within vision, her dilemma resolved itself in one final moment of wild panic. 'Oh, please let it be Hunter! Oh, please,' she prayed the God Bird, 'please, please let it be him. Though ours was such a fleeting, brief encounter, I somehow felt as if I'd known him all my life. To talk with him, if only for a few moments before midnight, would give me back my dream again and restore my hopes of a richer, fuller life. Oh, please let it be him!'

But it was not Hunter. To Holly's disappointment and confusion, the owl who emerged from the darkness and landed beside her on the thick branch of the sycamore was none other than Westwood, the owl to whom she had been promised when she was still a fledgling.

'You've changed, Holly,' he said, once they had greeted each other with that shy and awkward reassessment of those who have long been separated and whom time has caused to develop in their different ways.

'You're even prettier than you were before, and very fully fledged as well.'

'That's hardly surprising, is it?' Holly said, attempting to keep the tone between them light and friendly and at least for the moment nothing more. 'It's a long time since we last met.'

'Too long,' said Westwood, edging his big, bony frame closer to her on the branch and staring at her with those bulging eyes and faintly manic stare that she now remembered well.

'You've changed a bit yourself,' she said, leaning backwards as he thrust his tall, clumsy body closer to her on the branch. 'Though you still have that lean and hungry look, as though you'd never eaten well.'

'I'm so glad you're still alive,' said Westwood, staring at her now with that burning intensity she dreaded and had hoped to avoid altogether, or at least delay. 'It's been hard for all of us,' he added, beginning to breathe heavily. 'But in spite of great peril, I have survived, as you can see.'

'And now you've come back to claim your own?' asked Holly. 'It's still all yours, you know. There's no one in the whole valley but for me and mother, and she won't be with us for much longer, I'm very sad to say.'

Westwood looked at her solemnly and then slowly shook his head. 'I'm not coming back,' he said. 'You know how I feel about this place and about my inheritance.'

'I thought you might have changed,' said Holly. 'What with losing your parents, surviving the invasion and growing older, I thought you would have wanted to come back to the old traditions.'

'Oh no, I haven't changed,' said Westwood. 'My beliefs are like a fixed star. I gave up my inheritance for them and I shall continue to dedicate my life to the twin principles that all Barn owls are equal and all Barn owls are free.'

'Aren't we free anyway?' asked Holly. 'Except, of course, for personal commitments. Didn't we enjoy the freedom of the sky at night for centuries before the monster came?'

'No, no!' said Westwood, shaking his head energetically. 'You don't understand, Holly. Like your parents, mine and their ancestors before them, your philosophy is based on primitive owl nature, not on the new dogma and dialectic which will free us all and eventually create unity among the different species.'

'If you say so, Westwood,' Holly murmured, wishing that his eyes would not bulge with such passionate conviction when he spoke of the things that for some reason he had always held most dear. 'But tell me,' she continued, 'if you've not come back here to claim your ancestral land, what is the reason for your visit?'

'To see you again,' said Westwood, with alarming intensity. 'And to ask of you a great favour and a sacrifice. Not for myself, you understand, but for the very survival of our Barn owl species.'

'Ask it then,' said Holly, feeling a flood of generosity flow from the relief that Westwood was not staying and no longer wanted her to mate with him.

'It's a matter of the utmost gravity and essence,' Westwood said. 'To start with you must know that I have been elected leader of the territory where I settled before the invasion and the war.'

'Congratulations,' Holly said. 'A Barn owl usually has to live in a new territory for many springs before he has a chance of being chosen for the council, let alone becoming leader.'

'Exactly,' said Westwood, with a brief, smug smile that faded quickly to an expression of deep dissatisfaction and concern. 'But now that I've been elected leader, a great misfortune has befallen us. A threat to the survival of our local population and perhaps to the future of the entire Barn owl species.'

'Not another monster!' Holly said. 'Don't tell me there's going to be another war.'

'It might be worse than that,' said Westwood, with an almost cadaverous expression on his long and bony face. 'It's something that affects our reproductive systems and interferes with breeding.'

'What do you mean?'

'It's the fledglings,' Westwood said. 'This spring most of the eggs produced so far have had such thin shells that they've cracked before the proper time for hatching. Either that, or else the fledglings were stillborn. And most of those that have been born alive are either feeble or deformed and will almost certainly be too weak to survive the coming winter.'

'How awful!' Holly said. 'I've heard that sometimes happens when the mother hasn't eaten proper food.'

'I've had a survey done,' said Westwood. 'Discreetly, of course, so as not to cause the rest of the population any needless panic. Hardly any of the mothers have eaten anything unusual.'

236

'What is it then?' asked Holly. 'And what are you going to do?'

'First I have to find out if other territories have been affected,' Westwood said. 'I have to find out if this phenomenon is widespread, or if we are the only ones affected.'

'I can't help you there,' said Holly. 'I've told you, no one has bred here since the war.'

'That's the whole point,' Westwood said. 'That's why I've come. To ask you to breed with me.' He stared down at her with his great bulging eyes and as Holly returned his gaze a little thrill of fear shivered up and down her spine.

'To breed and not to mate?' she asked, struggling to clarify the proposal he was making. 'To stay here and have your chicks while you return to play your role as leader?'

'I've already told you,' Westwood said. 'I'm committed to my duty and to the whole community. In the interests of survival, all other Barn owls should be, including you. Even a young female should be prepared to make a sacrifice for the survival of our species.'

'But what good would it do?' asked Holly. 'Even if we bred successfully, it wouldn't prove a thing.'

'It would be a great help,' Westwood said. 'You see, it might not be the food. It might be some kind of disease or sickness that has infected either the males or the females of our species, and that sickness might be only local. If I breed successfully with you, it will help to prove that our females are the ones affected.'

'Of course it won't!' said Holly, her alarm increasing as Westwood edged his bony body closer to her on the branch. 'It could be all the males but you, and in that case you'd have to breed with one or more of your own females to make sure.'

'That is just what I intend to do,' said Westwood, with a pained, heroic expression on his face. 'As leader, it is a sacrifice I have to make.'

'You could delegate,' said Holly, who was growing more and more horrified by the whole affair. 'Being leader doesn't mean you have to make every sacrifice yourself.'

'In this case, I do have to,' Westwood said. 'I must do it myself to avoid spreading needless alarm among the population.'

'Well, I'm sorry, I can't help you,' Holly said. 'I don't want to be used for experimental purposes, and when I breed I want a father for my chicks. You know a female can't rear fledglings on her own. In any case, I'm not ready yet for mating. I want an education and some independence first.'

'You are mature and fully fledged,' said Westwood, beginning to breathe heavily again. 'I appreciate your desire for independence and I totally approve of emancipation for the female owl. In our New Apostasy, there will be no sexual discrimination whatsoever. All owls, male and female, will be equal in every way.'

'But how could I feed them on my own?' asked Holly.

'I would come on frequent visits,' answered Westwood, having now inched her so far down the branch that she was swaying on the end of it and close to falling off. 'If they were not stillborn, I would come here from time to time and help you with their education.'

'My mother wouldn't like it,' said Holly, nearing panic now as he peered down at her with those burning, bulbous eyes. 'She's fading fast and a thing like that would kill her off at once.'

'Your mother doesn't enter into this,' said Westwood. 'It's you I'm asking, Holly. Your mother's much too old to understand these things.'

'Come and talk to her,' said Holly, clutching at any excuse to put a safer distance between herself and Westwood. 'She's so ill and so much alone, it would be a wonderful surprise for her to see you back again.'

'The chicks will cheer her up,' said Westwood. 'They will be a great comfort to her, if they hatch.'

'If they hatch!' cried Holly, her pent-up anger at his proposal finally breaking through the embarrassment and fear. 'And what if they hatch as weaklings, as you say so many have in the territory where you are leader? What if she and I have to watch them fade away and die? Will that cheer her up? Will that make her happy, do you think?'

'You can have all my territory,' Westwood said. 'All the land my father left me in return for this vital experiment.'

'No!' Holly said. 'The idea doesn't appeal to me at all.'

'I could evict you,' Westwood said. 'I won't, of course, but as you said yourself, all this territory still belongs to me by right. Even the bit my father let your parents settle on when they came as refugees from their home that had been swallowed by the spreading city.'

'That's not true!' said Holly, angrily. 'Your father gave this land to mine. The rest is yours, all of this deserted valley between the woodland and the iron tracks. But not our bit. Your father gave it to us, you know he did.'

'It was a favour,' Westwood said. 'He gave you this bit of land so that your parents could breed and provide a home for you. Don't you think it's time you repaid the favour and did something for the survival of the species, too?'

'No, I don't!' said Holly. 'When I was young my parents wanted me to mate with you, and for their sakes I agreed. But I was little more than a fledgling at the time, many moons have passed since then and now I've changed my mind.'

Breathing laboriously, Westwood stared down at her with burning eyes till Holly was terrified that he would throw himself upon her there and then. But somehow he managed to control the raging urge, grunted and brushed his forehead with one weary wing. 'Very well, then,' he said harshly. 'Fly home with me. We can mate there, in the place where I am leader, and afterwards I'll see to it that you get a further education.'

'I can't. Mother's fading fast and I intend to stay with her until the end.'

'All right,' said Westwood, his eyes bulging with frustration as he spoke. 'Come later, when she's dead. You fly north for six nights along the iron tracks. Listen carefully and I'll give you precise directions.'

'Oh, and when you get there, don't ask for Westwood,' he said, when he had finished. 'In the territories where I'm leader, they don't know me by that name.'

'Why not?' asked Holly. 'Your father, your grandfather and all your ancestors were known as Westwood. Why did you have to change?'

'My background does not fit in with the new philosophy,' said Westwood. 'I do not choose for the owls there to know that my ancestors held sway over this valley for so many centuries. It would not be consistent with the message that I preach or with the new dogma and dialectic by which I seek to subdue a primitive breed of owls who hoard and sleep and feed and must be converted to the new philosophy. After all, I gave up my inheritance to bring enlightenment to them.'

'Who shall I ask for, then?' enquired Holly, holding his gaze, though she knew full well that when she did fly north it would not be in search of him.

'Just ask for the leader,' Westwood said, preparing now for take off.

'But you weren't called that in the beginning,' Holly said. 'And if I'm to have a mate and a father for my chicks, I want to know him by his name, not just by his status or his position in society.'

'Very well, then,' Westwood said. 'Just ask for Winger. Winger is my new name and I advise you to learn it well. Like Grumwell, it is a name to be conjured with. It will be remembered in our Barn owl history as the name that marks the beginning of our New Apostasy and the end forever of the ancient, solitary reign.'

With that, Winger took off and as Holly watched the darkness swallow his great white shadow, the tension drained slowly from her taut young body and left her limp and tingling with relief. But it was relief that proved to be short-lived, for when she flew back to the long deserted church in which she had always lived, she found her mother had fallen from the rafters and now lay unconscious and hardly breathing on what had once been the altar before the ancient building had fallen into ruin.

Distraught, Holly landed beside her mother, gazed sadly at the crumpled feathers on her chest and listened to the faint, tortured breathing that told her the end was now much nearer than she had thought. Though there was nothing she could do, Holly sat beside her mother as the night wore on, watching and waiting for the moment that she had been dreading for so long. Well before dawn she realized that after the coming of that dreadful moment, the abandoned church could no longer be her home, and though she was afraid, the memory of Hunter came back to her and shone above the church and the deserted valley like a star of hope. To give her courage in those silent, lonely hours of darkness she dreamed that one day they might meet again. She had no idea of how or where or when, but some day, somewhere, they would perch side by side at twilight and look up together at those other stars that told of so much promise and so many secrets that in time they would learn to share, to cherish and to understand.

CHAPTER
6

For a long time Hunter remembered nothing. When he came to he was at first bewildered and blinked several times before he could be quite certain he was still alive. Then he grew slowly curious about his whereabouts and increasingly concerned about his state of health.

Gingerly, he moved his aching head and looked around him at the inside of the small, wooden barrel in whose belly he had somehow come to rest. There were leaves, grass and twigs at the bottom of the barrel where he lay, and by stretching his sore head he could see upwards through the open top of his coffin-like container towards the sky. He was pleased at first to see the moon and stars, blurred and muffled as they were by a thick yellow haze of city lights and smoke. 'So I'm still here,' he thought, initial relief now tempered by his fear and loathing of the town. Vague, painful memories began to stir and he saw again the cruel eyes of the wild cats he had fought and remembered the sudden blaze of light that had preceded his oblivion. Hard as he tried, he could remember nothing more and so turned his attention once again to his aching head and bones. Tentatively, stretching and twisting in the barrel, he explored his body bit by bit and was overjoyed to find himself quite whole, with many minor aches and pains but nothing really broken.

Filled with a new optimism he stretched his head upwards towards the hazy sky and for the first time saw the bars that would prevent him from flying towards the moon and stars and back to his beloved rural home. Slowly, Hunter sat up straight, peered through one of the small holes that had been punched in the side of the barrel and saw a solid wall. Unable to spread his wings inside the barrel, he began to climb with a growing sense of panic, using strong talons to claw his way up towards the open-ended top. When his head emerged and he looked all around him, he saw to his horror that he had been incarcerated in one of the owl houses belonging to the prison. His barrel was fixed to the wall three feet above the floor and there was another wall in front of him, while the two remaining sides of the cell were enclosed by iron bars through which he himself had peered at the inmates when May Blossom had introduced him to the prison. Behind him, perched on a wooden bar that stretched high across the back wall of the cell, slept the incarcerated Barn owl for whom he had felt such sympathy and sorrow on the occasion of his own brief and terrifying visit.

'The humans must have brought me here,' thought Hunter, who was shocked and filled with mounting horror and revulsion. 'They must have knocked me out and then dumped me in this cell alongside the only other member of my species in the city.'

As Hunter stared upwards at his cellmate with a sort of morbid fascination, the sleeping owl stirred, awoke, blinked twice and then peered down at Hunter with what seemed like merely passing interest. 'Hello,' he said, after looking at him for some time. 'You've come to your senses, then?'

'Partly,' said Hunter, staring round him at the walls and the iron bars on two sides of the cell. 'But seeing where I am, I rather wish I hadn't.'

'How are you feeling?'

'All right,' said Hunter, almost reluctantly. 'There's nothing crushed or broken that I know of.'

'There wouldn't be,' his cellmate said. 'There's another place for sick and badly injured birds. They only bring the well ones to the cells. Oh, by the way,' he added, stifling a healthy sounding yawn. 'My name is Humanoid. What's yours?'

Hunter told him, wondering at the same time what kind of parents could have been so insensitive as to curse their fledgling with such a truly abominable name. 'How long have you been here?' asked Hunter, pulling himself right out of the barrel now and perching on its rim.

'Oh, for a long time,' Humanoid replied. 'For almost half a lifetime, you might say.'

'How awful!' Hunter said, and then froze as the most bloodcurdling cry that he had ever heard burst from one of the gigantic foreign owls imprisoned in the neighbouring cell. 'How have you survived?' he continued, as the dreadful howl died vibrantly away. 'How have you kept your health and sanity, surrounded by man and by monsters like the one that we've just heard?'

'That's a long story,' said Humanoid. 'I'll tell you in the daytime. At night, in this place, you must learn to get a little sleep.'

'Sleep at night?' asked Hunter, puzzled. 'Why not in the day?'

'You'll see tomorrow,' said his cellmate. 'After one day here, you won't need an explanation, I can promise that! Sleep now, while you can. We'll talk in the daytime when the men keep us awake.'

Hunter looked up at Humanoid in sorrow and bewilderment, but the older owl merely shifted on his perch, rested his head on one sloping shoulder and dropped off at once into a deep, untroubled sleep.

Hunter looked around him once again and listened, growing more and more aware of the other owls imprisoned in their neighbouring cells. Their signals, coupled with the proximity of so many other unknown birds and animals, filled Hunter with a dreadful blend of claustrophobia and despair. Slowly, he let himself slide down to the bottom of his barrel and lay there crumpled and huddled in a ball, unable to think or react to his cruel fate until at last, when the murmur of the waking metropolis grew into a mighty rumbling that heralded the break of day, he dozed off at last into fitful and unhappy sleep.

When he stirred again to full consciousness it was to find the sun already high and the foul city air around him loud with a cacophony of sounds from the imprisoned birds and animals who had been steadily awakening since the early dawn. Humanoid was already wide awake, still perched on his wooden bar but blinking now with pregnant interest into the morning light as if he expected something of importance to occur from one second to the next. Sure enough, before Hunter had had time to realize what was happening, two men appeared beyond the iron grille and opened the door of the owl house on their right. 'They feed the Tawnies first,' said Humanoid. 'It will be our turn next.'

Terrified, Hunter slipped to the bottom of his barrel and listened to the men stomping and clanging in the next door cell. He had never had a man so close before – at least, not while he was conscious – and the thought that one or both of them would soon be within striking distance made him feel quite faint with fear. Soon, all too soon, he heard another loud clang as their cell door opened and almost at once the light above his head was blotted out by a looming human head. As Hunter stared upwards in horror, the head turned sideways and uttered odd, unmelodious human noises, whereupon a second head appeared beside the first and stared down into Hunter's barrel. Then two big arms were thrust inside the barrel and began to reach downwards to the bottom.

As Hunter rose to attack the descending arms and sell his life as dearly as he could, he heard Humanoid call out loud and clear from his perch on the bar above the humans' heads. 'Don't fight!' he shouted. 'They won't hurt you. Let yourself be lifted up and held.'

But as two strong hands seized Hunter's wings and pinned them to his sides, he ignored his cellmate's warning and drove his bill hard into the nearest arm, whilst at the same time trying desperately to bring his talons up into the attack. Though the man emitted a strange human grunt, he did not let go but pulled Hunter clear of the barrel and turned him round so that his head and dangerous bill faced away from the hands and arms that held him. Furious, Hunter turned his head right round, as only owls know how, and struck out as best he could, though this time without the angle or the force to hurt the man who held him.

'Don't attack!' shouted Humanoid again. 'They won't hurt you. They want to see if you're all right.' Powerless in the hands that gripped him, Hunter's whole body shook and throbbed with rage. The shame and humiliation of being manhandled in this way was so great that it took his breath away, and when the man holding him suddenly let go he was obliged to flap his wings in a frantic, undignified manner to stop himself from falling. He fluttered there, seething with anger and impotence, and then with a mammoth effort managed to control his rage and instead of attacking those who had defiled him, he flew up to the wooden bar, landed beside Humanoid and let out an indignant and frustrated little gasp.

The two men looked up at him and uttered more of their strange human noises. Then the one who had held Hunter moved to the door of the owl house, opened it and left, while the other plunged one hand into a bucket he had brought with him and then strewed the floor of the owl house with the dead bodies of half a dozen day-old chicks.

'You see?' said Humanoid, when the second man had left. 'I said they wouldn't harm you. They only come in here to clean the cell and bring us food.' At first, Hunter was too shocked by his experience to answer but eventually he pulled himself together and nodded downwards at the ugly little corpses of the day-old chicks.

'Food?' he said, contemptuously. 'You call that food? No self-respecting Barn owl will eat carrion and those wretched little chicks look to me as though they've been a long time dead.'

'Oh well, it's all you'll get,' said Humanoid philosophically. 'Except for the odd mouse as an extra treat, but even then they're always cold and dead.'

'Horrible!' said Hunter, with an outraged little shudder. 'Barn owls feeding on dead meat, like some common rook or crow!'

'You'll get used to it in time,' said Humanoid. 'In fact, to survive in this place you must become accustomed to many seemingly unnatural things, and quickly, too. Otherwise you lose your mind, or starve. Or both.'

'Or die of sorrow and despair,' said Hunter. 'The way I'm feeling at the moment, that seems a very likely end.'

'There is a high rate of mortality among the prisoners,' admitted Humanoid. 'And for some reason it seems highest among Barn owls like ourselves.'

At that moment Hunter's attention was distracted by a great mass of movement outside their cell and to his horror he saw a crowd of humans converging on them from behind another prison building which contained some great catlike creature that Hunter had never encountered in the wild. 'Look, Humanoid,' he said, in a voice that was hardly louder than a whisper. 'Look at all those men!'

'Oh yes,' replied his cellmate, with a casual little yawn. 'They always let them in about this time. If you don't mind, I'll get my breakfast now. Although I'm quite used to humans, I still don't like strange ones peering at me while I eat. If I were you, I'd fly down with me and do the same.'

'I can't face it,' said Hunter, to whom the thought of eating carrion while being gaped at by a gang of humans was the ultimate in degradation. 'I can't eat, Humanoid. You're welcome to my share as well.'

'Well, I'll leave two dead chicks for you, anyway,' said his cellmate casually. 'You never know, you might feel hungry before they bring more food this afternoon.'

With that, Humanoid flew down from his perch and began to devour the dead chicks as if they were a delicacy like mole that he had hunted, caught and had the beauty of hot. Hunter watched with a mixture of revulsion and amazement as his cellmate polished off three chicks, paused before the fourth and then swallowed that as well, remaining entirely unabashed as the first of the humans arrived outside the cell and began to point ánd cackle through the bars. Humanoid merely cocked his head on one side and looked at them with familiar unconcern before taking off again and flying up in a leisurely manner to his perch beside Hunter on the wooden pole.

Astonished, but not quite so frightened as before, Hunter watched while the first of the humans moved on and others came to take their place. A few peered in and muttered in their strange human mumbo-jumbo, whilst others merely glanced up at them and walked on by.

'Not many stay and look at us for long,' said Humanoid, as if he had read his cellmate's thoughts. 'Most of them are more interested in the great big foreign owls in the next cell.'

'Who are they?' asked Hunter, who had already noticed that the majority of humans seemed more interested in the owl on their left than in the Tawnies, Humanoid or him, and whilst he despised all humans and held them in contempt, he was still peeved that some foreign owl merited more attention than he did himself.

'I don't know who they are or where they're from,' said Humanoid in the bland indifferent tone he always seemed to use when discussing other owls. 'To tell you the truth, I can't understand a single word they say. But I do know that the male is very fierce and the female's great with eggs. So great, in fact, that I imagine the chicks will be out at any moment.'

'Is that what they do?' asked Hunter, in surprise. 'The men, I mean. Do they normally put a male and female of the species together in a cell?'

'They do, indeed,' said Humanoid. 'The men seem to encourage breeding in captivity, though exactly why I cannot tell.'

'You mentioned a high rate of mortality,' said Hunter. 'Perhaps they want to encourage the inmates here to maintain the prison population?'

'Perhaps,' said Humanoid. 'After all, it's true that in the wild owls of all species must be very hard to catch.'

'But why catch us at all?' asked Hunter, turning to his older companion with a puzzled frown. 'And why create this dreadful prison in the first place?'

246

'I don't know,' said Humanoid, speaking slowly and gravely as he pondered. 'I have my theories, but though I probably know more about men than any other living owl, I still can't be quite sure.'

'I can't see any sense in it,' said Hunter, who was surprised by the boastful claim his cellmate had just made. 'I mean, we owls are the oldest and certainly the highest form of life on earth, yet we don't incarcerate whole colonies of men, mice, bats, crows or any other kind of living creature. And if the humans do want us to breed in captivity, why have they put you and me in here together? Don't they know that we're both males? Perhaps they just pick two owls at random and then hope for the best.'

'I'm afraid it's my fault we're together,' said Humanoid, looking away from Hunter in what seemed like sadness, embarrassment or both. 'They put female Barn owls in with me before,' he added quickly, still looking away from Hunter in the direction of the Tawny cell next door. 'They tried three times, but nothing ever happened, so I suppose by now they've simply given up on me.'

'It must be very difficult,' said Hunter, feeling a surge of embarrassment for Humanoid's predicament. 'I mean, one can't just mate with any female, can one? There has to be mutual attraction, compatibility and all that sort of thing.'

'I'm afraid that, in my case, it's rather more than that,' said Humanoid, turning back to Hunter, who was now feeling mortified and wishing that he had never brought the subject up. What on earth did he mean by something more than that? Had he had some sort of accident or sickness, or – and Hunter felt a sudden rush of panic at the thought – or, oh dreadful to conjecture, was he like Bardic and certain other owls he had heard of who for some reason preferred male partners and could not mate with owls of the other sex? By some irony of fate, had he been shut up in a cell with one of those?

'There are good reasons for it, but the fact is I don't feel the urge for female owls at all,' said Humanoid, immediately echoing Hunter's worst suspicions. 'In some ways it's unfortunate, I admit. Or at least, it was unfortunate for the three unhappy females who were imprisoned here with me. Mating and breeding would have at least given them some motive for survival, some reason to go on living in these cramped, unnatural surroundings.'

'What happened to them?' asked Hunter.

'They pined away,' said Humanoid. 'One by one they gave up hope, succumbed to captivity and died.'

'Does the same fate await me, do you think?' asked Hunter, who was shocked and anxious to make it plain in a firm but tactful way that there was no chance of his entering into an unnatural relationship with his cellmate.

'I'm afraid so,' said Humanoid, with a sad little sigh of resignation. 'Unless you can adapt to these conditions and then find some reason to go on living, I'm afraid it's quite likely that you'll simply fade away and die.'

They sat in silence for some time while Hunter let the terrible reality sink in. Then he glanced up at Humanoid, wondering what it was about his cellmate that made him so different from any other owl he had ever met. Was it because he could not mate with females? But surely that would not explain the curious way he spoke. His discourse was slightly hesitant yet almost too perfect, too correct, as if he had learned it as a second language and therefore formulated the words with an effort, from the head, and not with the spontaneous earthiness that springs from the belly or the heart. But most of all, Hunter wondered at how well he looked, for though smaller and less powerful than the average Barn owl, Humanoid seemed very spritely still and was clearly in the best of health.

'How have you managed to survive for all this time?' Hunter asked, eventually. 'What reason have you found to go on living in a place like this?'

'It's different for me,' said Humanoid. 'I told you that before. For me, prison is not really so different from my natural habitat.'

'How can that be?' asked Hunter, irritated by the obscurity of Humanoid's reply. 'Captivity can never provide a natural environment for any kind of owl. None of us was ever conditioned for survival in such a place as this.'

'I was, in a way,' his companion said quietly. 'In a manner of speaking, I was brought up in captivity, though since I knew nothing else, I never thought of it that way.'

'I don't understand,' said Hunter. 'You weren't born here, were you?'

'No, but when I was a fledgling I fell out of the nest. I must have been very tiny because I have no recollection of my father, my mother or of the place where I was born. My first memory is of a female human feeding me a cold, dead, day-old chick just like those two down there on the ground.'

'A female human?' asked Hunter, in amazement. 'You mean a female picked up the chick for you and fed you with her mouth?'

'Not exactly with her mouth. She did it with a sort of instrument. The same type of thing they use to feed themselves.'

'I wouldn't know,' said Hunter, with a stunned shake of his head. 'Where did this human feed you? Where you had fallen, outside on the ground?'

'Oh no,' said Humanoid. 'She kept me where she lived, inside her house.'

'And you grew up there?' asked Hunter. 'She fed you till you were strong enough to fly away?'

'For much, much longer,' answered Humanoid, with a sad expression of nostalgia on his face. 'I stayed there for a long time, until after I'd first felt the urge.'

'So she trapped you there?' said Hunter. 'She kept you in a sort of prison, like this one, only smaller?'

'No,' said Humanoid. 'She didn't keep me there against my will. I chose to stay myself.'

'Why?' asked Hunter, whose imagination had made a tremendous effort to picture the whole thing and miserably failed.

'Because I loved her,' said Humanoid, with great simplicity. 'To all intents and purposes she became the mother that I'd never known. She fed me, she cared for me, she gave me security and so naturally I stayed.'

'Naturally!' said Hunter. 'Forgive me, Humanoid, but to a normal owl like me the word seems out of place.'

'Naturally? Yes, to someone with your background, I suppose the idea of cohabiting with humans must seem rather strange. To you the city is not natural, but it is here! To you, the foreign owls and the strange animals whose cries we hear are not normal, and yet I assure you that they're very, very real. You rustic owls imagine that the world ends beyond the borders of the meadows, fields and woodlands where you live, but in fact there are more things and places in the world than you or I have ever dreamed of. It's good to remember that sometimes. It's a concept that will help you learn humility.'

Shocked and chastened, Hunter said nothing in reply but fell to thinking about the story he had just heard. Humanoid took no further notice of him but peered down through the cell bars at the passing humans. Some of these seemed to stimulate great interest in him, so that he stiffened on his perch and stared hard at them, whilst others seemed to leave him cold. Watching, Hunter wondered why this should be the case and what it was about certain individuals that seemed to evoke such an excited reaction from his cellmate.

The day wore on, the warders returned with more dead chicks and once more the cold and clammy corpses filled Hunter with revulsion. Although he was ravenously hungry, he could not bring himself to eat. Forced to stay awake all day, Hunter was exhausted by the time the shadows began to lengthen and the light began to fade.

Not long after the last of the human visitors had left the prison, Humanoid began to question him about his past and as the darkness deepened and the roar of the city faded to a distant, intermittent rumble, Hunter gave him a brief synopsis of the story of his life. As soon as he had finished, Humanoid yawned, said goodnight and promptly fell asleep, leaving Hunter worn-out but wide-awake and dreading the weary hours of darkness that lay ahead.

His was to be a slow death, he realized with bitter sadness and regret. A long-drawn-out and lingering decline, not a quick, heroic end like his father and his comrades who had fallen in the war. Not a young owl's death like the one he had always hoped for, but a slow drifting into premature senility – a gradual rotting of the brain and body brought about by pollution and captivity, but fostered most of all by sorrow and despair.

As the weary night dragged by, Hunter sought for comfort in the remembrance of time past, but every image that he conjured of his beloved countryside brought with it a vision of transience and death. He saw the long grass scythed down and dying in the fragrance of new-mown hay. He saw the spring flowers wither and give way as the sun burned the corn from gold to burnished copper, and then saw the corn fall, too, in the heat and dust of harvest time. He saw the leaves rotting in the swirling autumn mist and felt the first bitter frost that killed the last living berries in the hedge, just as his captivity would surely but more slowly put an end to him. Even the memory of Holly, whom he had met only briefly, but long enough to know that one day they might share a dream, was now rendered sad and bittersweet and relegated to one of the many things that might have been.

As he dozed off at last, the only living thing that still warmed the bleak midwinter of his vision was the love that he had once shared with little Alba among the mysteries of the lost domain and in the shelter of the abandoned farmhouse where he had found peace and independence and where he knew now he would never return again. And the one faint hope that soothed his troubled dreams was one he dared not cherish in his hours of waking. Namely, that Dapple had been right and that he would meet his little sweetheart once again in the place where he would soon be going.

CHAPTER 7

The next day Hunter forced himself to swallow one dead chick, and by the end of his first week in prison he had conquered his revulsion sufficiently to manage two. But this was still only half the food he needed, and as time went by he lost weight and slowly weakened. Gradually, his wings and limbs lost all their spring, his feathers grew dowdy and dishevelled, his eyes turned inward as he pined and soon lost all the bright lustre of a Barn owl in his prime.

As time went by, he ceased to converse with Humanoid, limiting his answers to a monosyllable or a phrase at most. He no longer watched the passing humans in the daytime or heeded the mournful night-time cries of the prisoners in their cells, but sought nourishment only in memories of the past and in the evocation of his much-loved rustic home.

High summer came and went in the stifling, airless city and Hunter tried to conjure scenes of the coming season in the country, knowing that he would never again fly above the hedgerows when the blackberries began to ripen, or perch with Yoller on the willow branch and watch the leaves fade from green to russet brown and then drift down to be buried slowly by the acrid earth beneath.

'At this rate, you'll soon be dead,' announced Humanoid, early one twilight as the autumn days were drawing in. 'If you don't soon find some reason to go on living, you'll simply fade away.'

'That's the problem,' agreed Hunter. 'The Tawnies have a proverb which says "better one day as an eagle than twenty thousand as a rat" and as far as I'm concerned, they're right. I'd give anything just for one day's solitary soaring over woodland or open country, or even among the dangers of the lost domain. As it is, stuck here in this cell, I might as well be dead.'

'Well, you'd better find a reason to go on living very soon,' said Humanoid. 'I don't want a fourth dead Barn owl in my cell, or the men will begin to think I carry some disease.'

'What reason did you find?' asked Hunter, who was anxious to return to the solace of the past and the remembered glories of the wild country that had once been his.

'My studies,' answered Humanoid. 'In single-minded dedication to my subject, I found a reason to go on.'

'In your Human Studies?' Hunter asked. 'Or more widely, in the general search for knowledge?'

'In my speciality, of course,' said Humanoid. 'Total concentration on your subject is the only way to intellectual excellence. If you fail to achieve this single-minded dedication, you will become a mediocre owl who hoards and covets like the rest and who can never know the joy and satisfaction that pure science brings. Too many owls forget this as they grow older and degenerate into creatures scarcely better than a starling or a crow. Of course, as a mature student you would find it hard to adapt to a strict curriculum. You would find it more difficult than a younger acolyte to give up things of the flesh, such as the desire for certain kinds of food, for comfortable, secluded quarters and, of course, the urge. Tell me, do you often feel the urge?'

'From time to time,' said Hunter cautiously. 'But I suppose that's normal, since I've long been old enough to mate.'

'Normal!' exclaimed Humanoid, turning his bright gaze away from Hunter and out into the murky darkness that was still smudged with a haze of yellow light. 'There you go again, with your natural and your normal! Just what is normal, can you tell me that?'

'The urge is,' answered Hunter, speaking calmly, though he feared that his worst suspicions about Humanoid were about to be confirmed.

'Yes, but for whom, or what?' asked the older owl, turning his penetrating gaze to Hunter, who was desperately trying to think of a polite way to rebuff him when the moment came, though he knew this would be very difficult because he had never before been propositioned by an owl who wanted to mate with one of his own sex.

'The urge can manifest itself in many ways,' said Humanoid, still fixing Hunter with the full intensity of his bright stare. 'Ambition, greed, politics, religion – an owl can sublimate the urge in the pursuit of many different things. And the wrong choice can mean disaster.'

'But why should an owl sublimate the urge in any other but the natural way,' said Hunter, remembering Holly's lilting voice and lovely little hips. 'Why can't it just be the urge, all by itself, and quite separate from all those other things?'

'Because it is a curse!' said Humanoid, with passionate conviction. 'If you cannot control it, or sublimate it in some other way, it will destroy you before you reach the ripeness of your days. Coupling, finding a home and getting food for chicks are all fatal for one who wishes to pursue pure knowledge. And in any case, there aren't any female owls in here. In my opinion, the only hope you have is to take advantage of this unique opportunity, eschew things of the flesh and dedicate yourself to higher education.'

'How?' asked Hunter, somewhat ungraciously. 'I can hardly study owls in here.'

'Why not? That female Tawny did, and you're surrounded here by more species than you could ever hope to meet elsewhere.'

'May Blossom? But she wasn't trapped inside a cell like I am. And even if I could talk to them, I wouldn't understand a single word they said.'

'There is an alternative to owlology,' said Humanoid. 'There's something you could study without stirring from this cell.'

'Humans?' asked Hunter, not sounding in the least bit enthusiastic.

'Of course!' said Humanoid. 'You are surrounded by them all the time. I can think of no better opportunity than here.'

'But I'd be very difficult to teach,' said Hunter. 'I'm not in the least interested in man, so somehow or other I'd need to be inspired.'

'I don't know about inspire,' said Humanoid. 'No one can teach successfully unless the student really wants to learn. And knowledge of the subject doesn't necessarily make a teacher, either, although I'm an experienced pedagogue as well. You see, I was once Man Owl on our local council.'

'Where?' asked Hunter, whose interest was suddenly awoken on hearing that his cellmate's life had not been spent entirely with man.

'Not far from here,' the older owl replied. 'In what was once the first truly rural territory to the north of this great city. From what you've told

254

me, it's even possible that you flew across it on the way here with your Tawny friend.'

'I assumed you'd always lived with humans till you came here to the prison.'

'I didn't come here voluntarily,' said Humanoid. 'Like you, I was shut up in here against my will.'

'I don't understand,' said Hunter. 'You told me you chose to stay with the female human who adopted you.'

'I did,' said Humanoid. 'I would have stayed with her forever, but one day she betrayed me.'

'How?' asked Hunter, who did not see how on earth a human could betray an owl, any more than an owl could betray a fox, a sparrow or a horse.

'One day she put me in a box,' said the older owl, as his breast heaved suddenly and his face contorted with remembered pain.

'A box!' said Hunter. 'But why did you let her? Surely you were strong and fully grown by then?'

'I loved her,' said Humanoid, almost choking with emotion as he spoke. 'I let her do anything. I thought it was some kind of game. She and her mate took the box to their machine and carried me two hundred meadows' distance, to the first rural territory outside the town. Then they opened the box and let me out. I was so frightened and indignant that I flew up at once into the branches of a nearby sycamore. They watched me for a moment or two and then got back into the machine, which immediately moved away. I was suffering from shock and it took me some time to realize exactly what was happening. By the time I flew after them, it was much too late and the machine had disappeared. I was betrayed, abandoned and I nearly died,' continued Humanoid bitterly, his breast heaving as he attempted to keep control of his emotions. 'I had no education and no training. I didn't even know the words. Not only the Barn owl credo, but any words at all. The only thing I knew about was man.'

'So what did you do?' asked Hunter, who had now become quite interested in the miracle of Humanoid's survival and in any case deemed it better to go on talking and thus distract his cellmate from the memory of his betrayal.

'I flew back again,' said Humanoid. 'I flew back to the house where I'd grown up with my human mother.'

'But how did you find it?' asked Hunter in amazement.

'Oh, I don't know. Homing instinct, I suppose.'

'And what happened when you got there?' Hunter asked. 'Were they pleased to see you back?'

'They'd gone away,' said Humanoid, with a sad shake of his head. 'They'd moved. There was another family of humans living there, but the new ones were afraid of me. At twilight I plucked up courage and flew in through the window, but the older male and female were terrified, so I flew out again. When I tried again at daybreak the windows were all closed and they wouldn't let me in.'

'What did you eat?' asked Hunter. 'By this time you must have been on the point of starving.'

'I ate some little sparrows,' said Humanoid, with a pained expression of distaste. 'It was late spring, they were still fledglings and therefore not very hard to catch. Then I perched in the chestnut tree at the bottom of the garden and waited to see whether these new humans would stay or go away again. After all, I was there first, so it was my territory more than it was theirs. But that evening the young female came out into the garden and that was when it happened! Though I did try later, that's when I first found out that I could never lead a normal life.'

'What do you mean?' asked Hunter, looking very puzzled.

'I got the urge,' said Humanoid.

'The urge?' asked Hunter. 'Why, was there a female Barn owl passing by?'

'No, I got the urge for this human female. I called to her, she looked up to the tree where I was sitting and answered back.'

'But you can't feel the urge for female humans!' said Hunter, who found this story quite unbelievable and also most offensive. 'It's impossible,' he said, rejecting the whole concept. 'You can't feel the urge for anyone but a female of your species.'

'Can't you? Then how do you explain your feelings for that little immigrant? And what about those males who feel the urge for owls of their own sex? I suppose that up to now you suspected that I was one of those?'

'That's different,' Hunter said. 'At least little Alba was an owl, and however unnatural it may seem for male owls to fancy one another, it's been going on for centuries. But a female human! I simply don't believe it. It's like telling me you felt the urge for a crow, a kestrel or a fox.'

'It was the urge all right,' said Humanoid, who seemed to be taking some sort of perverse satisfaction in telling Hunter this lewd and most disgusting story. 'In fact, after I'd called and she'd answered me, I flew down from the tree and tried to get closer to her.'

Horrified, Hunter sat back on his perch and boggled at Humanoid in speechless disbelief, whilst struggling to decide whether his cellmate was a dangerous maniac or merely a lost and helpless mutant deserving of his pity.

'How was I to know?' asked Humanoid, who seemed stubbornly determined to continue his vile confession to the end. 'It's called implant and it can happen to creatures of any species, animal or bird. If you take a duckling from its nest and put it with a hen, it will think the hen's its mother. Worse than that, as it grows up it will think that it's a chicken, not a duck. Only much later, when the time comes for him to mate will he realize he was wrong.'

'What did the female do when you flew down?' asked Hunter, hoping that his cellmate would have the tact to spare him any lurid detail.

'She screamed and ran back to the house,' said Humanoid. 'She wouldn't even let me touch her. It was the first time I'd had the urge. I was hurt and frustrated, as you must have been with your little immigrant.'

Trying to be fair, Hunter rocked slowly on his perch, thought of little Alba and winced when he remembered the pain he had felt when she refused to mate with him. He remembered the agony and the frustrated rage which had caused him to attack and kill the kestrel and realized that even if Humanoid had suffered only half as much, his was still an ordeal worthy of compassion and respect.

'I'm sorry,' he said, gently. 'Tell me, what happened next?'

'I went back to the wild. I flew back to the place where my human mother had abandoned me. It was my only point of reference. And though I didn't know the hardest lesson then, it did occur to me that my mother would have chosen a place where there was a chance I might survive. After my first unfortunate experience, I realized she might have known that no human female would ever feel the urge for me and that my only hope of happiness lay in returning to the wild and learning to become a normal owl.'

'And did you learn?' asked Hunter, doubtfully, for there was still a strange otherworldliness about the Man Owl that had bothered him from the beginning.

'I tried,' said Humanoid. 'I soon learned to hunt and to eat small animals instead of birds, and I eventually adapted to that mystic quiet and solitude of the countryside, that deep slow peace of hidden copse and meadow that you long for and you love so well. And in a way, I was lucky. The leader of the local council was obsessed by man. He was afraid that what you call the asphalt blight would one day spread so far as to engulf the rural district where we lived. So as soon as I had learned to understand and speak, he made me Man Owl on the council. That way I was able to pursue my Human Studies to the exclusion of all else.'

'But how did you get into prison?' Hunter asked. 'You told me you'd spent half a lifetime here.'

'Our leader was right,' said Humanoid. 'Bit by bit our territory disappeared, slowly swallowed by the flood of the ever-spreading city. The other owls all emigrated to the north in search of virgin countryside, but I stayed where I was. It was partly the lure of human females, I suppose. That and my work. It's much easier to study humans when you're living in their midst. I stayed on as the fields and meadows were wiped out by the flood of buildings and until the only green place left was a big park like this one round the prison. I made my home there, in the hollow of a dying elm and went back to eating starlings, pigeons and any other town food I could find. From this hiding place, in the very middle of his territory, I tried to study man. And every twilight, I flew out in search of my ideal female human. You must understand that most of all it was love and affection that I craved. I was alone. I'd lost my mother and her mate, who were my only friends.'

'Did you find one?' Hunter asked. 'Did you find a female human you could love?'

'I found several,' said Humanoid, with a sad, nostalgic little sigh. 'At nightfall, gliding through the parkland, the gardens and the quiet, tree-lined roads I saw many human females. Only a few of them attracted me, but whenever I flew down to make contact their reaction was the same. They screamed and ran away. Night after night I searched, between sunset and midnight, when most of the humans go to sleep. Then, early one summer, a man tried to kill me with a firestick. Three nights later, in the same place, he tried again. Not long after that they traced me to the elm tree in the park and trapped me in a net. They fed me and then the next day they brought me here. Again I was lucky I suppose. They could easily have killed me, but instead they locked me up in here.'

'What an amazing story!' said Hunter, who was still not sure whether to believe it all or not.

'I've never told it all to anyone before, especially not the bit about the female humans. I feel it's done me good to get it off my chest. I only wish I'd dared to tell the three female owls they put in here with me. If they'd known the truth, they might not have pined away and died.'

'I'll try,' said Hunter, making a spontaneous decision, more with a view to helping Humanoid than in any real hope of delaying his own slow drift into decrepitude and death.

'I'll be your prison pupil, if you'll have me. But I warn you, I'm an absolute beginner. I know nothing about humans, though I suppose I'm one of the few owls ever to have lived in an abandoned house. In spite of this, in spite of my journey to the city and of the time I've spent here in this cell, I know absolutely nothing. I don't understand their body language or the noises that they make. I can't even tell their sex.'

'That doesn't matter,' answered Humanoid. 'What does matter is that here, with me, you will concentrate exclusively on man. Other owls, birds, animals, religion or any kind of dogma will be absolutely no concern of ours. I am an expert, the greatest living expert, and with me you will concentrate entirely on your subject. Is that clear?'

'I suppose so,' said Hunter, reluctantly. 'But after all, I am an owl, and that is a fact I may sometimes find difficult to forget.'

'You must try,' said Humanoid. 'I repeat that total concentration is the only way. We will begin at once. We'll work all night and every night. That way we'll both take to sleeping in the day which will be good for your health and your appetite. All we need to do is to wake up twice to eat. And it will stop me from the torment of ogling human females that I can never reach.'

So they started, and on that first short night Hunter learned so many new and utterly surprising things that he thought his poor, overloaded brain would burst.

As the city came to life again and the predawn rumble swelled into the thunder of a bright autumn day, Humanoid at last stopped teaching and promptly fell into a deep, exhausted sleep. Before sinking into weary oblivion himself, Hunter snatched at one last waking thought which made him smile in grim and bitter irony. Though this learning process could neither set him free nor do more than stretch his life out for a little longer, it at least meant that he would die a great expert, unknown, forgotten and unsung, but armed at last with rare and priceless knowledge that he would never, ever be able to use or to transmit.

CHAPTER 8

Time passed more quickly after Hunter had made his big decision and for a long time he was so deeply committed to his new course of study that the last streaks of snow had melted from the park outside the prison before his enthusiasm began to flag and in his heart of hearts he realized that the experiment had failed.

'How can I ever tell him?' Hunter wondered as he sat awake and worried on the wooden pole after Humanoid had fallen peacefully asleep before the breaking of that first spring dawn. 'How shall I ever dare tell him that commitment to Human Studies and to the pure quest for knowledge will never be enough for me? That I dread everything connected with these wretched humans who reared him and by whom he is so utterly obsessed? With or without him, I must escape from here,' Hunter decided as the faint hum of the city swelled into a throb and then a mighty roar. 'I shall continue to work with Humanoid, but from now on escape will be my first priority. I don't know how, when or if ever, but in the meantime I will eat more, take more exercise and study till I find a way.'

Hunter stayed awake until the sun had risen high and as the sap rose in the warm spring breeze he saw the brown stained wallflowers spring to life outside his cell and dreamed of flight to distant valleys and to woodland in rich array of blossom where bees would soon awake and buzz round the dozing cuckoo in his hollow tree. That night he found it hard to concentrate and shortly before daybreak Humanoid broke off the lesson to offer his first praise and encouragement since their course of lessons had begun.

'You're learning very fast,' he said. 'Though you're obviously tiring now and still only at what I'd call an intermediate stage, I must say that you're one of the quickest students that I've ever taught.'

'I still mix the sexes up,' said Hunter. 'Hard as I've been trying, I just can't seem to get it right.'

'It's no wonder,' Humanoid replied. 'Since the beginning of their war, male and female plumage has grown more and more alike.'

'But you don't make mistakes,' said Hunter. 'You can distinguish every time.'

'With me it's second nature,' the Man Owl replied. 'I grew up with them, remember?'

'And their plumage is another thing,' said Hunter. 'I still don't understand how they can put it on in the morning and take it off at night.'

'That's because you've never seen them do it,' said Humanoid.

'And the war you've just mentioned,' Hunter said. 'The human war I mean, not ours. If the enemy men wanted to move into this territory, why did they make fire fall from the sky and try to burn it down?'

'I don't know. But men are destructive creatures. Even when there is no war, they're always busy pulling things down and then putting them back up again. In that respect, they're more like ants than owls.'

'The Tawnies say we live too close to them. They say it will be our downfall in the end.'

'It's possible,' admitted Humanoid. 'I've taught you about pollution and contamination which to us are far more dangerous than their wars because they can change the environment in which we live. In my view, men are a transient species and will eventually destroy themselves. But if we are to survive we must learn more about them and learn to adapt to what they are doing. Though a young, upstart form of life, they learn very fast. Much faster than we owls do. I mean, what's the use of having twelve million years of history behind us if we haven't yet discovered a way of recording information?'

'Recording information?' Hunter asked. 'Can men do that?'

'They can,' said Humanoid. 'Somehow they have invented artificial memories and that is the secret of their power.'

'You mean they don't have to remember everything by heart?'

'Exactly! Just think how much more knowledge we could store if we weren't limited to the memory of each individual brain.'

'And how do they do it?' Hunter asked. 'If we knew, perhaps we could copy them.'

'I don't know for certain,' admitted Humanoid. 'But it may be connected with the talking boxes they have in their homes and sometimes carry round with them. You've seen men with them here inside the prison. You've heard the boxes speaking, singing and making human music. That may be one of their artificial memories, or it may be a way they have of communicating with their dead.'

'But how can they speak or make music if they're dead?'

'I know nothing yet,' admitted Humanoid. 'But I'm determined to get there in the end. And then we Barn owls will have discovered the greatest secret ever known. A secret that will help our species to gain ascendancy over all other forms of life, including man.'

'But how can you discover these secrets unless you get outside?' asked Hunter. 'And what good will all this knowledge do us if we're stuck here in this prison? Have no prisoners ever escaped from here?'

'To my knowledge, only once. But that was in the war.'

'How did they do it?' Hunter asked, experiencing a sudden surge of hope.

'There was an explosion. Fire fell from the sky, part of the prison was on fire and several birds escaped in the confusion.'

'Any owls among them?' asked Hunter eagerly.

'Only one. An Eagle owl. He was a real monster, one of the fiercest birds I've ever seen.'

'And do you think there'll be another war?' asked Hunter. 'Will fire fall from the sky again?'

'I hope not,' answered Humanoid. 'The Eagle owl escaped, but several others were burned to cinders in their cells. There was confusion everywhere and for some time no warders came to feed us. Personally, I should not care for a repeat performance.'

'Confusion,' said Hunter, grasping at the concept eagerly. 'The men were confused and so some prisoners were able to escape. What else causes confusion among men, apart from fire falling from the sky?'

'In this prison, nothing,' said Humanoid, after thinking carefully for a while. 'In the house where I grew up with humans there was confusion when the male and female mated, and even more so when they had a quarrel. And with the fledglings, of course. Fledglings nearly always cause confusion.'

'And they never mate or quarrel here?' asked Hunter, sounding disappointed.

'There are no female warders now,' said Humanoid, shaking his head sadly. 'We had some in the war, but then they disappeared. Take my advice, Hunter, and forget it. There's no escape from here. And in any case, why bother? You get fed twice a day. There are no dangers here and ample opportunities for education. If you did escape, and even if you did find your way back to the wild and to the distant rural territory you say you love so well, you'd find that everything had changed. Nothing would be exactly the same as you remembered it. Remember the hardest lesson. You can't go home again.'

'But your research,' said Hunter. 'To track down the secret of the artificial memory, you must get out of here some day.'

At this mention of his main objective, a gleam lit up in Humanoid's bright, penetrating eyes. 'There is another reason,' he said slowly. 'Another reason why I need to get outside, but at the same time a reason why I'm much safer shut away in here.'

'Why's that?' asked Hunter, sensing that after a long period of acting strictly as his tutor, Humanoid was about to revert to their personal relationship in order to unburden himself of yet another shocking secret.

'The urge!' said Humanoid. 'I've tried hard to suppress it, and for long periods I've succeeded. But now the spring is here and it's come back again. And it's not for Barn owls but for human females that I feel it. It's a torment to see them staring at me through those iron bars. Some gaze at me with tender eyes and I know they'd like to touch me if they could. Outside this cell the temptation would be too strong for me. I'd try to get close to one, she'd scream and run away and then one of the males would fetch a firestick and destroy me. No, I must stay here and continue my research as best I can. And if you take my advice, young Hunter, you will do the same. Life in the wild is vastly overrated. Strife is endemic in our species and you will find few owls who understand or care for more than eating, sleeping, mating and the essential business of survival. As I've already told you, pure science transcends the petty things of yesterday, tomorrow and today, so eschew things of the flesh and find salvation in pursuit of knowledge.'

Having spoken these brave words, Humanoid yawned, stretched his wings and then fell sound asleep, while Hunter dozed as the darkness faded and then slept at last and dreamed of flight, first to Holly's hidden valley and then north through the ever wilder country till at last he reached his home.

He slept deeply until habit stirred him from his dreams and he woke for morning feeding time. He yawned, blinked drowsily around him and then snapped wide-awake as he saw that Humanoid had turned rigid with excitement and was staring in fascination at the two warders who were now approaching with the food. It was only when the cell door opened and they entered that he noticed that one of the humans was new to him, smaller than the other one and almost certainly a female.

Glancing at Humanoid, he saw that his tutor was transfixed. The male warder threw down their morning ration of dead chicks and then pointed up at the wooden pole where they both perched, at the same time making those odd, unintelligible noises that pass for human speech. The female followed the pointing finger with her eyes, looking first at Humanoid, then Hunter and then turning her gaze back to the older owl again. Glancing sideways again, Hunter saw that his tutor was trembling as if gripped by some deadly rheum, or else suffering from some acute form of Barn owl fever. Then the female human looked away from him and followed her companion's finger as it pointed to the various objects in the cell. Though she did not speak, she nodded her head from time to time and glanced back only once at Humanoid and Hunter before she and her fellow warder left the cell.

For a long time after they had gone, Humanoid said nothing, but sat quietly trembling on the wooden pole. First Hunter asked him what the matter was, then whether he was going down to eat and finally if he wanted food brought up to where he was sitting on his perch, but no reply was forthcoming to any of these questions. The Man Owl merely sat staring straight in front of him with a dreamy glaze suffusing those eyes that were normally so keen and bright.

Eventually Hunter flew down himself and ate his ration of dead chicks. When he had finished and flown back to the wooden pole, he found that Humanoid was trembling slightly less and so he tried him with another question. 'The small one was a female, wasn't she?' he said.

'Beautiful!' breathed his tutor in reply. 'Just like my human mother, only younger.'

'And did you feel the urge for her?' asked Hunter, half-dreading the reply.

'I did!' replied the Man Owl fervently. 'In fact, it's worse than the mere urge. As you see, I tremble. I am completely smitten.'

'Remember your previous disappointments,' Hunter said. 'Remember your commitment to pure science.'

'How can I, when she's here in the cell with me?' asked Humanoid. 'It's amazing, it's incredible! Did you see the way she looked up at me? If the male had not been with her she'd have tried to touch me, I can tell.'

'Do you think she'll come back again?'

'She must!' said Humanoid. 'She'll come back with our second feed this afternoon and I can't sleep or teach till then. From now on our lessons are suspended.'

'Be careful!' Hunter said. 'Remember what you said about the urge. It is a curse. It can destroy you whether you feel it for another owl or for a female human.'

'I can't help it,' answered Humanoid. 'You have your obsession with the wild and I have mine for female humans. Dream your own dreams of lost valley, copse and woodland, but while you wake, breathe gently upon mine.'

'Don't try to mate with her,' said Hunter. 'She won't like it and if the male fetches a firestick there'll be no escape this time.'

'I shan't make the same mistake again,' said Humanoid. 'This time I shall woo her first, as if she were a female owl. That much I did learn in the wild. This time I shall have skill and patience and in the end I shall ·prevail.'

Though Hunter tried to reason with him, the Man Owl would not listen. In the afternoon, the female keeper returned with her companion and on the following morning she came back alone.

As soon as she was inside the cell, Humanoid puffed himself up into a pompous ball and began to strut up and down the wooden pole uttering guttural little love calls and rolling his big eyes in the way that male Barn owls do when they are well and truly smitten. For Hunter this behaviour was both mortifying and indecent to behold, especially when the female human looked up at Humanoid, cocked her head on one side and cooed back up at him.

'You see, she is responding!' cried Humanoid, once the female warder had gone about her business and left them in the cell. 'All I need now is to repeat my display of courtship and then present her with the ritual gift of food. Then she will give herself to me. She will let me perch on her shoulder and rub my head against her cheek.'

'But not in here!' protested Hunter. 'You can't do that in front of me. I couldn't bear it.'

'You can look the other way,' said Humanoid. 'I'm sorry, but this is the chance of a lifetime and it's obvious that I can't follow her outside.'

'How do you know?' asked Hunter, who was desperate to prevent this attempt at union from taking place, especially in front of him. 'If you fly to the door of the cell and flap your wings, she might even take you somewhere private. Or are humans accustomed to mating in public, with a lot of other creatures looking on?'

'That's not my biggest worry,' answered Humanoid. 'The immediate problem is what to find her as a ritual gift.'

'Hardly one of her dead chicks,' said Hunter. 'You'll just have to be patient till something comes along.'

'But I need it now!' said Humanoid. 'The right time to give it to her is straight after my next display of courtship. If I wait any longer she'll think I'm shy or even impotent, just like those three female Barn owls did. For the sake of the God Bird, Hunter, tell me how I can get hold of human food?'

Hunter clamped his bill shut and said nothing, though a simple solution to the Man Owl's problem had just flashed into his brain. To his horror, the same idea occurred to Humanoid a few moments later and at once he told Hunter what he planned.

'The human fledglings!' he shouted out in a state of great excitement. 'When the warders aren't watching, they push bits of human food through the bars of the entrance to our cell!'

'I've never seen them do it,' lied Hunter, trying to sound as convincing as he could.

'Of course you have,' said Humanoid. 'The Tawny next door often perches on the floor at the entrance to his cell and cocks his head this way and that to attract the passing humans. When there are no adults looking, the human fledglings poke food at him. Of course, he doesn't eat it. It's just a mindless occupation to pass the time of day.'

'It's useless asking him. He doesn't understand a single thing you say.'

'I know,' answered Humanoid. 'His long imprisonment has driven him insane. But you could try it. You could do the same. You could perch at the entrance to the cell, peer out through the bars, rock your head from side to side and roll your eyes to attract attention. That way I'd get the ritual gift I need.'

'Me?' said Hunter in disgust. 'I don't want any of your wretched human rubbish. If you need it that badly, then do the grovelling yourself.'

'Oh, all right!' said Humanoid. 'I just thought you'd get more because you're bigger, younger and much better-looking, but if you're going to be like that about it, I'll just have to do my best.'

Having said this, Humanoid immediately flew down from the wooden pole and took up his begging position on the floor at the entrance to their cell. While Hunter watched in horror, his tutor began to pose and posture in the most grotesque of fashions, swaying his body, rolling his head from side to side and uttering strange cries in a ludicrous attempt to copy human speech.

Though more humans paused for longer periods to stare down at him, no young ones came and none of the adult visitors attempted to poke food or other objects through the iron bars into the cell.

High noon came and went on that fickle day in spring and as afternoon feeding time drew nearer, Humanoid was still without success. Then, suddenly and unexpectedly, as Hunter had already begun to breathe a great sigh of relief, a large man accompanied by three human fledglings paused outside the cell and for some time all four stood looking in at Humanoid's grotesque routine. Then, while the adult drew their attention to Hunter who was watching anxiously from high up on his wooden perch, the youngest of the fledglings slipped a tiny hand into his pocket, extracted a small object wrapped in silver paper and surreptitiously stuffed it through the iron bars into the cell. Humanoid at once seized the object in his bill, flew back to the wooden pole and deposited the gift with great care in a crevice high up in the back wall.

Seeing what had happened, the large man turned on the youngest fledgling in what seemed to Hunter like a fit of human anger. Expostulating, he waved his arms about and then pointed up at Humanoid, who had now rejoined Hunter and was perching complacently beside him on the wooden pole.

'I got it,' the Man Owl muttered a few moments later, when the adult and his human fledglings had moved on. 'I got my ritual offering of human food.'

'What is it?' asked Hunter, who could not help being curious and also quite impressed in spite of his dreadful fear of what might happen next.

'I told you, food!' said Humanoid. 'My mother's human fledglings used to eat them all the time, only first they take off the silver skin. Inside the meat is not red but rich dark brown like the colour of the winter earth.'

Hunter looked away from the Man Owl and saw to his dismay that the female warder was approaching their cell with their second daily ration of dead chicks.

'She's coming,' whispered Humanoid, and rapidly began to preen and puff himself up to impress the object of his passion. As she began to open the cell door, he turned to the crevice in the wall, seized the silver object in his bill and flew down to the entrance before the female human had time to close the door behind her.

Mistaking Humanoid's intentions, she cried out in fear and flung both arms up to protect her face. Instead of retreating to his perch, Humanoid continued to flap around her, poking his bill forward in an attempt to stuff the silver object into his loved one's face. The harder he tried to do this, the more she flailed her arms about and screamed.

Watching in horror, Hunter saw her male colleague running from across the prison courtyard towards their cell. In that split second he took off, flew down from his perch, swerved past the whirling frenzy of flailing arms and flapping wings, shot through the half-open door, scattering curious spectators as he went, and then thrust up skywards just as the male warder made a desperate lunge to catch his soaring legs.

Airborne and out of reach, he wheeled round once, stared wide-eyed back at the cell and yelled out for Humanoid to follow. But in that same fleeting glimpse he saw the Man Owl still flapping in his frantic love fight with the female human, while the second keeper flung himself through the cell door to her defence.

Hunter dared not pause or look back again but gained height as quickly as he could and flew south-east, intent on reaching one of the great trees in the park in which he could hide and wait till darkness came. No longer used to sustained or rapid flight, his wings ached and his lungs were bursting before he left the last of the prison buildings in his wake. With the green haven of the park beneath his wings, he slowed down slightly, gasped for breath and then looked around him to select the safest, most accommodating tree.

After wheeling twice high up in the cloud-flecked sky, he chose an ancient towering cedar standing alone and majestic in the centre of the park, flew into the dark cover of its massive crown and perched on a hidden branch close to the centre of the mighty trunk. 'Will they search for me?' he wondered, when he first began to think again after the panic of the flight. 'Which way are the iron tracks that I must follow to get back to the place where I belong? Or should I simply fly north-west at nightfall and keep travelling until the city's far behind me and I can find an owl who may be able to tell me the right way?'

Still scared, he sat quite still and indecisive on his hidden perch until the shadows lengthened and the late afternoon drifted slowly into dusk. But it was not until long after darkness had engulfed the last of twilight and the roar of the city traffic had dwindled to a distant, intermittent murmur that Hunter first fully realized he was free.

CHAPTER 9

'Look at it my way,' Hunter said as he and Quaver perched in a beech tree in the heart of the secret forest. 'How would you feel if you came back to discover that Bardic had occupied your home, Winger was leader and there was about to be a civil war? How would you feel if you'd been in prison all that time and came back to be forcibly enrolled in this so-called resistance movement and then told to go into hiding in the lost domain? I mean, of all the places to be banished to, Rivers could hardly have picked a worse exile for me than this. Doesn't he realize that I've got very painful associations with the place?'

'You had to go into hiding,' said Quaver, apologetically. 'This is the only place where you won't be seen or recognized. Rivers says it's essential for you to stay under cover till his final plans are made. And this is our secret headquarters. It's the only place where those of us in the resistance can meet without the risk of being seen.'

'And then there's this deal he's made with Falco,' said Hunter angrily. 'In exchange for being permitted to hide out in the secret forest, I am to investigate the changes men are making in the lost domain. I have to fly around the great house, the parkland and the gardens and then tell Falco who these new humans are and what they're trying to do. It will be a miracle if I'm not blasted to pieces before I've seen Dapple or had one decent meal.'

'Think of it as your first mission on behalf of the resistance move-ment,' said Quaver, trying to soothe his brother but not sounding at all convincing. 'And it was your fault, in a way. You did tell us you'd been studying men and their behaviour patterns, so what else could you expect?'

'Well, not a hero's welcome, but nothing quite as bad as this. You all seem to have gone quite crazy since I've been away.'

'We live in dangerous times,' said Quaver. 'It was lucky no one saw you on your way back into the territory last night. It was lucky that Bardic was out eating when you arrived back at the abandoned farmhouse and it's very lucky that you've learned something about man so that you can do this survey for Falco and the Little owls, otherwise they might not have let us use this place for our headquarters.'

'But what's lucky about all that?' asked Hunter, in exasperation. 'Why can't I simply fly up to Winger and tell him I've arrived? And why should I join this so-called resistance movement anyway? After all that time in prison I'm entitled to my freedom and a bit of peace.'

'You won't get that with Winger,' Quaver said. 'I've told you, we're on the verge of civil war.'

'What nonsense!' Hunter said. 'All it needs is for me or the History Owl to have a quiet word with Yoller. He and I sat in this very tree in this same clearing the night that Ferocity and Ripper began their survey of the secret forest and we both said then that another war between us and the Tawnies would be quite unthinkable.'

'Would it?' answered Quaver, as his patience began to wear a little thin. 'Frankly, Hunter, you've been away too long. You need time to adapt to all the changes. May Blossom leads the Tawnies now, not your friend Yoller. You'll find he's not the same owl now as the one that led us to victory in the war. The iron female has bent him to her will.'

'I don't believe it!'

'It's true,' Quaver said. 'And if Winger decides to annex Ferocity and Ripper's wood, she'll send a task force to take it back again.'

'Then let me talk to Winger.'

'You can't negotiate with Winger,' Quaver said. 'You don't know how ruthless and how devious he is!'

'And what do Yoller and May Blossom say will happen if there is a war?' asked Hunter. 'What role will your resistance movement play?'

'He says if it happens Rivers and the other owls who fought beside the Tawnies in the war should keep well out of it. If we don't participate, he says he'll make sure that none of us gets killed.'

'I still don't believe it,' Hunter said. 'I sat with him in this very clearing and he said that if the men stayed away the Tawnies would one day take back this forest in the lost domain, which belongs to them by right. But he never spoke of taking Barn owl country. Tawnies don't like open farmland any more than I like living in the middle of this wood, so whatever possessed Winger to think of colonizing Ferocity and Ripper's place?'

'We don't know,' said Quaver. 'But we think it may be connected with this secret crisis. Something so grave that Winger hasn't even told the council yet. Our priority is to find out what it is in the hope that this information will help to bring him down. But Rivers will tell you more when he comes on his next visit. Until then you'll just have to wait and be patient, I'm afraid.'

'What I don't understand is how Winger got himself elected,' Hunter said. 'As a newcomer to the district he was only appointed Owl Owl when poor old Beak Poke died, and that wasn't long before the war.'

'I've told you Rivers' theory about Barn owls wanting to forget the conflict,' Quaver said. 'Then, of course, when he was campaigning he made many promises that will be impossible to keep. And as soon as he'd been elected leader he began to replace dissident members of the council with his own disciples – those who believe blindly in the new dogma and dialectic and are prepared to see all our history and tradition swept away. Geography is the latest victim. At the last meeting he was voted off the council on the excuse that his war wounds prevented him from keeping up with all the latest changes.'

'It reminds me of a religious poem Dapple taught us,' Hunter said. 'Do you remember it? It sums up my feelings perfectly. "I returned and saw under the moon that the sky was not to the swift, nor battle to the strong, nor food to the wise or happiness to owls of understanding, but that time and chance happens to them all."'

'I remember it well,' said Quaver. 'And talking of Dapple, I have something to confess.'

'Oh, what's that?' asked Hunter, looking at his younger brother with impatient curiosity.

'She àsked me to go in search of you. She asked me to fly far south to the great city and bring back word of you, or else let her know the time and manner of your death.'

'And you didn't go?' asked Hunter, guessing that a quest of that nature lay beyond his brother's powers.

'No,' said Quaver. 'I talked to Yoller instead. He told me about the fight with wild cats and how he'd seen you killed by that machine. But he made me promise to invent another story to tell Dapple. Something that would help to keep her hopes alive.'

'Under the circumstances, it's a good thing that he did. Anyway, what exactly did you tell her?'

'I told her that you had met a female called Holly who lived in a secluded valley in the last rustic territory before the beginnings of the ever-spreading city. I told her that you'd fallen in love with this female who had a lilting voice that sang of summer flowers and sparkled like a mountain stream. I said that after Yoller had lost you in the city, you'd probably decided to go back and mate with her instead of coming home.'

'And did Dapple believe you?'

'I don't think so. But Yoller was right. At least it gave her hope.'

'Well, apart from the five seasons that I spent in prison, the story was a pretty good invention,' Hunter said. 'I did meet a female called Holly and on my way back from the city I called in to see her. I was going to bring her back here with me so that she could get an education, but with Winger as our leader and judging from everything you've said, it was just as well she wasn't there.'

'She wasn't there?'

'No, when I arrived in the deserted valley there were signs that someone had just died, but whether it was Holly or her mother I don't know.'

'Were you disappointed?'

'Very,' Hunter said. 'It's spring, and you can imagine what the urge is like after spending all that time in prison! And I needed to talk to another owl to prove I was still normal. It's not easy to stay sane when you're shut up in a cell with an owl who thinks he's half-man and even tries to mate with female humans.'

'Perhaps this Holly thought that you were dead. After all that time, she must have thought that you were never coming back.'

'I suppose so,' Hunter said. 'But she was a gentle, attractive creature and it seems a shame, especially when I find myself exiled to the lost domain where there are no female Barn owls to be seen. You must understand that after all that time in prison, the urge is becoming an obsession.'

'Of course I understand,' said Quaver. 'But it could be dangerous. In a

274

state like yours it would be easy to pick the first female that you met and risk making a terrible mistake.'

'It's a risk I wish that I could take,' said Hunter. 'By the way, Holly said she might come looking for me when her mother died. You've not heard of any female strangers passing through?'

'Unfortunately not. Be realistic, Hunter. As I said before, after all that time she must have thought that you were dead. To tell you the truth, Dapple was the only owl who always believed you might still be alive, and even she might have given up all hope if it hadn't been for the story I invented. And since Winger's return from his secret mission, he's been telling everyone you're definitely dead, so what can you expect?'

'Stuck here in the lost domain, I suppose I might as well be,' said Hunter, sounding very sorry for himself. 'For the God Bird's sake, get Rivers to come soon and tell me what his plans are or else I shall rebel.'

'I'll tell him,' promised Quaver, wondering more and more what this miraculous resurrection of his brother's might bring forth. 'I must leave you now,' he said. 'I've been away too long already and Bardic's in a panic because we've got to get this new version of the ballad ready by the next full moon.'

Hunter nodded and forced a friendly smile, but as Quaver took off and headed north across the forest of the lost domain, he wondered once again what events might be precipitated by the return from the dead of one armed with who knows what strange power and knowledge, culled from his travels and from his adventures in places where no other Barn owl had ever flown. As he sped silently through the dark, mysterious forest, Quaver was troubled by the uneasy feeling that one so mature and confident as his brother had now grown would not be content to stay out of sight for long, and that when the time came for him to emerge and make his presence felt, things might never be the same again.

Back in the clearing, Hunter sat unhappily in the beech tree and pondered on the series of disappointments that had befallen him since his escape from prison. The more he thought about it all, the sorrier for himself he felt and eventually he almost began to wish that he had not risked his life to make the long flight home but had stayed on by himself in the fertile, empty valley and waited for Holly to come back. As the lonely night wore on Hunter was more than ever tormented by the urge, which filled him with bittersweet memories of little Alba and with a sudden, acute yearning for the female Barn owl whom he had met only once yet seemed always to have known.

As dawn rose slowly and the mists began to clear, the secret beauties of the lost domain burgeoned into a deep dark sea of green which seemed to heave and throb with grief for the dead that lay long buried beneath the fullblown thickness of late spring. And deep within the throbbing of this grief, Hunter sensed a late-flowering violence that now threatened to burst forth from the seething cauldron of buried blood and bones, for he knew that this was the place where Grumwell's army had fought with the Tawnies three hundred springs ago and he was sorry now that he had lied to Quaver about what had been said when he and Yoller had sat in this clearing so many moons before. 'Can you imagine the two of us fighting?' he had asked then. 'Why, the treaty between us has lasted for centuries. Why should it ever break?'

'Things change,' Yoller had answered, staring out into the forest that surrounded them. 'And centuries go by very quickly, even with a short history of twelve million winters like yourselves.'

'It would be the end of civilization as we know it.'

'Oh, I agree,' said Yoller. 'But all good things must finish sometime, I suppose.'

In the early dawn Hunter stared out into the forest as Yoller had done so long ago and saw that the path the men had made, overgrown at the time of Yoller's warning, had recently been cleared again, meaning that humans could once more penetrate to the very heart of the ancient woodland and walk to the beech tree in the clearing where he sat. At this point Hunter realized why Falco and the Little owls were worried by these changes and by this human intrusion into the place they called their promised land. He also realized that in order to keep his promise to them and discover what kind of humans had now come to violate the lost domain, he would have to spy on the great house by daylight and fly back once more to the tragic scene of little Alba's death.

As the sun rose higher and the last mists faded above the ancient forest, Hunter decided to delay his dangerous mission no longer and so reluctantly set out to put his knowledge of Human Studies to the test. It was a test that he would fail if Humanoid had not taught him well, and more than bringing disappointment to Rivers and the Little owls, he knew that failure might mean loss of liberty or death.

CHAPTER 10

At midnight two days after Hunter started his dangerous mission in the lost domain, Holly flew into the district from the north, convinced that she had completely lost her way.

On the night after her mother's death she had set out above the iron tracks and flown north for six long nights, following the instructions Hunter had given her so long ago. But on the sixth night she found a growing town in place of the tiny hamlet and the other landmarks Hunter had so carefully described. It occurred to her then that Hunter might have timed the flight by the strength and speed of his own wings and that the same journey he could fly in six nights would take her seven, or even eight, especially since once or twice she had lost the tracks and missed her way.

So, weary but still full of hope she had flown on around the murky glow of yellow light and continued her journey to the north and deeper into the unfamiliar countryside. But by the end of the ninth night she realized she must have flown too far, and although anxious by now and almost totally exhausted, she turned and flew back until once again she came to the moonlit rubble of new buildings that scarred the rural landscape and marked the rising town. Only then did it occur to her that this spreading sore of cement and brick might have grown from the hamlet Hunter had once known and that somewhere behind the buildings and the glow of murky yellow light lay the farmland and the barn where Hunter had been born, so she skirted round it once again and then headed due east until the last of the winking lights was far behind her.

As she flew, Holly was troubled by a vague feeling that the route she now followed was similar to the one that Winger had given her, but she could not be sure of this because she had deliberately forgotten his directions for fear of confusing them with Hunter's. Thus it was that she found herself at once and unwittingly in the territory where Winger lived and from which he ruled the district. Not only was Holly unaware that she had entered the lair of the owl to whom she had been promised as a fledgling, but she was by no means sure that she had yet found the remote, rural district which Hunter had described so well and to which he had declared that one day he would return.

Weary and anxious, she flew on above a wide expanse of ripening corn that rippled softly below her in the silver moonlight. Beyond the cornfield she glided downwards over sloping grassland towards an empty barn which stood in lonely isolation at the bottom of the meadow before the beginning of a wooded glade. As she began to drift down towards the barn, intending to rest for a while and take stock of her position, she sensed the presence of another Barn owl approaching fast across the open country that rose gently upwards beyond the low lying shelter of the leafy glade.

Holly slowed down as she approached the barn but did not attempt to change direction for she knew that it was in any case too late to avoid confrontation. 'Better this way,' she thought, as she landed on top of the old, dilapidated building. 'At least this local owl may be able to tell me if this is the right district and how far I am from Hunter.' A few moments later the rapidly approaching incumbent homed in through the darkness and landed on the roof beside her. For a long time both owls stared at each other, speechless with surprise, till Holly found a faint voice and heard her own words tremble in the night time breeze. 'Westwood?' she said, her heart sinking as she spoke. 'Is this your territory? What a coincidence!'

'It's you!' said Winger, who also looked as if he had had a nasty shock. 'What on earth are you doing in this district?'

'Mother died,' said Holly, who could see that for some reason Winger was as unhappy about this meeting as she was herself. 'So I flew north to find an owl that I once met. He comes from the deep country place where Barn owls and Tawnies combined to bring the monster down. He gave me directions and after twelve long nights of flying, I thought that at last I might have reached my destination.'

Winger stared hard at her and as she looked back at him, Holly saw that he seemed quite badly shaken, though she had no idea why this should be the case.

'You never told me,' said Winger, making a visible effort to pull himself together. 'Where did you meet him and what was this owl's name?'

'His name is Hunter,' Holly said. 'You may have heard of him? He's one of those that fought against the monster in the war.'

To Holly's surprise, she saw Winger tremble as though something had struck him in the chest. His bill dropped open and then snapped to again as he regained his composure.

'When did you meet him?' asked Winger, phrasing the words of his question very slowly, as if he were speaking to a fledgling. 'When did you first meet, and why did you set out in search of him?'

'He was very kind,' said Holly, who was worried and confused by Winger's attitude. 'He told me he had some influence in the territory where he lived and said he would use it with the local council to find a place for my further education.'

'Hunter has no influence here,' said Winger, whose flat, deliberate tone and supercilious manner failed to conceal the shock he was still trying to suppress. 'The owl you're looking for is dead.'

Holly gazed back at him in complete dismay, unable to take in what he had said. 'Dead?' she asked, still unwilling to believe her ears. 'But that can't be true, and this can't be his district, not if you are leader here.'

'This was Hunter's district,' repeated Winger flatly. 'But now I am leader here and he is dead.'

'But how?' asked Holly. 'How did he die, and when?'

'A long time ago,' said Winger. 'Soon after the war he flew south to the great city and that is where he died. Some say he was devoured by wild cats and others that the firestick brought him down. In my opinion, he was done away with by the Tawnies in whom he put his trust. No one knows exactly how or where he met his end. The one certain fact is that he's dead.'

Trying desperately to hide her great distress, Holly caught her breath and clung to the one hope that she had left. If Winger did not know exactly how or where it happened, then how could he be as certain as he sounded that Hunter was really dead?

'When did you meet him, by the way?' asked Winger, whose attempt at a casual tone failed to mask the suspicion and concern behind his question. 'It couldn't have been recently, of course.'

'Oh, I never knew him well,' she answered, stalling for a reason that she could not quite define, unless it was because she had known Winger as a fledgling and learned even then that it was sometimes better not to tell too much until you knew exactly why the information was required. 'And you?' she asked, countering to play for time. 'From something in your tone, I gather that you didn't really like him?'

'I hardly knew him either,' answered Winger. 'As a matter of fact, we never even met. But since he's dead and gone, let's change the subject. What do you intend to do now that your long journey has proved to be in vain?'

'I suppose that depends on you,' said Holly, still clinging to the faint hope that Hunter might still be alive and knowing that her only chance of ever seeing him again would be somehow to stay on in the territory that had once been his. 'You know that I came here in search of an education. As leader, you must be in a much stronger position to help me than Hunter would have been.'

'That's very true,' said Winger, smiling with grim satisfaction and seeming much more like himself again. 'Of course I can help you, but I'm afraid that there will have to be conditions.'

'What conditions?' asked Holly, suddenly feeling defenceless, exhausted and very much alone.

'First, you will tell no one where I come from. You must pretend that we met for the first time when you came here looking for an education.'

Surprised, Holly nodded and said nothing. She knew she had no choice but to listen and to play a waiting game.

'Second, don't ever mention meeting Hunter. That owl caused a lot of trouble in his time and the sooner he's forgotten, the better it will be.'

'What kind of trouble?' asked Holly, grateful that her intuition had stopped her from telling Winger her true feelings.

'That's too long a story,' Winger answered. 'I'll tell you some other time.'

'And the third condition?' Holly asked, realizing as she saw Winger hesitate that this would be the one she would on no account be able to accept.

'You will help with my experiment,' said Winger. 'The one I mentioned to you on my recent visit.'

'I don't understand,' said Holly, worried by the manic gleam that was now beginning to appear in Winger's bulging eyes. 'To test your theory, you told me it was essential to mate with a female in another district. What use can I be to you now that I'm not at home but here?'

'I have another theory. I have discovered that the Tawnies have not been affected by this infertility. Neither have the Little owls living in the lost domain. Therefore, our inability to breed may be connected with the farmland and the food we eat.'

'But this is farmland,' said Holly, edging backwards along the roof as Winger leaned his bony frame much closer to her body. 'What would be the use of mating with me here?'

'I don't mean here. I intend to mate with you in what was once a Tawny wood. I will take you there tonight, and from now on, both before and after we have mated, you will eat only food taken from the wild woods, far away from agriculture and from man. If your chicks hatch properly and thrive, that will be a partial confirmation of my theory.'

'What about the Tawnies?' Holly asked. 'Since when have they welcomed Barn owl settlers on their ancestral land?'

'There are no Tawnies in Ferocity and Ripper's wood. The three incumbents were all killed in the war.'

'But surely more will come to take their place. To survive, the Tawnies must conserve every patch of woodland they can find.'

'For the moment, they are too few in numbers,' Winger said. 'In this district, they were decimated by the war.'

'But one male and one female won't be enough to test your theory,' protested Holly. 'For a conclusive experiment, you'd need to run the programme on a much wider scale.'

'There will be three of you,' said Winger. 'I already have two other females earmarked for this experiment.'

'Lucky them!' said Holly. 'Do they know about it yet, or are you planning a surprise?'

'One knows already, I intend to tell the other when the time is ripe,' answered Winger, in deadly seriousness.

'And the males?' asked Holly, who could hardly believe all this was happening. 'Have they been told, and have they met their partners yet?'

'There will be no other males for the time being,' said Winger, breathing heavily and straightening his awkward, bony frame as if squaring up to the task that lay ahead. 'I intend to undertake this sacrifice all by myself.'

'But Barn owls are monogamous,' said Holly. 'And come to that, so are all other kinds of owl. Aren't you afraid that this experiment of yours could be seen as setting an example for promiscuity?'

'The project is top secret,' Winger said. 'And conventional morality is merely a set of rules by which the masses live. Rules followed by leaders, too, in times of peace. But in times of great crisis, we cannot prejudice the chances of survival by tying ourselves to the dictates of a meaningless, worn-out religion.'

'But supposing we three females all breed successfully?' asked Holly. 'What will you do then? You can't move the entire Barn owl population on to Tawny land.'

'No,' admitted Winger. 'But we can annex some of it and use it for breeding in rotation. Couples would be able to mate there and then return to open country once their fledglings were old enough to travel.'

'The population wouldn't stand for it,' said Holly. 'Owls are very private creatures and families need secure, traditional homes. If you suggested that, there'd be a revolution.'

'The revolution has taken place already,' Winger said. 'If there is any opposition to my plan, I shall dissolve the council and declare myself sole ruler of the district. I have sufficient following and power to do so. This is a desperate situation, and desperate situations call for bold and drastic remedies.'

Holly looked at the lean and bony frame towering awkwardly above her and flinched from the burning conviction in Winger's bulging eyes. 'He's gone mad,' she realized lucidly, but with a little chill of fear. 'Perhaps he always has been, or perhaps this new dream of dictatorial power has totally corrupted him. In any case, if I am to survive till I meet other owls, I must pretend to go along with him.'

'And how long must I live in this woodland and diet on wild food before we mate?' she asked, forcing a faint smile as she looked up at him wide-eyed.

'Not long,' said Winger. 'Four or five nights at the most. The season is nearly over and I can't wait until next spring. I must come up with an answer to this infertility to show the population that I'm in control.'

'And what do I get in return for taking part in your experiment?'

'An education and afterwards a territory of your own,' said Winger. 'And who knows, a place on the council one day, if I should decide to keep it going.'

'All right, I accept,' said Holly, calculating that even if she failed to find out more about Hunter, she would still have time to get away before Winger appeared in the woodland territory to subject her to his awful, experimental mating. 'Just tell me one more thing,' she said, searching for a weapon to use against him in case her escape was in any way prevented. 'Why don't you want me to tell anyone we met before, or that we were both born and bred on your father's territory?'

'This is a time of great austerity,' replied Winger promptly. 'We shall all have to make great sacrifices in order to survive. Bigger territories must be broken up and traditional privileges will vanish in the interests of complete equality. I shall set the first example, but if certain of the council members knew my family history and that I had inherited a whole valley in the south to which I could return at any time I wanted, they might be less prepared to make the sacrifices that are so necessary for survival.'

'You mean, if you were taking land from them, they might wonder why you didn't go back home and claim your own?'

'Precisely,' Winger said. 'I gave up my inheritance because of my convictions, but you are right, I can hardly expect them to believe it. Therefore you must say nothing now or at any future time. Is that clear?'

'If you say so,' answered Holly, relaxing now that Winger had given her a weapon she could use against him should the time ever come for this experimental mating. She would refuse and if he insisted on going through with it, she would threaten to tell the local owls about his aristocratic past and his inheritance.

'We shall leave at once,' said Winger, squaring his gangling, bony frame again. 'I will take you to the territory once known as Ferocity and Ripper's wood. There you will meet the first of your female companions who is a passionate believer in the New Apostasy and has therefore agreed to take part in this experiment. I will introduce you and together the three of us will celebrate a new point of departure in the twelve million years of Barn owl history, the liberation of a Tawny wood! To celebrate this most important landmark, we shall rename Ferocity and Ripper's wood in honour of a former Barn owl leader who has much influenced my thinking. From this night forth for evermore the place where three brave females will transcend superstition and religious prejudice and sacrifice themselves for the future of the New Apostasy shall be known as Grumwell's Haven. Or, for short, the Graven, a most suitable abbreviation, since his name and our New Apostasy will be carved forever in the future of all Barn owl thinking.'

'To me it sounds too much like images of death,' thought Holly, but did not say so. 'What are they called, the other two?' she asked instead, being curious to find out more about these females who believed so blindly in the new philosophy as to lend themselves willingly to Winger's lewd and unromantic plan.

'The one already waiting there is called Dawn Raptor,' Winger said. 'The other, who does not yet know that she's been chosen, is the daughter of Dirge, the Owl for Dogma and Dialectic. Her name is Ivy Perch.'

'Can you tell me any more about them?' Holly asked. 'It's so long since I talked to any other owl but mother that I'm afraid I've grown rather shy. And it's important that the three of us should get on well together, don't you think?'

'Ivy Perch is rather common, but a very pretty bird indeed,' said Winger, with a horrid gleam of anticipation in his eye. 'And as for Dawn Raptor, it may interest you to know that she's the sister of the dead owl you came looking for, but fortunately found me instead. And I must say I'm delighted that you did. I have a feeling that this experiment is going to work out very well.'

As Holly took off and followed Winger towards her unknown destination, she wondered briefly how Ivy Perch could be described as common by a leader who believed implicitly that all owls must be absolutely equal, but this tiny anomaly troubled her tired brain only for a fleeting moment to be replaced at once by the much greater enigma of how a sister of Hunter's could ever bring herself to mate with an owl like Winger, even though Holly remembered that she had once considered doing so herself. 'Perhaps she is young and innocent, as I was,' Holly thought. 'Or perhaps Winger has coerced her in the same way as he is forcing me.'

The more she thought, the more she was convinced that this must be the case and she decided to confide in Hunter's sister, her fellow victim, at the earliest opportunity, for Holly had made up her mind that if

Hunter was really dead and she had nothing left to live for, then the least that she could do was to protect his sister and prevent this nightmare experiment from ever taking place.

CHAPTER

 11

Having finished his survey in two long, dangerous days of flying and spying on the new humans living in the lost domain, Hunter sat at twilight in the beech tree by the clearing and told the leader of the Little owls the conclusions that he had reached.

'The odd thing is that most of them are females,' Hunter said. 'And stranger still, most of these females are aged from ten to seventeen or twenty springs. In human terms that means they're little more than fledglings.'

'But why so many fledglings of the same sex together in one place?' asked Falco. 'And are they dangerous? In human terms, as you've just put it, is the female of the species more deadly than the male?'

'Not for owls or other wildlife,' said Hunter, with a swift shake of his head. 'Of course, the fledglings cause confusion, but they're no more or less dangerous than the young of any other species that we've studied. The adult females are seldom seen with firesticks, and although they are known to be physically weaker than the males, they may be killers in some other subtle way that hasn't been discovered yet.'

'But it's not a family, is it?' asked Falco. 'Or are human families composed of a hundred or more fledglings, as you say you've counted, nine adult females and three males?'

'Definitely not,' said Hunter. 'The only thing I can suggest is that these human fledglings have been brought here to the lost domain to undergo some form of collective education. We know there was a human war not long ago and it may be that the fathers of these fledglings are all dead. In any case, since all of them are females, it's highly unlikely that they're being trained to kill. Also, since they've left the gardens, the parkland and the forest exactly as they were before, it does not look as if they intend to farm here or clear the woodland to build houses.'

'They have cleared some of the paths that lead into the forest,' Falco said. 'That must have been the first thing that you noticed.'

'The paths are for the fledglings in the daytime,' Hunter said. 'On the whole, I'd say the news for you is very good. There's no sign yet of agriculture, which might bring pollution, and from the game that now abounds here I'd say these new humans don't kill pheasant, duck and partridge as the others used to do. So at this time of the year, the pickings for your population should be very good.'

'Thank you,' Falco said. 'And my congratulations. You learned a great deal in the city. You must know more about man than any other living owl.'

'There is, or was, one who knows much more than I do,' said Hunter, remembering Humanoid and thinking that with its hundred human females the lost domain would have been paradise indeed for him!

'You are very welcome to remain here,' Falco said. 'Because of your heroism in the war and because of what you did for little Alba, we offer you sanctuary and refuge from Winger for as long as you should wish. Our memories, it seems, are longer than those of your own species. But it cannot be official. We cannot create a precedent. As far as we are concerned, you are in a permanent state of transit. You do not reside here, you are merely passing through. I have put the word about and ordered that none of us shall notice the ghostly presence of a great white bird. You do not exist, so no one will come near you. You will be left alone and no one will ask you how or why you're here.'

'Don't worry, Falco,' said Hunter, as the fierce Little owl peered at him from the opposite branch in the centre of the beech tree. 'You won't be haunted for much longer. Your ghost will soon be gone.'

'Where to?' asked Falco, with no change in the expression on his scarred and weathered face.

'Home first and then back to the south,' said Hunter, sounding sad and bitter now that the final decision had been taken. 'Nothing in these territories is the same as I remembered. It is a different world from the one that I once knew. I should have listened to my tutor. You can't go home again, he rightly said. First I shall say goodbye for the last time to my mother and then I shall fly to an empty, sheltered valley that I found far to the south of here. I shall settle there and live in peace, with my memories and my dreams, far, far away from all this ancient blood and strife.'

'You're not the type,' said Falco. 'Your brother, maybe, but not you. You're the kind of owl things happen to, and if that's your destiny, it's no good trying to escape. I'm afraid that's another lesson you must learn. However far you fly, your history and your own past will always catch up with you. Better by far to stay and fight.'

'Against owls of my own species?' Hunter asked. 'Or against Yoller, who was once my friend? Must I fight against him for a so-called New Apostasy with whose philosophy I don't agree?'

'Go home and see your mother,' Falco said, as the darkness deepened in the primeval forest all around them. 'Go back to the place where you were born and make your decision then. If you decide to stay, then your ghostly white presence will be welcome here again.'

'Goodbye Falco,' Hunter said, struggling to suppress the choke in his voice as he stared into the immigrant leader's kind but steely eyes. 'May the Great God Bird protect you and all your species, and may you live long and prosper in your promised land!'

The Little owl stared back at him, nodded once and then took off and disappeared into the surrounding forest with the funny, bouncing little flight that once more evoked sweet, bitter memories of little Alba. Sweet because he had loved her, and bitter because he was the homeless squatter now.

Hunter waited till the last of the twilight had dwindled into darkness and then took off himself, heading purposefully across the forest towards the confines of the lost domain. As he approached the edge of the woods and the beginnings of the open country that had once belonged to Brook, he sensed the presence of a female Barn owl perched ahead at the very limits of the forest, in roughly the same spot where he had been stationed as a decoy and had seen the monster overhaul and murder Yoller's brother.

'Dawn Raptor,' Hunter thought immediately, for he had been told that she now lived in that lonely stretch of farmland, together with the Owl for Dogma and Dialectic and his daughter, Ivy Perch. 'If she recognizes me, then my cover's blown and Rivers will be furious.'

For a while he hesitated and hovered in mid-flight among the trees. There was still time to turn and fly back into hiding deep inside the forest where she would not dare to follow. 'No,' he decided firmly. 'What does it all matter, if I'm leaving here forever? It's a good opportunity to say goodbye. By the time she tells Winger, I'll be gone.' So he picked up speed again, glided on to the edge of the forest, flew into the sycamore where he had sensed his sister's presence and perched there to be greeted by the most glamorous-looking bird he had ever seen.

'Hello stranger,' she said, wriggling a little on her branch as she preened her magnificent plumage into place. 'Who are you and where are you going, may I ask?'

'I beg your pardon,' said Hunter, his brain racing to exploit this opportunity for a reprieve. 'I'm afraid I'm a total stranger here. If I'm trespassing, I'll turn around and go back the way I came.'

'No, don't do that,' the sexy female said. 'We call that place the lost domain, and it's lousy with ghosts, little squatters and dangerous human beings.'

'It's quite all right,' said Hunter. 'Actually, I'm conducting a survey for the Little owls. You see, they need my expertise.'

'Expertise?' enquired the glamorous female, swaying and rocking slightly on the branch as if dancing to some silent inner rhythm. 'And what do you know, big stranger, that we don't?'

'Not much,' said Hunter modestly. 'Not much about anything except man. I'm an expert on Human Studies. I grew up with them, you see. Then I became a Man Owl in the wild, but after that I got caught again and put in prison. Now I've escaped from there and I'm just wandering till I find a place to settle down.'

The female stopped her rhythmic swaying and stared at Hunter in amazement. With her mouth hanging open and a dull, opaque glaze in her smallish eyes, she was less attractive than he had thought at first, and now that a few of her carefully-groomed feathers had slipped out of place, it struck Hunter that the preening of her plumage was perhaps slightly on the gaudy side for the best of Barn owl taste.

'Go on!' she said. 'Owls can't grow up with humans, and what's a prison, anyway?' So Hunter told her, pretending to be Humanoid. Briefly, without mentioning his lust for female humans, he outlined the story of his life, from the time he had fallen from the nest until the female warder had left the cell door open and allowed him to escape. She listened to him in open-mouthed astonishment, still moving her hips absent-mindedly to the beat of the silent music in her inner ear.

When he had finished she closed her mouth at last, lowered her eyelids, cocked her head coquettishly and subjected him to a long, hard, half-sexy and half-suspicious stare. It was obvious that she had understood only half of what he had said and was still uncertain whether to believe the rest.

'What's your name?' asked Hunter, struggling to drag his eyes away from the mellifluous movement of her hips.

'My real name is Ivy Perch,' she said. 'But that's rather common, don't you think? My friends all call me Honeysuckle Rose instead.'

'Honeysuckle Rose!' repeated Hunter, who could not help noticing as he looked deep into this glamorous female's eyes that they were indeed rather on the small side and perhaps set too close together. Also, the glazed, opaque look in them made it seem as if her mind were really somewhere else, but in spite of these slight imperfections, the way she twitched her head and shoulders in time to the swaying of her hips stirred Hunter so deeply that in spite of himself he began to feel the urge. 'This will never do,' he thought, shifting a little on his perch. 'I'm the Man Owl now and I must remember that in the role I'm playing, no female owl can be of any sexual interest whatsoever.'

'And what do they call you?' asked Honeysuckle Rose, alias plain Ivy Perch.

'Humanoid,' said Hunter promptly. 'That's the name the other owls gave me when I first joined them in the wild.'

Ivy Perch took cognizance of this, cocked her head on one side again and looked at him through half-closed eyes.

'Want to meet a member of our council?' she asked, giving an extra delicious little wriggle to her hips in response to the music in her head. 'I can fix it for you if you want.'

'Thank you,' said Hunter, with his brain racing once again. 'It's very kind of you, but I'd really rather not. You see, I'm very shy, and it's such a long time since I had anything to do with other owls that I can hardly remember the right way to behave.'

'But you've got to find some place to crash down. You can't go back in there.'

'Oh, it's not so bad,' said Hunter. 'Unlike most Barn owls, I don't mind living in the woods. It's easier to stay private and secluded.'

'Well, if that's what you want, I'll take you to our leader,' Ivy said, as the gleam of an idea shone through the dull glaze in her eyes. 'There's a bit of woodland territory that he badly wants to settle, but like you said, none of the local owls are very keen. Just think, big stranger, if you got it, we'd be neighbours. It's only just over there,' she continued, jerking her left hip provocatively in the direction of Ferocity and Ripper's wood.

'Perhaps later,' said Hunter, trying not to panic. 'At the moment, as I've already told you, I'm doing this survey for the Little owls on human behaviour patterns in the lost domain. After that I'll decide whether to settle somewhere in the district or move on.'

'I kind of like you,' said Ivy, with her eyes half-closed once more. 'You're different. You've got more about you than most of the rustic, joskin owls round here.'

'I like you, too,' said Hunter, feeling the urge well up again. 'But do me a favour, Rose, please don't tell anyone you've seen me. Don't let's get involved in protocol. Let's keep it to ourselves.'

'All right, big stranger,' said the self-styled Honeysuckle Rose. 'I'll meet you here the same time tomorrow night. But just make sure you get here. If you don't turn up, I'll tell.'

'Oh, I'll come all right,' said Hunter. 'Just let's keep this thing between ourselves.'

'I like secrets,' said Ivy, looking at him with her head cocked to one side and treating him to one last wriggle of those titillating hips.

'Till tomorrow, then,' said Hunter, and took off to fly back into the lost domain with one longing backward glance at the most instantly seductive female that he had ever met.

'Well, I couldn't have flown on,' he told himself as he headed back towards the clearing in the middle of the forest. 'Not once I'd told her I was Humanoid. If she'd told her father about me, the Owl for Dogma and Dialectic might have had me intercepted, or Dawn Raptor might have seen me, which would have been even worse. I've blown my cover, I won't be able to visit Dapple and so now I'll have to think again.'

But in his heart of hearts he knew that none of this would matter if he was really moving on and he knew, too, that there was one reason and one reason only for his sudden change of plan. 'The urge is a curse,' Humanoid had said. 'And choosing the wrong partner can destroy you.' Hunter shuddered in mid-flight as he remembered his tutor's ill-fated attempt to mate with the female warder and realized that his own lust for Ivy Perch was much less complex than the feelings he had had for little Alba or the instant affinity that he had known with his potential soulmate, Holly.

Deep in his heart he knew that he did not even like her and that a liaison with the self-styled Honeysuckle Rose would in the long term be bad for both of them. He knew all of this as he landed on the beech tree in the middle of the lost domain. He sat and brooded darkly on the implications as the night moved on towards morning and the urge waged a raging battle with his potential guilt and shame. During that tempestuous inner conflict he told himself a hundred times that he would never return to keep his secret tryst with Ivy Perch, and yet when dawn broke dull red and glowing above the riot of bud and blossom in the lost domain, he also knew that nothing but death or some kind of miracle could stop him from going back again.

CHAPTER
12

After mating with Ivy Perch for the first time on that following night, Hunter knew that things would be even worse than the Man Owl's bitter warning had foretold.

Before, it had been different. Before there was the impeccable, seductive plumage, those hips swinging to the inner music, those dull eyes lighting with a glow of pleasure when he gave the ritual gift of a young rabbit, which they consumed together on the branch of the sycamore on the very edges of the lost domain. Then came the courtship, the foreplay, the warmth of togetherness and finally the thing itself which was so good, so transcendental that it almost drove you wild. That was one thing to be said for Ivy Perch. The urge with her was very, very good.

It was only afterwards he realized that her eyes were vacant, small and far too close together and that her plumage looked dowdy and dishevelled when she had not spent all of the gloaming or the dawn on grooming it. 'Oh, Hunter,' she whined plaintively when it was time to find some supper. 'Do catch something for me while you're at it. I'm tired out, it's all such a nuisance and in this blustering wind I just can't seem to get my feathers right.'

As she spoke the gentle spring breeze blew so softly that the fresh green leaves of the sycamore in which they sat were barely stirring, and it was at times like these that he understood why she had had to give up her education because the lessons made her head ache half way through and why in response to any kind of mental challenge her mouth turned sulky and her feathers drooped till the whole of her body looked listless and bedraggled.

In spite of all this, the power of the urge prevailed and on the second night Hunter went back again, part driven by the same brute lust and part by the desire to sink deeper and perhaps even drown in the mire of guilt and shame he had created for himself. And when at midnight, all dowdy and dishevelled, she asked him to hunt for her again and then enquired tetchily what territory he would find on which to raise their chicks, he knew finally that they could never be true partners or make each other happy, but that he would come to resent her more and more as time went by and that she would never understand anything but the bartering of her female body for the good things in life that he could give her.

'We could settle in Ferocity and Ripper's wood,' she said later, when Hunter returned with a juicy mole. 'It's empty and Winger's longing to move some Barn owls in to claim it.'

'There's no hurry, is there?' Hunter asked. 'We don't even know if you're pregnant yet.'

'Oh, I'm pregnant all right,' said Ivy with a simper and a smirk. 'With a big strong beast like you, who wouldn't be?'

Only two nights ago, Hunter would have revelled in a compliment like that, but as things stood it made his heart sink and filled him with despair. 'Anyway, I can't wait to get away from home,' continued Ivy, before swallowing her generous slice of mole. 'Dirge bores me with his endless dogma and dialectic and as for Dawn Raptor, she's too stuck-up for words.'

'Dawn Raptor is his pupil?' enquired Hunter, remembering his role as Humanoid.

'She's his pupil but she's really mad on Winger,' Ivy said. 'It makes you sick to see the way she hangs on to every word our leader says.'

'And are the feelings mutual?' Hunter asked. 'Does Winger intend to mate with her some day?'

'Not in the normal way,' said Ivy sarcastically. 'He says he's too busy in his work to settle down and raise a family. But if you ask me anything, he'd mate with all the pretty females if he could. That's what drives Dawn Raptor wild. To start with, she knows he fancies me.'

'You haven't told Dawn Raptor anything about me?'

'I haven't said anything to anyone. So far it's been a secret, just as we agreed.'

'Then don't, just yet. Let me try to find an alternative territory first.'

'How can you?' asked Ivy, narrowing her eyes suspiciously. 'You're just a stranger here. You don't have any rights at all.'

'If those woods belonged to the Tawnies once, they'll send a task force to take them back. That means we'd all be killed.'

'Winger wants someone to settle there,' repeated Ivy stubbornly. 'He's even suggested that me and Dawn Raptor should go and live there now. To stake a claim, he says, and to make the Barn owl presence felt.'

'Two young females? What a strange idea! To protect the place, you'd think he'd want at least one male.'

'That male could be you,' said Ivy, coaxing now instead of cross. 'It could be our chance to live together straight away.'

'Let me think about it first,' said Hunter, his heart sinking still further at this dreadful mess the urge had landed him in.

'All right,' said Ivy, with a sulky, disappointed little pout. 'But you'd better find one soon, or else I'll tell!'

'I'll start straight away,' said Hunter, grateful for an excuse to get away from Ivy and fly back to the seclusion of the lost domain.

'Wait!' cried Ivy. 'There's a Barn owl coming towards us, over there.'

Sure enough Hunter sensed the intruder as she spoke and a second later he saw a great white shadow descending from the darkness towards their secret trysting place in the middle of the sycamore. 'I'm going,' he whispered, bracing his wings ready for a sudden take-off.

'Too late, he's seen us,' Ivy said. 'Funny thing though, it doesn't look like Dirge or Winger. I wonder who he is?'

Hunter hesitated for a second longer and then froze with guilt and panic as Rivers, the History Owl, landed on the branch above them and peered down to establish their identities.

'I'm Humanoid,' said Hunter, blurting the words out quickly before Rivers had a chance to greet him. 'And this is Honeysuckle Rose, though I suppose the two of you have already met. I'm just a stranger passing through and Rose here is the first local owl I've seen.'

'Hello Ivy,' said Rivers, nodding at her briefly before turning back to gaze at Hunter in surprise. 'Humanoid?' he said, as his eyes first narrowed with suspicion and then lit up suddenly with relief and understanding. 'That's an odd name, isn't it? Have you travelled very far?'

'A long way,' said Hunter, heaving a sigh of relief at this temporary let-off. 'From the great city in the south, where the humans held me captive. You must forgive my manners, but I was brought up by humans and in many ways I am more man than owl.'

'How extraordinary!' Rivers said, with the flicker of a twinkle in his eye. 'And do you plan to stay long in our territory?'

'That depends,' said Hunter, with a quick, anxious glance at Ivy Perch. 'It depends on whether your council can find me a spare place to live.'

'Where are you staying at the moment?' enquired Rivers, with his eyebrows raised in the same mock curiosity.

'In there,' said Hunter, nodding behind him at the great forest of the lost domain. 'In captivity, I studied under the greatest living expert on Human Studies, so in return for their hospitality, I'm helping the little immigrants with information about man.'

'That's a coincidence,' said Rivers. 'I'm heading there myself, in my official capacity. As History Owl, I have to observe the latest developments in their collective and chronicle any social progress they have made in what they call their promised land. We could fly in there together, if you like?'

'With pleasure,' replied Hunter, and then turned back to face a petulant stare from Ivy Perch. 'Shall I see you tomorrow?' he enquired politely. 'Same time, same place?'

'Find a place to live,' she said, sulkily. 'And tomorrow, don't be late.'

Hunter nodded, smiled at Rivers and then took off quickly before the situation had a chance to deteriorate. They flew in silence until they came to the clearing in the centre of the forest. Hunter perched in his usual place in the beech tree and Rivers landed on the opposite branch and looked at him with eyebrows raised, waiting for an explanation.

'I'm sorry,' Hunter said at length. 'I've blown my cover now and spoiled the plans you made.'

'All is not lost,' said Rivers, with a wintry little smile. 'At least you've convinced her that you're someone else.'

'I was going home,' said Hunter. 'I was on my way to see Dapple and to tell her that I was leaving these territories for good.'

'I see,' said Rivers, nodding slowly. 'The changes are too much for you?'

'It's not the place I knew,' said Hunter quickly. 'It's not the place we fought for. The place for which so many died.'

'That's why we need your help,' the History Owl said quietly. 'Winger has made these changes and we must bring him down. Was it true when you said Ivy Perch was the only local Barn owl that you'd met?'

'Yes, apart from Quaver, but it's enough to ruin everything. When Dirge and Winger hear about me they'll obviously want to meet this strange Man Owl who's lurking in the lost domain.'

'Has Winger ever met you?' Rivers asked, after a brief pause for thought.

'No,' said Hunter. 'And neither has Dirge.'

'Good! Since neither of them will recognize you, you can go on pretending to be Humanoid.'

'What about Dawn Raptor?'

'Of course! I'd forgotten her.'

'I'm afraid it's hopeless,' Hunter said. 'Two or three more nights, at the most, and then they'll find out that it's me.'

'Not necessarily,' said the History Owl, frowning with concentration. 'Ivy thinks you're Humanoid. She'll tell the others, but no one will come looking for you in the lost domain. Just keep out of the way and after a while they'll think you've gone back the way you came.'

'No good,' said Hunter, taking a deep breath and shaking his head slowly as he summoned up the courage to confess and tell Rivers what had really happened. But before he could open his bill and tell the History Owl the worst, Rivers got in ahead of him.

'Between you and me, old boy,' he said, sounding a little embarrassed by what he was about to say, 'there's another good reason for keeping well away from Dirge's territory.'

'Oh, what's that?' asked Hunter, half-relieved at having to postpone his confession and half-dreading what he was about to hear.

'That young female, Ivy Perch, or Honeysuckle Rose, as the silly creature likes to call herself.'

'What about her?' Hunter asked, groaning inwardly again as he guessed the answer in advance.

'She's on the make,' said Rivers. 'She's looking for a mate. She's desperate to get away from Dirge, and who can blame her? But if you don't mind my saying so, it might be dangerous for you to go on seeing her. She's sexy enough, poor Ivy, but not over endowed with character or brains, so what she's really looking for is someone to provide her with food and shelter for the rest of her natural life. If I were you, I'd stay away.'

'It's too late,' Hunter muttered miserably. 'I was just going to tell you. We've already mated.'

Having got it off his chest, Hunter looked away at once, unwilling to witness the bitter disappointment that he knew must be registered on Rivers' face. He heard a sharp intake of breath, and then, after what seemed like an age of silence, he heard the same breath whistle out again.

'It was my fault,' Rivers said eventually. 'If I'd come sooner, this might not have happened.'

'What can I do?' asked Hunter, spreading his wings in a gesture of despair. 'She'll be pregnant, and I can't abandon my own chicks to struggle for survival on their own.'

'No,' said Rivers, slowly. 'But on the other hand, there may still be some hope.'

'What hope?' asked Hunter, wearily. 'She's hardly got the energy or brains to feed herself, let alone a hungry brood of fledglings.'

'Oh, I agree,' said Rivers, frowning with concentration once again. 'But don't despair just yet. The worst may never happen.'

'I'm not impotent, you know, in spite of all my time spent in captivity.'

'Of course you're not,' said Rivers. 'And I don't suppose for a moment that Ivy Perch is barren. But strange things have been happening lately.'

'What do you mean?' asked Hunter impatiently. Whilst eager for any hope, however slight, of escape from his bond with Ivy Perch, he was bitterly ashamed to be speculating on the fate of the innocents who had barely been conceived and were still a long, long way from being born.

'There's been a lot of trouble,' Rivers said. 'We still don't know the full extent of it. Winger's keeping the details secret, even from the council, but it seems that breeding has become a problem. At least, in these territories it has. Several couples that I know of have failed to produce any eggs at all. Others have laid theirs, but with shells so thin that they've broken before the eggs have hatched. And even among the fledglings that have been born, the mortality rate is exceptionally high.

Nobody but Winger knows the full extent of it and nobody knows why, but I suspect our leader is trying to find out. That was probably the aim of his recent mission to the south.'

'So it's happening here as well?' said Hunter. 'That's very bad. It could be catastrophic.'

'It's an ill wind,' said Rivers, cautiously. 'It may help us to bring Winger down.'

'How so?' asked Hunter, slightly shocked by the cynical attitude of the History Owl.

'Because any leader stands or falls by the events that take place during his administration,' Rivers said. 'Just as many of the stupid electorate associated us with the war, so will they blame this infertility on Winger, whether he's got anything to do with it or not.'

'So we depose him and take over? A fat lot of good that will do us, if we're all extinct!'

'That won't happen,' Rivers said. 'As soon as we've overthrown him, we'll find out what the cause is and put things back to rights.'

'I know what's causing it,' said Hunter flatly. 'And there's nothing we can do to put it right. Unless, of course, you can communicate with humans.'

The History Owl looked at Hunter in amazement. 'You?' he said. 'You know what's causing it? But how on earth did you find out?'

'In captivity,' said Hunter, and then told Rivers everything that he had learned about pollution from Humanoid, the greatest living expert on man. 'So it's the humans who are contaminating the environment,' he concluded. 'This breeding failure happened in the southern territory where my tutor was Man Owl on the council and he was the one who first discovered what was causing it.'

'But why are they doing it?' asked Rivers. 'If men put poison in the ground to grow more of the food they eat, then surely the first creatures they contaminate must be themselves?'

'Not so,' said Hunter, grateful now for the education he had received. 'You see, it depends on something called the food chain,' he continued. 'That means the first creatures to eat these contaminated crops do not suffer from the ill effects at once. According to Humanoid, it may take generations before the poison really filters through and strikes at the reproductive systems of men and all the other creatures who eat the polluted food raw as it comes up from the ground. But when we eat the birds or animals that have digested this contaminated food, the effect on us is instantaneous, as it is with hawks and falcons.'

'I still don't understand,' said Rivers. 'Like us, men eat birds and animals that feed on these contaminated crops. Why don't they suffer from the same effects?'

'They suffer, but more slowly,' Hunter said. 'Humanoid says this may be because humans butcher the meat first and burn it before eating, instead of swallowing the raw creature whole. But he says that sooner or later, the effects on them will be the same.'

'And when the men discover this, will they stop?' asked Rivers, who was clearly struggling to digest this concentrated knowledge all at once.

'I suppose so,' Hunter said. 'But by that time, we Barn owls may well be extinct.'

'Thanks be to the Great God Bird that you came back when you did!' said Rivers, who seemed more excited than depressed. 'Thank heavens we have found out about all this before Winger does!'

'I don't see that it makes much difference,' Hunter said. 'If our homeland is polluted and we face extinction, I don't see that it matters who the leader is.'

'Of course it does!' the History Owl replied. 'One day man will see the error of his ways, the earth will be purified and cleansed and we Barn owls will begin to breed again. In the meantime, the important thing is to overthrow Winger and his New Apostasy.'

'I must warn Ivy Perch,' said Hunter. 'I must tell her not to catch any food on cultivated land. I shall tell her to hunt in no man's land and on the edges of the lost domain.'

'Don't!' said Rivers. 'You mustn't tell her anything. She's not the type to keep a secret and word might get back to Winger or to Dirge.'

'I don't want her to suffer,' Hunter said. 'It would be dreadful if the eggs hatched and she lost the chicks.'

'Hunter, don't talk to her yet. Just give me time to think. If Winger finds out who you are, he'll have you banished, or even hunted down and killed.'

'Think quickly,' answered Hunter, returning the History Owl's compelling gaze. 'I'll give you two more nights and then I'll tell her. I must do. They may be unwanted, but they're still going to be my chicks.'

The History Owl stared at him for a few moments longer, but Hunter did not flinch. Soon Rivers took a deep breath, sighed and then smiled as wan resignation replaced the anger on his face. 'All right,' he said. 'I'll discuss this with the other members of the resistance movement and meet you back here the night after tomorrow at the same time. And in the meantime, for the sake of the God Bird, get your priorities right. The first thing we must do is to get rid of Winger.'

'I'd put pollution before politics,' said Hunter. 'But you're the History Owl, so I suppose that you know best.'

'Thank you,' said Rivers, smiling more broadly as he prepared for take-off. 'And Hunter, one last word before I go. When we have taken over, I intend to make you Man Owl on the council. It's a trifle premature, but I just thought you'd like to know.'

It was very premature, thought Hunter, as he watched the white shadow of the History Owl flit away among the upper branches of the great, stately trees that crowded so close together in the teeming forest of the lost domain. 'A great future!' he said to himself sarcastically. 'That's what Rivers sees for us. I don't see much of a future for me with extinction facing us and with a mate like Ivy Perch.'

In the lonely darkness he began to worry then about the future of her chicks and about the dual responsibility he had of warning Ivy without betraying the secrets of the resistance movement of which he had become a part not out of choice, but by destiny and chance. In the midst of these worries he remembered little Alba and the last thing she had said to him as she lay dying in the parkland of the lost domain. 'Promise me one thing,' she had said, as the last light in her eyes began to fade. 'You're the nicest owl I've ever met. Don't change. For my sake, please try to stay the same.'

'I'll try,' he had said. Dawn filled the sky with deep, red streaks and the acrid richness of the earth rose up around him in the morning light. When he had torn himself away from Alba's dead body, he had promised that one day the world would be a better place. 'Some day owls will be more enlightened,' he had told himself. 'There will be more knowledge, and out of greater knowledge, greater kindness and tolerance will grow. And I shall devote my life's purpose to that end.'

Remembering his promise and comparing it with the way he himself and the world around him had become, Hunter was so overcome with anger and with shame that he broke down and wept.

CHAPTER

 13

As twilight deepened on the night after his long meeting with the History Owl, Hunter winged his way to the edges of the lost domain to visit Ivy one more time before Rivers was due back at midnight.

Though the History Owl had told him not to, and though Hunter liked her less and less each time they met, he somehow did not have the heart to stay away. Since mating, she had grown ever more peevishly dependent on him, and in spite of his increasing irritation, he fretted and worried for the future of their chicks. In fact, such was his concern for the mother and her fledglings that in spite of Rivers' warning he had decided to tell Ivy about the possible dangers of pollution and to make her promise to catch her food wild along the teeming borders of the promised land. She was waiting for him in her usual tree, and as soon as Hunter saw her, he knew that something had gone wrong.

'Oh, Humanoid,' she said, even before he had had a chance to settle on the branch beside her. 'So much has been happening, I'm really glad you came.'

'Tell me,' said Hunter, preserving a calm exterior although every nerve and muscle tingled in preparation for the shock. He knew it would be a bad one as she had not even reproached him for breaking his promise by not visiting her the night before.

'Promise you won't be angry?' she said, cocking her head to one side and emitting the words in a coaxing little whine.

'What's happened?' Hunter asked, finding it harder to control his apprehension as he noticed a suppressed glint of triumph in her beady little eyes.

'I had to tell,' she said, ruffling her plumage with a coquettish little sigh. 'To save myself from Winger, I had to tell the truth.'

'What do you mean?' asked Hunter, stifling his temptation to take hold of Ivy with his talons and shake her till every soft feather on her preened and pampered body trembled like frail leaves of aspen in the wind.

'He wanted to mate with me,' said Ivy, with a coy smile and a mock little shudder. 'So I had to tell him, didn't I?'

'I suppose so,' said Hunter, trying to stay calm until he had heard everything she had to say. 'Tell me, when did this happen?'

'Last night. He wanted to take me to the Graven.'

'What's the Graven?'

'It's the new name for Ferocity and Ripper's wood. Winger's always giving things new names. He says it will help us create the New Apostasy and forget the ancient reign. He's already got Dawn Raptor there.'

'Dawn Raptor?' said Hunter, carefully. 'She's your father's pupil, isn't she?'

'Yes, I told you she was mad on him. Just think of it, he wanted me as well!'

'What? Mating with two females at the same time? That's bigamy. It's against the constitution.'

'Not anymore it isn't. Winger says there's a crisis on and he has to mate with three females at a time in the interests of survival.'

'Three!' said Hunter in amazement. 'Whatever did your father say?'

'Oh, he agreed,' said Ivy. 'He's so thick he agrees with everything that Winger says. That's why I had to tell them, but Winger wasn't angry. In fact, he was very interested. He wants us to go there as well.'

'To Ferocity and Ripper's wood? You know we can't do that.'

'Well, tell him yourself then,' said Ivy, staring back at him defiantly. 'He'll be here to see you any moment now.'

'What, Winger will?'

'Yes, he's coming straight on here from the Graven. But there's no reason to be scared. He won't do you any harm. When I told him you'd grown up with humans, it didn't put him off at all. In fact, it made him all excited and he said he wanted to see you as soon as possible.'

'Is Dawn Raptor coming with him?' asked Hunter, making every effort to conceal his rising panic.

'I shouldn't think so,' Ivy said. 'He wants to talk to you alone.'

At that very moment, Hunter picked up the signals of a lone Barn owl flying towards them fast across Brook's old territory from the direction of Ferocity and Ripper's wood. Panic urged him to fly to his sanctuary inside the secret forest of the lost domain, but at the last moment a sudden, reckless desire to stay and confront Winger made him hesitate until it was too late and the leader's gangling body loomed up through the darkness and landed on the branch just opposite.

'Good evening,' he said, leaning forward with that slightly manic look of his. 'Humanoid, the Man Owl, I presume?'

'At your service,' said Hunter, gazing back into those strangely bulging eyes. 'I take it you are Winger, leader of the local council?'

'I am indeed,' said Winger and then turned his compelling gaze on Ivy Perch. 'Honeysuckle Rose, my dear,' he said, in an unctuous, patronizing sort of way. 'Will you leave us now and join Holly and Dawn Raptor in the Graven? In your present condition, it is vital for our experiment that you should avoid all farmland food.'

Ivy Perch looked at Hunter for his approval, but Hunter's bill had fallen open at the sound of Holly's name.

'I'll see you later, then,' said Ivy, as she gathered her feathers ready for the journey.

'What? Oh yes, of course,' said Hunter, managing to raise a wan and feeble smile. 'Goodbye Ivy, and be careful how you go.'

Ivy glanced sulkily at the two males, obviously somewhat offended by her summary dismissal. But Hunter and Winger were still scrutinizing each other so closely that they seemed quite oblivious of her presence. Unnoticed by either of them she pouted once and then flapped her wings and left.

'Well now, this is most interesting,' said Winger. 'You're living in the lost domain, I hear?'

'Not living,' Hunter said. 'Just passing through and helping the little immigrants with some information about man.'

'I see,' said Winger. 'And in the meantime, you've mated with our Ivy Perch?'

'I have,' said Hunter, averting his eyes from Winger and feeling wretched at this latest reminder of his folly.

'Such a charming little creature,' Winger said. 'Have you noticed how it pleases her to be addressed as Honeysuckle Rose? Her father is a member of my council,' he continued, after Hunter's unhappy little nod. 'A splendid, loyal owl, old Dirge. Not overbright, of course, but then he hasn't had our advantages.'

'I've never met him.'

'That's a pity! Of course, as a newcomer you should have approached me first. Now that you've decided to mate and settle here, you'll need a place to live.'

'You must forgive me,' answered Hunter. 'In many ways I am more man than owl. You might say I was more familiar with human behaviour than I am with Barn owl lore.'

'Well, I dare say we can forget your little misdemeanour, providing you cooperate, of course. We need your expertise,' said Winger, leaning forward on the branch and thrusting his long, bony face uncomfortably close to Hunter's. 'We need your knowledge of our neighbour, man.'

'Don't you have a Man Owl on your council?'

'Yes, of course, but he's not had your unique experience or education. To be quite frank, his was more of a political appointment than the choice of a true expert. Do you follow what I mean?'

'I think so,' said Hunter, speaking slowly and uncertainly in his role as Humanoid. 'You mean he knows nothing about man?'

'Well, hardly anything,' admitted Winger. 'About as much as Dirge knows about dogma and dialectic. But what the leader of a social revolution most requires are loyal supporters on his council. True specialists make indifferent politicians, don't you think?'

'Perhaps,' said Hunter, nodding slowly as he remembered Humanoid. 'You mean that sometimes they are blinded by scientific truth?'

'Exactly!' said Winger, who seemed very pleased with this reply. 'How aptly you put it, Humanoid,' he added, leaning back on the branch and treating Hunter to a meaningful yet supercilious sort of smile.

'But you need a true expert now?' asked Hunter, wondering how he was going to obey his instructions from the History Owl and withhold the information Winger so much needed.

'Yes, I do,' said Winger. 'And in the greatest confidence, I will tell you why. Whatever happens, you must promise not to divulge a word of what I am about to tell you to any other owl. The last thing I want is panic or discontent among the population.'

'Your secrets shall be mine,' said Hunter and then sat back and pretended to pay the closest attention while Winger told him about the infertility crisis, about his efforts to find out the cause of it, about the conclusions that he had come to and finally about the experiment he had set up in Ferocity and Ripper's wood.

In reality, Hunter knew nearly all of this already and listened only superficially whilst working out what line to take when Winger finished. And most of all, he wondered how he could stop Winger from using Holly's body, if it really was his Holly and if this despotic leader had not subjected her to his vile experiment already. And as he listened, Hunter once more reviled his own inconstancy and cursed the overpowering urge that had driven him to mate with Ivy Perch.

'So first I need all the scientific information you can give me,' said Winger in conclusion. 'And second, I need you in the Graven to help with my experiment.'

'I have two reservations,' said Hunter immediately, having decided that with an owl like Winger attack would be the best form of defence. 'First, I fear that the common owl might interpret your sacrifice merely as bigamous self-indulgence and that in consequence your reputation as leader could be badly damaged.'

'You are right. If I fail to solve the problem of infertility, I shall be branded as a tyrant and a lecher. But if I find a way for us to breed in safety, I shall be hailed as a great leader and maybe even as the saviour of our species. It is a risk I have to take.'

'I can see that,' said Hunter, pretending to agree, but secretly coming to the conclusion, as Holly had done earlier, that Winger was quite mad. 'However, my second reservation is more serious. Ferocity and Ripper's wood is Tawny territory and sooner or later they'll send a task force to take it back.'

'I don't agree,' said Winger coldly. 'I don't think the Tawnies will retaliate and even if they do, it won't be the Graven they attack. To start with, they won't get a task force through the lost domain. Our History Owl is currently conducting a survey of what the little squatters call their promised land. He says they have multiplied in numbers since the war and are now strong enough to repel anything but a full-scale invasion. But what is your opinion? You're staying with them, after all.'

'They have a very powerful garrison,' said Hunter. 'I agree that they could repel a Tawny task force if they wanted. But suppose they let them through in return for some territorial concession? For example, a promise that the Tawnies would give up their claims to the secret forest and never try to recolonize it again?'

'I suppose that is just possible,' admitted Winger, still gazing at Hunter with those bulging eyes. 'Before you leave the lost domain question the little squatters and find out what you can.'

'But the Tawnies don't even need to cross the lost domain,' continued Hunter. 'Assuming the task force sets out from Yoller's territory, they could circumnavigate the promised land and approach the Graven from the west.'

'Too far!' said Winger, with a vigorous shake of his big, bony head. 'It would take too long, and they'd have to cross the heartland of our Barn owl country first. No, if they do retaliate, they'll attack the Barn owl territories that lie on the borders of their ancient woods. They could take those easily and with very little risk.'

'But wouldn't you defend them?' asked Hunter, thinking of Bardic and his brother, whose territory would be one of the first to fall if what Winger said was true.

'How could I?' replied Winger, with a careless little shrug. 'There are too many. I couldn't keep a garrison in each.'

'So what do you gain?' asked Hunter, satisfied that so far he had received more information than he had given. 'Are you really prepared to sacrifice Barn owl lives and territory in exchange for the Graven and for one dubious experiment?'

'In the long run, does it matter?' Winger asked. 'If I am right and our farmland is polluted, we must find new territory or eventually become extinct. You are an owl of the world. You have travelled far and like me you have seen the villages begin to grow and swallow up our land. Even the countryside itself is changing as men flatten the hedgerows to make great barren wastes of field with no trees and no cover for raptors of our kind. What do a few lives matter now if we can find new, unpolluted territories and new ways to survive?'

'Don't underestimate the Tawnies,' Hunter said. 'In spite of their ancient woodlands and their feudal ways, they are more adaptable than we are. They can survive in villages, in parks, in cities and in all sorts of places where we can't. And when it comes to fighting, we don't stand a chance. With Yoller as their military leader, it's hard to imagine them losing any kind of war.'

'How do you know?' asked Winger, his great, bulging eyes narrowing slightly with suspicion. 'It struck me just now that for a stranger you seemed to know his name and the layout of his territory very well. Have you ever met him?'

'Of course not!' said Hunter, thinking very quickly. 'But news of his exploits has travelled very far. And you must know more than anyone about their military strength. You were doubtless one of those Barn owl heroes who fought beside them in the war.'

Winger was clearly embarrassed by this reference to war heroes. 'By the way,' he said, 'on your travels, did you ever come across an owl called Hunter? He came from this district and flew south to the city in the spring following the war.'

'I think I've heard of him,' said Hunter cautiously. 'He was one of your great war heroes, I believe?'

'A foolish, swashbuckling sort of bird,' said Winger quickly. 'Most of the stories about him are pure myth and legend, and partly for that reason it would be useful for me to know exactly how he died.'

'He was eaten alive by wild cats,' Hunter said. 'But don't rely on it, it's only what I've heard.'

'Hardly a heroic death,' said Winger, with a grim gloat of satisfaction in his eye. 'But I must say it is the kind of end one might have expected. He was a reckless, iconoclastic sort of owl who would have caused problems here had he returned.'

'Is that so?' said Hunter, and then, unable to resist it, added, 'I've heard he was courageous, though. And quite clever, in his way. In fact, some say he was almost a legend in his time.'

'Pure fantasy!' said Winger. 'A folk tale with no substance in reality. But anyway, he's dead and we are wasting time. Tell me, what do you think of my theory and how does it equate with scientific fact?'

'You could be right about pollution and the breaking eggs,' said Hunter, who had just hit upon a wild idea that might save Holly, at least for a while, from the leader's lewd abuse. 'On the other hand, contaminated food is not the only cause of infertility.'

'But how can I be sure?' asked Winger, bending his bony frame forwards and staring at Hunter with renewed intensity. 'How can you help me to find out if the food here is polluted, and if so, how and where?'

'I shall need time,' said Hunter, trying not to flinch as he returned the leader's gaze. 'I shall need time to conduct a survey of this territory and examine every corner bit by bit. For that, I need your authority to fly as freely as I please.'

'You have it,' Winger said. 'You have my authority to do exactly as you wish. But report to me at once with any progress that you've made.'

'Don't start your experiment until you hear from me,' said Hunter. 'Wait three or four days until you get the go ahead.'

'Why?'

'Because if the cause of this infertility is not human pollution, but disease, and if you go ahead with your experiment and fail, the local owls will blame you for starting a permissive society and perhaps even for spreading the disease.'

'It's too late,' said Winger, looking paler and somewhat shaken by what Hunter had just said. 'It's already started. I impregnated the first of the two females yesterday.'

'Which one?' asked Hunter, holding his breath and trying not to betray the agony of his suspense.

'Dawn Raptor.'

'The local one?'

'Yes, she's Dirge's apprentice and a passionate believer in the New Apostasy.'

'That's good,' said Hunter, as his heart lifted with immense relief. 'But whatever you do, don't touch the other one! Ivy tells me she's flown in from the south.'

'What's that got to do with it?'

'You never know,' said Hunter, darkly. 'She might be carrying some disease. You don't know where she's been!'

'But if I mate with her and she has healthy chicks, it will mean that she and the Graven are both clean and my theory about infertility is right.'

'Wait!' said Hunter. 'It's too soon to take the risk. Wait until you get the go-ahead from me.'

'Very well then, you may go,' Winger said. 'And remember, Humanoid, if you can help me solve this problem, there will be a great future for you in the New Apostasy.'

'Thank you,' said Hunter, unable to suppress the ghost of an ironic smile as he nodded deferentially at Winger before taking off and flying back into the depths of the lost domain for his midnight meeting with the History Owl.

As he glided silently towards the clearing in the heart of the secret forest, he warmed himself by the glow of the one small satisfaction he could find in the crumbling world around him. For the time being, at least, he had saved Holly from Winger's despotic, lewd experiment. She was safe now, for three or four nights only, but what all-consuming changes might occur between twilight and the dawn at such a fluid time in history as this?

CHAPTER 14

As his brother flew to meet the History Owl in the middle of the lost domain, Quaver left the abandoned farmhouse in a rage and sped fast across the Bard Owl's territory, propelled by the anger and frustration of one who has been humble and silent for too long.

'I can't stand it anymore,' he muttered, fuming as he flew, furious with himself and Bardic for the cowardly, servile manner in which they were proceeding with Winger's version of the epic ballad. 'That great, foppish bird is nothing but a fawning opportunist!' he shouted to no one in particular as he headed for the hollow oak that stood in no man's land between the borders of the Bard Owl's domain and the beginning of the Tawny woods. 'He's nothing but a slimy, servile toad!'

Quaver began to feel better once he had squeezed himself through the oval opening and got inside the hollow tree. It was a novel experience for him and a pleasant one. Though rather cramped, he felt well protected there and as he curled up into a comfortable position deep inside the belly of the oak, he began to experience a mellow, womb-like feeling of well-being. He remembered that this place had once been little Alba's funk hole and he was surprised to see that even after all that time there were still faded traces of her feathers in the secret, hidden chamber.

'Fawning, cringing sycophant!' he muttered to himself, as he struggled to put the final touches to a vitriolic little jingle he was secretly composing to lampoon his tutor and thus defuse his own rage and exasperation. Curled up inside his funk hole and hidden from the sky outside, Quaver stretched himself, sighed contentedly and recited the

little parody which in his opinion summed up the story of the Bard
Owl's life.

'The pompous Bard Owl lies,
Or tells the truth invented.
His own success in such a wise
Was by himself fomented.

His friends all know, the council too,
His fame at bottom's hollow,
But he himself proclaims it true
And the facile critics follow.

He puffs and blows his bumptious noise
Till most must surely hear him.
So devious are his little ploys
That few would dare to jeer them.

The moral then my friends rings thus:
If fame is your ambition
Create your own enormous fuss
And the fickle world will listen.'

Quaver smiled to himself as he spoke the last words of his jingle,
soothed by the feeling that he had struck a small blow against hypocrisy.
He sat on inside the hollow tree, wallowing in his freedom and wondering how soon he should go back, when suddenly he sensed a great
commotion in the night sky above his head. Quaver stiffened and then
poked his head cautiously through the hole in the trunk to identify the
cause. To his utter astonishment, he saw three Tawnies flying in
formation from the copse to the north of him and heading fast across
Barn owl country towards the abandoned farmhouse he had just left.
With his heart racing furiously, Quaver pulled his head back inside the
hollow of the tree and tried desperately to think. 'Is this it?' he asked
himself. 'Has Winger taken Ferocity and Ripper's wood, and is this a
Tawny task force on the way to win it back?'

Trembling with fear, Quaver clambered out of the hollow in the trunk
and flew off in the wake of the three invaders, terrified that they might
turn at any moment and tear him limb from limb. Though he had lost
sight of them by his initial hesitation, Quaver's radar soon told him that
the Tawnies had reached the abandoned farmhouse and then stopped.

As he forced himself to fly onwards through invisible barriers of fear, Quaver wondered how on earth Bardic would stand up to the shock.

Then, behind him, he sensed the rapid arrival of a fourth Tawny, hesitated, turned and saw to his surprise that the lone owl bringing up the rear of the task force was none other than their former military leader, Yoller. Quaking inside, Quaver slowed down and waited for his old acquaintance to catch up with him. Then, without a word of greeting, they flew on fast together towards the farmhouse roof.

'What's going on?' asked Quaver, now struggling to keep up with the Tawny's swift and powerful flight.

'I dread to think!' said Yoller grimly. 'I'm no longer in charge of this task force, and I've only just been told. That's why May Blossom held me back. It's on account of my having lost a talon, or at least that's what she says.'

'Who is the new commander?' asked Quaver, who was shocked by this news and even more frightened than before.

'There he is,' said Yoller, attempting to mask his humiliation as he strained his neck forward in full flight to indicate a lone Tawny who was now perched in a commanding position on the roof. 'His name is Birch and he's undoubtedly the finest warrior we've got.'

'And what's your role now?' asked Quaver, as they flew the last half-meadow's length to the Bard Owl's abandoned farmhouse.

'Oh, I'm still responsible for strategy,' said Yoller, adopting a casual tone to hide the bitter shock of his disappointment and betrayal. 'But on the battlefield, Birch has been placed in sole command. That's why I dread to think what we might find.'

A moment or two later they landed beside Birch on the roof and as they did so a bloodcurdling howl of pain came from the bedroom below them, followed by a choking, pleading kind of gibberish and then another dreadful, drawn-out scream of pain.

Though almost paralysed by terror, Quaver flexed his shaking limbs and prepared to fly down through the window, but as he was poised for take off Birch turned towards him, raised one mighty claw and placed all three talons squarely on Quaver's chest. 'Stay here,' he said, in the steely, chilling tones of a practised killer. 'It's all over now. There's nothing you can do.'

As Quaver stared at him in horror there was a noise at the bedroom window just below them and peering over the edge of the roof he saw two Tawnies heaving Bardic's torn and bleeding carcass up on to the windowsill. There the body lay suspended with the lifeless head lolling out above the ground, blood still welling from a great gash across the severed throat.

'Shall we eat 'im?' one of the killers called up to the roof.

'Of course not, Cleaver,' the new leader shouted back. 'I want his body left there hanging and dangling as a warning!'

'It be a pity, that,' said the first assassin, glancing down at the mangled body of his victim. 'Oi've never tasted Barn owl meat afore.'

'Us'll get our chance,' the second killer said, dragging his vicious talons across Bardic's bloody chest as if he wished he had had a chance to inflict more damage to the body before the Bard Owl died.

'Quite right, Hook. You'll get plenty of opportunity quite soon,' Birch said. 'You'll get the chance of something young and tender. Something much more succulent than that puffed-up old minstrel bird, you can be quite sure of that.'

The new Tawny commander was much better-spoken than Hook and Cleaver who had done the killing. His voice had an aristocratic drawl a bit like Yoller's and this somehow made him seem even more sinister and frightening than the two fierce thugs who had butchered the Bard Owl in his inner sanctum.

'Let me introduce you,' said Yoller, sighing slightly as he turned his head from Quaver to the owl who had taken over his command. 'Quaver, this is Birch, the leader of my troops. Birch, this is Quaver, one of the Barn owls you are not to harm, unless, of course, he interferes or makes himself a nuisance.'

'How do you do,' said Birch, with a suave, ironic little bow, while Quaver continued to gaze at him in horror. 'Did you hear that, you chaps?' he asked, calling down to the two killers. 'Take a good, long look at this one here. As a member of the Barn owl resistance movement, he's strictly not for eating.'

'That be a pity!' Cleaver said. ''E do look young and tender by comparison with this 'un us 'as killed.'

'That's enough, you fellows!' said Yoller, his hesitant drawl hardening into the sharp tone of command. 'We don't jest over dead bodies and we don't eat our victims in a war.'

314

'You shouldn't have done it,' said Quaver, finding a voice at last and surprised at how firm and strong it sounded, in spite of his great fear. 'It wasn't necessary to kill him.'

'Oh, but it was, old boy, it was,' said Birch in his most affected drawl. 'We had to kill at least one member of your council. As an example, you understand? And the Bard Owl can hardly be described as a great loss. In future, when you're over the shock, I hope you'll come to see it as a favour. I heard he was a lousy poet, anyway.'

With that Birch grinned sarcastically and flew off to join Hook and Cleaver who had abandoned Bardic's lolling body on the window sill and now sat together on the far end of the roof, laughing as they compared their steely, blood-stained talons.

'That was murder!' Quaver said, as his shock and anger hardened into an unexpected courage. 'He didn't stand a chance.'

'This is war, old boy,' sighed Yoller. 'And Winger started it, not us. If Bardic's dead, it's his fault and the fault of the Barn owl resistance movement for not acting sooner.'

'But Bardic couldn't fight,' protested Quaver. 'You know yourself he was terrified of any kind of violence. You wouldn't have had him killed if you'd still been in command.'

'Perhaps not, but I've told you, this is war,' said Yoller, sighing once again. 'And in a state of war you must be one thing or another. Bardic knew better, yet he was prepared to distort the truth and compose Winger's lying propaganda. Nobody is sorrier than I am that this thing has started, but having entered into it, we shall make absolutely certain that we win. Go to your brother now and tell him to lie low till this is over. Tell him not to intervene in any way or he'll be killed. And the same applies to you.'

'Give me time!' begged Quaver. 'Let me take a message to the History Owl. It may be that we can bring Winger down, form a new government and give you back Ferocity and Ripper's wood. Give me one more chance to stop all this blood from being shed.'

'I've told you, it's too late,' said Yoller, shaking his head with slow regret. 'May Blossom's directives are quite clear. We retake Ferocity and Ripper's wood and slaughter any Barn owls that have settled there. The harder we strike now, the sooner the whole thing will be over.'

'But think of the dangers you will face,' pleaded Quaver. 'You have to fly a long way across Barn owl country, unless you risk a dangerous short cut through the lost domain. Your whole task force could be wiped out before you reach Ferocity and Ripper's wood.'

'You think so?' asked Yoller, with one eyebrow ironically raised. 'Look at Hook and Cleaver! They are crude fellows but trained killers, both of them, and eager for the fray. And as for Birch there, he's the best warrior we have. He could kill your brother easily, and Hunter is the strongest and bravest Barn owl fighter that I've ever seen.'

'There are only four of you, and you have lost a talon.'

'No, this is the time for action,' said Yoller, very firmly. 'That's the trouble with your so-called resistance movement. Like all Barn owls, you're much too democratic. You've thought too much and talked too long and now your chance has gone. Go to your brother now and warn him before it is too late.'

At that very moment, Birch issued a sharp word of command. Hook and Cleaver immediately prepared for take off and a few moments later they were airborne and winging their way south-west, with Yoller in their wake, ready to carry death and destruction from their ancient woodlands into the heart of Barn owl farmland.

Quaver watched from the roof until the powerful formation had disappeared from sight. Then he flew down to the gap that had once been a window and perched on the sill beside Bardic's torn and bleeding body. Though it was an effort, he said the last words carefully, faltering from time to time before he found the courage to go on. Then, shortly before midnight, he set off with fear and sadness in his heart to search for his brother in the secret forest and to tell him that after three hundred springs they were at war with the Tawnies once again and that what was unthinkable to all owls of good will had finally and irrevocably happened.

CHAPTER 15

'Yes, of course I'd made a plan,' said the History Owl, who had arrived in the clearing in the centre of the secret forest shortly after midnight. 'I'd made quite a good plan, as a matter of fact, but now that you've met Winger, everything is ruined.'

'I'm sorry,' Hunter said. 'But there are some advantages. At least we know his plans, and we know he has guessed the cause of this infertility.'

'That was a good idea of yours,' said Rivers pensively. 'To put him off the scent with that warning about disease. When you next meet, keep him guessing. Say you still think that could be the cause. In the meantime, I will spread the word about this bigamous experiment. That should help to discredit him and to gain us the support of the older, more religious owls.'

'What if the Tawnies send a task force in the meantime? What will happen to the females in Ferocity and Ripper's wood?'

'I daresay they'll be killed,' said Rivers, casually. 'But does it really matter? It's unfortunate about your sister, but luckily you've never liked her much and in any case she's one of Winger's acolytes. Just think, you'd be rid of Ivy Perch, and the third female isn't from this district anyhow. No, in many ways I hope the Tawnies do retake the so-called Graven and don't attack the Barn owl territories that border on their woods, as Winger seems to think they will.'

'Why's that?' asked Hunter, who was deeply shocked to discover that the History Owl seemed as ready as Winger was to sacrifice both existing and unborn lives in his ruthless pursuit of power.

'Because most Barn owls know that Ferocity and Ripper's wood truly belongs to the Tawnies, not to us. They'll say the Tawnies are only taking their own territory back again. But if the Tawnies attack the vulnerable borderlands instead, the population will see it as an outside threat. They'll band together behind Winger to defend the heartland and for the time being we'll have missed our chance to bring him down and form another government.'

'I can't allow it,' Hunter said. 'I can't allow those three females to be slaughtered. Apart from Dawn and Ivy Perch, I know the third one very well. I met her in the south and she came here in search of me. I only wish I'd waited to mate with her instead of Ivy Perch. The three females must be warned and told to leave at once.'

'You can't go!' said Rivers sharply. 'Dawn Raptor would expose your true identity, and where would you be then?'

'You do it then!' said Hunter. 'We can't just leave them there to die.'

'Relax,' said Rivers soothingly. 'The Tawnies haven't sent a task force yet. For all we know, it may never happen.'

'You could warn them anyway. Or does it suit your strategy to have them killed?'

'Take care, Hunter!' said the History Owl, leaning forward on his branch and peering through bright eyes that showed pain and anger at one and the same time. 'You are too subjective. You don't realize how serious this is. The future of our species is at stake and yet you allow yourself to be swayed by emotional attachments. First that little immigrant, then Ivy Perch and now some female that you picked up on your travels. It's just not good enough. Heroes of the resistance must be made of sterner stuff.'

'They must be warned,' repeated Hunter stubbornly. 'If you don't go, I will.'

'But I can't!' protested Rivers, who was now burning with exasperation. 'Don't you see? As a member of the council I can't countermand an order Winger's given. That would be tantamount to treason.'

'What were you saying about stern stuff in the resistance?' Hunter asked sarcastically. 'Or doesn't that apply to you, as leader?'

'Of course it does,' said Rivers, fuming. 'But don't you see, I can only countermand his orders once? Once and once only, when we strike our decisive blow and take away his power.'

'Then I will warn them. I'm sorry, Rivers, but I can't leave Holly and two pregnant females there to die.'

'You must!' commanded Rivers, with all the strength and authority that he possessed. 'You've already frustrated all the plans I've made for you and the resistance, first by mating with Ivy Perch and then by meeting Winger. For the God Bird's sake, do as you're told this time! Lie low and wait until the time is ripe.'

'I'm more concerned with preservation than with power,' said Hunter, who knew that the time had now come to make his middle way position plain. 'You won't like this, Rivers, but in my opinion, Winger is not altogether wrong. He's mad, he's power-drunk and he's dangerous – all that I'll admit. But he's right about pollution, he's right about the changing countryside and he's right to be concerned about the environment in which we live. I don't like lying to him about contamination. I want to put all my experience and all the education that I got in prison into the interests of science and survival. I don't want to waste it playing power games.'

'Think carefully,' said Rivers, breathing very deeply to control his anger. 'Winger may think he needs you in your role as Humanoid, but if he knew your true identity, you'd be destroyed. Therefore your only future lies with us in the resistance. But you must be either with us or against us. In dangerous times like these, there's no room for the middle way. And I can assure you that we're not playing games.'

Hunter was about to reply when he picked up a Barn owl approaching fast across the secret forest from the north. Though this was unusual in itself, the rapidly strengthening signals revealed an even stranger thing. The lone Barn owl was being escorted by a squadron of little immigrants who were flying above him and round him in formation. Rivers had picked up the signals, too, and both he and Hunter stared up at the night sky above the beech tree in the clearing until presently they saw the white shadow of Quaver appear above the tree tops. He was surrounded by four fierce-looking Little owls with Falco at their head.

Looking very frightened, Quaver settled on the branch beside his brother, while the little immigrants fluttered to strategic positions in the tree above them.

Falco landed next to Rivers, glanced sideways at him without any form of greeting and then stared hard at the two brothers sitting opposite. Then he turned back to Rivers and said, coldly: 'Quaver has a message for you. He may give it to you here, but then you and he must leave. Hunter, you may stay here if you wish, but only in your role as Humanoid. For the duration of the war, no other Barn owl or Tawny will be allowed to enter here. We shall not permit two other species to turn our promised land into a battlefield.'

'War? What war?' asked Rivers, widening his eyes in consternation.

'It's started,' said Quaver, still looking very shaken. 'Bardic has been murdered and a Tawny task force is now on its way to reconquer Ferocity and Ripper's wood.'

While the History Owl's eyes narrowed in steely concentration and Hunter sat and listened in dismay, Quaver told them what had happened. 'Of course, the worst thing from our point of view is that Yoller is no longer military leader,' he concluded. 'May Blossom told him it was due to the fact he'd lost a talon, but I don't believe it and I don't suppose that he does either. The real reason is that Yoller knows us, we once fought side by side and she thinks he'd be too soft. With Birch in command, there's no risk of compromise, mercy or compassion. He's young, ruthless and ambitious. He'll carry out her orders blindly and kill until his task force is wiped out or till he gets the unconditional surrender that May Blossom wants.'

'But will they ever get to Ripper's wood, the long way round?' asked Hunter, while his brother sat back on his perch in a crumpled heap of feathers, still suffering from emotional exhaustion and from shock. 'Or will Winger's forces intercept and kill them over open country?'

'He'll have no time to organize defences,' said the History Owl, with a quick shake of his head. 'The first thing he'll do is to convene an emergency meeting of the council.'

'It will be too late by then!' said Hunter, remembering the last war. 'Unless we act at once, those females in the Graven will be killed.'

'I know,' said Rivers. 'But this is a surprise attack and Winger has no choice. He'll let the Tawnies through to Ripper's wood, muster his forces in the meantime and attack them on their way back home again. I must fly back at once to consult with Language and Geography and then attend the meeting.'

'Remember that you can't come back again!' said Falco, leaning forward as he spoke. 'From now on, the promised land will be closed to all refugees until this war is over.'

'Fly back with me,' said the History Owl to Hunter and to Quaver. 'There will be great confusion at the emergency council meeting and this may be our time to strike.'

'Too late,' said Hunter firmly. 'By that time the three females and my unborn fledglings will all be dead. I shall go to them at once, before the Tawnies get there.'

'Think carefully,' said Falco. 'I've told you, you may stay. You once sheltered a Little owl on your land, you warned us before Ferocity and Ripper came to kill those few of us who first settled here, and now you have solved the enigma of the new men living in the lost domain. For this, we offer you protection here until the war is over. But only as Humanoid. If you left here and your true identity were discovered, for us the risk would be too great.'

'Don't be hasty, Falco,' said the History Owl. 'You offered our resistance movement refuge and a headquarters here in the secret forest. If you keep that promise we will respect your territory once the war is over. Otherwise, once we have taken power and made peace with the Tawnies, what's to stop us making a treaty with them and joining forces to invade your so-called promised land? That way, the Tawnies would get their ancient forest back, we could colonize the parkland and you would be banished back into the no man's land from whence you came.'

Falco did not reply at once but stared hard at the History Owl who returned his gaze unflinchingly. After a few moments' silence, Falco threw his head back and barked out one sharp call of command. Then he leaned forward on his perch, cocked his scarred head to one side and thrust his fierce little bill forwards into the space that separated him from Rivers. 'There is one good reason why neither you nor the Tawnies will ever recolonize the promised land,' he said, stabbing the words out in tones of icy calm, while his four warriors stiffened on their perches and glared down at the three Barn owls below them as if longing for their leader to give the signal to attack. Then suddenly the branches of the beech tree shook as six more Little owl warriors appeared from nowhere and settled in strategic positions to reinforce their comrades who were already poised for the assault.

'As you see, we are very well prepared,' said Falco, with the flicker of a smile at the visible anxiety on Rivers' face. 'You must go now, History Owl, and when the war is over we will talk again. But there will be no more conditions, do you understand?'

Surrounded by a circle of immigrant warriors, Rivers looked up and around him and then slowly nodded his assent. 'Come with me now,' he said, turning and fixing Quaver with his bright, commanding stare. 'Come with me and leave your brother here to make his own decision. I have warned him, but he doesn't seem to understand that at times like this no one can survive alone. If he stays here as Humanoid he will always be an exile, reviled by Winger's party, or by the ancient reign, whichever of us wins. And if he flies his mercy mission to the Graven, he'll die there inglorious, forgotten and unsung, the second blood victim of this senseless war and of Winger's New Apostasy.'

Quaver stared back at the History Owl and hesitated still. Then he turned and looked at his brother with a desperate, pleading expression on his face. 'Come with us, Hunter!' he implored. 'Come with us or else stay here in the lost domain. You haven't seen the Tawny task force. They'll tear you limb from limb. For the Great God Bird's sake, Yoller's warning was quite clear. If we stay away from the conflict and the action, we're quite safe, but if we interfere in any way, we shall be ripped to pieces like poor Bardic.'

Hunter glanced quickly at his brother, at Falco and last at the History Owl. Then he looked away from them into the deep throbbing of the secret forest, remembering the place in the parkland beyond the sea of trees where he had watched over little Alba's body till dawn came and she died. He remembered the promise he had made her not to change and as the last war flashed back into his mind he recalled the pain of his own wounds and how close he had come to death. But above all he remembered flying into battle with that brief vision of a better, cleaner life that lay ahead. 'Go with the History Owl,' he said, turning back to Quaver with a wry half smile. 'I shall fly to Ripper's wood, warn the three females and then wait there for the Tawnies. Who knows, I may be able to negotiate a settlement.'

Quaver stared at his brother for a moment longer, glanced at Falco and then turned to the History Owl and sighed with the deep resignation of one who suspects that his time upon this earth has but a little space to run. 'I shall go with Hunter,' he said, sounding surprisingly calm as he uttered what he thought would be his own death sentence. 'I must,' he added simply. 'We were both born of the same mother and I can't let him die alone.'

'Very well,' said Rivers, his face twisting into bitter disappointment. 'In that case I'll say goodbye, for I doubt whether we three shall ever meet again.'

'Farewell, then,' Hunter said. 'And remember me when you take power. Remember Humanoid, who warned you that the main threat to survival came from man and not from the transient Winger and his New Apostasy.'

'I shall remember both of you,' said Rivers, with a formal little bow. 'And now let us depart and face our separate destinies.' The History Owl looked round him then, nodded once to Falco and then took off and headed south-west across the secret forest towards the borders of the lost domain.

'May your own God Bird fly with you both!' said Falco, as the two brothers prepared for take off. 'And if he wills it, we will meet again in times of peace.'

Hunter nodded, smiled at Quaver and then took off, with his brother following close behind, on what both well knew might be the last short journey of their lives.

CHAPTER

 16

They emerged from the lost domain and travelled onwards fast, crossing Dirge's flat farmland and flying high over the place where Steeple had fallen in the war. Soon they reached the no man's land that began as the valley sloped upwards in the darkness beneath their wings and the low-lying fields and meadows gave way to the rising spinney on the borders of Ferocity and Ripper's wood.

As the trees thickened and they entered the dense darkness of the wood itself, Hunter sensed the presence of a female Barn owl ahead of them in the clearing beside the battlefield where the monster had been slain, and he prayed that it might be Holly so that he could see her alone for a few precious moments before meeting Dawn and Ivy Perch. But as they entered the ghostly clearing, Hunter saw his sister seated in the great beech tree where the Barn owl contingent had perched in serried ranks so long ago and waited for the final battle to begin.

He slowed a little in his powerful flight, allowing Quaver to catch up with him, and as they both landed on the branch opposite Dawn Raptor he saw at once that she looked much older than he had expected. Her smile, once enigmatic and supercilious, had now hardened into a sour and disapproving glare as she greeted her younger brother Quaver.

'What are you doing here?' she asked ungraciously, and then looked away from him at Hunter without waiting for a reply. 'We were expecting an owl called Humanoid. I imagine this is him?'

The two brothers glanced at each other sideways in surprise and then Hunter looked back at her, his face breaking into a rueful little smile.

She stared back at him and the sour expression on her face gave way to amazement as the dawn of recognition rose slowly in her eyes.

'Hunter!' she gasped, eventually. 'It can't be Hunter, come back from the dead?'

'You don't sound very pleased to see me,' Hunter said.

'It can't be!' Dawn repeated, staring at him in a state of growing consternation. 'You must be Humanoid. Hunter died in the city long ago, yet the likeness is amazing.'

'That's hardly surprising,' said Hunter, with another rueful little grin.

'What do you mean?' asked Dawn, turning away from him and glaring at Quaver for an explanation. 'Who is this owl? Is it Humanoid, or is it really your brother come back from the dead?'

'He's both,' said Quaver, who wished they would both get on with it and stop wasting precious time.

'Don't be ridiculous!' said his sister, and then turned impatiently to Hunter. 'You must be the Man Owl who's just mated with Dirge's daughter Ivy Perch.' Then she leaned forward and peered at him more closely. 'And yet you're not!' she added, gasping on the intake of her breath. 'You really are my brother Hunter, born again.'

'Quaver's right. I'm both. Or put it this way, there's no such bird as Humanoid. There was, but I left him in prison in the city and took on his identity.'

'You mean you're pretending to be someone else?' asked Dawn Raptor, as rising anger began to take the place of her perplexity.

'Exactly!' Quaver said. 'As far as Winger is concerned, he's Humanoid, and you'd better not forget it.'

'So it's true!' Dawn said, still too amazed to give rein to her full invective. 'When Winger finds out, he'll be livid. Dead or alive, he doesn't want you back.'

'Is Winger here now?' asked Quaver, who was almost bursting with impatience.

'No,' Dawn Raptor said. 'He's gone back to his headquarters for a special meeting of the council.'

'Good!' said Quaver. 'Where are the other two?'

'Ivy Perch has gone to call her father to the meeting. She should be back at any moment. Holly's gone to eat somewhere in the centre of the wood.'

'Then call them, please,' said Hunter. 'We haven't got much time.'

'Call them yourself!' Dawn Raptor answered back. 'You can't come flying back here from the dead giving everyone instructions. Winger is our leader and he's left me in charge here. I take orders from him and from no one else.'

'Don't be silly, Dawn!' said Quaver, who by this time was almost in a frenzy. 'This is an emergency. If you don't call them soon, we'll all be dead.'

'Dead, why?' asked Dawn Raptor, looking stubbornly at her two brothers.

'Because the Tawny task force is on its way,' said Quaver.

'They've already murdered Bardic and they'll kill any Barn owl they find in this place you call the Graven.'

'How many of them are there?' asked Dawn Raptor, after a brief pause to take this in.

'Four,' said Quaver. 'Yoller, the new leader Birch and two dreadful killers known as Hook and Cleaver.'

'Good!' said Dawn Raptor, with a decisive little nod. 'You have arrived just in time to help us defend this place for Winger and the New Apostasy. With Dirge and Ivy, there'll be six of us. That should be enough.'

'You must be mad!' said Quaver, hopping up and down on his branch with impatience and frustration. 'You haven't seen them, or what they did to Bardic. Hook and Cleaver are killers like Ferocity and Ripper, and against Birch even Hunter wouldn't stand a chance.'

'Nonsense!' said Dawn Raptor, who looked very frightened in spite of the bold stand that she was taking. 'Anyway, they probably won't get this far. Winger will bring them down over Barn owl country to the west of here.'

'He won't!' said Quaver urgently. 'That's what this council meeting's all about. For the Great God Bird's sake, call the other two and let's get out of here before they arrive and tear us all to pieces.'

Dawn Raptor still hesitated and Quaver was about to put out the call himself when he sensed two separate Barn owls approaching from opposite directions.

'Here they come!' said Hunter, who had also picked up the signals, and sure enough only a few moments later Ivy Perch appeared through the tree tops to the north-east as Holly flew into the clearing from the west.

'Oh, Humanoid, you're here at last!' cried Ivy as she landed beside him on the branch. 'What kept you so long? We thought you were never coming!'

'That's not Humanoid,' snapped Dawn Raptor, while Hunter looked up at Holly as she perched on a branch just above his sister's head. 'That's my brother Hunter and he's mated with you under false pretences.'

'There's not time for all that now,' said Quaver, who was getting desperate. 'For the Great God Bird's sake, let's get out of here before they come!'

'What does she mean?' asked Ivy, looking at Hunter in a peevish and bewildered manner. 'You are Humanoid, aren't you? You'd better be! You're going to be the father of my chicks.'

'Who's coming?' asked Holly calmly, looking down at Hunter with a smile that was forgiving, though both hurt and sad.

'The Tawnies are, and Quaver's right. You must all get out of here at once. I shall stay and attempt to negotiate a settlement.'

'I see it now!' Dawn Raptor said, her eyes blazing with the fury of one who has been betrayed. 'This is a conspiracy. You and Quaver are in league with the Tawnies and this is all part of a plan to bring Winger down and destroy the New Apostasy.'

'Oh, don't talk such sparrow shit!' said Hunter angrily. 'Go with Quaver, all of you, before it is too late!'

'Where shall I take them?' asked Quaver, who had been driven almost to distraction by this ridiculous delay.

'To Dapple's place.'

'Not all of them. There's not enough to eat for five.'

'True!' said Hunter. 'Take Holly, then. And you, Dawn Raptor, fly back with Ivy to Dirge's abandoned cowshed. That's where the three of you have been living anyway.'

'I'm staying,' Dawn said bitterly. 'I'm staying to defend the Graven and to frustrate this conspiracy. In Winger's name, I order all of you to do the same!'

'Don't be insane!' said Hunter, and was turning to beg Quaver to reason with their sister when he picked up the distant rhythmic beat of Tawny wings as the task force powered its way through Ferocity and Ripper's wood.

'Go now!' Hunter said. 'Not to Dapple's, it's too late. Dawn and Ivy, go to Dirge's, and you, Quaver, take Holly to the edges of the lost domain.'

Quaver took off without further hesitation, called for Holly to follow and flew towards the north-eastern reaches of the wood. Holly fluttered in the air above her perch and called out to Hunter in despair. 'Come, oh please come now!' she cried as the quiet thunder of the Tawny wings moved closer and filled the midnight air. But Hunter shook his head, swallowed hard and pointed one wing towards the confines of the Graven. Holly hesitated for a moment longer, then gave a little gasping sob and flew off following fast in Quaver's path.

'Get out, Ivy!' shouted Hunter, who was now at the very limits of despair. 'Do you want our fledglings killed?'

Ivy looked back at him, too bewildered and too terrified to move. A moment later, with Birch leading, the four Tawnies burst into the clearing and made straight for the beech tree where Hunter, Dawn and Ivy sat petrified by the sight of so much savage yet coordinated power. At the same time Hunter picked up the signals of a Barn owl entering the clearing from behind him. At first he thought it must be either Holly or Quaver making a suicidal return, but Dawn Raptor turned and called out 'Dirge!' just as the four Tawnies paused, hovered in mid-flight and turned their terrible attention to the new intruder.

'Wait, Yoller!' Hunter shouted. 'Don't attack! He's innocent, he doesn't live here. He knows nothing!' In the meantime Dirge stopped and hovered in mid-air, staring in astonishment at the three Barn owls in the beech tree and the four Tawnies who barred his path across the clearing.

'Dirge is one of Winger's owls!' cried Birch. 'Kill him, Hook, and this time do it cleanly!'

Hunter's mouth opened in horror but before he could call out again, Hook's back arched as he hurled himself across the clearing towards the hesitant, bewildered Dirge.

'Stop!' shouted Hunter. 'He doesn't know what's happening!' But it was too late. Warned of the attack in time, Dirge instinctively flexed the muscles in his portly frame and prepared to do battle in his own defence.

It was only a few moments before the two owls clashed, but to Hunter it all seemed to take place very slowly as Hook surged closer and closer to his prey, spreading his vicious talons for the kill. As the distance between the two owls diminished in a nightmare of slow motion, Hunter dominated every instinct and forced himself to stay still and frozen to the branch of the beech tree, knowing that any hostile movement made by himself, Dawn or Ivy Perch could cause a widening of the conflict and provoke a bloodbath in which they would all be killed.

With a few moments to recover from the shock, the slow-witted, solid Dirge had gained a little height, placing himself fractionally above the Tawny at the moment of their impact. Over-confident and contemptuous of Barn owl opposition, Hook flung himself recklessly upwards into the attack and as he did so, Dirge struck downwards hard and unexpectedly. It was a clumsy, panic-stricken lunge, but his powerful talons caught Hook unprotected and off-balance in his upward swing and ripped his head wide open just above the eye.

Hook howled with pain, fluttered furiously and then climbed higher and flung himself head-on at Dirge who lunged and wounded Hook's head again before the Tawny's dreadful talons tore into his chest, ripping clawfuls of flesh and feathers from the bone. Dirge clamped both talons into the Tawny's side and drove his bill deep into the gaping wound he had made above the eye. Hook howled out in rage and pain again and tore into the Barn owl's body in a frenzy of furious destruction.

Then Ivy moved. Before Hunter had noticed or could stop her, she took off from her branch in the beech tree and flew fast across the clearing towards the two fighting owls who were now locked in one flailing ball of feathers, blood and tearing flesh. Before Ivy had time to reach her target, Cleaver ceased his hovering watch and launched himself forward in an attempt to intercept the female before she could fling herself at his comrade's unprotected back.

As soon as he saw this, knowing that the end had come for all of them, Hunter took off and hurled himself across the clearing, ready to take on the entire Tawny task force in defence of Ivy and her unborn chicks, though even as he raced into combat he knew that this would be a fight to the very death and a fight he did not stand one single chance of winning.

CHAPTER

 17

From his vantage point high up in the great oak on the edge of Ripper's wood, Quaver saw all this begin to happen and not for the first time in his life he wished he had become a warrior instead of a composer and a poet. 'I can't go on,' he had said, as Holly joined him high up in the giant oak. 'I know it's dangerous, but I have to see what happens next.'

And from their high position they both saw it come to pass, as Hunter had done, in slow, excruciating motion. They saw Ivy drawing nearer and nearer to Hook's vulnerable back, saw her waver once in flight, as if she had sobbed, and then watched her drop and sink her talons into the Tawny's neck as he tore the dying Dirge to shreds. They saw Cleaver reach the scene a split second before Hunter did and watched in horror as he dived and half-decapitated Ivy with one single stroke of his lethal talons. Even as she died, Ivy clawed once more at Hook's unprotected neck, and Cleaver was himself struck down as Hunter ripped his left eye from its socket in a late, despairing dive.

Now, with Hook dying and Cleaver badly wounded, Birch raced across the clearing to dispose of Hunter, while to his amazement Quaver saw his sister leave her branch and launch herself towards Yoller to prevent him from joining the attack.

'Now!' said Holly urgently. 'We must save Hunter now!' Quaver groaned in misery, glanced at Holly and saw in a flash how happy the two of them could have been if they had escaped together and shared a gentle life of poetry and song instead of being caught up by their destinies in all this conflict, blood and strife. Then he took a deep breath, threw himself down from the high branch and headed towards the battle in the clearing, with a frightened but determined Holly flying by his side.

Hunter heard Birch coming and had time to turn before this most dangerous of enemies could strike him from behind. When the Tawny came straight at him, with vibrant outstretched talons, Hunter dived forward low beneath his assailant's feet and then climbed high up into the air as Birch turned to attack again. From his brief vantage point above the battle, Hunter saw Ivy's dead body fall in a lifeless heap of feathers to the earth beneath and land beside the place where Dirge and Hook already lay dead, still clasped in that same mortal embrace with which they had grasped each other in the battle. He saw the one-eyed Cleaver climbing towards him slowly, blood streaming from his empty socket and heard Yoller's cry of pain as Dawn Raptor slashed through his bemused defences with her furious female claws.

'Of course, he's lost a talon,' Hunter remembered suddenly, as the ferocious Birch drew face to face with him again and Cleaver struggled higher towards him in the sky, half-dead but still bent on the most terrible revenge. 'This is the end,' Hunter told himself, steeling every muscle and determined to take both Birch and Cleaver with him to his death.

Then he saw Quaver and Holly race into the clearing side by side and his heart leaped high with sudden hope. As Birch lunged for him, Hunter swayed to one side and then slashed the Tawny just behind the ear. As Birch turned to attack again, Hunter dived suddenly downwards, met Cleaver climbing towards him and with one perfect blow took out his other eye. Cleaver howled, fluttered once and then crashed downwards, dying not long before he hit the ground. As Birch was about to drop on Hunter, he too saw Quaver and Holly coming towards him, so he hesitated and then climbed higher in the sky.

'Help Dawn Raptor!' Hunter shouted. 'Leave this one to me.'

Quaver and Holly paused, hovered face to face with Birch and then veered off with one accord and sped across the clearing just as Yoller, stung by the wounds Dawn Raptor had inflicted, recovered from the shock of being attacked by a female, regained his lost confidence and began to tear his opponent limb from limb.

'Just you and me, then!' Birch said, as Hunter rose to meet him. 'I'm going to take your eyes out first, just like you did to Cleaver, and then I'm going to cut your body into tiny little shreds!'

'We'll see about that!' Hunter said and lunged unexpectedly into the attack, swerved at the last moment and then set off across the clearing, following in Quaver's flight path, while Birch was left behind clawing at thin air. Ahead of him, Hunter saw Quaver and Holly racing towards Yoller's unprotected back, but the Tawny heard them coming and let Dawn Raptor go. She fell at first, then sank fluttering feebly to the branch of a nearby sycamore, her head and body both bleeding profusely and torn beyond repair.

Yoller braced himself for Quaver and Holly's twin attack, but just before they reached him the two Barn owls divided, veered to either side of him, joined up again and then turned to dive down on the Tawny from behind. Yoller turned to face them and thus exposed himself to Hunter, who was closing on his target fast, well ahead of Birch who had set off in pursuit.

Homing in on Yoller, Hunter knew that he must hit his old friend hard and kill him with one blow so that he could then turn his attention back to Birch, for in spite of all their courage, neither Holly nor Quaver had any fighting skills and would therefore stand no chance if either one of these two Tawnies stayed alive.

With Holly and Quaver racing towards him from the other side, Yoller did not sense Hunter's arrival until it was too late. He heard Birch's howl of warning and half-turned as Hunter's talons ripped the top of that massive, rock-like head. As Yoller lost consciousness, ceased to hover, turned over in mid-air and fell headlong to the ground, Holly and Quaver flew on above his falling body and headed straight for the fast approaching Birch. As before, they veered to either side of him just before colliding with the vicious Tawny killer in mid-air. Birch turned to face them, just as Yoller had, while Hunter rose rapidly high into the sky and prepared to hurl himself down on Birch in one death or glory dive the way he had killed the kestrel in wild fury on that now long-distant dawn.

As he started his long dive, he saw Quaver and Holly turn and fly back towards Birch, who had now lost sight of Hunter in the sky straight up above him. Hunter dropped then, straining every nerve and sinew, knowing he must kill or maim the Tawny with that first vital blow. But at the last moment, Birch turned up to face him and Hunter's plunging talons missed the head and neck and instead sank deep into Birch's powerful chest. The Tawny grunted with pain and blood spurted from his breast. Winded and badly hurt, he gave Hunter time to extract his talons from the bone and flesh and rip upwards at the unprotected throat. More blood spurted, but Birch found the strength to claw at Hunter's body, ripping flesh and feathers from both shoulders while Hunter ignored the pain and struck again and again as trickles of his own blood began to mingle with the fountains that now welled from Birch's throat and breast. This Tawny warrior was stronger and more skilful than either Hook or Cleaver and in spite of his mortal injuries he fought on, lusting for more of Hunter's blood before his own red fountain ceased to flow.

'I'll have your eyes for Cleaver's,' he growled, and gathering the last of his fast fading strength he made a mighty effort, wrenched himself free from the fierce grip of Hunter's talons and was about to launch one final attack in the full fury of his dying spasm when Quaver dropped from the sky above him and delivered a powerful but inexpert blow to the back of Birch's neck. He turned fast to slash at his new assailant but Quaver slipped quickly from his grasp, sustaining only one deep scratch and the loss of several feathers from his wing.

Hunter was about to attack his apparently indestructible opponent once again when Birch's head arched backwards in a sudden spasm, straightened and then lolled forward on his chest. His great round wings beat once more as a kind of reflex to keep him in the sky and then he turned over slowly in mid-air and nose-dived stone dead into the ground.

Hunter watched him fall and then flew at once to the low branch of the sycamore where Dawn Raptor sat bleeding profusely and propping up her wobbly, lacerated body against the mighty trunk. Even as he reached her she lost consciousness, slipped off the branch, toppled the brief distance to the ground and lay there on her side, her breast heaving as she struggled for the last few gulps of breath that she would draw before going to the great beyond.

Hunter landed beside her and touched the torn and heaving body with one wing. Her eyes opened, she looked up at him and across her ravaged features there flickered weakly the ghost of that once infuriating, enigmatic smile.

'Tell Winger that I died for him,' she whispered. 'Tell him that I died to defend the Graven and our New Apostasy.' Hunter nodded and she smiled up at him for one last time. Then her eyes closed, she gave a little shudder, her breathing stopped and Dawn Raptor died.

'My sister, Dirge, Ivy Perch and four Tawnies dead!' said Hunter bitterly, as Holly and Quaver landed beside him on the ground. 'Six dead for Ferocity and Ripper's wood!'

'Seven,' said Quaver, quietly. 'You've forgotten Bardic.'

'Nine or ten,' said Hunter sadly. 'If you count poor Ivy's unborn fledglings.'

'Say the last words for your sister,' murmured Holly gently. 'Then we'll all fly across the clearing and do the same for Dirge and Ivy Perch.'

'What about Yoller?' Quaver asked. 'We don't know if he's dead yet, or just very badly injured.'

'And you?' asked Holly, gazing at Hunter anxiously. 'Are you very badly hurt? I've never seen an owl or any other living creature so completely soaked in blood before.'

'Not much of it is mine,' said Hunter gruffly. 'The injuries I have will heal much sooner than the sorrow. Let's say the words and then go and look at Yoller.'

When they had observed the last rites for Dawn Raptor, the three of them flew the short distance to the centre of the clearing and found Yoller sitting upright in a daze with blood still seeping from the body wounds Dawn Raptor had inflicted and still only semi-conscious from the near-fatal blow that Hunter had delivered to the head.

'He's still too stunned to speak or fly away,' said Quaver. 'Let's say the last words for the others before we decide what to do with him.'

'I know what to do with him,' said Hunter. 'The only problem is, I don't know exactly how.'

'Are you going to kill him?' Quaver asked, looking in awe first at the semi-conscious Tawny and then at his blood-soaked elder brother.

'Of course not!' Hunter said. 'There are far too many dead already. No, I'm going to use him to bring Winger down and to put an end to this senseless civil war.'

'The last words for Dirge and Ivy,' prompted Holly gently. 'For the moment they're much more important than Winger and the civil war.'

So they flew back to the edge of the clearing and landed on the ground beside the three lifeless bodies. Still entwined with Hook's, Dirge's corpse was torn and mangled almost beyond recognition, but Ivy still looked very much the same as when she had been alive. Only one deep slash and the odd angle of her lolling head showed that she had been killed outright when Cleaver broke her neck. Even her well-groomed feathers were only slightly ruffled and with a stab of pain and guilt Hunter realized that she had probably preened her plumage specially for her reunion with him before flying bravely to her unexpected death.

'At least she didn't suffer much,' said Quaver, who seemed to guess what must be going on in Hunter's mind. 'She died instantly and could have felt no pain.'

'I should have saved her,' Hunter said.

'Don't blame yourself,' said Holly. 'You did your very best.'

'Holly's right,' said Quaver, who was feeling very queasy at the sight of all these corpses and above all at the crimson, blood-soaked apparition of his brother. 'You very nearly lost your life in the attempt.'

Hunter nodded unhappily and then Holly began to say the last words in that soft lilting voice which at that poignant moment no longer sparkled like a mountain stream but still reminded Hunter of freedom and of summer flowers. Quaver spoke all of the words with her as the three of them stood with their heads bowed in reverence above the corpses in the clearing, but Hunter was too choked with remorse and grief for Ivy and the unborn chicks and did not join in until they reached the very end. 'Through knowledge and self-sacrifice you will survive until the sun no longer sets and until the moon fails to rise and give us light at night. Know that with us and among us still you will survive for all eternity and beyond the boundless limits of all wisdom and all time.'

As they finished saying the last words, Hunter once more remembered the way he had felt when he had finally left little Alba's body and flown off towards the deep red streaks of rising dawn. 'One day the world will be a better place,' he had promised, and though he no longer believed that to be true, he decided that the time had come to put aside his dream of a solitary, uncommitted life and take action here and now to try to make it so.

In the centre of the clearing they found Yoller fully conscious, though still bleeding and still unsteady on his feet. When the three Barn owls perched on the ground in a circle round him, he looked his old friend Hunter in the face, raised one broad blunt wing, stroked the top of his battered, lacerated head and winced. 'That was a good one, old boy,' he said, with a glum and rueful grin. 'So good that with slightly better timing you'd have killed me!'

'Unhappily, that was my intention,' said Hunter, who was now very glad he had failed.

Yoller moved his magnificent, blood-stained head in a slow circle round the clearing and for the first time took in the full toll of the wounded and the dead. 'A bad business, this,' he said, his eyes at last resting on the body of Dawn Raptor, with whom he had sparred so long and reluctantly before the kill. 'I'm sorry that I killed your sister,' he said, with a rueful shake of his badly wounded head. 'But your brilliant strategy left me very little choice.'

'What do you mean?' asked Hunter.

'Keeping those two in reserve for the surprise attack,' said Yoller, wincing once again as he nodded at Holly and at Quaver. 'All right, call it tactics, then, not strategy, but in any case, it did the trick. Like the two of them flying at us in tandem to divert attention from the real attack. Brilliant, old boy! Quite frankly, I didn't think you had it in you.'

'It was an accident,' said Hunter. 'Quaver and I came here to warn the others and it was my intention to stay on and meet you here alone.'

'In any case, you won a great and unexpected victory,' said Yoller. 'You'd best kill me now and get the whole thing over with. I'd much rather die here on the battlefield than go into hiding and wait to be hunted down by Winger's lot. In any case, as you can see, I'm too badly wounded to defend myself.'

'I'm not going to kill you,' Hunter said. 'You are our prisoner and our hostage, and as such you will be protected. You will fly with us now to Winger's council meeting and when I have deposed him you will be granted safe passage across Barn owl country and back to your ancestral wood.'

'That's good of you, old boy, but I'm not sure of the reception that I'd get. I can't go back as the ex-leader and the sole survivor of an annihilated army. There is the question of my honour to consider, and in any case, what would May Blossom say?'

'I don't give a crow's turd for your honour or for what May Blossom thinks! You must go back and help me put an end to this stupid civil war.'

'She won't stand for that, old boy,' said Yoller, sadly. 'She won't be satisfied until she's taken this place back. She'll simply wait until she can raise another task force and then try the same thing again.'

'She can have it back, in exchange for Beak Poke's old domain. That

336

way you can tell her that Birch lost the battle but you achieved your objectives just the same. If she won't agree, you must take her place as leader, or else find another owl who knows how to compromise and choose the middle way. To survive, our two species must learn to co-exist.'

'I'll do my best,' said Yoller, with a little sigh. 'But if you knew her as well as I do, you'd realize that rather than approach her with an ultimatum of that kind, it might be better to be dead.'

'Get ready for the journey,' Hunter said, and then turned to the two Barn owls standing by his side. 'My purpose now is to fly to the council meeting and have it out with Winger,' he continued. 'And in this vital mission, I shall need your help.'

'I have some information,' Holly said. 'His real name is Westwood and he still owns all of the secluded valley where I lived. He was the young aristocrat to whom I was promised as a fledgling.'

'Tell me all about it on the way,' said Hunter. 'Time is of the essence in this enterprise and at all costs we must reach the council meeting before dawn.'

So they took off and flew south-east through the sleeping trees of Ripper's wood, while behind them a strong breeze blew across the clearing, rippled through the tall grass of early summer and gently stirred the ruffled, blood-stained feathers of the dead.

CHAPTER

 18

Though slowed down by Yoller's wounded, limping flight, the four owls reached Winger's territory well before daybreak, flew over the great wide field of ripening corn and then across the grassland that sloped down sharply to the leader's isolated barn.

Hunter flew around the barn and landed in a tall oak tree on the borders of the wooded glade. The others followed and he waited until all three had settled before he announced his plan. 'I'm going to fly straight into the council meeting and confront him,' he announced, in clear, decisive tones. 'I want you to come with me, Quaver. You, Holly, stay here and keep an eye on Yoller.'

'But are you sure that's wise?' asked Quaver, looking rather scared. 'There are eleven of them in there with Winger. If they gang up on us, we could be cut to pieces.'

'There are only nine,' said Hunter. 'You forget that Dirge and Bardic are both dead. The History Owl and the Language Owl are both on our side, so that makes only seven. Eight of them, including Winger, against five.'

'Seven against six,' said Quaver, becoming visibly less apprehensive as he analysed the odds. 'Don't forget Geography. He's in the resistance – an original member of the gang of three.'

'Winger's got rid of him,' said Hunter. 'The excuse was that his war wounds prevented him from attending all the meetings.'

'He's been reinstated,' said his brother, sounding almost cheerful now. 'Winger probably needed his territorial knowledge to help solve the problem of infertility. 'He can't fight, though,' added Quaver, with a frown. 'So that still makes it seven against five.'

'There won't be any fighting,' Hunter said. 'And even if there is, I'm quite certain we shall win. Are you ready now? We're going in.'

'Aren't you going to clean that mess off first?' asked Quaver, looking at his brother in awe and trepidation.

'No time,' said Hunter firmly. 'And if it puts the fear of the God Bird into them, so much the better.'

'Winger could never stand the sight of owl blood,' said Holly. 'At least, he couldn't when I was a fledgling.'

'Old boy, you look awful,' said the wounded Yoller, wobbling slightly on his branch. 'You look ghastly. Much better not to wipe it off.'

'Come on, Quaver,' said Hunter, turning his blood-stained features to his brother. 'We're going in there now. There won't be any initial opposition. When they pick up our signals, they'll think we're Dirge and Bardic turning up late for the council meeting.'

Quaver nodded, pulled his shoulders back and then took off in Hunter's wake and flew the short distance to Winger's barn, ready for the second major confrontation of the night. Hunter flew in ahead of him through a gap in the barn roof and as he followed Quaver saw the ten assembled Barn owls flutter on their beams at the shock of his blood-soaked brother's sudden apparition.

'Humanoid!' exclaimed Winger, as his eyes bulged even wider open and his bony frame shrank back on the beam from which he had been conducting the assembly. 'What's happened? We thought that you were Dirge.'

'Dirge is dead!' said Hunter. 'So is his daughter Ivy Perch, and Dawn Raptor, killed by the Tawny task force because of your mad scheme to colonize Ferocity and Ripper's wood and mate with three females all at the same time.'

'Where is the Tawny task force now?' asked the Environmental Owl, one of Winger's major allies, who now looked only slightly less shocked and sickened than his leader. 'Did they do that to you? How big an air force shall we need to bring them down?'

'They are all dead,' said Hunter, who had perched with Quaver on a big beam high above the whole assembly. 'All except their ex-leader, Yoller, who is wounded and now my prisoner in the spinney just outside.'

'Dead?' said the ancient War Owl, who had been old and decrepit even at the time of the invasion and the previous war. 'But who did such a deed? Were they destroyed by man?'

'No, I killed them,' Hunter said. 'With the aid of my brother here and of those who died in the battle, Dawn Raptor, Dirge and his daughter Ivy Perch.'

'Your brother!' exclaimed Winger, as this second shock rocked him backwards on his perch. 'Then you're not Humanoid at all!'

Hunter stared down at him and at the upturned eyes of all the members of the council. 'I am the owl you knew as Humanoid,' he said. 'But I am also Hunter, son of Steeple, and I have returned to expose you, Winger, and to bring you down.'

'Don't listen to him!' shouted Winger, recovering his commanding manner, though still pale and shaken by the sight of so much blood. 'That owl is an impostor! Leave this barn at once and go back to your exile in the lost domain, or I will have you tried and put to death for treason on the spot.'

'You are the impostor!' Hunter countered firmly, still holding the attention of the whole assembly which was now so tense and silent that you could have heard a feather drop. 'Your real name is Westwood. You are the last of the Barn owl aristocrats and you still own a sheltered, fertile valley in the south which you abandoned before the invasion and the war. You have lied to the council about infertility and you have caused a bloody civil war by stealing Tawny territory which you set aside as a private lair in which to satisfy your lust by fornicating with three helpless females all at the same time.'

'It wasn't lust or fornication!' shouted Winger, his bulging eyes blazing with righteous indignation. 'It was pure science! An experiment in the interests of survival!'

'You see, he confesses it,' said Hunter, turning his blood-stained head to take in the entire assembly. 'I can also prove that he's been planning to disband the council and take on dictatorial powers. You are finished, Westwood! Go back to the fertile valley that your ancestors have owned for centuries. Take any disciple of your New Apostasy who is brave enough to face the long journey to the south. Here we shall return to a modified, more enlightened version of the ancient, democratic reign, and the election of a new leader will take place at once.'

'We can't have an election now,' protested the Environmental Owl.

'The Owl for Dogma and Dialectic is not with us and therefore cannot cast his vote.'

'Of course he can't, you idiot!' interrupted Rivers. 'He and the Bard Owl are both dead.'

'Then let their successors be appointed first,' commanded Hunter.

'Only the leader can do that,' said Winger's Man Owl, who knew nothing about man. 'But what's the point of Winger choosing council members if he's on the point of being banished?'

'No point at all,' said Hunter, thinking very quickly. 'Unless, of course, he appoints the candidates that I suggest. Winger!' he continued, thrusting his blood-soaked head and body down towards the leader of the New Apostasy. 'Appoint Quaver instead of Bardic and make me the Owl for Dogma and Dialectic. Do it now, for it is your last task as leader and your very life depends on it.'

Winger sat slumped on his perch and neither looked up nor answered. For a few moments there was great tension in the barn as murmurs of dissent began to rise up from supporters of the New Apostasy. Then Hunter spread his wings, hissed and flew down towards Winger's perch while as one owl the whole assembly gasped and drew its breath. Winger looked up and as he saw his blood-soaked enemy approaching, his gangling body twitched with panic, he covered his big head with one wing and cowered on his perch in a state of abject fear. Hunter veered to one side before he reached his target and landed on a lower beam beside Rivers and the Language Owl. 'Speak, Winger!' Hunter commanded. 'Appoint us now, before it is too late!'

Still covering his head with one trembling wing, the banished leader mumbled something unintelligible, his bulging eyes averted from the foul spectacle of so much blood and gore, whilst all around his supporters on the council gazed at him in disappointment and perplexity.

'Good! That's excellent!' said Hunter, elated by his own success and beginning to understand how it was that power went to your head. 'And according to tradition, as the newest member of the council I'll cast the first vote in this leadership election. I hereby propose Rivers, the war hero and History Owl.'

'I second that,' said Quaver.

'My vote goes to Rivers, too,' said Quirk, the Language Owl, as he raised one wing enthusiastically.

'Mine, too,' said the Geography Owl. 'And that makes four out of eleven.'

'Five!' said the decrepit old War Owl, who had only just worked out what was happening and was obviously relieved. 'I vote for Rivers. About time, I say, and a jolly good thing too!'

'Me as well!' the Owl Owl cried at the same time as the Man Owl raised his wing and shouted 'Rivers!' Having seen which way the wind was blowing they were both anxious to ingratiate themselves with the new leader by being seen to cast the sixth, decisive vote.

'That's settled, then!' said Hunter, looking at the History Owl with a grim smile of satisfaction on his blood-stained features. 'You are our new leader, Rivers, and your first task is to appoint someone to take my place as Owl for Dogma and Dialectic. Only I suggest you return to the habit of the ancient reign and call him the Religion Owl again.'

'I want you as Man Owl,' answered Rivers. 'Having lived in the city and studied under Humanoid, your knowledge is unique. You can be Religion Owl,' he added, turning to the current Man Owl on the council. 'Since you don't know anything about man or religion either, it won't make any difference.'

'No!' interrupted Hunter. 'I don't want a place on your council, either now or in the future. My experience and above all tonight's events have shown that I can contribute more as an outsider, both to your new council and to the survival of our species. Though I will give you all the help I can, my role must be untrammelled by politics or protocol. I must be free, for my purpose holds to follow knowledge like a sinking star and roam these territories until I find the secrets that will save us from extinction. I shall strive for enlightenment until it is safe for us to breed again, or until my own day wanes, the darkness deepens and I die.'

There was a solemn pause, then Rivers nodded and looked around at the entire assembly. 'Very well, Hunter,' he said, sounding composed and already very much the leader. 'You are a hero and a legend in your time and so we gladly give you leave to be a law unto yourself. But I don't agree with setting Winger free. He has caused the deaths of Bardic, Dawn Raptor, Dirge and Ivy Perch. Do you want to take your own revenge, or shall the council punish him with death?'

'There has been enough killing for one night,' said Hunter. 'Let him go now and begin the long journey back to his ancestral home before the break of day. And remember, from Winger we have much to learn. Some of his dogma we must keep and many of his ideas must be adopted and cultivated in the course of time. His main fault was the lust for power, and blind belief in a system which belies the essential nature of the owl. Let him pass into history, but keep the best of him and always remember that our most dangerous enemy is man.'

'And Yoller?' enquired Rivers, who clearly did not care for what Hunter had just said but at that moment did not think it politic to answer back. 'Shall we kill him now, or do you want to do the job yourself?'

'No, we need him to help us stop this stupid civil war. Dismiss the council now and I will tell you what we're going to do.'

Rivers reluctantly nodded his assent and there was a stir in the barn as the assembled owls prepared for their departure. While Rivers said goodbye to each member of his council, Hunter flew across the barn and perched beside his brother. 'Go back to Holly and to Yoller and make sure that no harm comes to him,' he said to Quaver quietly. 'With Winger gone, from now on this place will be your new domain. Rivers can lead the council from his own ancestral home. As Bard Owl, you can stay here with Holly as your pupil.'

'With Holly?' asked Quaver as his heart leapt unexpectedly. 'But you're the one she travelled all this way to find. Surely you're going to mate with her one day?'

'I hope so, but not yet. Not with Ivy and her unborn fledglings barely dead. And first I must solve this problem of infertility. In any case, Holly's first objective is an education. Poetry and singing are the subjects she prefers, so what solution could be better?'

'Oh, I'm happy with it,' Quaver said. 'But will she be? That's the question. Forgive me, Hunter, but understanding females is not your strongest point.'

'Perhaps not,' said Hunter, frowning as he remembered his ill-starred affair with little Alba and the awful mistake he had made in mating with Ivy Perch. 'But in any case it's too late to mate this season, there are problems to be solved and I have to find a safe territory for us first.'

'If you say so,' answered Quaver, with a little shrug. 'But you've got to tell her, Hunter, and what's more you must point out that the whole thing was entirely your idea.'

'I'll tell her when I've finished here with Rivers. In the meantime, go and bring Yoller here inside the barn. I don't want those ghouls from the council gawping at his wounds and gloating over a victory they did nothing to achieve. Here, in your new inner sanctum, he can sleep in peace till twilight and the beginning of his long, inglorious journey home.'

Quaver sighed and raised his eyebrows as he looked at his brother in a sort of affectionate despair. Then he took off and followed the last of the council members through the barn roof and out into a darkness that was already pregnant with the coming dawn.

Later, when Hunter had cleansed himself of all the blood and gore, he sat beside Holly in the mighty oak and told her of his future plans. 'The sun burns all around us and no wind stirs the summer haze, yet my brother tells me that Dapple has now come upon the deep midwinter of her days. For this reason I shall go back to the place where I was born and stay with her until the coming spring. I shall keep her company by day and by night I shall fly the length and breadth of all our territory to solve the problems of pollution and infertility. I shall fly until I find a wild green place where nature is not spent, where no human foot has ever trod and where next spring we may safely have our chicks.'

'Home is where you are,' Holly said. 'In a barn, in a hollow tree, in the abandoned farmhouse where you once lived or even far across the salty waters. As long as you are there, it will be home to me.'

'I shall also fly close to the new town and study the question of an artificial memory,' continued Hunter. 'If we are to survive the scourge of man, it is clear that we must understand more and more about his ways.'

Holly listened while Hunter told her about Humanoid and his theories, but all the time she longed for him to put one strong wing around her and cuddle her close and hidden in the shady oak, not moving all the basking, burning day, but blending slowly together until twilight came and with it the mellow flowering urge she knew that neither of them would be able to resist. Gazing up into his eyes, she seemed to take in all he said, but her mind was really wondering whether they would ever mate and whether it would be better for both if she turned down this tempting opportunity to study under Quaver.

Troubled, she glanced away from him and briefly watched the red dawn glowing on the pale copper of the ripening corn. If only he would hold her close to him and let her rest her head against his chest! If only they could stay together until the sun had reached its southern heights and then sank slowly down to twilight in the west. She knew that when the evening shadows lengthened they would come together as one owl and in their own small, local way they would struggle tenderly to create at least one last generation of their species in the natural manner of the last twelve million years.

But Hunter did not stay. When he had finished speaking he put one wing around her, rubbed his cheek gently against hers and drew forth from Holly a trembling, heartfelt sigh. 'If the God Bird wills it, we will mate at the beginning of next spring,' he said. 'In the meantime I shall be close by and I shall visit you from time to time at twilight or in the early dawn, but now I'm going home to begin my quest for a lost and silent place where the deep down things are fresh and clean enough for us to mate.'

'But you can't go now,' protested Holly. 'You can't begin your journey when the sun is high.'

'I've often flown by daylight,' Hunter said. 'And today I'm going to break another Barn owl rule. At long last, I'm going home again.'

He took off then and Holly watched his strong shape fade into a white speck against the clear blue sky as he flew back after so long in prison, in exile and at war across the countryside he loved so well to the place where he had first seen the sun rise and the first spring day begin.

CHAPTER

 19

High summer came and went and Hunter flew to every hidden corner of the rustic territories, using Dapple's barn as his home base. As he pursued his quest for a safe haven in which to mate with Holly, the first gusts of colder wind swirled the red and golden leaves in a last flurry through the air before they fell to shroud the pungent earth of summer's russet grave.

Still he searched, but almost everywhere the story was the same. Fledglings either stillborn in the broken eggs or else too sick and weakly to survive the rigours of the coming winter, whilst in some territories the older owls were dying mysteriously, much sooner than expected.

Hunter flew on with despair growing in his heart as the great black clouds began to drift in from the west, borne in by fiercer winds which stripped the last clinging leaves and bared the shivering branches till old nests stood out like blotches in the gaunt and naked trees. Behind his home territory the hamlet that had grown into a town spread still farther and swallowed the Barn owl district to the west, so that there was no longer any buffer between Dapple's land and the growing inferno of cement and brick from which yellow smoke and foul fumes billowed and whose distant rumble disturbed the slumber of the owls by day.

'Give up, Hunter,' said Dapple, one wet and misty dawn when he flew back from yet another weary, unsuccessful mission. 'Rivers is right. Man will stop this pollution soon enough, when the poison gets to him. In the meantime, you're as safe here as in any other place. For all you know this territory may be fertile still, like the two or three others you've discovered.'

'Our world is shrinking,' Hunter said. 'Yoller was right. We are a dying race and this disaster comes from living far too close to man.'

'The stupidity of both owls and men never ceases to amaze me,' Dapple said. 'Even at my age! The best thing you can do is to bring this Holly home to roost with you and have your fledglings here. The chances of my surviving this coming winter are very slight, so you'll soon have the whole place to yourselves. And even if I'm still alive I eat very little and there's food enough here for four or five.'

'It's ironic,' Hunter said. 'The Little owls are thriving in the lost domain, the territory we once thought was so dangerous. And the Tawnies are holding their own, too. They've already recolonized and bred successfully in Ferocity and Ripper's wood. So unless I move back to the abandoned farmhouse, which has been deserted since poor Bardic's death, there's nowhere else for me to go.'

'Stay here,' said Dapple in firm but gentle tones. 'Stay here, and when you've mated, take up your position on the council. To survive, our species needs sincere and altruistic owls like you.'

'The danger is men use this barn much more than they did when I was a fledgling. I don't like it. I'm afraid it would upset Holly and the chicks.'

'They've never harmed us,' Dapple said. 'But if you prefer it, use the hollow elm tree in the second meadow between here and the spinney. The hollow is very high above the ground and there's room in there for a family of five or six.'

'The elm trees are all dying,' said Hunter, with a sad shake of his head. 'Few of them will ever flower again, and when they've rotted, the men will come and cut them down.'

'The cowshed then,' said Dapple, nodding across the barn yard to a building that had not been used by man since Hunter's early youth. 'It's low down, I know, and quite exposed to man, but they've got a new place for the cattle and no humans ever go there any more.'

'It's a possibility,' admitted Hunter. 'But first I'll try just one more time to find a wild place that is still free from all trace of man. In my soul I know that somewhere such a place exists.'

'You'll never find it,' Dapple said. 'Not unless you fly to the far north or far across the salty waters. Come home, Hunter. Come in out of the

347

hail and wind and stop seeking after places and secrets that you'll never find.'

'I'll keep trying till the spring. Then, if I've found nowhere I'll fetch Holly and we'll settle for the cowshed.'

So Hunter searched again while the days grew even shorter and black rain lashed down on barren field and ragged hedge and the gnarled trees creaked and trembled in the driving wind. Then the wind and rain gave way to pale winter sun and night-time frost which thatched both field and hedge with hoary white and traced silver patterns on the bare branches of the trees.

Still Hunter's quest continued till the first snow fell and drifted in the wind. The snow froze, more fell and Hunter flew on in search of a wild, virgin place where nature was still clean, until one day in deep midwinter Dapple died.

Returning one flaming sunrise he found her body lying frozen on a great white grave of driven snow and he knew that at last the time had come to end his hopeless quest. 'She was right,' he thought, looking down at her frail body with the remorse one feels when it is too late to make amends. 'I'm searching for something I shall never find. I have survived prison and two wars, I have travelled far, seen many die and at long last I have come back to this. It is my portion under the moon and stars and for Dapple's sake I shall make the best of it.'

He bent his head then over his mother's body while above him the flaming sun rose higher and bathed the whole of his domain in radiant, blinding white. He said the last words slowly and with great feeling, while in the new town not far across the frozen winter meadows, the low rumble of another alien day began.

At the same time, in the seclusion of his inner sanctum, Quaver watched the early sunlight streaming through the roof and for the first time spoke his heart and mind to Holly. 'Hunter will be coming for you soon,' he said, as she arched her graceful neck with the effort of memorizing the last verses of the epic ballad they had composed.

'How do you know?' asked Holly, her eyes shining with a strange blend of pleasure and regret.

'I have a premonition,' said Quaver, with an unhappy little shrug. 'I don't know exactly what, but something's happened, I can tell.'

'He won't want me to go at once,' said Holly. 'If he does, how can I help you to revise the ballad?'

'The question is,' said Quaver, his voice suddenly becoming husky as he looked away from her and watched the beams of sunlight dancing on the rafters of the barn. 'The question is, do you really want to go at all?'

'I must,' said Holly, as their eyes met for a fleeting, furtive moment before each looked rapidly away again. 'I gave him my promise, after all.'

'A female owl can always change her mind,' said Quaver, sounding unhappy and uncertain of himself. 'After all, that's her prerogative.'

'Oh, Quaver,' said Holly sadly. 'I've seen this happening. I've seen it in your eyes.'

'I can't help it. With true love, I don't suppose one can.'

'I love you, too,' said Holly, leaning forward on her perch and pleading with her lovely eyes. 'I love you, too, Quaver, but not in the same way.'

'That would come later. It would come in the spring, if you stayed here and we mated.'

'It might,' admitted Holly, turning her face away from Quaver's in confusion. 'I must confess it might. But Hunter trusts us. How could we do a thing like that after all that he's been through? And in any case, it would never be the same.'

'Why not?' asked Quaver, looking at her with unhappy longing in his eyes. 'We have so much in common, you and I. We have poetry and singing, for which you have a natural talent. We have the same sense of humour, we're good friends and we get on with each other in almost every way. We've lived, worked and even fought together, side by side. What more could you want than that?'

'We've grown to love each other, I admit,' said Holly, gazing at him with her lovely, troubled eyes. 'But with me and Hunter it was different. Even the first time that we met it was as though we'd known each other all our lives.'

'The urge, then,' said Quaver, with a tortured little smile. 'You mean he's bigger, bolder, stronger and you have the urge for him?'

'It's not only the urge. Oh, how can I explain it? It's more of an instant recognition in the soul. If I'd never met your brother I'd be overjoyed to spend my life with you. But I did meet him and I loved him instantly for some sort of dream I knew we could share with each other and with no one else. It sounds silly but it's true. We have the same secret dream that neither of us could put into words. Maybe it's a dream that won't come true, but we must try to make it happen if we can.'

'Perhaps it's just as well,' said Quaver, with another unhappy little shrug. 'I don't suppose I'd have ever dared to tell him even if you had accepted. But Holly, if anything should ever happen to him, promise that you'll come back here to me. I, too, have a tiny, feeble little dream and you're the only female I could ever share it with.'

'That's very sweet of you,' said Holly, with tears starting in her eyes. 'I do love you, Quaver, and in spite of what I feel for Hunter I want to stay and work with you until the spring.'

'I have a premonition,' said Quaver, with a sad shake of his head. 'Something has happened and Hunter will be here tonight.'

'I don't see how you can be sure, yet it's uncanny how your premonitions are so often right.'

'It's the poet and minstrel in me,' said Quaver, bitterly. 'You could call it seeing where science hath no light.'

'I'm sorry,' Holly pleaded. 'I've told you, if it hadn't been for Hunter . . .'

'Forget it!' said Quaver, managing a wry and twisted smile. 'I'm only glad that it's my brother and not some other owl. That I would have fought against, but only the best is good enough for Hunter. After all, he is a legend in his time.'

'And you will be the best Bard Owl for centuries. You have your art, Quaver, and in that respect you're the luckiest owl I know.'

'They say suffering is good for a poet's soul,' said Quaver. 'If that's the case, then my songs and verses should improve dramatically this coming spring.'

'You'll find someone else. Time and another love will ease the pain.'

'All this is getting rather trite,' said Quaver, pretending to yawn with the fatigue most Barn owls feel when the sun has risen high. 'Think of all the millions of conversations just like this that must have taken place since the dawn of history and the beginning of recorded time. There should be some new way of saying things, but I fear that even in Winger's New Apostasy the pain and the commonplace would stay the same.'

'Sleep now,' said Holly. 'If your premonition is right you must be prepared for your brother and for whatever tidings he may bring.'

'He'll come,' said Quaver. 'Or another will, if it is not him. I can feel it in the wind.'

So they slept till twilight and then hunted and ate together for what proved to be the final time, for at midnight Hunter came, told them of Dapple's death and announced his decision to take Holly back with him to the place where he had been born.

'Do you want to take her now?' asked Quaver, after Holly had left the two brothers alone in the barn to grieve for their mother's death. 'Or do you want her to stay here until the winter's gone?'

'Now would be better,' Hunter said. 'She needs to settle in before the spring.'

'It's a dangerous place to raise a family,' warned Quaver. 'Men use the barn more often than before and the new town is creeping closer to the borders of your land.'

'It can't be helped,' said Hunter. 'When Dapple died, I saw it in a blinding flash of light. The place where I was born is the place where I must come to terms with all these changes. There is no escape. Like my old tutor Humanoid, we must study man in order to survive.'

'Let Holly stay with you here,' said Quaver, in a burst of noble generosity that he at once regretted. 'You will both be safe in this sequestered place and the spreading town will threaten me much less. I am a loner and a minstrel with no mate or fledglings to protect.'

'That's kind of you,' said Hunter, smiling as he shook his head. 'It's good of you to offer, but you need peace, routine and seclusion for the great songs and poems you have it in you to compose. And in any case I need the vicinity of humans, for my purpose holds to help our species survive these changes and this erosion of our habitat by man. But there is something you can do for me,' he added, glancing quickly round to make certain that Holly was still nowhere within hearing. 'I want you to promise that if anything should happen to me, you'll take care of Holly and the chicks. You may have a mate yourself by then, but remember the offer you've just made and find a place where they may thrive and grow in safety.'

'I promise. You have a charmed life, Hunter, and I don't intend to mate, but I make you my solemn promise just the same.'

'Good!' said Hunter, with a smile and a solemn little nod. 'Goodbye Quaver. I'll take Holly with me now. You must come and see our fledglings in the spring.'

'I will,' said Quaver, forcing a wry smile that he hoped would hide his pain. 'Tell her goodbye from me,' he added, as Hunter shifted on the beam and spread his wings for take off.

'Come outside and say goodbye yourself. You must have grown quite fond of her after all this time.'

'Oh, I have,' said Quaver, with a depth of feeling he could no longer hide. 'I've grown very fond of her indeed. Just say I'll be thinking of her and I'm sure she'll understand.'

'As you wish!' said Hunter, who was so excited at the prospect of taking Holly home that he failed to notice anything amiss. 'Till spring, then, Quaver. And thanks for everything.'

'Till spring,' repeated Quaver and watched his elder brother fly through the gap in the barn roof to begin a new life with his beloved Holly, while he was left alone to fill his solitude with the birth pangs of fresh verse and the melancholy solace of old song.

He did not stir again that night but sat and brooded on what might have been if Holly had accepted him and Hunter had really been betrayed. In his mind's eye he saw Holly still beside him on the beam and his brother flying heartbroken and alone in his endless quest for knowledge that would mean the survival of their species. He tried hard to imagine how he and Holly would have felt, building their nest with the broken feathers of his brother's grief, and although he realized how wrong and impossible it would have been, he also knew to his own shame that the sudden loss of Holly had cut him deeper than his mother's death.

To expiate the guilt he felt for having the wrong feelings, Quaver forced himself to compose a dirge for Dapple's death, a task he had completed by the time day broke and began to lighten the darkness of the frozen landscape all around him. Peering out into the rising dawn he recited the verses he had composed, declaiming them loud and clear in case by some unheard-of miracle his mother could still hear him.

'Did you see the years roll by
As you lay dying? Did the joys
And sorrows of so long ago
Drift past you like the driven snow?

Did you hear time heave
And see the ebb and flow
Of brief untidy lives
That interrupt eternity?

I like to think you did
And realized at the very end
How little in our tiny world
Is worth the striving and the stress.

And did you vanish into clay,
Or do you soar above us still
And does your smoky wisp of owl soul
Sail free forever in the wind?'

'It would be nice to think it did,' said Quaver to himself, feeling slightly better now that he had asked his departed mother this series of enormous, unanswerable questions. For a long time he gazed out at the frozen landscape, searching in vain for some sign of the coming spring and wondering how long it would be before he and all the other owls he knew joined Dapple in the sky, in the ground, in the great beyond or wherever it was that they would all be going in the end.

Then, as the sun rose high outside, he thought of Holly once again and wept before sleep came at last and in its mercy numbed the ache of loneliness and loss.

CHAPTER

 20

Spring came at last and between the flowering of primrose and wild hyacinth Holly gave birth to two healthy chicks.

Thriving on abundant food they grew quickly and learned fast as the green corn thickened and the soft wind of coming summer breathed their names to the newborn grass and to the hawthorn blossom bursting in the hedge. As they flourished and learned to fly around the barn yard on clumsy, fledgling wings, the only threat to their existence seemed to come from the drifting fumes and distant rumble of the growing town.

One day at dusk, when May had melted into June, Hunter sat beside Holly on the cowshed roof, watching the man with a firestick as he wandered down the new lane that now led deep into their territory from the distant town. In silence, they watched him disappear into the copse beyond the meadow and the barn yard as the sun sank slowly behind him in the west.

'They walk here more often than before,' said Hunter warily. 'Soon, when high summer comes and young Steeple and little Alba are strong enough, for their sakes we must move farther from the town.'

'Don't hunt yet,' said Holly, as she sensed the hidden man still moving steadily through the copse in their direction. 'Wait until it's darker and he's gone away again.'

'The chicks must eat,' said Hunter. 'At dusk they're at their hungriest, and in any case, that firestick's not for us. The humans on this farmland haven't killed a single owl in living memory. In the breeding season they don't even kill the wild birds they eat. He must be looking for a fox.'

So saying he took off, circled low over the meadow as the last glow of sunlight spent itself behind the copse, soon caught a full-grown mole to still his fledglings' hunger and flew back with it through the gaping hole in the sagging cowshed roof. Waiting on the beam beside her chicks, Holly carved it quickly, gave her chicks half each and then turned to Hunter and spoke urgently but quietly into his ear.

'He's getting nearer,' she said, softly. 'He came right through the copse and now he's moving across the meadow towards the cowshed and the barn. I think he must have seen you coming back.'

'No,' said Hunter, peering out at the meadow and the slowly moving shadow of the man. 'I don't think he saw me. It was very nearly dark.'

'I won't panic,' said Holly, glancing at the chicks who were both much too happy swallowing their food to notice the tremor in their mother's voice or the tension in Hunter's powerful back.

'He's still coming,' said Holly, no longer able to conceal her fear from Hunter as she turned away from the two chicks and stared out again to see the man leave the meadow and enter the deserted yard between the cowshed and the barn.

'He's stopped,' said Hunter as the intruder paused and stared up at the abandoned cowshed until his eyes rested on the huge gap in the low and sagging roof.

'Perhaps we should get out now, while there's still time,' said Holly softly. 'Even little Alba can fly a meadow's length and that would take us to the high hollow in the elm where all of us could hide.'

Hunter thought carefully for a moment, his eyes still fixed on the stationary man. 'No good,' he whispered in reply. 'There's no cover between here and the hollow tree. The chicks could make the distance but they're still slow and clumsy in their flight. It's not yet quite dark and they'd be sitting targets for the firestick.'

'He's coming closer,' breathed Holly as the man took several paces forward and then stopped to gaze upwards through the gap in the low roof. As Hunter stared back at him the man moved forward again until he was close enough for both owls to peer down into his curious human eyes.

'What do you think he wants?' Holly whispered, as behind her the two chicks huddled closer to each other in response to their mother's fear.

'I don't know. But he's not one of our men from the farm.'

'Are you sure?' asked Holly, still filled with wonder at her mate's ability to tell one human from another.

'As certain as I can be. I learned to distinguish between them when I was in prison. He's looking directly up at us,' continued Hunter, without taking his eyes off the intruder for a second. 'I don't know what he wants but there's something that he's after, that's for certain.'

'You told me about all those owls in the city,' Holly murmured. 'Those in captivity. Have you ever asked yourself how they were trapped?'

'Of course I have,' said Hunter, for the first time taking his eyes off the man and glancing sideways at his mate. 'Most must have been taken as fledglings from the nest before they were strong enough to fly.'

Holly held his glance for a long moment and from the expression on her face he knew that both of them were thinking the same thing.

'Don't worry,' said Hunter, as he looked back at the intruder. 'If he comes any closer to us, I'll attack.'

'Don't!' pleaded Holly. 'Let me act as a decoy. I'll flutter down there pretending I've got a broken wing and then drag myself across the yard to lead him farther from the chicks.'

'No! He knows where they are. The only hope is to frighten him away. If anything happens to me, wait until it's safe to fly and then take the little ones to Quaver, stage by stage.'

'He's coming!' Holly cried, and for the first time there was panic in her voice as she sensed Hunter tense his muscles ready to do battle. Before she could stop him he took off, flew through the gap and climbed high above the cowshed, startling the man who stopped as he was about to enter and looked up as the great white shadow rose high above him, wheeled in the twilight sky and dived downwards to attack.

Hastily the man lifted the shotgun to his shoulder and started to take aim. As Hunter dived with talons stretched he saw the firestick wheel on the man's shoulder until it was almost in line with his trajectory. Still he dived and at the last moment the barrels jerked away from him as the man pulled his gun down and crossways to protect his face and head. Then he howled out loud as the owl struck and his talons tore one hand and gashed the forehead just above the gun. The man staggered back, blood spurting from his hand and trickling down his face as Hunter rose swiftly into the air and turned to dive and strike again.

This time the man gripped the shotgun firmly with both hands and blasted as the owl came down. Though badly aimed, about half the first barrel load of grape shot took Hunter in the stomach and the chest, smashing him sideways in the air, where he hung momentarily and fluttered once before the strength went from his wings, he wavered and then crashed headlong to the ground.

Cursing, the man pulled out a handkerchief, fumbled to staunch his bleeding hand and then ran stumbling back across the meadow towards the distant farmhouse in search of first aid for his wounded head and hand.

Lying in the dirt and dust of the barn yard where he had first played as a fledgling, Hunter was surprised to find he felt no pain. 'Dapple was right,' he murmured to himself as he lay gazing up at the moon, the stars and the freedom of the sky above. 'I am dying in the place where I was born. I have come home to roost at last.'

Though one lung and half his guts were shot away, Hunter was still sufficiently conscious to sense the intruder's ignominious retreat across the darkened meadow. He knew that Holly was watching from the barn and would fly down to his side and say the last words as soon as the man had vanished and it was safe to leave the fledglings on their own.

As the strength drained from him and the moon blurred in his dying vision, Hunter was happy that he had saved little Alba and young Steeple and now that his life was nearly over and there was nothing more that he could do, he felt a strange sense of well being and relief. 'At least I died for a true purpose,' he told himself as his vision blurred still further and the end drew very near. 'A young owl's death is better, after all. Not for me a long slow agony from poison, pollution or the sickness of old age. I'm going so fast that there's hardly any time for sorrow, pain or fear.'

But then the earth heaved beneath his dying body, the sky above him went completely blank and instead of the moon and stars he saw all the other owls he had known in a sudden, agonizing flash and was filled with piercing sadness at the certain knowledge that in this world they would never meet again. Yoller, Humanoid, Falco and Winger, Bardic, Dapple, his father, his sister and the self-styled Honeysuckle Rose, what would happen to those still living and what became of the long dead?

And in his last, searing vision he saw that the only thing they had in common, all these owls, was that he had once known them and remembered at the end. This break in continuity, the fact that this one microcosm of a world would die with him made him sadder by far than the thought of his own fast approaching end.

Still in his inner vision he saw Quaver, Holly and the chicks and was filled with a fervent hope that some fragments of his world might live on a while in them. But at the very end his last thoughts were of the first war that he had fought in so very long ago and of the idyll that he had shared in times of great danger with little Alba in the lost domain. He knew then that his true home was and always had been with his first love in the lost domain, or in that realm of faith and hope that somehow, some day the world will be a better place.

And he died in the belief that they might come together once again in the place where he was going, so far away above the highest mountain and beyond the moon and stars. His had been a hard life in which he had known sorrow, war and pain but also great happiness and joy, so it was fitting that his last thoughts on earth were of faith and hope for a cleaner future for his species and for himself at long last a deep, eternal peace.